About the Author

BERNARD CORNWELL is the author of the acclaimed and bestselling Saxon Tales, which include *The Last Kingdom*, *The Pale Horseman*, *Lords of the North*, and *Sword Song*, as well as the Richard Sharpe novels, the Grail Quest series, the Nathaniel Starbuck Chronicles, the Warlord Chronicles, and many other novels, including *Stonehenge* and *Gallows Thief*. He lives with his wife on Cape Cod.

CRACKDOWN

Books by Bernard Cornwell

The Saxon Tales

THE LAST KINGDOM*
THE PALE HORSEMAN*
LORDS OF THE NORTH*
SWORD SONG*

The Sharpe Novels (in chronological order)

SHARPE'S TIGER*
Richard Sharpe and the Siege of Seringapatam, 1799

SHARPE'S TRIUMPH*
Richard Sharpe and the Battle of Assaye, September 1803

SHARPE'S FORTRESS*
Richard Sharpe and the Siege of Gawilghur, December 1803

SHARPE'S TRAFALGAR*
Richard Sharpe and the Battle of Trafalgar, 21 October 1805

SHARPE'S PREY*
Richard Sharpe and the Expedition to Copenhagen, 1807

SHARPE'S RIFLES
Richard Sharpe and the French Invasion of Galicia, January 1809

SHARPE'S HAVOC*
Richard Sharpe and the Campaign in Northern Portugal, Spring 1809

SHARPE'S EAGLE
Richard Sharpe and the Talavera Campaign, July 1809

SHARPE'S GOLD
Richard Sharpe and the Destruction of Almeida, August 1810

SHARPE'S ESCAPE*
Richard Sharpe and the Bussaco Campaign, 1810

SHARPE'S FURY*
Richard Sharpe and the Battle of Barrosa, March 1811

SHARPE'S BATTLE*
Richard Sharpe and the Battle of Fuentes de Onoro, May 1811

SHARPE'S COMPANY
Richard Sharpe and the Siege of Badajoz, January to April 1812

SHARPE'S SWORD
Richard Sharpe and the Salamanca Campaign, June and July 1812

SHARPE'S ENEMY
Richard Sharpe and the Defense of Portugal, Christmas 1812

SHARPE'S HONOUR
Richard Sharpe and the Vitoria Campaign, February to June 1813

SHARPE'S REGIMENT
Richard Sharpe and the Invasion of France, June to November 1813

SHARPE'S SIEGE
Richard Sharpe and the Winter Campaign, 1814

SHARPE'S REVENGE
Richard Sharpe and the Peace of 1814

SHARPE'S WATERLOO
Richard Sharpe and the Waterloo Campaign, 15 June to 18 June 1815

SHARPE'S DEVIL*
Richard Sharpe and the Emperor, 1820–21

The Grail Quest Series

THE ARCHER'S TALE*
VAGABOND*
HERETIC*

The Nathaniel Starbuck Chronicles

REBEL*
COPPERHEAD*
BATTLE FLAG*
THE BLOODY GROUND*

The Warlord Chronicles

THE WINTER KING
THE ENEMY OF GOD
EXCALIBUR

The Sailing Thrillers

STORMCHILD*
SCOUNDREL*
WILDTRACK*
CRACKDOWN*

Other Novels

STONEHENGE, 2000 B.C.: A NOVEL*
GALLOWS THIEF*
A CROWNING MERCY*
THE FALLEN ANGELS*
REDCOAT*

* Published by HarperCollinsPublishers.

CRACKDOWN

A Novel of Suspense

BERNARD CORNWELL

HARPER

NEW YORK • LONDON • TORONTO • SYDNEY

HARPER

First published in Great Britain in 1990 by Michael Joseph. A paperback edition was published in Great Britain in 1993 by Penguin Books.

First Harper paperback published 2008.

Library of Congress Cataloging-in-Publication Data is available upon request.

ISBN 978-0-06-143837-0

10 11 12 /RRD 10 9 8 7 6 5 4

Acknowledgements and Dedication

It is usual, and prudent, to claim that no characters in any novel are based on real people, which claim is certainly true of the characters in *Crackdown*, yet the fictional island of Murder Cay is based on the all too real Bahamian island of Norman's Cay, and for details of that island, as well as for much other information about the *narcotraficantes*, I am indebted to the book *The Cocaine Wars* by Paul Eddy, Hugo Sabogal and Sara Walden.

I must also acknowledge my extreme debt to Dr Laura Reid, erstwhile Medical Director of the Gosnold Treatment Center in Falmouth, Cape Cod, who educated me about cocaine, and about the difficulties faced by her patients who are trying to break their cocaine addictions.

It seems to me that the true warriors of the drug war are people like Laura Reid and her colleagues whose battles and victories are rarely headlined. To them, and to all their patients who have defeated the evil, *Crackdown* is respectfully dedicated.

PART ONE

You cannot cheat death. It is not an illusion. It does not melt into air, into thin air, it is instead a clumsy thing of the night, to be discovered in the dawn.

And it was in the dawn, in a gentle Bahamian dawn, that I discovered *Hirondelle*.

She had been a cruising yacht; a pretty thirty-eight-foot fibreglass sloop. She had been a graceful thing, and she had been butchered.

When I found *Hirondelle* she was nothing but a barely floating derelict, so low in the water that I might have missed her altogether except that a heave of her sluggish hull flashed a reflection of the sun's new wan light from a polished deck-fitting into my eyes. I was so tired that I almost took no notice, assuming that the scrap of light had been mirrored from a discarded and floating beer can, but something made me pick up my binoculars and there she was; a dead creature which rolled under the blows of the short dawn chop.

I could see no one aboard the rolling hull. Her apparent abandonment, together with my weariness, tempted me to ease my helm to starboard and thus slip past the stricken boat that, like any other piece of floating junk, would have been out of sight within moments, and forgotten within hours, but curiosity and my sense of duty would not let me ignore her. There was still a slight chance that a wounded mariner was aboard, and so the wave-drenched wreck had to be boarded.

At least the weather was being kind. There was no steep chop or gusting wind to make boarding the waterlogged hull difficult. Instead the dawn was a calm, lovely finish to what had been a perfect tropical night during which I had been reaching northwards with every sail set; jib, staysail, foresail, mainsail and both jackyard topsails. *Wavebreaker* must have looked unutterably beautiful in that ghostly sunrise until the moment when I ran her head into wind and pressed the buttons which controlled the electric motors that furled her sails. I still found it odd to be sailing a boat on which everything was mechanised, electrified or computerised

3

because by inclination and income I was a sailor of simpler tastes, but for the present I was *Wavebreaker*'s hired skipper, and *Wavebreaker* was a luxury charter schooner, and the kind of people who rented her expected to find her loaded down with as many gadgets as a space shuttle.

We had no charterers aboard on the morning I discovered *Hirondelle*. Instead we had been 'dead-heading', meaning that *Wavebreaker* sailed with only her crew aboard. The three of us had just spent four weeks off the western coast of Andros where *Wavebreaker* had been hired to make a television commercial for cat food. The notion of the commercial had been that an extremely wealthy cat had chartered the schooner to search the world's oceans for the best-tasting fish, only to discover that Pussy-Cute Cat Food had already caught and canned the taste. The commercial must have cost Pussy-Cute millions of dollars, and *Wavebreaker* had been overrun with camera crews, designers, visualisers, scriptwriters, cat-handlers, fish-handlers, directors, account executives, make-up girls, hairdressers, line-producers, assistant-producers, real producers, as well as all the girlfriends and boyfriends and hermaphrodite-friends of everyone involved. Serious adults had argued passionately about the motivation of the rich cat, and even I, who had thought myself immune to the insanities of the film world, had been astonished when an elderly actor had been specially flown down from New York to imitate the beast's miaow because the real thing had not been considered sufficiently authentic. The elderly actor, coming aboard *Wavebreaker* for the first time, had stared at me in astonishment; then, though he had never seen me in his life before, he spread his arms in familiar and lavish welcome. "Sweet Tom!" He had called me by my father's name, and I had smiled wanly, then confessed that I was indeed Tom Breakspear's son. "How could you not be?" the New York actor had demanded. "You're the very image of him! Will you remember me to the old rascal?" Everyone knew my father. Everyone wanted me to know how they just loved my father. Everyone told me just how like my father I looked, though very few dared ask me from which of my father's wives I had been whelped.

4

But now, thank God, I was free of miaowing Thespians, and *Wavebreaker* was sailing back to her home port on Grand Bahama where, in just twenty-four hours' time, she would begin her last charter of the season. Then came *Hirondelle* to spoil the dawn.

I had been alone on deck when I first saw the wreck. Ellen had been sleeping in the stern-cabin's king-sized bed, and Thessy had been snoring in one of the clients' forward cabins. It was only when we were dead-heading that we were allowed to make free with the air-conditioned luxuries of the boat's staterooms. The brochure promised our charterers the 'authentic sea-salt taste of tropical seafaring', though sailing on *Wavebreaker* was about as authentic as Pussy-Cute's miaow.

The whine of the sail-furling motors brought an alarmed Thessy running on deck. He stood blinking in the new daylight, then stared in astonishment at the waterlogged white hull which rolled sluggishly under our lee. We were now close enough to read the name on her transom and could see that the derelict was called *Hirondelle*, and hailed from Ostend. The small waves slopped and splashed across the neat blue lettering. It seemed a terrible waste to have run from that grim North Sea port safely across the Atlantic to what must have seemed like the sunlit paradise of the Bahamas' sheltered shallow waters, only to meet this savage fate.

And something savage had happened to *Hirondelle*. She was a mastless mess, trailing a tangle of sodden rigging. Her coachroof and deck were riddled with holes; so many holes that groups of them had joined together to make dark, jagged and splintered craters. My first thought was that someone had run berserk with an industrial drill, but then I saw a glint of brass in her scuppers and I recognised an empty cartridge case and knew I was looking at bullet holes. *Hirondelle* had been machine-gunned. Someone had poured fire at her, but she had stayed afloat because she was one of the few production boats that were built to be unsinkable. Foam had been sandwiched between her fibreglass layers and crammed into every unused space inside her hull and that foam was now holding her afloat, fighting against the dead weight of her ballast and engine and winches and galley stove.

"Help me with the skiff," I said to Thessy.

"You think someone's on board?" he asked with a trepidation that matched my own, for God only knew what horrors might be concealed in the darkness of those cabins.

Thessy and I unlashed the skiff that hung from *Wavebreaker*'s stern davits, I climbed aboard, and Thessy worked the electric motors that lowered me down to the small petulant slap of the early morning waves.

Ellen appeared on deck just as I was casting off. She was dressed in a Winnie-the-Pooh T-shirt that served as her night-dress. She yawned, then scowled at the Belgian yacht.

"Morning!" I shouted cheerfully.

She scowled at me, but said nothing. Ellen was never at her brightest and best first thing in the morning.

I pulled the skiff's outboard into life, then puttered across to the waterlogged yacht. As I got close I saw that her underwater hull had been holed by bullets which must have been fired from inside the boat because all the splinters had been driven outwards so that the hull looked like some giant and exotic sea urchin with red and white fibreglass spines.

I tied the skiff's painter to one of *Hirondelle*'s cleats and climbed gingerly on to the foredeck where I cautiously lifted what was left of the forward hatch to peer into the bow cabin. I half expected to see a body, but there was only dark water sloshing a few inches beneath the deck. No blood had been diluted by the water, or none that I could see. I edged my way aft and stepped down into the flooded cockpit. I steeled myself to look into the main-cabin, but I need not have worried for the big saloon was as blessedly empty of horror as the fore-cabin. *Hirondelle* held nothing but flotsam; so much flotsam that the water in her main-cabin looked like sludge. My eyes adjusted to the gloom and I saw that the sludge was really a thick layer of floating cornflakes, loose cigarettes, and a million scraps of foam that must have been shattered out of the hull by the gunfire. Embedded in that heaving mess were a plastic mug, some wooden clothes pegs, a broken pencil, a red shirt and a mutilated, sodden chart. There was a dark smear on the lip of the coachroof that might have been blood, but could just as easily have been a spill of varnish.

"What happened to her?" Ellen shouted. *Wavebreaker* had now drifted so close to *Hirondelle* that the schooner's huge hull was casting a shadow over me.

"God knows." I pulled the flimsy remnants of the chart out of the water.

"Are we going to salvage her?" Ellen was leaning over *Wavebreaker*'s rail and the sun, rising behind her, turned her mass of red hair into an incandescent haze.

"She's beyond help!" I called back. The waterlogged *Hirondelle* was much too heavy for *Wavebreaker* to take in tow, and I had neither the time nor the equipment to patch the hull and pump it dry. Besides, *Hirondelle* had been so badly damaged that no yard would ever think of trying to rebuild her. Not only had the Belgian boat been riddled with bullets, but I could see great gouges where an axe had been taken to the boat's decking. It all seemed so pointless. *Hirondelle* had clearly been a beautiful boat, yet someone had wantonly tried to destroy her.

I tossed the soaking chart into the skiff and stooped to see if there was anything else I should take from the cabin. I was not searching for plunder, but rather for any clue as to who might have owned this boat or what might have provoked its destruction. I found nothing, except that as I stepped back from the companionway my bare feet trod hard and painfully on some lumpish sharp objects. I ducked down in the cockpit, groped on the grating underfoot, and came up with a handful of cartridge cases. Some were brass, but most were green-lacquered steel. They were 7.62 millimetre cartridges, military issue, and I had a half-memory from the dozy days when I had slept through the perfunctory Warsaw Pact familiarisation lectures that only a few East European countries lacquered steel cartridges green.

It was all very peculiar. A Belgian boat in Bahamian waters

with Warsaw Pact cartridges? What was clear to me was that someone must have stood in this cockpit and fired a machine-gun down the companionway into the main-cabin. They had hoped to shatter the bottom of the hull so that *Hirondelle* would sink without trace, but they had not reckoned with the foam sandwiched in the boat's hull, and thus the evidence of their crime, if crime it was, still floated.

Thessy had started *Wavebreaker*'s engines. The wind had been driving the big schooner down on to *Hirondelle* so now Thessy gave the schooner's propellers a burst of power that churned the sea white and drove her clear. The schooner's shadow vanished, letting the new day's sun slash at me with brilliant force and lance through a line of bullet holes that had pierced the side of *Hirondelle*'s coachroof. The shafts of new sunlight lay like spears of gold in the cabin's muck-ridden gloom. I wondered if I should explore the boat further, but decided that such an exploration was best left to the police.

I tossed my handful of cartridge cases into the skiff, then went forrard along *Hirondelle*'s flooded deck to where an undamaged whisker pole lay in its foredeck clips. I tied the red shirt to the pole's top, then rammed my makeshift flagpole into one of the bullet holes so that the treacherous hulk would be visible to any other mariner. Then I climbed back into the skiff, feeling oddly desolate. There is something very sad about mindless destruction, especially of a boat.

I went back to *Wavebreaker* where, as Thessy stowed the skiff, I called the Royal Bahamian Defence Forces on the VHF radio. I reported our position and my opinion that *Hirondelle* was a danger to navigation; then, feeling very virtuous, I revealed my discovery of the empty cartridge cases and my suspicions that the Belgian boat, and perhaps its crew, had met with a sinister fate. The Bahamian radio operator did not seem particularly interested.

Ellen, who had come below to pull on a pair of shorts and a shirt, listened to the last words of my transmission. "That was a waste of time," she said scornfully.

"Why?" I had long learned not to be offended by Ellen's

caustic remarks. She had an Irish-American mother and a Polish-American father, which volatile blend had produced a girl of startling beauty and nitro-glycerine temper.

"Just what do you think happened to that boat?" she asked me in a venomous voice. "You think it's something simple like an insurance scam? Or a clumsy waste-disposal job?" She paused, waiting for my answer, but I gave her none. "Drugs," she answered for me.

"We don't know that," I protested.

"Oh, Nick!" Ellen was exasperated. "These are the Bahamas! Whoever was on that boat was stupid enough to get involved with drugs, and if you get involved with that boat's fate, then you'll be just as stupid. Which means that you should chuck that chart and those cartridges overboard. Now."

"I shall hand them over to the proper authorities," I said stubbornly.

"God save me from feeble-minded males." She turned towards the galley. "You want some coffee?"

"The prime purpose of the Defence Forces is to guarantee freedom of navigation in Bahamian waters," I said very pompously.

"Oh, sure!" Ellen laughed as she pumped water into the kettle. Thessy was still on deck where he had reset *Wavebreaker*'s sails and taken the helm. I glanced at the fluxgate compass over the chart table to see that we were once again heading northwards. Ellen lit the galley stove, then unscrewed the lid from the jar of instant coffee. "The real purpose of the Bahamian Defence Forces" – she pointed a teaspoon at me to emphasise her words – "is to present the appearance of being zealously engaged in the war against drugs; which appearance of diligence is designed solely to placate the American government who otherwise might issue an official warning to its citizens that the Bahamas are no longer a safe destination for the vacation trade, which warning will effectively stifle the islands' tourist and casino trade which, after drugs, are its most profitable industries." She offered me the pitying and self-satisfied smile of someone who has just proved a debating point. "So no one will thank you for drawing attention to a visiting yacht filled with inconvenient bullet holes. Such things are bad for the tourist business."

"Thank you for explaining it, Professor," I said sarcastically.

She grimaced at me. Ms Ellen Skandinsky, PhD, never liked being reminded that she had abandoned a tenured professorship in Women's Studies to run away to sea; a decision that she liked to portray as quixotic, but which I suspected had been sparked by the pure boredom and pomposity of academic life. Ellen herself swore that she had made the change in order to discover 'real life', a commodity evidently unavailable on campus and one which she believed necessary to her true ambition, which was to be a writer. For Ellen, 'real life' had proved to be a one-room cold-water apartment behind the Straw Market, an unpaid volunteer's job with a Bahamian Literacy Project, and a paid job as a ship's cook, a job so traitorous to her former life and feminist beliefs that even she was astonished to discover that she enjoyed it. I think Ellen had been even more astonished to discover that she and I had become friends in the months we had worked together, no more than friends, but close enough for her to be wondering whether to sail away with me around the world. Not in *Wavebreaker*, but in my own boat that needed to be rebuilt before I took it across the South Pacific.

I heard a whine of servo-motors and guessed that Thessy had turned on the automatic pilot. He came down the companionway, holding the chart I had rescued from *Hirondelle* and which I had spread to dry on *Wavebreaker*'s deck. The torn paper was still sodden. "Nick?" There was consternation in his voice. "Do you know vere they vere two nights ago?" Thessy had the Bahamian out-islander's odd Dickensian accent. He was seventeen years old, skinny as a sopping-wet cat, and was *Wavebreaker*'s first and only mate, which also made him the boat's steward, gorilla, ship's boy, skivvy and mascot. His real name was Thessalonians, and he was just as

10

pious as that New Testament name suggested. "Do you see, Nick?" He was pointing at the wet chart that he had draped across the galley table. "They vere there just two days ago. Only two days!"

The chart had been soaked in sea-water, but salt cannot remove the pencil notations from a chart, and whoever had sailed *Hirondelle* had been a meticulous navigator. A pencil line extended from No Name Bay just south of Miami and reached across the Gulf Stream and into the Bahamas. *Hirondelle*'s navigator had sailed much of the course by dead reckoning, and I could see just where that navigator had finally taken a fix and discovered that he or she had underestimated the northwards current of the Gulf Stream, but by very little, so that the Belgian yacht had only been five nautical miles off its estimated course. That course had curved to the south of Bimini towards a tiny island, lost all by itself between the Biminis and the Berrys, with the unprepossessing name of Murder Cay. The pencil line ended there, punctuated by a small circle enclosing a dot beside which the navigator had written the date and time of *Hirondelle*'s arrival. And that arrival, as Thessy had noted, had been just two days before. No neat pencilled line betrayed *Hirondelle*'s departure from the ill-named Murder Cay.

I had never noticed the island before, despite its most noticeable name. It was a very small island, a mere speck that lay some twenty miles south-east from *Wavebreaker*'s present position, and that was exactly the direction from which the currents and wind would drive a derelict boat.

I fetched the pilot book and looked up Murder Cay, but found no listing for the grimly named island. "Try Sister Island," Ellen suggested laconically.

It seemed a perverse suggestion, but Ellen's perversity was often justified, so I duly looked up Sister Island and discovered that was the new name for Murder Cay. The Pilot Book offered no explanation for that change of name, which seemed a deal of trouble for what must be one of the smallest inhabited islands in all the Bahamas. Sister Island was only three miles long and was never more than a half-mile wide. The island's southernmost promontory was marked with a white light which was meant to flash three times every fifteen seconds and be visible up to five miles away, but the book ominously reported that the light was 'unreliable'. The whole island was surrounded by coral reefs called the Devil's Necklace, and I wondered what unfortunate sailor had given the island and its reefs their macabre names. The deep-water access to Murder Cay lay through a dog-legged and unbuoyed passage to the west of the island. The best guide to the deep-water approach seemed to be a tall skeleton radio mast that was conveniently opposite the passage entrance and was supposedly marked with red air-warning beacons. There was an airstrip on the island which should have displayed a flashing green and white light, but, like the white light and the air-warning beacons, the green and white light was also said to be unreliable. The eastern part of the lagoon evidently offered good shelter, but the pilot book noted that the island had no facilities for visiting yachts. In other words, mariners were being warned to keep away from Murder Cay, yet the pencil line on *Hirondelle*'s chart led inexorably to that island, and there it had ended.

"The government decided the old name was bad for the tourist business," Ellen remarked in an odd sort of voice, almost as if she was trying to reassert a commonplace normality over the sinister implications of that line on an abandoned chart.

"Perhaps the islanders shot the crew," I said, but in a voice that carried no conviction for, despite the missing crew and the all-too-present cartridges, I really could not believe that murder had been done on Murder Cay. I did not want to believe in murder. I wanted the boat's fate, like I wanted life, to be explicable without causing me astonishment. I had been brought up in a house that specialised in giving astonishment, which was why I had run away from home to become a Royal Marine. The Marines had toughened me, and taught me to swear and fight and screw and drink, but they had not taught me cynicism, nor had they obliterated the innocent hope for innocent explanations. "Perhaps," I amended my previous supposition, "it's just an accident."

"Whatever happened," Ellen said brusquely, "it's none of our business."

"And Mr McIllwanney varned us to stay avay from the island!" Thessy said.

I remembered no such warning, but Thessy went to the shelves under the chart table and found one of McIllvanney's green sheets of paper. I hardly ever read McIllvanney's self-styled Notices to Mariners, and I had clearly overlooked this warning that was brief and to the point. 'You will stay away from Sister Island. The Royal Bahamian Defence Forces have issued a warning that the island's new owners don't like trespass, and I don't want to lose any boats to that dislike, so ALL Cutwater Charter Boats will henceforth keep AT LEAST five nautical miles from Sister Island until further notice.'

I thought of the bullet holes that had shattered *Hirondelle*'s once elegant hull. "Those poor bastards," I said softly.

"It's not our business, Nick," Ellen said in warning.

I looked again at McIllvanney's notice. "Do you think the island's new owners are mixed up in drugs?" I asked.

Ellen sighed. She is much given to long-suffering sighs which are her way of informing the male part of the world that it is ineradicably dim-witted. "Do you think they smuggle auto-parts, Nick? Or lavatory paper? Of course they're into drugs, you airhead. And that is why it is not our business."

"I never said it was our business," I spoke defensively.

"So throw those cartridges overboard and lose that chart," Ellen advised me very curtly.

"The police should see them," I insisted.

"You are a fool, Nicholas Breakspear," Ellen said, but not in an unkind manner.

"I've already advised the Defence Forces that the police should look at the boat," I said.

Ellen gave another of her long-suffering sighs. "The dragons won, Nick, and the knights errant lost. Don't you know that?

You've delivered the message, so now forget it! No chart. No cartridges. It's over. No heroics!"

She meant well, but I could not forget *Hirondelle*, because something evil had stirred in this paradise of beaches and lagoons and palm-covered islands, and I wanted the authorities to take the damp torn chart and to find just what lay at the end of its carefully pencilled line. So I shrugged off Ellen's cynical and doubtless sensible pleading, and went topsides to take the helm. *Wavebreaker*'s wake lay white and straight across a brilliant sunlit sea on which, far to our west, I could see a string of grey warships that were American naval vessels come to the Bahamas for an exercise called Stingray. The sight of the flotilla reminded me of my time in the Royal Marines, and I felt a rueful envy of the American Marines who had this tropical playground with its warm seas and palm trees for their training. I had learned the killing trade under the bitter flail of Norwegian sleet and Scottish snow, but that was all in my past, and now I was a free man and I had just one more charter to skipper, after which I could mend my own boat and sail her on new paths across old oceans.

Just as *Hirondelle* had sailed to her adventure.

But, in its place, had found a coral scrap of land called Murder Cay. And there died.

We docked at midday. The deserted boatyard was swimming in heat. It was well into the charter business's low season, so the vast majority of Cutwater's yachts had either gone north for the summer or were sitting on jackstands out of the water. A couple of our bareboat yachts were still at sea, and *Wavebreaker* had one more paying charter to complete, but otherwise McIllvanney's yard had the torpor of tropical summer about it. Even Stella, McIllvanney's long-suffering secretary, had taken the day off, leaving the office locked, which meant I had to walk into town to find a public telephone from which I called the Bahamian Police and told them about *Hirondelle*, and added that I had rescued a chart and a handful of cartridges from the stricken boat. The police sounded surprised that I had bothered to call them, and I walked back to the boatyard feeling strangely foolish.

Ellen laughed at my punctiliousness. Doubtless the police had responded to my call by sharpening their cutlasses and charging their muskets, she mocked, in readiness for an invasion of Murder Cay?

"I didn't mention Murder Cay," I said. "I just told them about the bullet damage to the boat and about the chart."

"Well now that you've single-handedly won the war on drugs, perhaps you can do something useful, like scrub the deck?" We had only this one day to resupply and prepare *Wavebreaker* for her last charter, which meant the schooner had to be refuelled and provisioned, her carpets must be vacuumed, her bilges poisoned against rats and cockroaches, her galley made spotless, her deck scrubbed and her brightwork polished.

In the middle of the afternoon, when it seemed that the work would never be done on time, Bellybutton arrived at the yard. Bellybutton was McIllvanney's foreman, and for a few seconds I dared hope that he had come to help us, but instead he told me that one of the bareboat thirty-three-footers was in trouble. "The man radioed that his engine broke," Bellybutton grumbled, "so I have to fetch the idiot in *Starkisser*." He was pretending that the errand was a nuisance, though at the same

15

time he was grinning with pleasure at the thought of taking McIllvanney's brand new sportsboat to sea. *Starkisser*'s midnight-blue hull had metalflake embedded in its fibreglass so that the sleek boat seemed to scintillate with an internal and infernal dark blue light. She had to be one of the fastest production boats in the islands; her twin big-block engines could hurl the three-ton wedge-shaped hull at over eighty miles an hour, and it worried neither McIllvanney nor Bellybutton that at such a speed a man could not hear himself scream and that even the smallest wave shook the bones right out of their flesh.

"There ain't a girl in creation who don't melt after a ride in *Starkisser*," Bellybutton liked to boast. His real name was Benjamin, but no one ever called him Benjamin or even Ben. To the whole island he was Bellybutton. It was rumoured he had earned the nickname by biting the navel clean out of a whore who had displeased him, and I found the rumour all too believable for he was not a pleasant man. In fact he was a black version of McIllvanney himself; rangy, knowing, tall and sarcastic. "Mr Mac wants to see you tonight," Bellybutton leered at me, as though he suspected I would not enjoy the meeting. "He says you're to go to his place at sundown."

"Why isn't he in the yard today?" I asked.

"Mr Mac's taking a day off!" Bellybutton said in an indignant voice, as though my question had impugned McIllvanney's honour. "He has business to take care of. He had to take a boat to Miami, and that's why he give me the keys to *Starkisser*. You maybe want to take Miss Ellen for a ride in *Starkisser*?" He dangled the sportsboat's keys enticingly. "I won't tell Mr Mac, long as you give me a ride on Miss Ellen when you're done." He laughed and obscenely pumped his lean hips.

"You're an offensive shit, Bellybutton," I said in a very friendly voice, but he had already turned his attention away from me because a car had suddenly appeared in the yard. It was a long white Lincoln with black-tinted windows. The car slid quietly between the cradled yachts to stop just short of *Wavebreaker*'s pier. Apart from the crunching sound of the tyres the Lincoln's approach had been silent and oddly sinister.

One of the passenger doors opened and a very tall and very black-skinned man climbed slowly into the sunlight. "A friend of yours?" I asked Bellybutton, but his eyes widened, he muttered a curse and, instead of answering, he dashed frantically towards *Starkisser*'s pontoon.

The tall black man who had emerged from the Lincoln was dressed in a dark blue three-piece suit that looked incongruously heavy for such a hot day. He wore the elegantly cut suit over a white shirt and an old Etonian tie. He was impressively built; thin hipped and wide shouldered, like a boxer who could punch hard and dance lightly. He looked calmly around the yard, then put on a pair of mirrored sunglasses before slamming the car door shut.

Bellybutton had thrown off *Starkisser*'s lines and now let the sportsboat float away from the pontoon as he unclipped her jet-black cockpit cover. Then, plainly frantic to escape the elegant man, he punched the boat's engines into life. The echo of the twin motors crackled back from the nearby buildings like the sound of a battle-tank firing up for action. Scared pelicans flapped away, and Ellen came up from the galley to see what had caused the commotion. Bellybutton gave one last look at the man walking along the dock, then shoved *Starkisser*'s tachometers way into their red zones so that the dark blue powerboat stood on her tail and screamed out to sea as though the devil himself was on her tail.

"A guilty conscience is a terrible thing." The tall black man chuckled, then sauntered across *Wavebreaker*'s gangplank. Once on deck he stopped to admire Ellen who was dressed in a brief pair of shorts and a faded tank top. Even with her glorious hair scraped back into a loose bun, and with her hands and face smeared with soap and sweat from the exertions of scrubbing the galley stove, she looked utterly beguiling. The black man momentarily took off his sunglasses as though to examine Ellen more closely and I saw he had very hard and very cynical eyes that were suddenly turned full on me. "You must be Breakspear."

"Yes."

"My name is Deacon Billingsley –" he paused as though I should recognise the name, "and I am a police officer."

The arrival of Deacon Billingsley should have given me the satisfaction that my telephone call had been treated seriously, but I sensed this policeman was not going to offer me any satisfaction at all. He had spoken very flatly, making his introduction sound like a threat. The sun, mirrored in the obsidian brightness of his glasses, momentarily dazzled me. "What were you doing when you found *Hirondelle*, Breakspear?" Billingsley asked me.

"Making passage."

"Making passage." He mocked my British accent, then turned on Ellen who had stayed on deck to hear the conversation. "Where were you coming from, lady?"

"Hey! Count me out, OK? I didn't call any goddamn cavalry. You want to know anything about that boat, you ask Nick, not me." She twisted contemptuously towards the companionway.

Billingsley watched her walk away. "She's American?" He seemed amused rather than offended by Ellen's defiance.

"She's American," I confirmed.

Ellen dropped out of sight and Billingsley turned back to me. "Are you screwing the American, Breakspear?" I was so astonished by the sudden question that I just gaped at him. "Are you laying the girl?" Billingsley rephrased his insolent question as though I had not understood the first version. His tone of voice was so bland that he might as well have been asking my opinion of *Wavebreaker*'s sea-keeping qualities.

"The answer is no," I finally said, "and fuck off."

Billingsley lit a cigar. It had a red and yellow band on which I could just read the word *Cubana*. He took his time; first cutting the cigar, then heating its tip with a succession of matches that he carelessly and provocatively dropped on to *Wavebreaker*'s scrubbed deck. He used the toes of his expensive brogues to grind each dead match into the teak-wood so that the charred tips smeared black carbonised streaks across the wood's bone-whiteness. He finally drew the cigar

18

into red heat and discarded the final match. He raised his eyes to stare into my face, and I felt a surge of fear. It was not Billingsley's physical size that provoked that fear, for I was of a size with him, nor was it his profession that gave me pause, but rather the aura of incipient violence that he radiated like a blast furnace. "You mess with me, Breakspear," he said in a deceptively mild voice, "and I'll rip your spine out of your asshole."

I was damned if I would show him my fear. "Do you have a warrant card?" I asked him instead.

For a second I thought he was going to hit me, but then he reached into his jacket pocket and brought out a wallet that he unfolded and thrust towards me, giving me just enough time to see that he held the rank of chief inspector, one of the highest ranks in the Bahamian police force, then the wallet was snapped shut and Deacon Billingsley moved to stand very close to me, so close that I could smell the cigar smoke on his breath. "Where's the chart you took from *Hirondelle*?"

"Down below."

"Then fetch it," he said dismissively.

I obeyed. The chart had dried into stiff and faded folds, but Billingsley did not look at it, instead he just screwed it up and thrust it into a pocket of his expensive jacket.

"I also found these," I said, and offered him the handful of cartridge cases.

He ignored my outstretched hand. "What were you doing at Sister Island, Breakspear?"

The question puzzled me for I had not mentioned Sister Island, nor its old name of Murder Cay, to either the police or to the Defence Forces, nor had Billingsley troubled to look at the pencilled line on the chart, yet he had somehow connected *Hirondelle* with the mysterious island. "I asked you what you were doing at Sister Island," Deacon Billingsley said threateningly.

"We weren't anywhere near the island!" I protested. "You can check that for yourself! I reported the co-ordinates where we found *Hirondelle* over the radio, and those co-ordinates are twenty miles north-west of Sister Island. That's as close as we ever got to it."

He said nothing for a few seconds, and I sensed that I might have unsettled this policeman. I had also angered him, though his anger seemed directed at himself. He had come here on a misunderstanding; believing that *Wavebreaker* had been at Murder Cay when in fact we had not even been within sight of that mysterious island.

But Billingsley had clearly known about *Hirondelle*'s visit to Murder Cay, and I realised that this senior police officer had not come here to enquire into a crime, but to cover it up. *Hirondelle*'s owners, he said glibly, had decided to fly home and, despairing of ever selling the yacht in a glutted market, had simply abandoned it and someone had evidently used the hulk for target practice. "Maybe it was the Americans," Billingsley suggested airily, "you know there's a naval exercise in progress? Perhaps they machine-gunned the hulk?"

"Those cartridge cases aren't American issue," I said, holding out the green-lacquered steel casings. I should have kept my silence, for the only purpose my words served was to demonstrate my disbelief in Billingsley's outrageous explanation.

That disbelief was a challenge, and Deacon Billingsley was not a man to resist a challenge. He tipped my hand with his own strong grasp, spilling the cartridge cases into his left palm, then, one by one, he tossed the cartridge cases overboard. "You have a boat in the Bahamas." It was not a question, but a flat statement. "A ketch called *Masquerade*, presently marooned on Straker's Cay."

"She's not marooned," I said, "she's under repair."

He ignored my emendation, but just continued to toss the cartridge cases over the gunwale. "And how will you repair your boat, Breakspear, or even take her away, if I put your name on the Stop List? You do know what the Stop List is, Breakspear?"

I knew only too well. It was the list of undesirable aliens who were banned from entering the Bahamas, and if my name was put on that Stop List, and if I was then thrown off the islands, I would probably never see my boat again. The threat was effective and blunt.

"Do you understand me?" Billingsley asked as he threw the last cartridge overboard. I suspected that as soon as he left the boatyard the chart would be similarly destroyed. Doubtless *Hirondelle* had already been blown up, just as my own boat would be butchered if I insisted on challenging this man. "Do you understand me?" he asked a second time.

"Yes." I tasted the sourness of humble pie.

"So do you still find anything suspicious in the circumstances surrounding your discovery of the yacht *Hirondelle*?" Billingsley asked with a mocking punctiliousness that was intended to humiliate me, but the humiliation was my own fault for having challenged the policeman's lie.

"No," I said, and hated myself for telling the untruth, but I was thinking of my own boat standing propped on the sand of Straker's Cay, and I thought of all the work I had lavished on *Masquerade*, and of all the love and care and time I had poured into her, and I tried to imagine her rotting under the tropical sun with her paint peeling, her deck planks opening and her timbers riddled with termites. So I lied and said I detected nothing untoward in finding a bullet-riddled boat awash in the Bahamian seas.

Chief Inspector Deacon Billingsley raised his right hand and victoriously, patronisingly and very gently, patted my cheek so that I felt the cold touch of his heavy gold rings. "Good boy," he said derisively. "And when you see Bellybutton, tell him that I know where his brother is, and I'll pick the bastard up whenever I choose and then feed him head first into a cane-shredder." He turned abruptly away, not waiting for any answer. The gangplank bounced under his confident step. He walked down the quay without looking back, but he must have known I was watching him for he stopped a few yards short of his car and very ostentatiously took the incriminating chart from his jacket pocket. I thought for a second he was going to burn it, but instead he tore it into tiny scraps that he tossed into the warm wind.

"The bastard," I breathed. In that moment, *Hirondelle* and her crew had disappeared for good.

The Lincoln's driver was a uniformed constable who climbed into the sunlight to open the car door for Billingsley. "I told you not to bother," Ellen said disparagingly as she climbed the main companionway, and I guessed that she had been listening to my conversation with Billingsley by standing just under the saloon skylight which was propped open. Now she stood beside me and watched the white Lincoln drive out of the boatyard. "Didn't I say you'd be wasting your time?"

"Sod my time," I said angrily. "Did you hear what he asked about you and me?"

"Of course I heard." She seemed quite unfazed by Billingsley's impertinent question whether we slept together, doubtless translating the policeman's particular curiosity as a general confirmation of men's innate tackiness. Ellen was more irritated by my answer than by Billingsley's question. "Why didn't you just tell him the truth?"

"I did."

"I mean the truthful explanation." Which was that Ellen had sworn herself to celibacy while she worked as a cook, a decision that was to me as eccentric as it was both incomprehensible and frustrating.

"I shouldn't have told the arrogant bastard anything." I stared at the empty yard where Billingsley's car had stood. "My God! But I ought to report him! I know what I'll do! I'll bloody well call the Belgian Embassy!"

"Don't be so stupid, Nick!" Ellen was genuinely frightened for me, but she was also indignant at me. "Report him, and you'll be thrown off the islands before the week's end! Don't you understand what's going on? Are you entirely blind? Don't you understand that in small countries power is more likely to remain undisguised because there isn't sufficient societal depth to conceal the realities of institutionalised brutality beneath a respectable fiction?"

But I was not listening to the professor's explanation. I was feeling disgust at myself. It seemed to me that the stench of Billingsley's cigar smoke clung to the boat like the sulphurous reek of the pit, and with it lingered the realisation that I had been twisted into dishonesty as easily as a length of rope could be coiled into hanks. I had lied, and I had let myself be used by evil. But all for *Masquerade*.

Masquerade is my boat. She's a beauty; a forty-foot ketch built of mahogany on oak. She had been constructed in Hampshire before the Second World War by craftsmen who had taken pride in their work, but fibreglass had made wooden boats redundant and *Masquerade* had been laid up and left to rot at a boatyard on the River Exe.

I had found her when I was a Weapons Instructor at the Royal Marines' Lympstone camp in Devon. I had bought her for a song, then spent a fortune restoring her and, when my term of service expired and I could afford to become the gypsy-sailor I had always wanted to be, I left the Marines and made *Masquerade* my new home. For a couple of years she and I had knocked around the Mediterranean, then I had sailed her across the Atlantic. That voyage had been the first leg of a planned circumnavigation, but those dreams had been brutally shattered when *Masquerade* was stolen from an anchorage in the Florida Keys. She turned up ten days later, stranded on a coral reef in the Bahamas with most of her gear missing and her starboard bilges half ripped out by the savage coral heads. The thieves were never found.

That theft and recovery had taken place just over a year ago. Now, laboriously rescued by Thessy's father, a fisherman, *Masquerade* was standing in the sandy backyard of Thessy's house where she was cradled by timber props among the casuarinas and palm trees, and where chickens roosted in her cockpit. She needed repairs and she needed love. She needed to feel the sea about her long deep keel again. Her timbers needed to swell with the salt water. She needed me. Which was why I had bowed to the imperative of Deacon Billingsley's dishonesty, because otherwise I would have lost her.

And I would have lost the chance to sail across the Pacific with Ellen, because Ellen was on the verge of agreeing to come with me, and if I had not yielded to the policeman's blackmail I would have lost Ellen as well as my boat.

And so I had lied.

A few moments before sundown I extricated *Wavebreaker*'s folding bicycle from the big locker on the boat's after swim-platform, forced the rusting hinges open, then pedalled along Midshipman Road to the glittering block of apartments where our esteemed boss lived.

Matthew McIllvanney was not the real boss of Cutwater Yacht Charters (Bahamas) Limited, which belonged to a retired theatre owner who now lived in Bermuda and was a long-time friend of my father, a friendship that had secured me the job of skippering *Wavebreaker* when *Masquerade* was wrecked, but McIllvanney actually looked after the day-to-day running of the charter business. Cutwater's charter bookings were usually made by agencies in Fort Lauderdale and London, then faxed to McIllvanney's yard in Freeport where the boats were docked and maintained. McIllvanney also kept a few power-cruisers of his own for charter, and his yard ran an efficient yacht-servicing and marine supplies business, and thus the boundaries between his operations and Cutwater Charters were necessarily blurred and, for all intents and purposes, he could have been said to run Cutwater. He also ran a couple of other businesses that had nothing to do with boats and were probably much more profitable.

McIllvanney was certainly making money from somewhere. *Starkisser* had to have cost him close to a hundred thousand US dollars, and the Lucaya penthouse apartment, with its private docks and its view towards Silver Point Beach, probably cost ten times as much. He kept a BMW and an old open-top MG in the garage, though his vehicle of choice was a big Kawasaki motorbike. Matthew McIllvanney, even by the standards of the expatriate retired Americans who lived all around him, was a rich man.

I chained *Wavebreaker*'s bicycle to an ornamental fence outside McIllvanney's apartment block, and persuaded the uniformed ape on security that I was not a terrorist. The ape keyed the lift panel so that the elevator would go to the very top floor where it opened directly into McIllvanney's apartment. I had visited the apartment at least a dozen times, but I still found the fact of a lift opening directly into a living room incredibly impressive; a proof of wealth as convincing as the possession of gold taps or of mink rugs or of the girl who waited to greet me just beyond the lift doors. She was a very tall and very fair and dazzlingly beautiful creature whose skin was goose-pimpled under the impact of McIllvanney's air conditioning which was set to a level that might have made a penguin shiver. "Hi!" she said enthusiastically. "You've got to be Nick! Matt's expecting you. He's right outside." The girl, who looked as though she had been made in heaven out of peaches and cream, was wearing a few pieces of string arranged as a bikini, high heels, the goose-pimples, and nothing else. She nodded towards the screened porch that overlooked the sea. "You'll have a drinkie, Nick?"

"Irish whiskey," I said, "no ice, some water, and thank you."

"You're surely welcome. My name's Donna." Donna gave me a limpid hand to shake, then wiggled her way towards the liquor cabinet. Just to watch her walk threatened to break your heart. She waved a hand about McIllvanney's apartment. "Isn't this just the cutest place you ever did see, Nick?"

"It's very splendid," I agreed politely. The apartment was indeed attractive, perhaps because it had nothing whatever of McIllvanney about it. The apartment's previous owners had hired an expensive interior designer from New York and ordered her to trick out the rooms in a horse-country olde-English Spy-Cartoons look, which had been done to extravagant perfection, but McIllvanney was none of those things. McIllvanney was a Protestant bully from the Shankill Road in Belfast, who had learned his thuggery in the hard school of Northern Ireland's prejudices, honed it in the British army, and now put it to whatever good use he wanted in the Bahamas. If I had been asked to decorate a flat to reflect McIllvanney's character then I would have given him an East Belfast bar with sawdust scattered on the floor, King Billy strutting on the walls, and blood splattered across its tobacco-stained ceiling.

"Why don't you just go on through, Nick," Donna invited me, "and I'll bring you and Matt your drinkies."

I went on through, sliding the heavy plate glass aside to walk on to the humid porch where a morose looking McIllvanney slouched in a cane chair and stared through the insect screens at the darkening sea. "It's you," he greeted me without delight and as though he had been expecting someone else.

"You wanted to see me," I pointed out. Spending time with McIllvanney was not my idea of relaxation, and I didn't much take to his lack of enthusiasm.

"Sit down," he said grudgingly, "your Holiness." Calling me 'your Holiness' was McIllvanney's joke. It was not because I was particularly pious, but rather because my namesake, Nicholas Breakspear, had been the only Englishman who had ever become Pope. He had taken the name Adrian IV and had ruled the church in the twelfth century, a fact that very few people other than myself knew, but a fact I had been foolish enough to tell McIllvanney whose hatred of 'taigs', Catholics, ensured he would never forget my papal connection. In truth there was no connection, for my original family name was Sillitoe, but, long before I was born, my father had adopted Breakspear as his stage name and I had really known no other.

"Did that focker Bellybutton bring *Starkisser* back?" McIllvanney suddenly demanded of me in his sour Belfast accent.

"In one piece, even."

"He's getting too big for his focking black boots, that feller is." The complaint was a ritual, not to be taken seriously, a mere habitual statement made solely to impress on me how tough McIllvanney was. If he had to choose between me and Bellybutton, or between Bellybutton and his own mother, he would have chosen Bellybutton any day. They were two of a kind.

McIllvanney was a tall, harshly scarred and surprisingly handsome man, with a hard knowing face and a deceptively thin body. It was deceptive for he was brutally strong. He could also be excellent company, with a fund of stories that he told with an exquisite sense of timing, though such good moments were rare for he preferred to brood savagely over life's injustices; the chief of which was the inexplicable existence of Roman Catholics.

"Are you a Catholic?" he asked Donna as she brought out the drinks. I suspected the question was meant for my amusement rather than for his own enlightenment.

"Gracious, no! In our family we're all Episcopalians." She gave him a big smile. "From Philadelphia," she added for my benefit and with yet another winning smile. Donna was one of life's cheerleaders; her teeth were a triumph of the orthodontic trade, her hair was a confection of gel, spray and heat, and her body was a tribute to wholesome American food and exercise. "I've heard so much about you," she said to me, as though settling herself in for a long cosy chat.

"So now fock away off and forget him," McIllvanney snapped at her.

"It's just been so nice visiting with you, Nick!" Donna gave me a last dazzling smile, then, apparently impervious to McIllvanney's evil-tempered scorn, clicked away on her ridiculously high heels.

I waited till Donna was safely out of earshot. "Is she your newest?" Pretty girls moved through McIllvanney's life at an astonishing rate, though the last, who had endured a record six months, had left just a few weeks before.

He shook his head. "She's one of the girls, so she is. She'll cost you two thousand US a day, Nick, plus air-fare, food and a present. I had to bring her over from Miami today because the stupid cow won't fly. Can you believe that? She's frightened of airplanes, so she is! So I had to fetch her in *Junkanoo*."

Junkanoo was one of McIllvanney's boats, doubtless purchased on the profits of his call-girl service. He liked to boast that the service was very elegant, and certainly not crude like the part-time pimp service that Bellybutton enforced with his teeth. Instead McIllvanney was the Bahamian agent for a Miami-based business that claimed to provide the world's most beautiful girls to anyone with the money to pay for them. McIllvanney arranged the girls' visits to clients in the Bahamas and guaranteed their safety while they were in the islands. That made McIllvanney a gold-plated pimp, though he preferred to describe himself as a 'leisure-agent'; however, he usually had the grace to smile when he used that label. He showed a similar amusement now. "I hear that black bugger Billingsley scared the living daylights out of you today?"

McIllvanney enjoyed making the accusation. He did not like me. I was the son of a rich and famous man and, to McIllvanney, that accident of birth clinked with the corrupt sound of silver spoons. It did not matter that I had rejected my father's ways, that I had become a marine and was as poor as a church mouse while McIllvanney had become a rich man; the stench of privilege still clung to me and McIllvanney loved to discomfort me because of it. "How do you know what Billingsley did to me?" I asked him.

"How the fock do you think I know? He told me!"

I should have realised that in an island as small as Grand Bahamas two men like McIllvanney and Billingsley would know each other. McIllvanney must have been Billingsley's source for the policeman's information about my boat and my plans to repair her. Doubtless, before coming to the yard, Billingsley had talked with McIllvanney, and I guessed that he had also entertained the Ulsterman afterwards with an account of my pusillanimity. I suddenly felt an immense relief that I only had one more charter to complete for Cutwater, and that I would then be free of these men.

"So what did Billingsley tell you?" McIllvanney seemed amused by my silence. "That the Belgian owners got pissed off with sailing and trotted off home?"

"Yes."

"Billingsley's a lying black bastard, so he is. Those Belgians must have been in the wrong place at the wrong time, and they probably saw something they shouldn't have seen, so someone shut them up for good. They'll not have been the first tourists to be fed to the sharks and they won't be the last."

"You're telling me they were murdered?" I was feeling guilty at giving in so easily to Billingsley's blackmail.

"I don't know what happened to them, do I?" McIllvanney said tiredly. "And if I did know, would I be telling you? I'm just telling you what I think happened, so I am. And I don't think they pissed off home because they were suddenly hungry for Belgian waffles. I think they were sent for their tea by Billingsley and his friends, and I'll tell you something more, no one will ever know what happened to them, so forget it! If you know what's good for you, Thessy and Ellen, none of you even saw the Belgian boat this morning!" He glared at me, almost daring me to contradict his advice. I kept a cowardly silence that was broken by a strident and sudden eruption of Goombay music from one of the nearby beach hotels. The music triggered a burst of applause. "It's a convention," McIllvanney explained with a sneer, "off-season rates, car dealers and their wives from Europe, and the product is a five-speed piece of tin-plate junk. Man's a prick."

He had added the last three words with the same morose carelessness with which he had decried the car dealers' convention, but he offered no elucidation as to what the words meant. "Who is?" I finally asked.

"Deacon Billingsley, of course. He's as tough as old boots, but playing with drugs is still a mug's game. If the spics don't blow you away then the Americans will. The man's a prick to be involved."

"So he is involved?" I asked, and I was unable to hide my surprise even though McIllvanney was merely confirming my own suspicion that Billingsley was corrupt. Yet suspecting and knowing are two different things, and I was still naïve enough to want to believe that all policemen could be trusted. Ellen was amused by my naïvety, claiming that if she dug deep enough she would probably discover that I still believed in Santa Claus. I did not like the accusation of naïvety, preferring to believe that I was an honest man who found it hard to imagine how other people could live with a guilty conscience. Whatever, I sounded primly shocked at hearing my suspicions of Billingsley's corruption confirmed.

McIllvanney stared at me as though I was a complete idiot.

"Of course he's focking involved. He's up to his black eyeballs in the drug trade. He's even got a house on Murder Cay, so he has, and he's not the only one with his nose stuck in that particular trough, but it's not your business, and you don't mess with the man because he's got friends who won't think twice about feeding you to the sharks. I've got a job for you."

I almost ignored his last words because I was still thinking about Billingsley's dishonesty, but then I realised just what McIllvanney had said and I frowned. "A job? What kind of job?"

"What the hell sort of a job do you think it is? It's an extra charter for *Wavebreaker*, of course."

"I can't do it, you know I can't," I said instantly and very firmly. McIllvanney did not respond, except to stare at me with his unblinking and reptilian eyes, and thus he forced me to add an unnecessary explanation. "I want to sail *Masquerade* south before the hurricane season, so I'm going to need all that's left of this summer to repair her." That was entirely true, but it sounded very limp as I said it and my voice just tailed away. "Of course I'd like to help you, but . . ."

"The job will pay extra," McIllvanney said flatly. He was not looking at me any more, but was staring out to sea where a small tanker, her navigation lights glowing bright in the falling darkness, nudged gingerly towards the bunkering buoys. "A lot extra. And it's legal."

"If it wasn't for *Masquerade* – " I began, but McIllvanney cut me off.

"The client's offering 115 American dollars a day for the skipper, which makes the whole thing worth over ten thousand bucks to you. Ellen will clear eight thousand, so she will, and Thessalonians will make over three."

I was doing some swift mental arithmetic, and the result was so crazy that I paused to rework the sums in my head. The car salesmen cheered from the darkness beneath as I stared into McIllvanney's implacable eyes. "Three months?" I asked in disbelief. "The client wants the boat for three months! That's impossible. I've got *Masquerade* to repair."

"The client says he's an admirer of yours." McIllvanney managed to insert a sneer into the word admirer. "He wants you particularly, so he does. You remember Senator Crowninshield?"

"Of course I do." I remembered George Crowninshield very well, for he and his wife had been my very first clients on board *Wavebreaker* and I had been nervous, not just at the prospect of a new job, but because of the client's eminence. George Crowninshield was a US senator, one of the stars of that legislature, and these days it was impossible to see his name in a magazine or newspaper without the added speculation that he might soon become the President of the United States. He was not the clear favourite for the Oval Office, for there were other men whose achievements were more palpable than George Crowninshield's, but he looked good, sounded better and no journalist had ever discovered him with his fingers in the till or his legs in the wrong bed. His enemies said that he was a politician without a cause, but if that was the worst they could say of him then he could indeed look towards the White House.

I had liked the senator. I had expected an American senator to be as pompous and flatulent as a British MP, but George Crowninshield had proved affable and friendly. He had been intrigued by my relationship with my father, and sympathetic to my rejection of the theatre. My father, Sir Tom, was the second most famous man of the British stage, of any stage for that matter; a towering and famous figure, one of the great actors of all time, who accepted the adulation as his due and who had expected me, like the rest of his children, to follow in his footsteps. Instead, in rebellion against the illusions of the stage and films, I had run away from home and joined the Marines. Not as an officer, but as a marine. Sir Tom had tried to get me out, had failed, and had then left me to my own devices. What hurt him was how much I looked like him. I, the only one of his children who had not gone on to the stage, had inherited the famous Breakspear eyes, the Breakspear height, the Breakspear cheekbones, the brooding Breakspear presence that my father had used to break the hearts of unnumbered women. I was often called Hamlet because I so

31

resembled my father's appearance in his most famous film, the 'Coronation' Hamlet, so named because it had been released in Coronation year. Yet I was not my father. I was an ex-marine sergeant who was also a damned good sailor.

Senator Crowninshield had been sympathetic to the problems a child might have with a famous parent. The senator had a son and daughter of his own and, though he had never talked specifically of their problems, I sensed that in my life he was seeking an answer to his own family's complexities. He and I had talked long into the tropical nights and I had enjoyed his company, and I would have liked to have spent more time with Senator Crowninshield, but three months? "Just how can a US senator take off from his job for three months?" I now asked McIllvanney in astonishment

"The senator doesn't want the boat for himself." McIllvanney shook a cigarette out of a packet, then opened his briefcase that lay on the floor beside his chair. "He wants the boat for his two children. Except they're hardly children any more; the wee bastards are twenty-four, so they are. Twins, you see, a boy and a girl." He had found his lighter in the briefcase, as well as a letter that was embossed with a blue and gold eagle above the rubric 'From the Washington Office of Senator George Crowninshield'. McIllvanney held the letter out to me as though it explained everything. "The girl's called Robin-Anne, and the boy is Rickie. It's a graduation present for her, so it is."

I ignored the letter. "A graduation present?" I was accustomed to wealthy Americans treating their children to lavish rewards for completing extremely average educations, but three months' charter aboard *Wavebreaker* seemed uncommonly generous, even to a man as famously wealthy as Senator Crowninshield.

"It's his focking money," McIllvanney justified the senator's generosity.

"But it's my time," I said as I stood up, "and I can't spare it. I've got a boat to repair."

"Ellen will be disappointed," McIllvanney said slyly, "she likes her money, so she does."

32

He again managed to invest his words with a sneer. "She's only saving her money," I sprang to Ellen's defence, "so she has something to live on while she writes her first novel."

"She should shack up with a man, then, like the other women writers do," McIllvanney said nastily and, when I did not respond, he jabbed a finger at me. "If she's so keen to save a spot of money then she won't thank you for cheating her of eight grand."

"Find someone else to skipper the charter," I said. "Why don't you ask Sammy Meredith? He'd love to do it." Sammy was another of Cutwater's skippers, and a good one.

"Because the senator asked for you personally," McIllvanney said. "He wants you, not Sammy or anyone else, and if you won't do it, then you're not just putting Ellen's money at risk, but you're putting my commission on the line too, and I might not like that."

"Get lost." I would not be threatened by McIllvanney. "Ask Sammy Meredith."

"A hundred and twenty-five dollars a day?" McIllvanney offered.

It never occurred to me that something quite extraordinary must be implicated in the charter if George Crowninshield was willing to pay such an egregious price for an out-of-season charter. "The answer's still no," I said.

McIllvanney shrugged acceptance of my refusal, then held up a hand to stop me leaving. "Talking of Ellen," he said casually, "is the silly bint still refusing to fock?"

"Jesus wept!" I was wondering if the world had gone mad. "You're as bad as Billingsley!"

McIllvanney was quite unmoved by my anger. "Because if she can't make money from the senator's charter," he went on, "I was thinking of offering her a job or two on my own behalf. I mean, she's an attractive girl, so she is, despite her ideas, and she could make a pretty penny out of her looks. Know what I mean?"

I knew exactly what he meant, and I felt a seething of anger at his suggestion. "Ask her yourself. I won't bloody pimp for you." I snatched his sliding door open and went back into the arctic cold where I punched the button to summon the lift. Donna was on the telephone. She smiled at me as the lift doors opened, then mouthed a silent farewell and fluttered her fingers at me till the lift doors closed.

I rode the bicycle back to the darkened and empty boatyard. Ellen had gone to her one-room apartment in town while Thessy was reading his Bible in the main-cabin, so I heated myself some baked beans in *Wavebreaker*'s microwave, spread them on buttered toast, soaked them in brown sauce, then ate a morose supper on deck until the bugs drove me to the screened sanctuary of the staterooms below. Thessy asked me what McIllvanney had wanted, but I said it had been nothing very much for I was too disgusted with the man to tell Thessy the truth. I felt dirtied by the corruption of pimps, yet I would soon be free of them for I had just one more job to do, and then I would be loosed to the consolations of *Masquerade* and to the joys of the South Pacific's winds. Just one more job; then home to the sea.

Next morning the sky was clear, the wind steady, and the barometer high. The customers' beds were made, the galley was stocked, and the black scorch marks of Deacon Billingsley's matches had been scrubbed out of *Wavebreaker*'s pale decks. Her fuel tanks were filled with diesel, the last fresh water was aboard, there was sun-tan lotion and lip-salve in every cabin, and the rotted chicken heads were safe in the freezer. We were ready.

McIllvanney made his usual inspection. *Wavebreaker* was the flagship of Cutwater's fleet and McIllvanney liked to see her sparkling before each charter. That morning, as usual, he found nothing to complain of, so instead he wheeled on me to demand whether the boat's electronic instruments were functioning properly.

"Ask Ellen," I replied laconically, for Ellen was the only person who truly understood all the fancy gadgets though, perversely, she had still not mastered a sextant. She confirmed to McIllvanney that the weather-fax machine and the Loran and the Satnav and the radar and all the other things that hummed and winked and glowed in the night were working properly.

McIllvanney flicked a non-existent scrap of dust from the varnished rail, then gave Thessy a sly glance. "I suppose His Holiness Pope Breakspear told you about the senator's offer, eh, Thessalonians? And I dare say you're disappointed about it, because it's not every day that an out-island lad gets offered that sort of money, is it now? It's even better money than you could earn in high season, so it is, but of course your father isn't Sir Thomas Bloody Breakspear and as rich as a pig in shit, so you need the money, while his Holiness here doesn't. And the senator was most particular in wanting Pope Break-spear. No one else, the senator said, just his Holiness." McIllvanney favoured me with a jackal-like smile.

Thessy hesitated, torn between curiosity and his loyalty to me, but he finally shook his head. "I don't know about the senator's offer, sir."

McIllvanney pretended astonishment. "Did I speak out of turn? That's terrible, if I did. Forget I even spoke." He shot a glance at Ellen, making sure that she had understood him as well as Thessy, then he looked at his watch and shouted for Bellybutton to start up one of the workboats. "I'll see you in a week's time, so I will." He gave me an evil grin, knowing just what dissension he had sown in *Wavebreaker*'s crew, then he was gone.

"What offer?" Ellen asked icily when McIllvanney was out of earshot. "And what senator?"

So, just as McIllvanney had intended, I was forced to tell Ellen and Thessy about George Crowninshield's offer, and how the senator was willing to pay above the odds if we would all abandon our summer plans and take his precious kids to sea for three months. I tried to make the prospect unattractive, but McIllvanney's vision of money had dazzled both Ellen and Thessy.

"Why the hell did you say no?" Ellen demanded angrily.

"I didn't say no. I just said I couldn't go myself! But I told McIllvanney that Sammy Meredith could go instead of me."

Ellen did not like that suggestion. Sammy was a competent skipper, but he could not keep his hands to himself when Ellen was close. Sammy was presently delivering one of our Nautor Swans to its Massachusetts owner; many of the charter yachts were privately owned and only leased into Cutwater's care on condition that we delivered them back to their owners for the northern summer. I assumed McIllvanney had sent a message to Massachusetts asking Sammy to telephone as soon as he reached port, and I was certain that Sammy would jump at the chance of three months' extra salary, and if he did then Ellen and Thessy would similarly earn their small fortunes.

"But Mr McIllvanney said the senator vants you, Nick," Thessy said unhappily.

"He just wants someone to give his two spoilt brats a holiday. He doesn't care who skippers the boat!"

"But maybe he does," Thessy insisted sadly, and both he and Ellen stared reproachfully at me as though I was risking all their future prosperity.

"For God's sake," I said angrily, "you'll both get your money. Sammy Meredith will jump at the chance of three months' work. I can't do it, OK? I've got a boat to mend." The two of them still gazed at me with resentful misunderstanding. Damn McIllvanney, I thought, and damn his blackmail. I turned away from my crew to demonstrate that I would not discuss the Crowninshield charter any further. "Thessy? Put up the flags."

The flags were our final welcoming touch. *Wavebreaker* was registered in the Channel Islands, and thus sailed under a defaced British red ensign with the Bahamian flag flying as a courtesy ensign from the main spreaders, but I always greeted arriving charter guests with their own country's flag – though such a gesture was considered bad flag etiquette by nautical purists, it was good for our final tip – and so Thessy now hoisted the Stars and Stripes to the mainmast's spreaders and a smaller Stars and Bars just beneath. The Confederate flag had been Ellen's idea, to be unfurled whenever we had charterers from the deep South, and this week's guests were three married couples from Georgia. I watched the two handsome flags uncurl to the warm wind, then went on my own tour of inspection. *Wavebreaker* looked good, and we, her crew, looked just as good in our matching blue and white clothes.

We were ready, even to the pitcher of orange juice, bucket of champagne and iced flask of vodka that waited on a table Ellen had carried up to the cockpit. The wind lifted the snow-white tablecloth and stirred the handsome red ensign at *Wavebreaker*'s stern. "She looks good," I told my crew, "well done."

"But suppose Crowninshield won't accept anyone but you as *Wavebreaker*'s captain?" Ellen, refusing to be sidetracked from her lost dollars, asked in a sulky and defiant voice.

The question annoyed me. "I'm supposed to abandon *Masquerade* just to give his spoilt bloody kids a holiday?"

"No, you're supposed to abandon *Masquerade* just so I can earn a few thousand dollars." Ellen smiled very sweetly at me. "And if I don't earn those few thousand dollars then I am sure as hell not going to sail away with you. As the psalmist says, dear Nicholas," and Ellen's smile became even sweeter, "you can blow that dream right up your ass."

Thessy gasped at such blasphemy, while I scowled at Ellen's blackmail. "You can earn your money with Sammy Meredith," I insisted, "then sail away with me."

"I can't if the senator demands you," Ellen said stubbornly, then turned away as Cutwater's courtesy taxi arrived from the airport in a salvo of backfires and black smoke. Thessy slid down the companionway, took the cassette from the rack, and waited by the boat's sound system for my signal.

The taxi doors opened. We knew very little about these last clients of the season except that they were two attorneys and a proctologist, all from Georgia and all vacationing with their wives, and we also knew that one of the wives was a vegetarian and that the proctologist hated pasta, but beyond that our guests were utter strangers and so we waited nervously to see what kind of people would be our companions and paymasters for the next week. Doubtless the arriving customers were just as anxious about us, and part of our job was to relax them quickly. "You have to remember," Ellen liked to lecture

Thessy and me, "just how absurdly wealthy they all are, and how desperately the wealthy want to be liked because they can't help feeling guilty about being so rich, so we only have to be obsequious, give them loads of booze, and pretend to be impressed by their entirely predictable and usually jejune opinions, after which they'll reward us with an outrageously large tip – which is, after all, the sole reason for being nice to the ghastly creatures in the first place."

The first man out of the Chevrolet was wearing blue and green Bermuda shorts, a pink and scarlet Hawaiian shirt and a blue tennis visor with the words 'Go Dawgs' inscribed on its peak. "He must be the proctologist," Ellen said sweetly.

"Vot's a proctologist?" Thessy, ever eager to extend his education, asked from the foot of the companionway.

"A proctologist is an asshole doctor, Thessy dear," Ellen explained, then gave me a smile that would have frozen the heart out of a blast furnace. "Or in Nick's case," she added loudly, "a brain surgeon."

"Now!" I interrupted Thessy's next earnest question, and he pushed the cassette into the tape deck and a steel band arrangement of 'Yellow Bird' thumped and jangled from the cockpit speakers to fill the marina with its bright and jaunty welcome. Bellybutton, a straw hat over his eyes, danced a few ludicrous steps on the deck of the workboat, thus looking for all the world like a simple Bahamian native welcoming the nice white folks from Georgia who now stood blinking in the bright sunlight beside a growing mound of their designer-label luggage. The man with the 'Go Dawgs' hat saw our rebel flag at the spreaders and let out an approving yell that sent two gulls squawking up from the garbage cans behind McIllvanney's office.

"Asshole," the Yankee Ellen said scathingly, then, joined by Thessy, we stepped forward to offer our practised and smiling welcome.

My last charter had begun; I had one week to work, then it would be back to *Masquerade*, and then to the long winds of the southern ocean that led to the uttermost ends of the earth, and thus to happiness.

Wavebreaker, despite her ethereal beauty, was not the most practical boat with which to cruise the Bahamas. She drew too much water, and the Bahamas, for the most part, are a shallow bank dotted with ripsaw coral heads and treacherous shoals where flat-bottomed boats might glide in comparative safety, but where a deep-keeled schooner was forced to creep with painful care. Whenever we reached coral or shoal waters Thessy was forced to spend hours perched at the foremast's lower spreaders to watch the water's colour. Deep safe water was a dark royal blue, while over a coral reef the sea shaded to green or, when perilously shallow, to brown, and Thessy, peering ahead, would shout at me to go to port or starboard, or even to go backwards as fast as the motors would catch hold. We tried to avoid such adventures by sticking to the deeper channels and harbours, but some guests demanded we anchor in the shallower lagoons where the rays glided above the bright sand and the grey snappers schooled and the barracudas patrolled. One way to discourage such demands was secretly to salt a shallow anchorage with a bag of rotted chicken heads which would quickly draw a sinuous and evil-looking pack of otherwise harmless sand sharks that would twist menacingly under our keel and persuade the paying customers to seek the deeper darker waters offshore.

Guests who still wanted to explore the lagoons and sea-flats could use *Wavebreaker*'s skiff. Our Georgia guests used the small flat-bottomed craft to go bonefishing one afternoon, and Thessy, well trained by his father, led them unerringly to a sea-flat by a mangrove swamp where, in just a few heart-racing moments, they landed four of the gleaming and elusive fish. None weighed more than three pounds, but the sheer savage strength of the mirror-plated fish astonished our guests. "Hey, beautiful!" the proctologist, back aboard *Wavebreaker* at sunset, called down the companionway steps to where Ellen was tearing apart a lettuce for the evening meal. "Can you cook me a bonefish?"

"I can cook it, doctor, but you won't want to eat it." Ellen gave him her sweetest smile, the one calculated to provoke cardiac arrest in a sworn celibate. "Eating bonefish is just like sucking fish-juice off a mouthful of tin-tacks."

"So what are you doing for my supper, darling?"

"French fries and New York strip steak."

"Who strips? You or the beef?" The proctologist whooped with laughter and punched my arm. "Get it, Nick? Who strips? You or the beef? Shee-it, I kill myself sometimes. Was she really a college professor?"

"So she tells me."

"They didn't look like that when I was at college. I tell you, Nick, the old bags who lectured us were all spayed before they were allowed near the students." He chuckled, then held his glass out for a refill of vodka and orange juice. Once the glass was full he held it up to the lantern that hung from the awning's strut and toasted whichever patient had paid for that afternoon's bonefishing. All week our doctor and two lawyers had thus credited their clients for their various pleasures. The proctologist drank the toast, then raised his glass once more, this time in tribute to Thessy's prowess as a bonefish guide. "Is the kid's name really Thessalonians?"

"It truly is," I confirmed.

"Weirdest goddamn name I ever did hear." The proctologist shook his head then turned to look at our private scrap of paradise. The evening was dropping like velvet and the lagoon was fading to a deep dusky richness in which the curving palms were reflected as cleanly as though the water were a dark-silvered looking-glass. We had moored off a deserted cay rimmed with a beach of clear sand above which the first stars were pricking the warm sky, while, beneath *Wavebreaker*'s bimini cover, half-moon ice cubes clinked in crystal glasses. "This is the life." The proctologist stretched his sunburned legs on the cockpit cushions and rested his head so he could stare past the bimini cover at the stars. "You're one hell of a lucky guy, Nick. You spend your life with Ellen, while I get to stare up assholes all day." He grimaced, then rolled his head to look at me. "Why didn't you become an actor like your dad?"

"I'm no good at it."

"Ineptitude didn't stop me becoming an asshole doctor!" The proctologist hooted at his own wit before asking which of my father's famous wives was my mother. I told him and he shook his head in admiration. "She was some looker, Nick! Wow."

"Wow," I agreed. In her time Mother had been almost as famous as Father, but presently she was in a home for inebriates where, on good days, she could remember who she was, but the good days were very rare and getting scarcer. I thought what a snakepit my family was; a snakepit dominated by a genius who knew how to create any illusion – even love.

"It must be pretty great having Sir Thomas as a father." The proctologist was fishing for gossip.

"It's wonderful," I said with suitable sanctimony. "He's a great man."

The doctor nodded agreement. "You can tell that just from looking at him." He was entirely serious, and had adopted a portentous tone suitable for expressing admiration for the Greatest Living Englishman. "Know what I mean, Nick? You look at Sir Tom on the screen and it doesn't matter what part he's playing but you can tell he's a great guy. What's the word I'm looking for? Help me out here, Nick." He snapped his fingers. "Integrity!" he said at last. "Your dad's got integrity."

Father would not know what integrity was if it sneaked up and bit his backside. "I know," I said humbly.

The proctologist swirled the ice in his glass. "You're a lucky fellow, Nick."

"I know," I said again, and I was too, but not for the reasons the proctologist believed. I was lucky because I had turned my back on illusion, pursuing instead common-sense reality. I had run away from Sir Tom because I needed to find a bedrock of truth on which to build a life. I had no time for my father's illusions. Illusion could not fix a position from a sextant reading, nor fight two hundred square feet of heavy flogging wet canvas in a tumbling sea and a rough wind. People envied me my birth and my childhood, but my secret

41

pride was that I had rejected both to make of myself a prosaic and common-sense fellow.

The proctologist was bored with talking about Sir Tom. "You reckon we can go bonefishing again tomorrow?" he asked me instead.

"It's your charter, doctor. You can do whatever you like."

"Hey, Ellen!" the doctor shouted down to the galley where Ellen was trying to disguise the fact that the frozen steaks were being thawed in a microwave. "Nick says I can do whatever I like! You want to come skinny-dipping with me tomorrow?"

"I don't think I could take the excitement, doctor."

By the week's end the proctologist was saying that it had been the best goddamned vacation he had ever taken, and as we passed the bunkering moorings near McIllvanney's yard I saw him take Ellen aside and I guessed he was offering her a job. In the year I had skippered *Wavebreaker* at least half of our married male charterers had either offered Ellen a job or pressed her to visit their offices the next time she passed through their city. It was almost tedious to watch it happen.

We docked ten minutes later, and Thessy and I carried the luggage out to the yard where the courtesy taxi shimmered in the heat. One of the lawyers' wives wanted to know the secret of Ellen's coffee, and Ellen modestly said she just followed the percolator instructions, while the truth was that she put a cupful of cheap instant coffee powder into every percolated pot. The proctologist handed me three envelopes, one addressed to each of us, then told me that if I ever had piles I could rely on him to cut them out for cost.

Ellen held her happy smile till the courtesy taxi had disappeared, then she tore up the proctologist's business card. "The creep suggested I might be his receptionist." She ripped open her envelope to find two hundred dollars. Mine had the same amount, while Thessy's only contained a hundred, though the proctologist had also given him the 'Go Dawgs' hat. Not that the inequity of the tip mattered, for we always pooled and shared the money evenly.

It took just over an hour to empty *Wavebreaker* of her

garbage and dirty linen, and then to hook up the shoreside electricity and pump diesel and fresh water into her tanks. Those chores done, and the synthetic fabric of the precious sails covered from the ravages of sunlight, I hefted my old marine kit bag on to the dock where Ellen was waiting to ambush me.

Ellen planned to return to her tiny apartment in the town where she kept her precious books and where, on an old manual typewriter, she wrote what she called her 'five-finger exercises', which she would never let anyone read. McIllvanney had offered to let her stay on board *Wavebreaker*, so long as the boat's air conditioners were disconnected, but his offer was not as generous as it seemed for Ellen would have been little more than an unpaid security guard and also subject to Bellybutton's endlessly tedious suggestions, and she far preferred her small hot room in the busy crowded apartment block that smelt of cooking all day and marijuana all night.

"I'll see you in a week's time, Nick?" Ellen now challenged me.

I shook my head. "You know you won't. I've got a boat to mend." I tried to edge past her, but she blocked my progress with her bicycle. "Sammy Meredith can skipper the boat," I suggested.

"Sam Meredith is a creep. Be here in one week, Nick, or you won't see me again!"

Thessy was already waiting at the yard gate where our taxi thumped and quivered. Ellen was still arguing with me as Thessy and I climbed in and backfired away, but I was no longer listening. I had *Masquerade* to mend and a life to live and, even if it meant living it without Ellen, my charter days were done. I was free.

I had been in New York when *Masquerade* was stolen. I had gone there from Florida because my father had pleaded with me to go. He was opening his celebrated King Lear on Broadway. He was old, he told me, and he was feeling his age, and he had played the Lear for five months at the National in London and he was tired, and he wanted to patch things up with me because it would make him feel better, and I was the only one of all his children whom he could trust, and he needed my youth to support him at this difficult time and so, like a fool, I had believed him and flown to New York where I had found the rogue ensconced in a suite of the Plaza with a frizzy-haired girl young enough to be his great-granddaughter. "The dear soul wishes to be in the theatre," he told me, "and her legs are good enough to allow me to encourage that ambition, though doubtless at the risk of slipping a disc or two in my back. Would you like to sleep with her?"

I went to his opening night. He was brilliant. I still don't know how he does it. He despises the method actors. "Grubby little players," he calls them, "vermin in greasepaint. They're not paid to be amateur psychiatrists, but to be players, to be actors. The stage is a job, dear Nick, not a mindfuck." On that first Broadway night I had stood in the wings where he was absent-mindedly fondling the breasts of his frizzy-haired admirer, and to me he had looked just like any other dirty old man; but then, as the royal fanfare sounded, he had twitched his grey gown, given me a wink, and walked into the stage's glare. "Attend the lords of France and Burgundy, Gloucester." He had spoken Lear's opening lines and I had felt a shiver run through the theatre's great darkness, because the voice was there, and the power of it, and he was suddenly not a dirty old man at all, but a great, kind, foolish and painfully honest King.

The performance was a triumph. Later that night, drinking champagne at the first night party, he gave me his usual disclaimers; how it was all an illusion, everything was an illusion, all life was an illusion, and how he, Sir Tom, was the master of illusion, but how his dear children were real because they alone could not be spawned from the imagination. "Sweet soul – " he took my arm in his, "come home to me. To England." He was drunk.

"Why?"

"You could succeed me. You have it in you, you know."

"Of course I don't."

"You are my bad conscience, Nick. That is why I need you."
He looked across the room to where a famous actress held
scornful court. "I screwed her in a hot-air balloon. Over
California. Her husband chased us in a jeep, and the oscillations
of the basket told him what I was doing to his wife, and the poor
man was jealous." My father had begun to giggle. "Do you
know what she told me, Nick? She said she could feel a shard of
genius enter her soul with my seed! Oh, Nick! How generous I
have been with my genius. Her silly husband shot himself,
which was hardly surprising because she was a rotten lay."

He talked me into staying two more days, and thus three
days passed before I discovered that *Masquerade* was missing.
It was another seven days before she was found grinding her
starboard side to shreds on a coral reef north of Straker's Cay
in the Far-Out Islands. Bonefish Straker reckoned that some
Bahamian kids must have stolen the boat as a means of getting
home, but we would never know who had wrecked her, only
that they had removed a dinghy load of gear including her
chronometer, sextant, VHF, barometer, spare sails, lines,
fenders, and even the mattress off the starboard quarter-berth.
They had stolen my good oilskins, but the thieves had never
found my small stash of money which had been hidden in a
redundant sea-cock, nor had they found the old Webley .455
revolver that I had hidden deep in *Masquerade*'s bilges. The
gun itself had been a prop in a film version of *Journey's End*
in which my father had starred, and when the filming was
over he had 'forgotten' to return the pistol which was still in
good working order. I had fewer than a hundred rounds for the
gun which I kept solely as a deterrent for those remote places
where cruising yachtsmen are seen as plump victims, ripe for
pillaging, and the Webley offered me good protection for,
though the gun was over seventy years old, it was massively
built and frighteningly powerful.

Bonefish Straker had rescued *Masquerade*, propping her up
in his own backyard and refusing to take any money from me
as a salvage fee. Bonefish Straker was Thessalonians' father,
and also father to two dozen other children, most of them

45

orphans who had been unofficially adopted by Bonefish and his wife, Sarah. Bonefish's real name was Hector, but he had earned his nickname because of his uncanny ability to find the elusive fish. He was reckoned one of the islands' best fishing guides, a man who could name his own price to the rich northerners who came to the blue waters to kill gamefish, but Bonefish believed that his family might stray from the path of righteousness if he spent too much time away from home so he restricted his guide work to just a few weeks of the year. The rest of the time he caught snapper or conch or lobster, and brooded over the souls of his ramshackle family; each of whom was named for a different book in the Bible. He had started at the back of the good book and was perversely working his way towards Genesis, which meant that his eldest daughter was called Revelation Straker; a young woman as pretty as her name, and as happy as all the other children who grew up under Bonefish's skinny care. Bonefish, in brief, was a very good man who had never heard of Sir Thomas Break-spear, and I was a very lucky man for the fortunate accident of having met Bonefish.

He watched in anxious silence as I ran a hand over the repairs he had begun on *Masquerade*. A Danish yawl had been wrecked on the far side of the island two years before and Bonefish had rescued some of her oak timbers which he had scarfed in to *Masquerade*'s broken hull. Only one rib had needed replacing and Bonefish apologised that he had fashioned that new one from a piece of his own Madeira wood.

"It's a wonderful job," I said respectfully. It was, too.

"I vould have done more, sir, but life is busy."

"Don't call me 'sir'. My name's Nick."

"Werry busy, sir," Bonefish went on as though I had not spoken. He called all white men 'sir'. To him we were still the missionaries who had brought God to his soul and law to his land. I had tried to tell him that the world had changed drastically, but Bonefish did not want to believe in change. He was descended from slaves who had accompanied their master,

46

one Rafe Straker, from Long Island in 1783. Rafe Straker, like many of the original white settlers of the Bahamas, had been an American loyalist who could not stomach life under George Washington. The white Straker family had long disappeared, their genes and blood melded into the vigorous bodies of their freed slaves, and only the Straker name lived on to be given new dignity by Bonefish and his family. "I don't know from vere ve'll fetch the copper." Bonefish drew his hand over the abraded edges of the copper sheathing left on *Masquerade*'s hull.

"I'll have some sent from England, and some bronze nails. But we can get the tar and brown paper locally?" The copper was bedded on to the wood with tarred brown paper.

Bonefish gave me a swift silent grin. "I think ve can manage tar and paper, sir."

Thessy, squatting nearby as he waited for his father's permission to join the conversation, looked up as a twin-engined plane howled low overhead. The plane's registration number was so faded as to be illegible, but I recognised the machine anyway. It belonged to the Maggot, whose real name was John Maggovertski. The Maggot was an expatriate American who ran a slew of businesses from his Grand Bahama home. All of the Maggot's businesses were perpetually on the fringe of bankruptcy. One of his shakier concerns was an air-taxi service with which he scared the wits out of travellers too innocent to know better than to fly with him. The shriek of the plane's engines drowned our voices, so Bonefish and I just watched as the plane sank towards Straker Cay's small airstrip. Once the machine had disappeared behind the trees Bonefish shook his head sadly. To him all aircraft were harbingers of dreadful change, mere noisy messengers of a Godless world; which, I realised, was a pretty accurate description of the Maggot himself.

I assumed the Maggot was delivering or picking up a customer, but it was none of my business, so I stripped down to my shorts and began work as Thessy, his brother Philemon and their father took a battered wooden skiff across the lagoon. Two brown pelicans flapped past as I began shaping the broken ends of *Masquerade*'s shattered planking. The sun was warm on my back, but the south-easterly wind took the edge off the stifling heat. A gaggle of Bonefish's children were in constant, but changing, attendance, sometimes helping me, but more often chasing each other in a complicated game of tag up and over *Masquerade*'s hull. Revelation came and sat in the shade of *Masquerade*'s bows where she plucked two chickens that I suspected had been killed in honour of my return to the island. The chickens' surviving relatives clucked and scratched in the dirt, oblivious to the drifting feathers. Revelation and I chatted idly, content to let the minutes drift pass like warm thistledown. "Thessy says he's been offered a lot of money for a charter?" Revelation eventually challenged me.

"That's true."

"But you von't do it?"

"I don't want to leave you, Revelation."

She gave that piece of gallantry the scorn it deserved. "Father vouldn't really vant him to go for all the summer."

"So it doesn't matter if I say no," I said with some relief, for I had been feeling somewhat guilty at risking Thessy's chances of making some money.

"But if you go on this charter, Father will let Thessy go." Revelation went sweetly on, thus impaling me on the hook of my own guilt once more. It was I who had introduced Thessy to McIllvanney and who had secured him the job with Cutwater, but Bonefish had only allowed his son into the wide wicked world because of his trust in me. I was not certain that the trust was deserved, but Bonefish was convinced I was protecting his son from iniquity, and no assertion to the contrary would convince him otherwise. "And if Thessy vent," Revelation continued, "then the money vould be good, because the outboard is broken and Father can't mend it and there's no money for another." She sighed, then twisted on her stool to gaze in astonishment because a car was thumping and crashing its way along the dirt road that led from the island's one village to Bonefish's sprawl of shacks. It was clear from Revelation's expression that cars were as uncommon at this end of the island as polar bears; indeed, the sight of one was so surprising that she picked up her skirts and, with the younger children around her, fled towards the safety of her mother's kitchen.

The car, an ancient Pontiac taxi that was painted six shades of yellow and purple, stopped outside the twin piles of broken coral that were Bonefish's proud gateposts. There was a pause, then the back door of the cab opened, and a very tall white man climbed out into the sun. He was dressed in checked golfing trousers, cowboy boots and a cowboy hat. He blinked uncertainly at the landscape. He looked lost and nervous, as though he was unsure of where he was or why he had bothered to come.

Then he saw me, waved, and began walking slowly towards me. I did not respond, for I was feeling nothing but astonishment. I could not even speak. I was struck dumb because George Crowninshield, senator and possibly a future President of the United States, had come alone to Straker's Cay. "Hello, Nick." He held out a hand and gave me a smile.

"Oh, bloody hell," I found my voice. Then shook his hand.

One night during our charter, when we had been sipping whisky under the stars, Senator Crowninshield had told me that no fat man could ever again become President of the United States. "William Taft will be the last really fat President," he had told me.

"Was he very fat?"

"Big as a house, Nick." The senator had frowned, then opined that it was not just the fat who were for ever barred from the Oval Office, but even the ugly. America, Crowninshield had said with a note of amusement in his voice, was doomed for ever to have toothsome Presidents, and all because television now ruled politics. He had sounded amused, but then he had turned to me and pointed to his chin. "See the scar?"

There had been the faintest mark against his tanned skin, so I had nodded.

"I had a dimple there," the Senator had confessed with his engaging frankness, "which my advisers determined made me look too baby-faced, and so we had it removed." He had laughed, simultaneously mocking the stupidity of government by cosmetics and confessing that he was also a part of it, just as he was part of government by voice coach and acting coach.

Not that the senator needed a beautician's help if he was to become President, for George Crowninshield was a good-looking man with a strong-boned face and a head of thick black hair. He had to be fifty, but he did not look a day over thirty-five, an illusion helped by his lopsided boyish grin that was so very full of charm. It was the candid charm that was his greatest public asset. He was popularly supposed to be a man who not only told the truth, but who could not tell a lie, and the senator's aides and publicists were not unhappy to promulgate that echo of a previous President's virtues.

Not everyone was so impressed by Senator Crowninshield. Ellen said he was a political lightweight whose stagecraft was better than his statecraft. The usual jibe was that Crowninshield was a politician without a cause, or rather that he would support any cause so long as it was fashionable, but his critics also attacked Crowninshield for being wealthy, claiming that his eminence was solely due to the vast amounts of money that he spent on his campaigns. One night, long after the senator had chartered *Wavebreaker*, I had defended him to Ellen, saying that it was not Crowninshield's fault that he had been born to wealthy parents, and that he had used his wealth well. "He's an honest man," I had said trenchantly, "and there aren't too many of those in politics."

Ellen had given me one of her pitying looks. "Honest? For God's sake, Nick, he graduated from Yale Law School! He's just pretending to be an aw-shucks-gee-look-what-happened-to-me-when-I-wasn't-trying kind of guy. He's nice to us because we don't threaten him, and because he's cultivated the vote-catching art of being modestly affable, but wearing cowboy boots and grinning like a demented Howdy-Doody doesn't turn a rattlesnake into a puppy!"

I had not believed her then, and I did not believe her now. I believed the senator was a thoughtful man whose wealth had elevated him above the need to make compromises with his convictions. He was also a man who seemed mighty pleased to see me again. He lightly punched my shoulder. "You look good, Nick, real good."

"So do you, senator."

"I ought to, Nick, considering how much I pay my fitness advisers and dietitians. You know what it costs to join a health club these days? Of course" – he offered me his ingenuous grin – "what really keeps me fit is all that prime USDA beef." The senator represented a beef-rearing state and never forgot to extol the benefits of a plateful of bleeding home-grown American steak, while in private, as I had learned when he and his wife had chartered *Wavebreaker*, George Crowninshield rarely touched red meat.

"How did you find me?" I asked him.

"One of my staff spoke to that guy McIllvanney. I had to be in Nassau anyway, so I thought I'd look you up. I can't stay long, but I had a particular reason to speak with you." The yellow and purple taxi was waiting for him. The taxi driver was squatting by one of Bonefish's gateposts where he surreptitiously smoked a cigarette. When the cigarette was finished the driver would be invited to wait in the shade of Bonefish's casuarinas, but not before.

"Did the Maggot fly you here?" I asked Crowninshield.

The senator nodded and laughed. "I remember him, of course, from when he played for the Giants. My Lord! He flies a plane in the same way he used to sack quarterbacks!"

The Maggot had played American football until he had come off his Harley-Davidson at eighty miles an hour and permanently damaged his left knee. Sometimes, when drunk, he would regale me with stories of his footballing prowess, but such stories went past me like galley smoke because I could not bring myself to enquire, nor indeed to care, about the differences between a Tight End and a flea-flicker. When the Maggot became too boring about football I told him cricketing stories until he shut up. We liked each other, and I was glad that the senator also liked him.

Now, fanning his face with his hat, Senator Crowninshield followed me into the shade of *Masquerade*'s hull and stared up at her scarred flank. "So this is your famous boat, eh?"

"What's left of her."

"She's surely pretty, Nick." He walked to the stern where her name was lettered in gold. "Sounds like a tribute to your father's profession, Nick."

"She was called *Masquerade* when I bought her. It's said to be unlucky to change a boat's name."

He gave me a shrewd look, clearly suspecting that I would have changed the name had I dared defy the superstition. He said nothing about his suspicion, instead asking me to remind him of how *Masquerade* had become damaged.

"Some swine stole her and ran her on to a coral reef," I said, "and I'm spending the next two months mending her."

Crowninshield walked a few paces in silence until he was standing under the palms which edged the lagoon. "So you're mending your boat instead of taking my twins sailing?"

"You got it." I mimicked his slow accent, and the mimicry made him turn and stare at me, and the look on his face instantly made me regret my mimicry. He was a man whose approachability made him seem so very affable, but no one, however wealthy, becomes a Presidential hopeful without some steel in the soul, and it was that sudden steel that I now saw in the senator's eyes. I had offended him, and the look he gave me was positively frightening. I tried to back away from my levity. "Someone else will take your kids to sea, senator. There's a fellow called Sammy Meredith who's every bit as good a sailor as I am."

"But I want you." He had evidently forgiven my mimicry. He now took a pair of sunglasses from his shirt pocket and pointed them at me. When I made no response he turned and gazed at the far line of coral reef that was marked by a fret of white breaking water. I could see Bonefish and his sons working the lateen-sail of their skiff way beyond the reef, perhaps looking for turtles which they could sell to the men who exported the rich flesh to the Japanese. The sun was flat and hard and brilliant on the nearer water, forcing Crowninshield to turn back to me. "I need your help, Nick, because my only son is dying and my only daughter is following his example, and I need a strong man who will save them." He said the words in the same light tone of voice he had used when speaking of my boat, and somehow the discordant contrast between the tone and the message threw me. I was not certain I had heard aright, then knew I had, and I suddenly felt a very British rush of embarrassment because of the senator's frankness.

"Your son is dying?" I responded inadequately.

"Rickie is a drug addict," he explained gently.

I said nothing for a few seconds. "Oh, shit," I then said, because that was how I felt and because I suddenly knew that the next few minutes were going to be extraordinarily difficult.

"Specifically Rickie is addicted to cocaine," the senator continued, "but I can't say he's particular in his tastes. He uses crack and cocaine and amphetamines, then more crack and more cocaine and perhaps even a speedball to round things off. You know what a speedball is, Nick?"

"No."

"It's an injection of cocaine mixed with heroin. It's real big boy stuff" – the senator's voice was very bitter – "and all of that garbage is washed down with alcohol and pickled in nicotine. My son is a dying junkie, but he doesn't want to die alone so he's encouraging Robin-Anne to keep him company and now she's become addicted to cocaine and it won't be very long before she's smoking crack and trying speedballs." The senator spoke with a sudden and incredible venom, and I realised it was only that angry force that was keeping him from weeping for his two children. "It seems," he went on in a

53

calmer voice, "that Rickie and Robin-Anne are among the sizeable minority of the population that is peculiarly prone to severe addiction."

I wondered why McIllvanney had not told me that Rickie and Robin-Anne Crowninshield were drug addicts, then I realised that McIllvanney would not have told me anything that might have risked my acceptance of the charter, but now that I had learned that the twins had such a severe drug problem I was even less keen to take on the job. "I'm no expert on drugs, senator," I said. "There must be hospitals they can go to?"

He nodded. "Of course there are such hospitals, and the twins are under the supervision of a clinic right now, but I believe they need extraordinary help." He paused, and gave me a flicker of his famous smile. "Help from an extraordinary person, Nick. You."

"I'm not extraordinary," I said flatly.

Crowninshield smiled. "You were a marine."

"They'll take anyone who isn't blind," I said with dismissive untruth.

"And you understand what makes a son rebel against a father," Crowninshield went on. "I remember those nights we shared our thoughts on that subject, Nick, and I think my son kind of needs the understanding you can give him."

I shied away from the very American-sounding compliment. "Get him a good doctor."

"I want you."

"I'm not an expert!" I protested.

"Yes you are," Crowninshield insisted. "You're an expert sailor, and that's good because it means you can take the twins to sea and keep them there until they're damn well cured. I don't care what hell they go through. I don't care if they have to be strapped to the mast. I don't care if they're hallucinating purple snakes and blue baboons, because the whole point of putting them on a boat is that they can't get off and swim home, and they can't get drugs on board, and they can't bribe you to take them to land, and that means they'll have no damned choice but to get cured."

I said nothing. I was thinking of all the work I needed to do on *Masquerade*; all the painstaking hours of sawing and planing and caulking and rigging.

Crowninshield stared at me through his obscuring lenses. "Nick," he said at last, "my son is going to die within a year if I don't do something very drastic. He's already lost the sight of his left eye because cocaine starved the retina of blood, and he's damn lucky not to be totally blind, or even dead, because the next time it could constrict the arteries of his heart or block the blood from reaching his brain. Or next time it could be Robin-Anne. So I have to do something because I can't just stand idle and let my kids die."

The pain in the senator's voice was awful, but I still did not want to become involved. I began walking along the track leading behind the beach towards the village, which was marked by the red tin roof of a tiny church showing above the casuarinas and palm trees. The senator fell into step beside me while some of Bonefish's smaller children followed at a safe distance. We stopped close to a small graveyard where a tribe of wild goats stared suspiciously at us from between the mounds of earth and bleak wooden crosses. The senator was looking at the sun-reflecting sea. "The truth is, Nick, I messed up my kids, and that hurts. It wasn't lack of love. Hell, I had a bumper sticker saying 'Have You Hugged Your Kids Today?' and, sure, I hugged them every day I could, but nowadays I sometimes wonder just what in hell is going on inside their heads. Especially Rickie. It's easier to extract sense out of a fruitfly than to get a civil word out of Rickie. They threw him out of college because of cocaine, and he was damn lucky that they didn't call the police, but all he'd say to me was to stay cool! To stay cool, for Christ's sake! Your only son is a college drop-out, and bleeding from the nose because his blood vessels are popping from all the cocaine in his system, and he tells you to keep your cool!"

I didn't know what to say, so said nothing. A tiny lizard watched me with unblinking eyes from a rock beside the lagoon, while above the trees the red tin church roof shimmered bright in the sultry heat.

"Did you ever take drugs?" the senator asked me after a long silence.

"No." My father had often urged me to try some of his marijuana, but I had never accepted, just as I had refused even to look at the cocaine that he kept in his dressing room.

"Lucky you," the senator said ruefully. "You're a happy man, aren't you, Nick? That's why I want you to take the twins to sea. I want some of your certainty and happiness to rub off on my kids."

I shrugged that embarrassing wish away. Ellen had once assured me that I was only happy because I did not think too deeply, and probably she was right, but it is still that shallow contentment which makes people bring me their troubles just as the senator was now bringing me his two children. "What I don't understand," I said harshly, and in an attempt to steer the conversation away from compliments, "is why you give the twins enough money to buy themselves drugs in the first place." What I really could not understand was why the senator did not beat ten kinds of nonsense out of a son who told him to cool it, but telling middle-class Americans to thump their kids is like asking them to burn their flag, so I did not waste my time.

"They've got their own money," the senator answered, "left to them by their grandmother. The twins are only entitled to the income, while Barbara and I control the capital, but all that changes on their birthday next month."

"When they scoop the pool?"

The senator nodded. He sensed my curiosity about how much the twins were worth, and for a few seconds reticence and candour fought across his face, but then he shrugged. "They'll inherit about six million dollars each."

"Jesus wept!" I stared at him. "And you let them use the income off that? Even though you know they blow it away on drugs?"

"The alternative, Nick, is much much worse."

"What alternative?"

The senator was again not looking at me but at the sea, and

his voice was immensely sad. "A drug addict will do anything to feed his habit. He'll steal, beg, pawn or sell his family treasures, anything. I let the twins use their money on drugs because I don't want to turn them into thieves –" he paused, "or hookers. Getting laid has never been so cheap in all history. Go to a crack house, Nick, and you can buy anything you want in the way of human flesh. Do you think I want to see my kids turning tricks for a smear of white powder?"

I felt his sadness and hopelessness, but I was still reluctant to embroil myself. There had to be agencies and clinics that were competent to deal with drug abuse, while the best I could be was an enthusiastic amateur, and that was rarely good enough. "So tell me about the twins," I said, not because I was interested, but because I wanted the senator to talk while I dreamed up a strategy to turn down his request.

"You'll like Robin-Anne," the senator said too quickly, thus betraying that I would probably not like Rickie. "She's always been the quiet one in the family. She was a Liberal Arts major at college, and has never really been any trouble." He must have read my thoughts, for he hurried on to explain how such a paragon could end up addicted to cocaine. "A boyfriend hooked her on drugs, and that boyfriend was a room-mate of Rickie's."

"And Rickie," I said sardonically, "is not the quiet one?"

"True." The senator did not seem to want to say much more.

"What was his major?"

"Girls? Sun-tanning? Skiing?" The senator found it hard to hide the rancour his own son provoked in him. "Cocaine? Actually he majored in Phys Ed, but to tell you the truth, Rickie was always a slow learner. He's not truly backward, but he suffers from some kind of learning dysfunctionalism."

I wondered why Americans always called a spade a manually powered entrenching instrument. The senator meant that his son was dumb, but psycho-babble made stupidity sound respectable. I walked to the water's edge where a coconut husk trembled in the backwash of the lagoon's tiny waves. "Are you sure you don't just want Rickie out of the way?" I felt nervous of challenging a man as important as Crowninshield with the truth, but I did it anyway. "I mean it can't help your Presidential prospects if the voters discover that your kids are drug addicts."

The senator responded with a practised smile. "What Presidential prospects? I haven't declared."

"Rickie's still an embarrassment," I accused him.

"Indeed," he accepted the charge, "and more of an embarrassment than you know. He was arrested two months ago on a charge of trafficking in drugs. Provisionally his trial is set for December, and till then he's released on bail." He hesitated for a few seconds. "Nick," he continued with a tone of wry honesty in his voice, "there are some mighty clever people who say I could be President of the United States three years from now, but what no one seems to realise is that I don't care about that. I just care about getting my kids off drugs."

He said it with such heartfelt force that I believed him. I felt guilty for challenging his motives and, even though a tiny corner of my mind was hearing an imaginary Ellen scoff at my naïvety, I believed the senator's sudden and passionate sincerity. Ellen would doubtless tell me that the senator was trying to turn an electoral liability into an advantage, meaning that if he could parade his cured children in front of the electorate he could then pose as both a noble parent and as an expert on drugs, but I preferred to ignore that imagined cynicism, choosing a different reservation. "You could spend a small fortune this summer," I told the senator, "and if Rickie doesn't want to stop killing himself, then he won't. I could take him to sea and keep him clean for three months, but how do you know that the moment the court case is done he won't just stuff his nose full of crap again?"

"I don't know that," the senator said simply. Above us the fronds of the palm trees clattered in the warm wind, while out to sea Bonefish's ragged and patched sail dipped in the steep waves beyond the reef. "But Rickie knows he's in trouble, big trouble, which is why he suggested this idea of isolating himself at sea."

"Rickie suggested it?" I could not hide my surprise. The senator had just told me how difficult it was to extract any sense from his son, yet apparently Rickie was not so far gone as the senator had suggested.

"It surprised me too," the senator confessed wryly. "Rickie calls it his 'cruise-cure'. I'm not sure he understands all that it involves. I think he's expecting a glorified vacation with a lot of scuba diving and board-sailing, but he does understand that a cruise-cure means giving up drugs. I guess he heard Barbara and me discussing the good time we had with you, and he kind of picked up on it, and he wondered why he couldn't come down to the Bahamas and isolate himself from drugs. Our lawyer took the idea to the court, and the judge altered the terms of Rickie's bail to let him come here for a therapeutic cruise. Even the judge thought it was a great idea, Nick, because on a boat Rickie will be far away from temptation."

I gave the senator a cynical glance. "Plenty of temptation in the Bahamas. The islands are awash with drugs."

"So take the twins for a proper voyage," the senator said with what he hoped was a contagious enthusiasm. "You can teach them navigation? Robin-Anne has always liked sailing, and I kind of think Rickie could take to it as well. You could go home! You could drink some of that warm English beer you were always telling me was so good."

"It isn't warm, and it isn't as easy as that, senator." I paused to marshal all my heartfelt arguments against the cruise-cure, but at the same time I felt a sudden and oceanic surge of homesickness. I imagined conning *Wavebreaker* into Dartmouth, and taking the power skiff upriver to one of my old and favourite pubs where the ale had real taste instead of the limp-wristed chill of North American beers. I suddenly wanted to see the green-leafed Devon river banks and to feel the grey sharp waves of the Channel buffeting my hull.

"It can't take too long to prepare *Wavebreaker* for a long voyage, can it?" The senator had sensed my vacillation and now pressed me.

"It can be done," I allowed, "but not by next week."

"But surely you can do some of that preparatory work at sea?"

"Some," I yielded the point, "but at this time of year I won't go far from land while I do it." This early in the summer most of the hurricane tracks lay well to the south of the Bahamas, but the islands could still be racked by ship-killing tropical storms and, till I was sure of *Wavebreaker*'s rigging, I would not go too far from safe harbours. Then I realised that I was actually contemplating accepting the senator's offer, and I told myself that the last thing I needed this summer was to babysit two spoilt rich-kid junkies. "And if *Wavebreaker* does sail across the Atlantic" – I was carefully not including myself in that statement, and I was also piling on the practical difficulties attendant on the cruise-cure – "she'll need a proper crew. She'll want at least another three watch-keepers, and preferably two of them must understand celestial navigation. I know *Wavebreaker*'s got more electronic toys than a battleship, but if the electricity fails then you're back to the sextant and the sharp pencil."

"You can have whatever and whoever you want," Crowninshield promised flatly.

"What I want" – I turned and pointed towards *Masquerade* – "is to have my boat mended and re-equipped, and then to sail her away."

"I'll have her repaired and re-equipped." Crowninshield sliced through my objections with all the brute force of his family's fortune. "You write the specifications for her repairs, and I'll guarantee to have them done at the best boatyard in America."

"But I don't know how to cope with drug addicts!" I returned to my first and most potent objection. "And I'm sure Ellen doesn't either, and I know Thessy can't cope. We're not medical people!"

"I wouldn't expect you to cope." The senator was seemingly prepared for every difficulty I raised. "I've hired a medical specialist from the Rinkfels Clinic to sail with you. He's a para-medic rather than a doctor, but his presence means you won't have to worry about the twins' health."

The senator had trapped me. I could have given him a straight rejection, but I suppose that was not in my nature. I wanted to overwhelm the senator with so many difficulties that he would abandon the idea, but instead I was the one who was weakening. I tried one last desperate objection. "We can't sail next week. It's impossible. There isn't another ferry off Straker's Cay till Saturday night and it's no good expecting me to get any preparatory work done on *Wavebreaker* till Monday at the earliest, and then it'll be two or three days before –"

"I'll have you flown back to the Grand Bahama today," Crowninshield said patiently, "and the twins can join you on Sunday morning."

"But I've only just got here," I said weakly.

"Listen, Nick." The senator had beaten down my last defences, and now offered me a compromise that might make my surrender to his wishes more acceptable. "Take my kids to sea for two weeks, just two weeks, and if at the end of those two weeks you really believe that the cruise-cure won't work, or if you're convinced that you're the wrong guy for the job, then send the twins home. Does that sound OK? You return the twins to me and I won't blame you one bit for failing, because all I'm asking you to do is to try. I'm not demanding that you succeed, only that you try. That's all we can ever ask of anyone, isn't it?" His voice was almost plaintive. "To try?"

I looked into his eyes. For all the senator's affability he was a proud man and I knew he had humbled himself to ask for my help and I also knew I could not refuse him. Which was exactly why, of course, he had taken the trouble to come all this way to look into my eyes as he asked for my help. "Shee-it," I said, and felt guilty that I was leaving the island without sharing the chicken dinner that Sarah Straker was doubtless cooking for me at that very moment. "I shouldn't be doing this!" I said to the senator. "I really should not."

He smiled. "But I'm glad you are, Nick, and thank you." He held out his hand.

I thought of all the extra equipment his money would buy

for *Masquerade*, and that's how I tried to justify my acceptance of the senator's proposal, but in reality it was because Crowninshield had invited me to play Galahad and I never could resist the lure of the dragon's breath even if it did mean charging into idiocy like a fool. So I reached for the senator's hand, and thereby couched my lance to face the dragon's fire. I should have thought more deeply before I agreed, but that's not how fools charge in. I didn't think before I went into the recruiting office and became a marine, and I didn't think now. Instead I consoled myself that Ellen would be pleased, and a pleased Ellen might become my shipmate all the way around the world, so really, I told myself, I was not doing this for the senator's happiness, and not even for the twins, but for my own, and so I shook the senator's hand.

The Maggot was waiting at the airstrip. He gave me a welcoming grin and an ironic bow to acknowledge the exalted company I was keeping, then he ushered the senator on to the starboard wing and so into the aeroplane.

It always seemed miraculous that the Maggot could fit himself into a small aircraft, for John Maggovertski was a huge man: six foot five and well over two hundred pounds, and none of those pounds was fat. I sometimes tried to imagine blocking the Maggot during a game of American football and simply could not. It would be like trying to stop a buffalo, because he was nothing but muscle, weight and bone. For exterior decoration he had a thick black beard, dark eyes, a shock of tousled hair, and weight-lifter's arms that were tattooed with snakes, naked ladies and the twin flags of the USA and the Maggot's home state of Arkansas.

He put the senator into one of the back seats, first shoving aside a tangle of camera equipment. Another of John Maggovertski's failing businesses was taking aerial photographs of rich folk's houses. He also refilled air-bottles for scuba divers, ran sports-fishing excursions and, despite his slow left knee, was a good enough tennis player to have been hired as a coach at some of the Lucaya hotels, though the Maggot's career as a tennis coach had been somewhat jeopardised by his insistence on helping only the prettier guests to improve their game. He sporadically published a newsletter about rare firearms, collected guns himself, and was the proud owner of a decrepit fishing boat that was called *Bronco-Buster* in honour of the Giants' Superbowl victory, though the Maggot himself never referred to the beaten team as the Denver Broncos, but always and ever as the Denver Fairies.

The Maggot referred to himself as a 'good old country boy', which description provoked Ellen, who could not stand the sight of him, to comment that John Maggovertski was to country what the serpent was to Eden. The Maggot, Ellen insisted, was an untoilet-trained redneck jerk whose only expertise was as a player of the most brutal and mindless sport to be devised since the lions took on the Christians. The Maggot, faced with these scathing judgments, countered by asserting that Ellen's education had ruined what might otherwise have been a useful bimbo, and loudly proclaimed that her extreme aversion to himself was positive psychological proof that she was secretly enamoured of him. On the whole I found it less tiring to keep the two of them apart.

The Maggot now ordered me into the right-hand pilot's seat and told me to keep my thieving hands off his knobs. As he fired up the twin engines I wondered just what instruments had once occupied the vacant holes in the dashboard, from which empty holes there now trailed forlorn scraps of wiring. It was best not to wonder, for I faced a long journey in what remained of the Maggot's plane. We were flying first to Nassau where the senator was to be guest of honour at an American Embassy reception for senior officers of the naval units taking part in Exercise Stingray, and after Nassau the Maggot and I would fly on to Grand Bahama where he lived and where *Wavebreaker* was docked. "Are you sure you don't want us boys to keep you company at the reception, senator?" John asked.

"I'd be surely delighted to have your company." The senator, ever affable, seemed unworried at the thought of taking the Maggot into polite society.

"Do I have to wear a tie?"

"I guess so. I'll be wearing one."

"Reckon I'll leave the embassy girls to you then, senator," the Maggot had to shout over the sound of the engines, "and me and Nick will just have to play with each other on account of forgetting to bring our ties." He laughed, then frowned at the aircraft's controls as if he was not entirely certain what most of them did. One reason why John's air-taxi service was less than successful was his habit of pretending not to know how to fly the plane or, worse, pretending to have forgotten how to land it once he had succeeded in becoming airborne. The performances made his customers understandably nervous, and nervous customers do not pass on glowing recommendations to their friends. "I suppose we should try and get this hot heap of shit off the ground," the Maggot growled now. It was indeed as hot as hell inside the aircraft.

We taxied away from the palm-thatched hut that was proudly styled as Straker's Cay Airport Terminal Number One. The hut was home to some lizards and to the island's one taxi driver who had sequestered it as his office and gasoline store. The airstrip itself had been built to serve a golf and diving resort that a consortium of Dutch and American businessmen had planned to build on Straker's Cay, but the money had run out before the hotel or marina had been built and all that was left of their grandiose plans was this pinkish runway made of compacted coral and a few abandoned cement mixers which rusted forlornly where the hotel's swimming pool was to have been built.

The Maggot, who refused to wear a seat belt, shoved his throttles forward, and I felt the sweat trickling down my belly as the brakes were released and the small plane thundered down the rough surface. "It plays hell with the tyres, senator!" The Maggot yelled over the howling engine noise.

"What does?" The senator shouted back.

"Runways made of crushed coral! As likely as not we'll blow a tyre, slew off, and become three small puddles of melted fat in a blackened and twisted plane wreck!"

The senator blanched and leaned back. I had heard it all before and so was a little more sanguine. The Maggot, pleased to have spoilt someone's day, pulled back the stick and we lifted safely off the runway and there was suddenly a wonderful rush of cool air coming from an overhead vent. We banked over Bonefish's house and I waved at Thessy who was standing beside *Masquerade*. Thessy would follow on the weekend ferry, arriving at Grand Bahama on the same day as the senator's twins.

The Maggot's Beechcraft clawed higher, its progress punctuated by the alarm sirens that the Maggot ignored and which the senator had learned not to worry about. Once, when an alarm became peculiarly insistent, the Maggot thumped the instrument panel until it stopped. "I think that goddamn racket means we should all be dead," he announced cheerfully, then carried on with an involved story of how he had once won undying glory by intercepting a pass against the Philadelphia Faggots. In the senator the Maggot had found a listener who was only too eager to hear his tales of goal-line stands and blocked punts, concussed running backs and sacked quarterbacks.

The one subject we did not talk about was why the senator had flown to Straker's Cay to meet me. I knew the Maggot was dying to hear the senator's business, but even the Maggot had enough delicacy to wait until we had safely delivered the senator to Nassau before asking. But once Crowninshield was gone, and when we had refuelled the Beechcraft and put a crate of beer on to one of her back seats, the Maggot demanded to know everything.

I suspected that he was hoping to hear that the senator had been arranging for an illicit love affair on board *Wavebreaker*. We had embarked two such affairs in the last year; the most memorable being an English lawyer who had arrived with his French mistress, but only after telling his wife that he was attending a legal conference in Brussels and, to preserve the lie, he had been forced to hide every inch of his pallid skin in case a sun-tan betrayed him. The French girl, to Thessy's infinite embarrassment, had strolled stark naked about *Wavebreaker*'s deck while the lawyer had cowered in the stateroom cloaked like an Ayatollah with impetigo. The Maggot, disappointed that the senator's business offered no such rich pickings of gossip, scowled at me. "You mean you're just babysitting two rich junkies?"

"You've got it."

"Shee-it." We had at last taken off from Nassau and were banking north to where three American warships sliced white water. I opened us each a beer, then idly unfolded the aviation chart that the Maggot had stuck down between our seats. It looked very different to a nautical chart and made little sense to me, but I gradually deciphered some of the meaning from its weird markings.

"You ain't going to have fun," the Maggot said suddenly.

"I'm sorry?"

"You ain't going to have fun with two goddamn cocaine addicts. That stuff is the hardest to kick."

"So the senator told me."

"And there ain't no magic pill that will do it." Maggovertski sounded unusually sombre. He lit a cigarette. "I hate cocaine," he said finally, and he surprised me by saying it for the Maggot had always struck me as one of life's rebels. If he discovered a new rule he would immediately seek a way of breaking it, and I had assumed that he would have some sympathy with those who flouted the laws against drugs, yet there was no denying the genuine anger in his voice when he talked of cocaine. He must have sensed my puzzlement, for he offered a reluctant explanation. "I knew a girl who got hooked on cocaine. She taught in a health club; aerobics, that kind of thing, and the next we knew she was wearing hot pants on a street corner in New York and strutting her stuff at the cars. Jesus, if you knew how hard we tried to get her off that damned powder."

"Did you succeed?"

He paused, and finally shook his head. "Last time I saw her she was doing a peep-show in Pittsburgh. Hell, Nick, I tried to get her out of that place, but she didn't care. All she wanted to do was shovel that crap up her nose, and if that's how someone wants to pass their time, then there's diddly-squat you can do to stop them."

He had sounded immensely sad as he spoke, and I wondered if the girl had meant more to him than being merely a casual friend, but I did not like to ask and Maggovertski was clearly disinclined to explain more, so I just stared down at the aerial chart, and I suddenly noticed, in an otherwise empty space beneath an intersection of two air corridors, the tiny island of Murder Cay. The chart, either printed before the government's name change or else blithely ignoring it, noted the existence of a 2500-foot paved airstrip. "Is 2500 feet long for a runway?" I asked Maggot.

"Two five? Short as a quarterback's dick." He was evidently still thinking of the girl, for the obscenity was automatic and his voice was clipped and distant.

"Have you ever flown into Murder Cay?" I asked him.

The big shaggy head turned to look at me. He frowned and sucked on his cigarette and I somehow got the impression that my question had annoyed him, but when he answered his voice was mild enough. "It's a snakepit, Nick. Leave it alone."

"So who are the snakes?" I insisted.

"The dickheads who bought the place, of course." He paused to pull on his beer bottle which, emptied, he tossed out through the tiny triangular window at his left elbow. "I ran a couple of passengers there before the dickheads bought the island. It was a real nice place two years ago; nothing but luxury houses for the super-rich, but then the snakes bought it and they've painted a big yellow cross on their runway. You know what a big yellow cross on a runway means? It means keep away if you want to go on living."

"So who are the new owners?" I tried again.

"Never been introduced to them, Nick."

"Drug people?"

"Of course!" The Maggot assumed I had already known that.

I looked down at the chart and saw that the island was not so very far off our course, and I knew that the Beechcraft was brim-full with fuel. "You fancy having a look at the island?"

The Maggot laughed. "What's made you feel suicidal? Did you get bored with waiting for Ellen to drop her panties?"

"I'm just curious," I said with as much innocence as I could muster, "but of course, if you're scared of the place . . ."

"Oh, damn you." I had reckoned that an accusation of fear would sting the Maggot, and even before he interrupted me he had banked the plane westwards. He snatched the chart off my lap and worked out a crude course for the remote island. "So why do you want to stir the bastards up?" he grumbled.

I told him about *Hirondelle* and how Deacon Billingsley had lied about the yacht's fate, and I confessed that though there was nothing I could do about a corrupt policeman, nor about what I strongly suspected had been the murder of a yacht's crew, I was still curious about the island.

"Billingsley's a bastard." The Maggot, who had lived long enough in the Bahamas to learn and relish all the important gossip, growled the verdict. "You want to stay upwind of him."

"McIllvanney says that Billingsley owns a house on Murder Cay."

"That figures," the Maggot said gloomily. "The dickheads know that the best way of keeping the Americans off their backs is by buying themselves a slice of the local law." His disgruntled voice made it seem as though the precautions of the drug smugglers formed a personal affront to his patriotism.

Yet if anyone's patriotism should have been affronted by what happened in the islands, it was the Bahamians, for they were forced to endure the indignity of having another nation's law-enforcement agencies operating in their waters. The islands had always been a smugglers' paradise, and had proved a perfect place to stockpile cocaine before running it across the narrow Straits of Florida to the waiting American markets. The American government had pressed the Bahamians to clean out the drug lords, but instead the trade had flourished until the Americans finally insisted that their own coastguard be allowed to patrol Bahamian waters. A scintilla of Bahamian pride was preserved by the presence of a native officer on every American boat or helicopter, but no one really believed the polite fiction that the local officer was thus in command.

"But we ain't in command either," the Maggot said sourly. "We can stop a boat at sea, but we sure as hell can't put a foot on dry land without Bahamian permission. And you can bet your pretty ass that your policeman friend is making sure that permission to search Murder Cay is never given, or if it is, that the guys on the island are well warned before our boys get anywhere near."

"We?" It was so incongruous to hear the Maggot aligning

69

himself with the forces of law that I was forced to ask the question. "Our boys?"

"I keep thinking of that girl in Pittsburgh," he said with a bitter ruefulness, "and how the bastards who run the peepshow have to put sawdust on the booth floors every hour. You don't get much lower than that, Nick, and if anyone wants to kick the balls of the people who put her there, then those are my guys." He paused to light another cigarette, then nodded through his scratched windscreen. "I reckon that's your snakepit, Nick."

Far ahead, and blurred by the heat haze, there was a bright green dot of an island ringed by coral-fretted water. No other land was visible. The Maggot turned in his seat and rummaged in his camera bag until he found a battered Nikon and a roll of black and white film. "Take some pictures for me. You never know, some customer might want a snap of Murder Cay one day."

By the time I had loaded the camera we were already close to the reefs that formed the Devil's Necklace. The shadow of our plane skipped across the bright sea, then flickered over the outer coral. We were approaching the island from the southeast, coming with the wind at a height of six thousand feet. The island was shaped rather like an anchor. The airstrip, with its unfriendly yellow cross that warned strange aircraft from landing, had been built across the curved flukes of the anchor, which otherwise seemed to be covered in low scrub, slash pine and sea-grape. The surprisingly big houses were all built on the western side of the north-south shank of the anchor that was thick with palm trees and vivid with bright blue swimming pools. The rest of the shank was a long narrow golf course, punctuated with sand traps. I twisted in the seat to see that there were a dozen or so boats moored in the protected crook of the easternmost anchor fluke.

The Maggot dipped the starboard wing to let me take a picture of the deep water channel that dog-legged in from the west. We flew above the skeletal radio mast and I stared down at the row of huge houses. No one and nothing stirred there.

"They spent a fortune developing the place," the Maggot said, "but the rich folks never came, so they sold it to the rich dickheads instead." We flew out across the northern reefs.

"One more pass?" I asked John.

"Why not?"

"And a bit lower?"

"Yeah, maybe." He had turned to fly around the eastern edge of the island's encircling reefs and was now staring intently at the houses, searching for any signs of danger, but it seemed as though Murder Cay was deserted. "What the hell," the Maggot said, and he wrenched the plane round in a tight turn until we were aimed plumb at the island's southernmost tip, then he dropped the nose ready to make one high speed and low level pass above the Cay. "That's friendly!" he shouted over the engine noise, and he pointed through the windscreen at the concrete airstrip which not only had the yellow cross painted huge at its western end, but also had two trucks parked in its centre line, thus making it impossible for any plane to land. Despite the obstructions it was clear that aircraft did use the runway, for it was marked by the black rubber streaks of fresh tyre marks, but the two trucks, together with the yellow cross, were evidence that the runway could only be used by invitation.

We slashed across the shank of the island, then we were over the anchorage and I had a glimpse of a sailing boat's shadow black on the bed of the lagoon before our own winged shadow whipped across a gaggle of powerboats. We were going too fast to see any details of the moored vessels so I just snapped a random photograph and, at the very same instant, the Maggot swore and banked and rammed the throttles hard forward.

We were side-slipping, starboard wing down, falling to earth with our engines howling. I flailed for support as the camera flew up to the padded ceiling. The Maggot whooped, dragged the stick back and our earthwards wing lifted and suddenly we were screaming just above the palm trees, close to the tiled roofs and at a speed that seemed to be doubled

71

because of our proximity to the ground. The camera, re-entering the world of normal gravity, dropped hard beside my shoes. Beer bottles were everywhere. One broke, shattering liquid across the side windows. I had a glimpse of a fair-haired girl staring wide-eyed and terrified from a tennis court, her racket held loose by her side and tennis balls scattered at her feet and, though the trees and buildings and gardens were nothing but a high-speed blur, my mind nevertheless registered with a startling clarity that the girl had been completely naked. The plane's engines were screaming. We whipped over the northernmost house, across the beach, and thus out to sea again. "What the hell?" I managed to ask.

"They fired at us! goddamn tracer bullets! Jesus!" The Maggot did not seem scared, but rather stung by the challenge. We were over the lagoon now, racing towards the northern strands of the Devil's Necklace, but low enough so that the wash of our twin propellers was whipping the blue water into a wake of white-hazed foam. "Shee-it!" The Maggot said with inappropriate exultation, then twisted his head to stare back at the island. "Let's go see them again!"

"Are you sure that's wise?" I asked, but I might as well have saved my breath because the plane suddenly climbed, banked, then began descending fast towards the island again. The Maggot was growling to himself, relishing the confrontation. Sunlight reflected from a window among the palm trees to lance a sliver of dazzling light at our cockpit, then the reflection was gone and we were at sea level, engines screaming, and I fumbled for the camera, prayed it had not broken when it fell from the ceiling, and took another picture just before Maggot lifted the aircraft's nose so that we swooped up and over the palm trees that edged the beach.

He jinked left, then right, throwing the plane into such steep and sudden turns that I was alternately jerked hard against the cockpit's side window and then against his broad shoulder. The Maggot was not taking evasive action but quartering the ground in search of our enemy. "There!" he said abruptly and threw the plane straight again, but this time dropping the nose, and I saw a jeep churning dust from the dirt road which ran the length of the island's long shank, between the golf course and the houses, and just as I saw the jeep so the red tracer bullets began climbing from a machine-gun mounted in the back of the vehicle.

"Oh, Jesus wept," I said, snapped a last picture, then ducked down in momentary expectation of the windscreen shattering into a million bright scraps.

"Fuck you," the Maggot screamed at whoever fired at him and I looked out of the Beechcraft's side window to see palm trees going past at over 150 miles an hour and above us. Above us. Truly. And I thought it really had been a very good life, a fun life, despite Ellen never having gone to bed with me, and I wondered if my father would even notice my death, then the Maggot whooped with glee, hauled back on the stick, and our plane was screaming up into the wide blue lovely bullet-free sky and the Maggot was laughing and slapping my shoulder. "Wasn't that just the best goddamned fun you can have this side of a blanket?"

"Was it?"

"You missed it?" He sounded aggrieved and astonished.

"Missed what?"

"I ran that turkey clean off the road! Shit, but I gave that bastard a headache!"

"I think you gave me one too," I said, then, very gingerly, I straightened up and twisted round to see that Murder Cay was far behind us and well out of machine-gun range. "You're mad," I courteously informed John Maggovertski.

He laughed. "You're the one who wanted to see the island." We were gently circling northwards now, heading for home. "So now you've seen it."

I tried to relax, letting the cold air from the vent cool the sweat from my face. My right hand shook as I re-membered the sudden fear of seeing the crimson tracer flick up from the ground. "Hell!" I protested. "They can't just open fire!"

The Maggot grinned through the black tangle of his beard.

"Nick, they are richer than your wettest dreams, and like all the very rich they think they are above the law." He was speaking very casually, but I saw that his right hand, like mine, was shaking. It is not pleasant to be shot at, and even the pleasure of being missed is spoilt by the mind's habit of constructing alternative scenarios; if the machine-gunner had been a bit quicker to react, or had led us with more skill, we would now be nothing but a heap of molten metal somewhere in the sea-grape. The Maggot shook his head. "Do you have any idea just how rich these people are?"

"Very, I imagine."

"There's an island not far from here that has just two thousand inhabitants, and last year, Nick, according to a banker I sometimes fly to Miami, those two thousand dirt poor and unemployed islanders deposited 24.3 million dollars in the one and only bank on their impoverished little island." The Maggot laughed. "Not bad, eh? And I do not believe that 24.3 million dollars a year is the average reward for selling coconut milk and conch shells to honky tourists. That money is pure commission, Nick, a mere ten per cent of the value of the cocaine that was stored on their island while it awaited transportation to the good old US of A; and neither you, nor I, nor even the dickheads in the Drug Enforcement Administration will ever know just how much money was not put in the bank, but stored in paper bags under the bed." He sounded depressed by the thought, but then cheered himself up by asking me for a beer.

I opened two bottles that I retrieved from the sticky mess on the cabin floor. We flew the rest of the way home in silence. It was not till we saw the captive aerostat balloon with its ever watching radar that the Americans had hoisted over Grand Bahama to probe for boats or aircraft smuggling drugs, that the Maggot again spoke, and by then he had recaptured all his old insouciance. "At this time, if you'd care to fold up your tray table and extinguish your hopes, we shall land this little sucker. Thank you for flying Maggovertski Airways; please return the stewardess her pantyhose, put her in the

74

upright position, and kindly pray that the tyres don't blow."

They did not, and thus I came back to *Wavebreaker*.

I went back to the Maggot's foul house, where he kept his killer dog and astonishing collection of guns, and we sat on his makeshift verandah that overlooked a noxious and polluted creek and shared a few whiskies as he told me an incredibly tedious tale of how he had once sacked the quarterback of the San Francisco Sugar Plums. I retaliated with detailed instructions on how to bowl off-breaks to left-handers on a drying pitch, and we eventually declared a truce as we watched the sun sink across the oil-storage tanks beyond the creek. He offered me his spare bed for the night, but I could not stand the stench of the creek, and I wanted to make an early start on the work I had to do on *Wavebreaker*, so I caught the bus to McIllvanney's boatyard. Naturally no one was there and the gate was locked and the top of the fence was rimmed with razor-wire so I could not climb it. I had not kept my old key, because I had hoped that my association with Cutwater Charters was done, so I was forced to carry my heavy pack into the tangle of dark alleys that lay behind the straw market and where I planned to find Ellen and borrow her key.

A tribe of stray cats scattered as I turned into the yard where Ellen's apartment lay. The archway was bright with the brass plates of the dozens of corporations who were registered at the address to avoid paying tax in their home countries. The courtyard was inhabited by three tethered goats that stared malevolently at me. The open-air stairways were shadowed with creepers and flickering with the eerie lights of televisions that glowed from within the screened windows of the small apartments.

I climbed the two flights of stairs and walked down the rickety balcony which led to Ellen's small end room. A child was screaming in one of the flats, while two dogs were snarling as they fought in the wasteland beyond the apartment house. The chorus of televisions was tuned to an American game show in which competing families were leaping up and down and screaming with apparent incontinence because they had won a trip to Disneyworld. Then, above all those discordant sounds, I heard Ellen's voice rise in sudden indignation. "No! No! No!"

I stopped outside her open window. Her room was lit by a single naked bulb which hung from the ceiling and shone harshly on Ellen who was standing in the doorway of her tiny bathroom. She was facing the window, but did not see me beyond its screen because she was staring at Matthew McIllvanney who seemed to fill the whole room with his malevolence. "I'm just asking you to think about it," I heard him say in a calm voice.

"I've thought" – I could see Ellen was trying hard to recover her composure – "and the answer is no."

"Six hundred." McIllvanney's persistence in the face of any refusal was monotonous and relentless. "And I won't even take my usual commission on that, so you'll get to keep it all, and remember the agreed price is just a guaranteed minimum and there's always a tip. Isn't there always a tip, Bellybutton?"

"This one's a big tipper, Miss Ellen." Bellybutton laughed suggestively. He was standing just inside the front door and was thus hidden from me.

"Shut up, you black bastard," McIllvanney snapped, then paused to light a cigarette. A small battery-powered fan whirled the smoke away and generally tried to stir up the humid air which played such havoc with Ellen's precious books in their orange-crate shelves. The Ulsterman blew smoke towards her. "Breakspear won't do the senator's cruise," he said, "so you'll lose that money, but if you work one night a week for me then you'll earn just as much anyway. And you're wanting to save money, isn't that right? So you can keep yourself while you write your book? So I'm offering you a good wage, girl! And this client's a good-looking fellow, isn't that right, Bellybutton? And he's already seen you, he likes you, and he's willing to pay you a professional's fee even though he knows you're an amateur, and –"

"No!" Ellen shouted again.

"He might go to seven-fifty," McIllvanney said dubiously, as though the price was the only possible objection Ellen might have to whoring herself.

That was as far as the conversation went, for I decided to end it by pushing open the screen door. All three stared in astonishment as I tossed my kit bag on to the floor. "I didn't have a key to the boatyard," I introduced myself, "so I thought I'd borrow Ellen's. I'm not interrupting anything, am I?"

"You are not, Nick, no!" Ellen almost flew across the small room and, to my astonishment and probably to everyone else's, greeted me with a warm kiss.

"What the hell are you doing here?" McIllvanney asked sourly, while Bellybutton just grinned maliciously at me.

"You sent the senator to see me? So he came, he saw, and he conquered me, which means I've agreed to do his charter. The Maggot flew me back, because if we want to leave on Sunday morning then we've got a heap of work to do first. God, I'm hungry."

Ellen still clung to my arm. "We'll go out and eat," she said quickly, "I'll get ready," and she twisted away to the bathroom, which also served as her wardrobe, and slammed the door to leave me alone with McIllvanney and Bellybutton.

"If the suggestion I heard just now," I said to McIllvanney, "was what I thought it was, then don't make it again. Not to Ellen."

McIllvanney found my defiance wonderfully amusing. "Who's to stop me."

"Just me."

He came and stood very close to me, trying to intimidate me as Billingsley had done. He blew cigarette smoke to sting my eyes. "Just because you were a poxy marine, your Holiness, doesn't make you tough."

"Piss off."

That also amused him. "Is there something going on between you and Ellen, now? Got your boots under her table, have you?"

"No," I said firmly, "so get out."

"Did you know she's a Catholic?" he asked me as though it really mattered, and he gestured with his cigarette at a crucifix that hung over the narrow bed, which I knew was there solely for sentimental purposes because it had belonged to Ellen's dead father, but to McIllvanney it was a challenge. "If I'd realised she was a taig I'd never have hired her." He used the Ulster slang, knowing I would have learned it during my tours of duty on attachment in Belfast. "Is it the papist meat that gets you going, Breakspear, is that it?" McIllvanney laughed, then stepped quickly back as he sensed I might bring my knee up into his balls. Then, as if counter-attacking, he jabbed the cigarette towards my face. "I'll do business how I like, with whom I like, and when I like, and I don't need your focking permission to do it, Nicholas Breakspear. Nor does the girl have to agree to anything I ask. I'm not forcing her, I'm merely making a business proposition. Do you understand me?"

"Get out of here," I said.

McIllvanney continued to stare into my eyes, but he spoke to Bellybutton who was cackling behind me. "He should have put on a pair of tights and joined his daddy in front of the fairy-lights." The Ulsterman's scorn was like a blowtorch, then he turned away, clicked his fingers at Bellybutton, and the two of them were gone.

Ellen and I did not go out to eat. She was too shocked by McIllvanney's offer and, at the same time, she was paradoxically surprised at herself for being so shocked. "I really thought I could handle something like that! I really did! I knew I wasn't in danger, because they weren't going to rape me, but it really, really upset me!"

"It upset me," I said.

"Shit!" Ellen was too angry with herself to be assuaged by or even interested in my sympathy. She paced up and down the tiny room while I sat on her bed, and she explained to me that McIllvanney had been approached by a client who had apparently seen Ellen and authorised McIllvanney to offer her the money. McIllvanney had made the offer very dispassionately, but that businesslike approach only seemed to add to

Ellen's fury. "What kind of a jerk pays that money?" she asked me.

"A rich and randy jerk?" I suggested, and decided not to tell her that for most of McIllvanney's girls six or seven hundred dollars a night was small change.

"And get this." She whirled on me. "This jerk has got something about redheads! But before he'd pay any money he had to be satisfied that I was red-haired all over! I mean, Jesus! How nauseating can you get?"

"Who was he?"

"McIllvanney wouldn't say." She shuddered, then plucked some typed sheets of paper from the small table under the window and stuffed them into a folder. The floor was crowded with cardboard boxes that were filled with leaflets for the Literacy Project that Ellen helped in her spare time. I idly picked up one of the leaflets which had two pictures on its cover; the first illustration showed a happy black family, all neatly dressed and reading books around a table that was filled with platefuls of food and with jugs labelled 'milk'. The second picture, clearly designed to demonstrate the rewards of illiteracy, showed a scabby-looking native dressed in a threadbare loincloth who crouched in the mud outside a grass hut and who seemed to be sharing his lunch bowl with a baboon. Ellen caught my eye, looked down at the ridiculous leaflet, and suddenly we both began to laugh helplessly. "I know they're absurd." She had tears in her eyes as she tried to recover from the laughter. "They were printed for Africa sometime in the 1950s and the United Nations sent them to our project, God knows why. There are too many to throw away all at once, so I take a handful out every day and hide them in someone's garbage can. They make rotten toilet paper, and I don't know what else to do with them, and, oh Nick" – she suddenly sat heavily beside me on the bed – "you're a good man and sometimes I think how nice it would be to have a good man in my life again."

"I'm available."

She kissed me on the nose, but then, as though rejecting her idea of adopting a good man, stood up briskly. "You reek of cheap whisky. I suppose you've been with that awful Maggovertski?"

"He sends his most fervent and undying love."

She mocked that assertion with a grimace. "If you want a sandwich there's some margarine and foul cheese in the cupboard and some not very fresh bread in the bin."

"You're sure you don't want to go out to eat?"

She shook her head. "I want to write up my notes."

"About what happened tonight?" I sounded surprised.

"Sure, why not? But I need a shower first." She went into the bathroom and I made my own supper by slicing some of the foul cheese and shoving it between two slices of greased plastic bread. Then I ate the sandwich as I walked back to *Wavebreaker*. Alone.

Ellen was perversely unhappy about the Crowninshield charter. She had nagged me to accept it, but now she behaved as though I had done her a disservice by doing so. "The senator obviously just wants us to drown his children so they can't embarrass him when the time comes to run for President," she told me next morning.

"I accused him of that," I said, proud of having anticipated Ellen's diagnosis, "and he told me he'd rather lose the election than lose his children."

Ellen put down her cup of coffee and stared at me as though I had gone completely mad. "He's a politician, Nick," she said at last, and in a voice she might have used to reason with a three-year-old, "and politicians would sell their mothers, let alone their kids, to win an election. He's just using us!"

I shrugged, but said nothing. Ellen had bought some melon and coffee on her way to the boatyard and we were eating a late breakfast in *Wavebreaker*'s cockpit. Bellybutton was pressure-hosing a hull across the yard, while McIllvanney was evidently taking another day off. I hoped that he was avoiding us because he felt ashamed of his offer to Ellen, but I doubted whether Matthew McIllvanney had ever felt ashamed of anything.

"God!" Ellen said in a tone which implied that I had entirely misunderstood the senator's motives, which she would now have to explain to me by the application of sound feminist arguments. Sound feminist argument usually means making the nearest male look like an idiot, which in Ellen's case was not a very demanding task. "We are talking about a man's image, Nicholas. If he runs for President next year then he's got to be clean, and that means that the issue of his drug-sodden kids will have to be defused. And above all, he's got to keep Rickie out of prison, and that's clearly our job. We have to clean the boy up so the judge will merely tap his wrist."

"Is that so bad?" I demanded.

"I just don't like being used by rich politicians," Ellen said angrily, though I silently noted she had no objections to taking their money.

"At least we'll be taking two kids off drugs," I said warmly, "and that's something to be proud of."

"Jesus wept," she said in disgust. "I do hate goddamn junkies, and I especially hate rich goddamn junkies. They don't even have the excuse of poverty for their addiction."

"I'm sorry," I said. I don't know why I apologised because it was not my fault that the Crowninshield twins were cocaine freaks, nor that their father wanted to charter *Wavebreaker*, but I sympathised with Ellen's distaste for cocaine and was foolish enough to say as much.

"Don't be so downright stupid, Nick," Ellen witheringly rejected my sympathy. "Of course I don't disapprove of cocaine. You forget that I was an academic."

I tried to work out an obvious connection between scholarship and cocaine and could not, but knew better than to ask. "But you can't possibly approve of drugs," I said instead.

"I neither approve nor disapprove. Cocaine is merely a recreational drug and, taken to excess, like alcohol or nicotine, it is undoubtedly dangerous, but judiciously used it can be a source of harmless pleasure, and even of intellectual stimulation. Eat your melon, it's good for you."

"I don't believe this." I stared in genuine horror at her. I was trying to imagine a girl in a Pittsburgh peep-show, put there by cocaine. "Did you feed that kind of intellectual garbage to your students?" I asked Ellen.

She stared defiantly across the cockpit table at me. "Nicholas Breakspear," she said at last, "there are times when you can be excessively tedious. You are a turkey–" she cast about for an even worse insult, "a puritan!"

"Rickie Crowninshield," I said stiffly, "has already lost the sight of one eye because of cocaine, and if he doesn't stop using the drug then he will almost certainly go to jail or even kill himself with an overdose."

"So Rickie Crowninshield is an irresponsible idiot," Ellen said coldly, "but you can't run society on the assumption that everyone is a retard, and you have to accept that there will be casualties in a free society. If you're so intent on keeping the young alive then why don't you ban rock climbing? Or surfing? Or motorcycles? Or alcohol? Or have you forgotten that America did once try to ban alcohol, and look what happened!" Her voice was scathing. "The vaunted land of the free became the last best hope of organised crime, and it has never recovered. The clear and obvious course for America is to legalise cocaine so the trade can be controlled, but there is no way that we shall ever persuade the airheads in Congress of that most obvious piece of wisdom. If you don't want the melon, I do."

"But you do believe the trade should be controlled?" I was seeking a scrap of common ground on which we could mutually back away from the argument.

"I naturally believe that the financial profits of the drug-suppliers are offensive," Ellen said, "which is why I've only used cocaine on a handful of occasions. I can't say I liked it much." She poured out the last of the coffee, then looked up into my horrified eyes. "Oh, come on, Nick! Don't be so innocent! And stop worrying, I won't reveal my views on the drug to the twins. The poor dim little creatures doubtless need all the help they can get, and I promise not to confuse them with anything so threatening as an idea."

82

"Robin-Anne's not dim," I said. "She passed her degree!"

"My dear Nicholas, a mentally retarded slug could get a degree in Liberal Arts! For God's sake, the silly little twinkie might as well have majored in handwriting or media studies!" Ellen gave me a dismissive glance. "Still, I suppose to the uneducated even a degree in Liberal Arts is impressive."

Cocaine thus became another of the subjects which Ellen and I decorously avoided, like the existence of God, the wisdom of my having been a marine, feminism and the cartoons in the *New Yorker*. Ellen was adamantly opposed to the first two and a noisy supporter of the last two, while my position was more or less the opposite. God alone knew why we wanted to sail to New Zealand together, except that in a strange way we were friends.

But for the moment we were friends who had to prepare *Wavebreaker* for a possible Atlantic crossing. Thessy and I would have a chance to strengthen the rigging during our two-week trial period with the twins, but some jobs simply could not be done at sea. Thus I stripped out all *Wavebreaker*'s unnecessary furniture and equipment, and I installed extra fresh-water tanks and fuel bunkers. I made storm shields for the big cabin windows and skylights. They were a delight for the charterers in the Bahamian lagoons, but in an Atlantic storm such wide windows could be our death warrants for if *Wavebreaker* fell off a big wave the glass could be driven out of the windows and the boat be filling with water in seconds, and so I cut and shaped sheet steel shutters that could be bolted over the boat's glass at the first sign of bad weather. The shutters' anchor points had to be welded to the hull and, especially at the stern where the windows wrapped round *Wavebreaker*'s counter, the bolts looked intrusive and ugly, but better that than to be a good-looking boat fifty fathoms down and still sinking.

Ellen and I worked hard that week and, on the Saturday, as though to commiserate with ourselves on this being our last day alone together, we stopped work at midday and took a bus to Mama Sipcott's Café on the beach where we ate lobster and drank too much of Mama's sticky-sweet white wine. Ellen proposed a toast to the prospect of her first Atlantic crossing under sail.

I drank to the toast, though I was not at all sure that we would actually make the crossing in *Wavebreaker*. The best season for an eastwards voyage was already past, though it was just possible that we might run far north and cross in the high latitudes where, even in summer, we could expect fog, rain and cold. I knew Ellen hated the cold, and I tried to warn her of the conditions we might expect in those latitudes. I told her of the big green seas, all crinkled and slow, heaving up astern as the icy wind scoured their tops into freezing spume.

Ellen smiled at my enthusiastic description. "My poetic and romantic Nick." She cocked her head on one side and gave me a long scrutiny, almost as though she had never seen me before. "You did inherit a lot from your father."

"You'll find that northern seas are oddly more threatening" – I ignored her insult – "because sunlight on water always makes it seem less formidable. But if we travel the northern route we probably won't see the sun for weeks, and the daylight is grey and the sea is green and grey, while at night you just see the cold white wavetops hissing out of blackness." It seemed curious to be describing such ice-cold seas while sitting in a palm-thatched Bahamian beach café that looked on to a shoreline where pelicans perched under the diamond-hard sun. "You'll need long johns," I went on gleefully, "and thermal underwear and layers of greasy-wool sweaters and good oilies and a woolly hat and a towelling scarf to stop the seas slopping down your neck and good sea-boots and as many pairs of gloves as you can find, because gloves never stay dry and –"

"Shut up," Ellen said firmly.

"I thought you wanted to go."

"I do, and I shall go. But I also want to enjoy the anticipation of going."

I smiled. "Just pray we don't get a North Atlantic fog, because in those latitudes we could roll in the swells for days, with the moisture beading the shrouds and the air as cold as charity, and always being terrified that a super-tanker will barrel out of the muck at full speed to thump you under her bows without even knowing you were ever there."

Ellen borrowed the adjustable spanner that Mama Sipcott provided as a lobster-claw cracker. "Don't come the Ancient Mariner with me, Nicholas Breakspear." She opened a claw and pulled out a sliver of succulent flesh. "If we encounter fog over the North Atlantic we will turn on the radar, switch on the Satnav, and start the engines. These are the 1980s, not the twelfth century when your namesake was Pope. He wasn't even a very good Pope."

"He was excellent!" I protested.

"Authoritative, unimaginative, anti-Irish, and a lousy politician," Ellen commented, then she smiled and pushed the lobster meat into my mouth. "God knows why I like you, Nicholas Breakspear."

"Because of my sexy legs," I assured her.

She laughed. Mama Sipcott's butter sauce was gleaming on her chin and she looked very beautiful. Beauty, I thought, was something to do with the way a face betrayed character. She seemed oblivious to my scrutiny. "I suppose I like you," she said after a moment's thought, "because you lack guile. You remind me of a cocker spaniel I once owned."

"Oh, woof-woof. Thanks a million."

She made a face at me. "You'd prefer to be villainous?"

I nodded. "I've always wanted to be mysterious and a little bit sinister and have girls swoon when they see me." Like my father, I realised, and tried to reject the thought.

To Ellen, my wish to be mysterious was a hoot. "Forget it. You have an open face, Nick, and you smile too easily, and you're much too honest, and you really can't resist helping people; and frankly, you're about as subtle as a Mack truck. As a villain, Nick, you just don't measure up."

I turned and looked at myself in the cracked Cutty Sark Whisky mirror behind Mama Sipcott's bar. Hamlet, not Macbeth or Richard III, stared back. I turned again to Ellen, pretty freckled Ellen with her high cheekbones and clever green eyes and flaming hair and mocking smile, and I suddenly wondered whether McIllvanney had spoken to her again in the last week. "Did McIllvanney –" I began tentatively.

"Oh, yes," Ellen cut in smoothly, and without any disgust in her voice. "In fact he increased the fee to a thousand dollars." She sounded perversely proud of her increased value, and again I thought it best not to inform her that a bubblehead like Donna could earn twice that fee in a single night. "I told him to go jump in a lake," Ellen said very calmly, "and then I told him that just as soon as I've finished with the Crownin-shield twins I shall be sailing away –" she clinked her glass on mine, "with you."

It was the first time she had actually said for certain that she would sail with me and I could not hide my joy, and Ellen, seeing that pleasure, laughed at it. "Of course I'm coming with you, Nick! I was always planning to sail with you! Do you think I'd pass up an adventure like that?"

So who cared about having a too-honest face? I was lucky Nick and she was pretty Ellen, and so I ordered another bottle of the sticky white wine and we let our dreams take wings. For we were going to sea.

Ellen and I lingered on in Mama Sipcott's for another hour and a half; indulging in the sailor's shorebound pastime of planning the perfect voyage. We decided that *Masquerade* would sail from the Bahamas to Panama, and thence to the Galapagos where we would find Darwin's giant tortoises. Then we would sail south to Easter Island to explore the mysterious statues before going to the mutineers' refuge on Pitcairn Island. After that we would go to Tahiti, and I saw the excitement grow in Ellen as she realised that these plans were so close to coming true. It was an excitement that matched my own, for I had never sailed the South Seas and I had long dreamed of that scatter of tiny, magically named islands strewn across one third of a globe. By the time we had drunk our third bottle of wine Ellen and I had long reached New Zealand and were already sailing north towards New Caledonia. We were happy.

We caught the bus back to Ellen's apartment and collected her clothes and notebooks. She was moving back on board *Wavebreaker* in preparation for the next day's early departure. I carried her luggage to the yard, noting that even Ellen's strident feminism evaporated in the face of two heavy bags and tropical heat.

Once in the boatyard Ellen ran ahead of me, evidently eager to reach *Wavebreaker*'s air conditioning. Then, as she reached the dock's edge, she suddenly checked. "What on earth is that? Oh, no!" She began to run again.

When I reached the water's edge I understood her dismay. A large sports-fishing boat was moored alongside *Wavebreaker*, but moored so crudely that whoever had brought the power-boat alongside the schooner had not bothered to put out fenders, but instead had gouged long ugly gashes in *Wavebreaker*'s white paint.

Yet even the gashes were not so ugly as the expensive boat that had caused them. There was nothing wrong with the boat's lines, which were sleekly functional, but her long powerful hull, her upperworks, and even the interior of her capacious working deck had all been painted with a wartime dazzle paint. The seemingly random and jagged-edged pattern of blue, black, silver, green and white had been designed to disguise a boat's shape from the prying eyes of U-Boat captains, so it seemed somewhat fanciful to thus camouflage a pleasure boat in the Bahamas. This boat was called *Dream Baby*, and she was clearly an expensive infant for rods and whip-aerials and outriggers splayed from her upperworks like the antennae of some outlandish insect. She boasted a harpoon walkway, a flybridge, and, above the highest wheel-platform, an aluminium canopy which held a radar aerial. The fighting chair on her aft deck had thick white leather straps giving it the appearance of a padded electric chair, while the dazzle paint gave the boat an oddly military look that was completed by the number 666 that was painted on her bows in silver-edged black numerals like those warships use to display their commissioning numbers. The boat's wrap-around windscreens were made of black polarised glass which only added to *Dream Baby*'s ugly air of menace.

Ellen, unencumbered with luggage, had already reached *Wavebreaker* and taken two plastic fenders from a locker. She swung lithely down to *Dream Baby*'s gaudily painted deck and cushioned the two hulls.

"How bad is the damage?" I called down to her when I reached *Wavebreaker*.

"It's scraped back to bare metal!"

"I'll give it some paint." *Wavebreaker*'s hull was made of steel and, while such hulls are marvellously strong and safe, they are soon weakened if their steel is exposed to salt air. I had to paint the gashes as soon as possible so that rust would not begin to bite into *Wavebreaker*'s long sleekness.

Ellen looked around the oddly painted powerboat. "You'd think someone rich enough to own a rig like this could afford a pair of fenders."

"Who cares? Just cut the damn boat loose," I said vengefully.

Ellen ignored my advice while I, obedient to the rule that if a job needed doing then do it without delay, found a pot of white paint and dug through the locker for a clean brush. Then, from behind me, an unfamiliar voice sounded: "Oh, ring my bells." It was a man's voice; drawling and lazy.

I twisted around and almost blinded myself by staring straight into the sun, but then, through the dizzying glare, I made out the long silhouette of a tall man who seemed, incongruously, to be dressed in a long, transparent dressing gown. He was emerging in stately fashion from *Wavebreaker*'s companionway and, though I could see he was tall and lanky and had a ponytail of hair, I could make out no details of his face. "Who the hell are you?" I demanded.

The man ignored me, walking instead towards Ellen who, dressed only in shorts and T-shirt, was climbing long-legged over *Wavebreaker*'s rail. "Be still my restless heart," the man had a strong, caressing voice and the slow luscious accent of America's deep south. "Dear lady, dear lady, to think that I might have lived my whole life through and never seen you. Oh, lay me down, just lay me down."

Ellen, usually so quick with a scornful reply, just stood and stared at the elegant stranger who stopped one pace away from her, took her hand, then bowed above her fingers. He kissed the air a fastidiously polite inch above her knuckles, then closed his eyes. "Dear sweet Lord above, I do thank Thee for Thy kindness in showing me this lovely woman before I died." To my astonishment and chagrin Ellen left her hand in his as he opened his eyes and smiled at her. "My name," he stroked her with his voice, "is Jesse Isambard Sweetman. And who, dear creature, are you?"

Ellen still said nothing. I had straightened up and moved aside so that the sun no longer dazzled me and I could see Sweetman properly, and what I saw I did not like. His face was old and young, sardonic and knowing, amused and handsome; the face of a man who has seen the world's wickedness and knows how to match it with his own. His long black hair was tied into its ponytail with a velvet ribbon, his skin was parchment pale, and his eyes dark. I put his age at forty, but even among men twenty years younger he would have been accounted handsome, and he knew it, for his expression showed both confidence and amusement as he continued to hold Ellen's hand, and he showed even more amusement when she suddenly realised just what liberty she was thus granting him and jerked her fingers swiftly away.

Thus released, Jesse Sweetman turned to look at me. The dressing gown had proved to be a long, stylish, ankle-length duster coat which was loosely woven from a delicate white cotton. Beneath the filmy topcoat he wore a black shirt and black trousers that were tucked into tall black boots. It was a dramatic and impractical outfit of a kind I only expected to see on the male models who posed in the more outlandish fashion magazines that our rich clients brought aboard *Wavebreaker*, yet Jesse Isambard Sweetman managed to wear the elaborate style with an elegant insouciance. The only incongruous note was a cheap round badge, enamelled in red and yellow, that he wore on his shirt, which bore the legend 'Just Say No!'. "You must be Nicholas Breakspear," he said carelessly, as though he did not much care whether I was or not.

"Is that gaudy piece of junk your boat?" I gestured to where *Dream Baby*'s aerials showed above *Wavebreaker*'s gunwale.

Sweetman turned and pretended to notice the sports-fishing boat for the first time. "No," he said helpfully, then bestowed a patronising smile on me. "You look so like your father. It's really uncanny."

"Did you bring that boat here?" I persevered.

"Oh, indeed I did," he said brightly, as though he merely indulged a rather dim child's curiosity. "Your mother was Malise Fielding, am I right? Or are you Lucy de Sills' son?"

"Why the hell didn't you use fenders when you tied alongside?"

He sighed, intimating what a bore I was being. "I did not use fenders, Breakspear, because I despise precautions. Precautions are the symptoms of small and fearful minds. Precautions will not conquer empires, they will not build great cities, they will not transmute dreams into gold or carry men across wide oceans, and precautions will not, emphatically not, win fair ladies," and here he turned to Ellen and lasciviousiy dropped his gaze to her long bare legs. Ellen twisted away and Sweetman laughed at her obvious discomfiture, then, as coolly as though he owned *Wavebreaker*, he stepped down into the central cockpit where he first brushed at, then sat on, one of the white cushioned seats by the ship's wheel. "I've had a look round the boat," he said very coolly, "and I approve of her. So tell me the cost of a week's charter."

"The man you want to see," I said, "is called Matthew McIllvanney and his office is the pink building with the outside staircase. He's not here this afternoon, but you can doubtless telephone him next week."

Sweetman took a pair of polarised sunglasses from his shirt pocket and put them on before inspecting me again. He did not seem to like what he saw. "You're really not being noticeably helpful," he said after a pause, "so let us try again shall we? Would you please tell me the high season price for one week?"

"How many passengers?" Ellen asked before I could refuse to answer.

Sweetman paused again, this time to light a long pale blue cigarette with a slim gold lighter. He shrugged. "Two, four, six passengers? Does it really matter?"

"One week in high season costs ten thousand US dollars for two people, and every extra couple is another thousand bucks." Ellen's voice was cold, as though she disliked satisfying his curiosity. "And to those prices you have to add the boat's running costs."

"Which are?" Sweetman asked carelessly.

"A lot." Ellen said flatly. "You're talking fuel, food and liquor, plus any toys you might want aboard like scuba equipment, snorkels, jet-skis or sailboards."

Sweetman drew on his fancy cigarette, then blew a plume of smoke into *Wavebreaker*'s rigging before smiling lazily at Ellen. "And tell me, sweet creature, do you count as a toy? Or are you a part of the initial ten thousand dollars?"

"Get off the boat," I said.

"Shut up." He turned on me like a snake. "You're nothing but a hired hand, Breakspear, so shut the fuck up." He glanced at the paint pot and brush that I was still holding. "Go and paint something. Be useful." He stared into my eyes, challenging me to defy him, and when I did not move he looked back to Ellen. "I asked you a question, dear heart. Please be so good as to answer."

"Get off this boat," I told him, but my anger only amused Sweetman who unfolded his long thin legs from the cushioned thwart.

"Dick off," he said to me.

I was surprised that he so eagerly sought to confront me. I am not a small man, nor am I a weakling, yet the thin Sweetman seemed unconcerned as I jumped down into the cockpit. Then I saw why he was so confident. He put a hand into a pocket of his elegant duster coat and brought out a small .22 pistol that he pointed at my face. "A ladies' gun," he said, "but remarkably effective at close range."

"Nick!" Ellen called warningly, as though I might not have seen the gun.

The gun's threat had not stopped my advance. I was calling Sweetman's bluff, confident he would not dare pull the trigger, and equally confident that my marine training would let me turn him into mincemeat. I was also half drunk, and thus filled with the Dutch courage offered by Mama Sipcott's worst white wine.

Sweetman stood. There was, at last, a look of alarm on his face, and I could see him wondering whether he really would have to pull the small trigger. He held the gun pointed at my eyes. I began to fear that he would fire, and a small sober part of my brain registered just how foolish this confrontation was; a contest caused solely by two male egos over a girl sworn to celibacy.

"Stop it! Both of you! I mean it!" Ellen's voice was suddenly a harsh scream, so harsh that we both looked towards her and saw that she was threatening both of us with one of *Wave-*

breaker's heavy-duty fire extinguishers that she had snatched from its rack at the head of the main companionway. The cylinder was filled with a compressed chemical that would have smothered both Sweetman and me in an avalanche of nauseating foam. "Step back, Nick!" Ellen said to me, her voice recovering its normal timbre.

"But I'm only going to kill him," I said reasonably.

"It is neither wise nor manly to get into a pissing contest with a skunk," Ellen said coldly, "so step back, Nick." She menaced me with the extinguisher's nozzle and, because I knew Ellen did not make idle threats, and because I knew she despised all displays of macho violence, I obediently stepped backwards and watched as she transferred the extinguisher's aim to Sweetman. "Leave us." she said.

"Listen, sweet lady —"

"I said leave us!"

He gave her his most confidently patronising smile. "Dear lady, I merely wish . . ."

Ellen squeezed the lever. There was a gulp from the extinguisher's valve and a trickle of yellow-white liquid dribbled pathetically from its nozzle. Sweetman crowed with laughter, but too soon, for, just as it seemed as though Ellen's gesture had indeed collapsed into an ignominious anti-climax, the extinguisher first coughed, then spat a vicious deluge of white muck that fanned from the flared nozzle to splatter spectacularly against Sweetman's chest. He staggered back, half tripped on the cockpit coaming, scrambled up to the deck and then to the ship's rail. Ellen, who was utterly delighted with her achievement, followed him to spray the churning mess over his hair, then down on to the decks of *Dream Baby* as Sweetman jumped panic-stricken from our gunwale. "Nick!" she called. "It won't turn off!" Ellen was laughing as she tried to stop the gunk that still spewed from the cylinder. Sweetman, safe under *Dream Baby*'s canopy, was starting his motors. He risked a soaking of foam as he darted out to cut his mooring lines, then twisted *Dream Baby*'s wheel and thrust her throttles forward. Ellen was laughing like a child let loose in a sweet shop. "It won't turn off!" she said again.

"Throw it overboard!" I didn't want to spend the rest of the afternoon cleaning foam from *Wavebreaker*'s decks.

Ellen hurled the still discharging extinguisher over the side. The cylinder bounced hard on *Dream Baby*'s dazzle-painted transom, then sank in the clear water where, resting on the sea-bed, it continued to discharge its disgusting foam. Sweetman turned a furious smeared face at us, then drove his garish boat hard at *Wavebreaker*'s hull to gouge a long scratch down to the bare metal. I heard the screech of protesting steel, then the powerboat bounced off our hull and accelerated away so that, within seconds, its powerful drives were swirling the sea into twin sprays of white water.

"Damn him." I leaned over the rail to inspect the new scratch in *Wavebreaker*'s paint.

"Didn't I do well?" Ellen asked proudly.

I had to laugh. "You did wonderfully!"

"He had a gun!" She sounded astonished, and I knew that the real danger of the moment was only just occurring to her.

"For someone who hates violence," I agreed, "you used force with great skill. You gained a victory over a piece of scum, and I congratulate you."

"A piece of scum?" Ellen turned to look at the rapidly disappearing *Dream Baby*. "I thought he was kind of cute."

"Cute!" I was astonished by her. "You thought that scabby creep was cute?"

"Yeah," she sounded defensive, "kind of."

"Bloody hell," I said, and decided that I would never understand women. "You'd better check that your cute friend didn't steal anything when he was down below."

It took me two hours to paint out the damage that Sweetman had caused to our hull. Ellen meanwhile cleared the foam from the teak deck, then searched *Wavebreaker*'s cabins. She reported that Jesse Sweetman appeared to have stolen nothing and, except for the padlock on the companionway, had damaged nothing either. Ellen and I both assumed that Sweetman's interest in *Wavebreaker* had been merely that of a prospective charterer who wanted to reconnoitre the boat's amenities.

So I forgot about him, at least until that evening when I gave Ellen some practice with the sextant. She was trying to master celestial navigation and I stood beside her as she trapped Altair in the mirror, then delicately and successfully brought the star down to the horizon. She read the star's altitude off the sextant's micrometer, and I dutifully jotted down the numbers and the time of day for her. "Does 666 mean anything?" I suddenly asked, remembering the numerals painted on *Dream Baby*'s bows.

"Of course it does." Ellen was already trying to identify another star. "It's the number of the Beast, the anti-Christ, the personification of everything that's evil."

"Seriously," I said, "does it mean anything?"

Ellen looked at me. "I'm not joking, Nick. It's from the Bible. Ask Thessy tomorrow. It's a bad news number, a kind of theological mindfuck."

I looked out to sea, almost as though I expected to see a puff of smoke and a beast with a forked tail appear from the darkness. "And you think Sweetman's cute?" I asked Ellen.

"I think he's best avoided," Ellen said in an unexpectedly sober voice, and suddenly, and for no particular reason on a very warm night, we both shivered.

If McIllvanney's yard had been deserted on Saturday afternoon, on Sunday morning it was unnaturally busy. Thessy arrived first, tired after an uncomfortable night on the ferry, and five minutes later Bellybutton half danced and half shuffled down the pontoon with a can of paint and a pocketful of rags and brushes. He arranged his materials on *Starkisser*'s long midnight-blue bows and, seeing my interest, offered an explanation. "Mr Mac wants a star painted on his sharp end, and what Mr Mac wants, Mr Mac gets."

Ten minutes later Mr Mac himself arrived, blasting his big Kawasaki into the yard before strolling down the quay to cast his sceptical gaze at *Wavebreaker*. "She looks all right," he said grudgingly, then he crossed the gangplank for a closer look. "Good holiday?" he asked Thessy.

"Thank you, sir, yes, sir."

"Well, it's over now, you lazy black bastard, and the client wants three scuba sets put on board." He tossed Thessy the keys to the storeroom. "So go fetch."

"Scuba?" I asked as Thessy ran towards the stores.

"Master Rickie Crowninshield likes to scuba," McIllvanney said sourly, "and his daddy's paying for the gear, so gear they will have. Good morning, Ellen." He stared defiantly at Ellen who, standing at the stern just above *Wavebreaker*'s swimming platform, nodded back very coolly. McIllvanney turned back to me and dropped his voice very slightly. "Ellen tells me she's sailing away with you?"

"Yes, she is."

"You're the lucky one, aren't you." He peered into the binnacle as though checking that no one had stolen the compass. "Screwing her, are you, Nick?"

"Piss off."

He laughed, clearly in high spirits. "And the senator tells me that you're only doing a two-week trial with his kids, is that right?"

"Yes."

"No, it isn't." He straightened up from the binnacle and jabbed a finger painfully into my chest. "You do the full three months, Nicholas Breakspear, because I want the commission on this one, do you hear me?" If a charter was booked direct by McIllvanney, and not through either the London or the Fort Lauderdale agencies, then the Ulsterman collected the full fifteen per cent commission, which meant that the senator's jaunt was worth at least eighteen thousand dollars to McIllvanney. "You cut this one short" – he jabbed my chest again – "and I'll cut *you* so short that you'll be singing falsetto."

"Has anyone ever told you that you're a filthy bastard?" I asked McIllvanney in a tone of genuine enquiry.

"The last creature who told me that is living in a greengrocer's shop now. You know what lives in greengrocers' shops, Nick? Vegetables do," He guffawed, then gave a grotesque imitation of a witless paraplegic slumped in a

96

wheelchair. "So everything's ready, is it?" he asked, suddenly businesslike again.

I nodded; then, on an impulse, I asked if McIllvanney had ever met a man called Jesse Sweetman.

McIllvanney did not even need to think about his answer, but just shook his head. "What kind of a name is Jesse?"

"It's a southern name," I said, "perhaps from South Carolina or Georgia? He runs around in a dazzle-painted sports-fisherman called *Dream Baby*."

"*Dream Baby*?" That name clearly struck a chord in McIllvanney, for he frowned at me for a few seconds, but the chord must have faded for he shrugged it off. "I've seen that boat somewhere, but I can't place it. Does it matter?"

"Sweetman and *Dream Baby* were here yesterday afternoon," I said, "and he gouged *Wavebreaker*'s hull and prised open the companionway. He didn't steal anything, but he annoyed me."

"He broke into the boat? The bastard." Whatever else, McIllvanney ran a good boatyard and hated to think of it being vandalised. "Bellybutton!" he shouted.

"I hear you!" Bellybutton had painted the outline of a five-pointed shooting star on the sleek deck of *Starkisser*'s bows. He had a surprisingly delicate touch and the silver star was going to look beautiful when it was finished. He had given the star a long fiery tail and surrounded it with darts of reflected light.

"What do you know about a sports-fisherman called *Dream Baby*?" McIllvanney shouted over the water.

Bellybutton, kneeling over his work, thought about it for a second, then spread his hands in a gesture of ignorance. "Don't mean nothing to me, boss."

"Well if you see the bugger, run him off!" McIllvanney said, angrily, then turned to look at the yard where a silver-grey stretch limo, its windows tinted black against the sun, rolled ponderously to park beside the stairs to his office. He scowled, because he never liked meeting the clients, and clearly the big car was bringing the Crowninshield twins for their cruise-cure.

Ellen came and stood beside me. Our usual nervousness about meeting clients seemed more intense this bright morning, for neither of us knew quite what to expect of the senator's children. One part of me, despite George Crowninshield's reassurances, anticipated that the twins would emerge as shambling twitching wrecks, and for a second, believing my worst fears, I bitterly regretted accepting the senator's charter. However, Rickie Crowninshield appeared reassuringly normal when he emerged from the limousine. At the very least I had expected him to be physically frail and mentally chastened; a boy worn out by his long addiction and frightened of the criminal charges that hung over him, but instead he came out of the limo and down the dock with the frisky energy of a puppy. He ran across the gangplank as enthusiastically as though he sought votes for his father's election campaign, then approached us with an outstretched hand and a voice full of bright greetings. "You must be Nick? Dad told me about you. He says you're one hell of a guy. Really!" His handshake was warm and firm, and his face redolent of his father's sincerity. "And, oh boy! I know who you are. Ellen Skandinsky! Wow!" He gave her an admiring grin that was very reminiscent of the senator's beguiling charm.

"Hello." Ellen's manner was almost British in its cool restraint, matching our welcome which we had deliberately pitched at a low key. We were not filling the marina with the steel band jollity of Yellow Bird, nor were any of us in our matching blue and white uniforms, for this was not a usual charter, and none of us were at Rickie or Robin-Anne Crowninshield's beck and call. Instead, if we were anything, we were their jailers. I introduced Rickie to McIllvanney who screwed his face into what he thought was a pleasant smile then, after exchanging an inanity or two, fled to his office.

"A terrific boat, Nick! Really!" Rickie looked appreciatively round *Wavebreaker*'s deck. He sucked on a cigarette and I saw that the fingers of his right hand were stained a deep yellow by the nicotine. "Just outstanding! My mom said she had just the greatest time with you all last year. She said it was a blast, really! So I thought we could have a really good time as well, yeah?"

"I do hope so," I said with polite enthusiasm.

"Just outstanding," Rickie said, but referring to what I could not tell. He was built like a basketball player; tall and as thin as a stick insect. I noticed a slight discolouration in his left eye that betrayed its blindness, but otherwise he looked as fit as a cricket. He had his father's black hair, a strong sun-tan, and seemed filled with a manic energy; ready and eager to enjoy both *Wavebreaker* and our company. "God, you look like him," he said to me, "like your dad, I mean. Really something. Wow." He turned as Thessy struggled aboard with a heavy scuba outfit. "You must be Thessy, right? Just great to meet you, just great! Do I call you Thessy or Thes-salonians?"

Thessy, forced to put the scuba outfit down to shake Rickie's hand, stammered that he did not mind what he was called, but Rickie had already forgotten his question. "Hey! Jackson!" He shouted towards a black man who was walking slowly along the dock. "You're just going to eat this up! Really! This is just awesome!"

The man who now approached *Wavebreaker* was as tall as Rickie Crowninshield, but, where Rickie was attenuated, this man was as broad shouldered and as heavily muscled as a pit bull. He was a black version of the Maggot, but this man appeared to have none of the Maggot's casual bonhomie. I guessed he was in his forties and he had a hard face with small wary eyes and tightly curled hair that was cut very short.

"That's Jackson Chatterton," Rickie introduced the big man, "and he's my minder! Really! Ain't that right, Jacko?" Chatterton carried two heavy suitcases across the gangplank and ignored the over-excited Rickie who shadowboxed two punches at his left arm.

Chatterton dropped the suitcases and turned to me. "Chatter-ton," he said flatly. "I'm a para-medic attached to the Rinkfels clinic."

"He'll tell you he's a male nurse," Rickie said, "but he's

really my bodyguard. A big bad black bodyguard. Ain't that what you are, Jacko?"

Chatterton continued to ignore Rickie, as did I. "My name's Breakspear," I said to the huge man, "and welcome aboard." Jackson Chatterton had not offered me his hand and appeared not to notice when I offered mine. Nor did he introduce himself to Ellen or Thessy, but instead looked warily up into the rigging as though he expected to be ambushed from the foremast's crosstrees. "You were a soldier," I said, not as a question, but as a straight assertion of fact, for almost everything about him spoke of the military.

"He was a killer!" Rickie answered for the giant Chatterton. "Really! Wow! Bang-bang."

"Airborne," Chatterton confirmed to me. "Sergeant."

"Vietnam?"

"Yessir! And proud of it."

Ellen opened her mouth, then had the brilliant good sense to close it unused.

"You?" Chatterton unbent enough to ask me the question.

"Royal Marines. Sergeant." I summed up my military career in Chatterton's own staccato fashion.

The big man gave me an approving nod, then gestured at the suitcases. "Not mine, the twins'. Where?"

"Ellen will show you."

Ellen offered me a poisonous smile, but I had no time to worry about her distaste for the militaristic para-medic. Instead I was looking down the quay to where a pathetically thin girl was walking beside a smartly dressed woman. "That's Robin-Anne," Rickie told me helpfully, "with Denise."

I crossed the gangway and Rickie came after me. "Were you really a marine?"

"Yes."

"A sergeant? Why not an officer?"

"I didn't want to be an officer."

"No shit! Really?" Rickie was literally dancing in circles around me as I walked down the dock towards his sister, but then he paused in his frenetic progress to light one cigarette

100

from the stump of another, and I wondered just what perverted fate decreed that such a boy should receive a legacy of six million dollars. "Is that your motorbike?" He had spotted McIllvanney's Kawasaki.

"No."

"Just awesome, Nick. Really! I mean, what a blast! Wow!" He ran on ahead, shouting at his sister. "He's a killer, Robbie! Really! He was a marine! Just awesome!"

Robin-Anne Crowninshield shyly offered me her hand. Like her brother she was painfully thin, but otherwise they seemed utterly unlike, despite being twins. Robin-Anne had her mother's fair hair, so fair that it looked bleached, and she had her mother's delicate good looks etched on to a face so pale that it seemed as though her skin must burn if it was exposed to anything more powerful than a light bulb. Her hand lay in mine as lightly as a bird's wing. "It's very hot," she said.

"It'll be cooler at sea," I reassured her, then I looked at her companion who was a very crisp and handsome black woman. "My name's Breakspear," I introduced myself.

"Denise Harriman," she responded. "I'm one of Senator Crowninshield's aides."

"She's from Washington," the manic Rickie explained, in a tone of voice which suggested I should be impressed. "She had to deliver us here, but she ain't coming with us because she gets seasick. Ain't that right, Denise? You barf in boats?" Rickie began mimicking an attack of vomiting.

"I don't just barf on boats." Denise Harriman shot Rickie a look of pure venom.

The sarcasm went airily past Rickie who had suddenly stiffened, and whose face now showed a look of the most terrible anxiety. I dreaded to discover just what symptom of drug dependency I was witnessing, and wondered if I should shout for the big Jackson Chatterton to come and rescue me, but then Rickie turned his terrified gaze on to me. "Jesus!" He punched one hand into the other. "My dad promised to ask you a question, but he forgot, and Mom couldn't remember. Shit!" He was clearly so fearful of the answer to his father's unasked question that he scarcely dared pose it himself, but then summoned up the courage. "Does this boat have a sound system, Nick?"

I nodded. "Sure. We've got a tape deck and a CD player."

His relief was palpable. "Really? A CD? Oh God, that's awesome! Come on, Robbie!" His good spirits thus restored, Rickie seized his sister's hand and dragged her excitedly towards the boat. Robin-Anne, who had been looking very apprehensive, seemed to go aboard *Wavebreaker* rather unwillingly.

Denise Harriman, the senator's aide, uttered a barely audible sigh which I translated as an expression of relief that her responsibility for the twins was ending. She took a thick manila envelope from her attaché case. "That envelope contains the twins' documentation, Mr Breakspear: their passports, emergency air tickets and medical records. There's also a full list of the senator's telephone numbers." She handed me that envelope, then took another from the briefcase. "And these are the papers concerning your own boat." She opened the envelope and handed me the forms which would be needed if the senator undertook the repairs to *Masquerade*. For the moment my boat was staying on Straker's Cay, and she would only pass into the senator's care if I agreed to extend the trial two weeks' cruise-cure into a full summer's excursion.

I spread the forms on the saddle of McIllvanney's Kawasaki. If I did take the twins away all summer then *Masquerade* would be taken to a boatyard in Florida, so I now signed the necessary customs forms and the insurance waiver and the dozen other pieces of paper that would be needed to keep the United States government and the delivery company happy. I signed the last sheet, hoped to God that the US Customs service did not discover the huge Webley pistol deep in its box in *Masquerade*'s bilges, and handed Denise Harriman back her pen. She put the signed papers in her attaché case, then shot a poisonous glance towards Rickie who was rummaging though his pile of luggage on *Wavebreaker*'s deck. "*Bon voyage*," she called aloud to him, and it was possible to discern a dance of relieved joy in her step as she walked back to the limousine.

Bellybutton, painting his delicate silver star, laughed up at the twins with his discoloured teeth, while McIllvanney leered at them from his office window. The last of their luggage was brought from the limousine and, as Thessy and I prepared to cast off, Rickie tested our sound system with a cacophonous cassette of rock music. Robin-Anne searched for a silent dark hole in which to hide, Jackson Chatterton scowled at us, Ellen looked exasperated and Thessy appeared just plain scared. I started *Wavebreaker*'s engines, used the bow thruster to drive her stem away from the quay and, with an apparent cargo of misery and mania, went to sea.

PART TWO

We beat southwards all that first day, slicing through a glittering sea, and propelled by an apparently changeless south-easterly trade wind. We hardly saw the Crowninshield twins. They briefly appeared on deck for lunch; a meal which Rickie hardly touched, while Robin-Anne, despite her apparent frailty, attacked the sandwiches and salad with the savagery of a starving bear. Afterwards, incongruously dressed in a rain-coat, she went to the bows and stared briefly down at the mesmerising onrush of sea where it split and foamed at *Wave-breaker*'s cutwater. She did not stay there long, but retreated from the fierce sun to the stern-cabin that she would be sharing with Ellen. The contrast between the two American girls was almost painful; Ellen was so healthy and strong, while the waif-like Robin-Anne was pathetically wan and list-less. "What do you think of her?" I asked Ellen that after-noon.

Ellen gave me an amused glance. "Little Orphan Annie? It's hard to believe she's about to be worth six million dollars. Still, she's got precious little else going for her."

I smiled at the severity of Ellen's judgment. "Is she that bad?"

"She has a distressingly simple mind, with only room for a single idea at any one time. Presently that idea is cocaine, and nothing but cocaine. She has an obsession with the drug that verges on monomania. She tells me she needs to understand it if she's going to defeat it."

"Don't you approve of that?"

"I think she'd do better to understand herself," Ellen said tartly. "She allowed a man to persuade her into taking the drug, so she can only blame herself for her predicament. She'd find it more useful to understand her own character short-comings than to take an elementary course in drug chemistry."

"What do you make of Rickie?" I asked.

"He's precisely what anyone would expect of a drop-out Phys Ed basketball-playing retard," Ellen said scornfully, "by which I mean that he's a jock with the brains of a dung beetle.

He reminds me of your Neanderthal friend, the Maggot, except Rickie is a great deal more handsome."

"Is he?"

She laughed at the suspicion of jealousy in my voice. "Yes, Nicholas, he is. But he's not cute."

At supper, as at lunch, Robin-Anne ate with the appetite of a horse, though her brother hardly touched his chicken and pasta salad. "Don't you like pasta?" Ellen, who was perversely proud of her skills in the salad department, asked Rickie with just a touch of asperity.

"It's great. Really awesome." Rickie lit a cigarette. "I just guess I'm not hungry."

Robin-Anne reached over and tipped her brother's food on to her own plate. "Kind of starving," she justified her theft, then poured herself some diet soda. For once we were carrying neither wine nor spirits on *Wavebreaker*, for Jackson Chatterton's drug clinic had utterly forbidden us to offer the twins any alcohol, saying that any mood-altering drug could hamper the success of a detoxification programme. We were thus officially a dry boat, though I had hidden some Irish whiskey in the engine room, and I was sure that Ellen would have similarly salted away some vodka.

It seemed that Ellen and I were not the only ones to take such a precaution, for late that night Jackson Chatterton lumbered on deck with a bottle in one huge hand. "Bourbon," he explained laconically. "Want some?"

"I thought you'd never ask."

He chuckled, produced two cardboard cups, and poured me a generous slug of the whiskey. We were alone on deck, though not the only ones awake for I could hear Rickie and Ellen's voices coming from the open skylight of the main saloon. I hoped Thessy was fast asleep for he would be taking the morning watch.

"Cheers," I said.

Chatterton raised his cardboard cup in silent acknowledgement, then stared ahead to where a great beam swept around the sky. "A lighthouse?" he asked in a voice which suggested that a prudent man avoided such things.

I nodded. "It's called the Hole in the Wall. Once we're past it we can turn out to the open ocean. Things will be a bit livelier then."

"Livelier?"

"We'll have a bit more sea, kick up some spray."

I had spoken enthusiastically, but Jackson Chatterton seemed unmoved by the prospect. "What are your plans?" he asked me.

I had nothing particular planned, merely an idea that it might be interesting to thrash our way out into the open ocean, though, mindful of the danger of tropical storms, I had no intention of going too far from the safe shelter of a Bahamian hurricane hole. But I fancied feeling the long hard pressure of ocean waves against our hull and, though we were short-handed, I reckoned that a few days out of sight of land would shake us all down quickly. I explained all that to Chatterton, but stressed that we would run for cover at the first sign of trouble.

He must have assumed that I meant trouble from the twins, for he suddenly became surprisingly loquacious. "They won't give you any grief in the next few days," he said. "Now that they can't get hold of cocaine they'll just crash out."

I grimaced. "Does that mean they'll be seeing green monkeys and blue snakes up the rigging?"

Chatterton poured himself more bourbon, then put the bottle within my reach on the binnacle shelf. "Coming off cocaine isn't like that. At first they'll just want to do nothing but eat and sleep. It's the opposite of a cocaine high, you see." He paused. "The difficult bit starts two or three days later. That's when the real hell begins."

"For all of us?"

"It won't be easy," he said grimly, and I was suddenly rather glad to have the taciturn Chatterton aboard. The big man had obviously come on deck to warn me what to expect from the twins, and for that I was grateful.

"I noticed that Rickie wasn't eating today," I said, "but Robin-Anne was?"

Chatterton nodded. "Rickie may have stopped his cocaine a day or two ago, which means he's probably already over the crash period. I promise you one thing; he's brought none of it on board. I searched him and his luggage, and he was clean." The big man thought for a few seconds, then laughed. "He'd better be clean! That turkey has got one chance of avoiding jail, just one, and that chance is by proving to the judge that he's cleaned up his act. And if he doesn't do that, then the man will send Rickie's plump young ass down to the gang-rape squad in the county jail." Chatterton did not sound unduly worried at that prospect.

"Can we be sure Robin-Anne didn't bring any of the drug aboard?" I asked.

"She won't have done that," Chatterton said with conviction. "That girl is serious about giving it up, real serious, heavy serious! That girl is really trying! She studies the drug, you know? Like it was her enemy." Chatterton had spoken with genuine admiration.

I glanced up at the sails, down at the compass, then ahead to where the lighthouse loom arced powerfully through the night. "So what are the twins' chances?"

"Depends on their will power, 'cause nothing else will do it for them. There ain't no pill to get you off the powder, Mr Breakspear, only will power. And let me tell you, coming off coke is the hardest damn thing in the world, and you're real lucky if you have a rich daddy who pays for people to hold your hand while you go through the hell of it. The twins' daddy has paid for you and me, Mr Breakspear, and for everyone else on board this boat, but even with all that money and all this boat, we still might not succeed with them."

"It's that hard?"

"It is that hard," he said ominously, and I thought of John Maggovertski's sadness for a pretty girl who had whored herself to pay for the white powder. "And it's even harder," Jackson Chatterton's voice was suddenly sinister, "for a poor person who has no one to help them."

I stared at Jackson Chatterton, and at last sensed the drama that lay behind his big calm presence. "Why did you leave the army, Mr Chatterton?" I asked after a long pause.

"I guess you can guess," he said.

I guessed, but did not make him confirm my guess. Instead I asked whether the American army had helped him to kick his drug habit.

"Sure they tried, they tried real hard, but back then I didn't want to be helped."

"But you still got off cocaine? On your own?"

"Eventually." The light inside the binnacle glossed his black face with a sheen of red, sparking his eyes like fire. He was not looking at me, but staring doggedly ahead into the turning white light of the Hole in the Wall. "And I had to lose a good, good woman before I came to my senses. But I did kick the drug, Mr Breakspear, and it was probably the hardest damned thing I ever did in all my life. But once I'd done it, I swore I'd help others do it."

"Even the very rich?" I asked provocatively.

"The rich trash pay the bills, Mr Breakspear, which lets me give my spare time away to the poor trash."

I looked at the tough, impressive face. "Are the twins trash?"

He paused before replying, then gave the smallest shake of his head. "She's OK, but him?" This time the pause was almost eloquent, then he gave a richly contagious laugh. "I'd have liked to have had Rickie Crowninshield in my platoon for just five minutes."

I laughed too. "Good to have you aboard."

"It ain't bad being aboard," he said, and held out his hand and, not before time, we shook.

By midnight I was alone on deck, and happy to be alone. I like sailing alone at night. I like to watch the phosphorescence curling away from the hull and I like to watch the brilliant specks of light fade in the black deep water far in the ship's wake. I like to be alone under the careless profusion of the stars, and alone on a moon-glossed sea.

I like the sounds of a boat sailing at night. The sounds are

111

the same as those of daylight, yet somehow the night magnifies and sharpens the creak of a yielding block, the sigh of air over a shroud, the stretching of a sail, the hiss of water sliding sleek against the hull, the curl of a quarter-wave falling away, and the thump as a wave strikes the cutwater to be sheared into two bright slices of whiteness. I like the purposefulness of a boat at night as it slits a path across an empty planet. I like the secretiveness of a boat in the blackness, when the only thing to dislike is the prospect of dawn, which seems like a betrayal because, at night, in a boat under sail, it is easy to feel very close to God – for eternity is all around.

I tacked the ship shortly after midnight, doing the job by myself and enjoying the work. Ellen was still awake, talking in the stateroom with Rickie, but everyone else seemed asleep. I wished that Ellen and Rickie would go to their beds, for the soft mutter of their voices was an intrusion on the dark and star-studded infinity through which I steered *Wavebreaker*.

I had just winched in the staysail's port sheet when the explosion sounded, or something so like an explosion that I instinctively cowered by *Wavebreaker*'s rail as my mind whipped back to the crash of practice shells ripping through the sleet in Norway.

The sound of the explosion melded into a terrible noise that was like an animal dying in awful, bellowing pain, but beneath that sound of agony was a harsh metallic scrape and clash that punched at my belly and eardrums. If anything the sound seemed to become louder as I ran down the deck. The noise was a foul but apt accompaniment to the schooner's fitful motion for, with her wheel lashed and her sails only half trimmed, *Wavebreaker* was bridling and jerking into the short hard seas that were driving through the North-East Providence Channel.

The noise rose to a scream; like the sound that a beast would make while being disembowelled. I stepped over the coaming and down into the cockpit where I cannoned off the binnacle before snatching open the companionway hatch. I put both hands on the rails and vaulted down to the accommo-

112

dation deck. I slipped as I landed and fell against the bulkhead. I scrambled up and reached for the eject button on the cassette deck. I punched the button and was rewarded with a blessed, ear-ringing silence as the offending cassette slid out.

"Shit! What is this?" Rickie, apparently still vibrating to the music, sprang up from the stateroom couch. "Hey! That was my tape, man! I was listening to that!"

Ellen was grinning from the other couch, but I was in no mood to humour her amusement. "Thessy's sleeping for the morning watch, for Christ's sake!" I accused her, wondering why she had let Rickie play such an appalling din at such volume at such a late hour.

"We're just listening to music!" Rickie was suddenly truculent, twisting off the sofa and dancing towards me on the balls of his feet. An inch of ash spilt from his cigarette as he raised his hands in a threat to hit me.

"Rickie!" Ellen called warningly.

Some grain of self-preserving sense must have penetrated Rickie's skull, for he suddenly dropped on to his heels and offered me a placatory grin. "You should like that sound, Nick!" he said happily. "It's really heavy English music."

I looked at the cassette which claimed to be music recorded by the Pinkoe Dirt-Box Band. "New shipboard rule," I said, "no English music on this boat, unless played very softly or through earphones." I tossed the cassette to Rickie who, turning away and thus leaving his blind eye facing me, fumbled the catch.

He stooped to pick up the tape. "Are you saying I can't play my music?" He was suddenly spoiling for a fight again.

"The man is saying that you keep the noise down, and I am saying that you do what the man says." Jackson Chatterton had appeared in canary yellow pyjamas at the far end of the stateroom. His looming presence utterly cowed Rickie who whined something about only wanting to play Ellen a little night music, and that he had not meant any harm, and what was a guy supposed to be doing on this boat anyway? It wasn't the goddamn navy, really, and he went on muttering all

113

the way past Chatterton's impassive gaze and so into the cabin that the two of them shared. Thessy's scared face appeared at the other cabin door, but I shook my head at him, mimicked sleep, and he ducked back inside.

"Sorry, Nick," Ellen said, though not with any great contrition.

"Forget it." I was still angry, but there was no point in pursuing what was over, so I went back topsides to trim the ship, and five minutes later I saw the stateroom lights go out, and half an hour after that the lights in Ellen and Robin-Anne's cabin were doused, leaving only a light in the forward starboard cabin to show that either Rickie or Jackson Chatterton was still awake. I wondered if they had simply forgotten to turn off the bulb which annoyingly cast its brightness through a porthole and on to the swirl and rush of white water, and I was half tempted to pull the fuse out of the circuit and thus surround *Wavebreaker* with darkness, but resisted the impulse.

The night became quiet again. *Wavebreaker* settled on her new course and, by the time the small hours were growing, we had left the island's lights well behind and I was cutting her prow hard into real ocean waves. We were on the starboard tack, fighting into the trades as we clawed our way out from the Bahamian shoals into the deep waters of the Atlantic. The difference in *Wavebreaker*'s motion was extraordinary. She had disdained the smaller waves in the shelter of the islands, but now she seemed to tremble as her hull soaked up the ponderous force of the ocean. This was proper sailing.

And, as if to celebrate her freedom, she dipped her cutwater into a sudden trough of the sea and then sprayed white water high over her bows. The shudder of the bigger wave sent a shock wave through the long hull, and I laughed aloud with the pleasure of it. Then, as I often did when I was alone at sea, I began to recite Shakespeare. I knew reams of the stuff, yards and yards of it, learned from my father; the one absolutely true gift of my childhood. I liked to hear the verse, and enjoyed declaiming it, but only if there was no one to hear me, for I knew that my voice held all the fine cadences of Sir Tom himself.

That night I belted out one of my favourite speeches, the one from the second part of *Henry IV* in which the new king, Henry V, rejects the friendship of Falstaff.

I know thee not, old man: fall to thy prayers;
How ill white hairs become a fool and jester!
I have long dream'd of such a kind of man,
So surfeit-swell'd, so old, and so profane;
But, being awaked, I do despise my dream.

I stopped abruptly. A movement had startled me and I turned to see Robin-Anne Crowninshield, dressed only in a white nightdress, standing in the main companionway.

"That was really great," she said. She was shivering violently.

"You'll find an oilskin jacket in the locker at the foot of the stairs," I said, "and you'll also discover that Ellen has left a Thermos of coffee on the stove, and I like mine without sugar but with milk. You may have to unscrew the stove-fiddles to release the Thermos, and you'll find the milk in the fridge to the right of the stove."

She nodded grave acknowledgement of all my instructions, then disappeared below for five minutes, eventually returning swathed in one of the vast, padded and multi-layered foul-weather coats, and carrying a mug of coffee. "I assume it's caffeinated?" she asked in her thin voice.

"It is indeed proper coffee," I confirmed, "but if you insist on the wimpish unleaded kind then you will find a jar in the locker above the sink. Are you hungry?"

"I'm OK." She sat at the edge of the cockpit, curled her legs into the warm shelter of the jacket, then hunched down into the thick collar so that all I could see of her face was her enormous, moon-silvered and lemur-like eyes beneath the pale gleam of her short bright hair. She yawned. "How long till dawn?"

"An hour. Couldn't you sleep?"

"I set an alarm. I wanted to be up. Mom said I shouldn't miss the dawn at sea, she said it's kind of beautiful." She rested her head against a cushion so that she could stare straight up through the network of rigging and past the light-blanched sails to where the stars wheeled their cold fire beyond the mastheads. "Where are we?"

"We've just left the North-East Providence Channel and we're in the open sea now. Did your brother's music wake you earlier?"

She shook her head, then seemed to shrink even lower inside the enveloping jacket. "You look happy," she said, almost accusingly.

"That's me. Just a dim, shallow and happy Brit."

I had meant her to laugh, but instead she frowned as though my happiness was a puzzle that needed to be understood. "Are you going to recite any more of that poetry?"

"No."

"It was Shakespeare, right?"

"Right."

"It was good," she said.

"He was a great poet," I said, as if she needed to be told.

"I mean your voice and delivery," Robin-Anne said fervently. "It was good."

"It was imitation," I said in self-disparagement, "just imitation." I suddenly heard my father's voice telling me that all acting is mere imitation. "That's all it is, dear Nick! Only imitation, mere mummery. Why do people take it so seriously?" The wheel suddenly pushed into my left palm and I could feel all the thudding pressure of the sea and the wind concentrated into that one polished spoke. I eased the wheel up, drawing *Wavebreaker*'s bows harder into the sea and wind, and I was rewarded with another shattering of white spray that exploded prettily about our bows before I let the hull fall away once more. I laughed for the sheer pleasure of playing such games with God's strong world, then remembered the senator had told me that Robin-Anne liked to sail. I asked her if she wanted to take the wheel.

116

She seemed to shudder at the very thought. "I'd be frightened."

"But you can sail a boat, can't you?"

"I used to sail a little cat-boat in Penobscot Bay, but that was a long time ago. Grandmother lived there in a house that looked over the water, but she's dead now." She spoke sadly, as though to a twenty-four-year-old there really was a time of lost innocence, and I suppose, if the twenty-four-year-old was a cocaine addict, then there was indeed such a time.

"I've never understood the appeal of a cat-boat," I said, "all that great big undivided sail and weather helm and barn-door rudder. It must be like going to sea in a haystack."

Robin-Anne nodded very earnestly as though she truly cared about my opinion, but her next question showed that she was paying no attention to my inanities. "What do you think of us?" she asked instead.

I glanced at her, trying to hide my embarrassment with a swift and flippant response, but I could think of nothing to say and so I looked back at the binnacle, then up to the long moon-burnished sea ahead.

"I feel really awkward, you see," Robin-Anne explained her question, "and ashamed."

"I'm just the skipper of this barge," I said, "so you don't have to explain anything to me."

"I feel like a circus animal" – Robin-Anne ignored my disclaimer – "because you're all expecting me to perform my antics, and I'm not sure I can do it."

"What antics?"

"To stop using cocaine, of course." She frowned at me. "You're all watching me, waiting to applaud."

"Is that bad?"

"It's patronising, and it's my own fault that you can all patronise me, and I hate myself for it."

"Come on!" I said chidingly. "We all like you!"

"That's what I mean." She fell silent for a moment and I saw she was watching the long heaving waves slip past our flanks. Then, with a rustle of the stiff jacket, she looked back to me. "Did you ever try cocaine?"

"No."

"You've not even been tempted by it?"

"No."

For a moment she was silent, staring at the sheen of night on the crinkled sea, then she smiled. "You're lucky. You're a cocaine virgin. Stay that way, because it's the most addictive substance on the planet."

Her last words had been spoken very portentously, and I rewarded them with a dubious shrug. "Heroin? Alcohol? Nicotine?"

"You have to persuade a laboratory animal to become addicted to any of those drugs, but you only need to give an animal one dose of cocaine and it's hooked."

The luff of the flying jib had begun to back and fill and so I let the ship's head fall away.

"But the real danger of cocaine," Robin-Anne continued softly, "is that it provides ecstasy, Mr Breakspear."

"Call me Nick."

"What cocaine does, you see, is to make the brain produce a thing called dopamine. That and a whole lot of other chemicals, but dopamine is the main one." Her voice was very earnest, as though it was desperately important that I understood what she said. "I know it's weird," she went on, "but pleasure is merely the result of naturally occurring chemicals secreted in the brain, and cocaine can turn those chemicals on like a faucet. Can you imagine a day of pure pleasure, Mr Breakspear?"

I did not need to imagine such a day, I could remember plenty. I remembered lying in bed with a pretty girl while the rain fell on a Devon river outside our window. I remembered the honesty of *Masquerade* in a force five wind, and then I thought of all the good days to come; days of Ellen and me and *Masquerade* in far seas, and I must have smiled, for Robin-Anne nodded approval of whatever silent answer I was framing to her question. "Think of all that happiness," she said, "and understand that a single hit of cocaine, just a single hit, will produce a hundred times as much pleasure-making dopamine as that one happy day. A hundred times! It's like making love to God. It's euphoria."

I looked at her, but said nothing, and she must have mistaken my silence for disbelief for she hurried to explain her evident knowledge about the drug. "I studied cocaine, you see. I had to. I wanted Rickie to stop using it, and I wanted a friend to stop using it as well, and so I learned everything I could."

"And did learning about it mean trying it?"

She nodded. "Yes."

"And thus you discovered euphoria?"

She nodded again. "And it's the euphoria that's so addictive, because you've been to heaven, and the real world seems a very dull place afterwards. So you begin to take more cocaine, and quite soon you need more and more cocaine to unlock the gates of heaven, and once you reach heaven you don't want to leave it and so you take still more cocaine, but by then it isn't working."

She stopped abruptly, perhaps fearing that she was boring me. I turned the wheel a fraction, waiting for her.

"The catch in this heaven," she went on, "is that the brain has only got so much dopamine to offer, and once the cocaine has used it all up, then that's the end of the pleasure. Except the brain is screaming for more dopamine, so you overdose because you can't accept that the drug isn't working any longer, and it's then that cocaine starts doing its other things to you. It shrinks the arteries, and that's what blinded Rickie's left eye."

I really had nothing useful to say, so I responded with a sympathetic noise that only made Robin-Anne shake her head impatiently. "There's worse," she said, "far worse."

"You mean a heart attack?"

"No . . ." She drew the word out, so that I heard in its simple syllable all the pain and hurt of the drug. Robin-Anne had been staring at the dark sea, but now she turned her big eyes back to me. "The worst thing about cocaine is that once it has exhausted all the dopamine from the brain, then what's

119

left is a black hole of depression so big and so awful that not all the misery in the world can fill it. People try to beat that misery with barbiturates, but nothing can cure it because you've taken away from yourself all chance of feeling pleasure. The doctors have a word for that misery; they call it anhedonia, which only means an inability to feel enjoyment, and that's what it is, but it feels like hell, like true hell, and it's a hell you can't even escape from in sleep because overdosing on cocaine gives you chronic insomnia."

Hell was being without God, I thought, but I said nothing, just stared instead at the white wash of cabin light on the rushing water, and I wondered why some people could take cocaine and just walk away from it, while others ended up in hell, or in a peep-show which was probably the same thing.

"Of course," Robin-Anne went on, "the brain eventually manufactures more dopamine, so after a day or two the cocaine can work again, and you go soaring up from hell into heaven. It's a roller-coaster, Mr Breakspear, up and down, up and down" – her thin white hand suited the action to her words – "from heaven to hell and back again, and if heaven is euphoria then let me assure you that hell is a terrible place."

"So remember the hell," I said, as though I really could help her with my tuppence worth of cheerful encouragement, "and perhaps that will stop you ever going back to it!"

"But there's another kind of hell," Robin-Anne's voice was dulled, as though my cheap optimism had depressed her, "which is remembering the euphoria, and having to surrender the means of creating it. That hell is giving up cocaine. I'm in the easy stage, the first few days when you just sleep and eat, but quite soon I'll be in the hell of denial, Mr Breakspear."

I looked past Robin-Anne to where the moon's path gleamed on the long waves, and then I glanced forward and saw another belt of silver, but this one diffuse and hazy, showing where the first crepuscular light seeped over the world's grey edge. "Dawn," I said in a hopeful voice.

But Robin-Anne did not react, and I looked down to see that she was not watching for the new day, but was crying. I did not know what to say or do. I should have knelt beside her and put my arms around her and promised her that she would be freed from the hell of anhedonia, and that there really was a God and that she did have the strength to tear herself free from cocaine, as others had freed themselves, and I should have assured her that there was true happiness without a drug, but I did not know her well enough to embrace her, so I just let her weep as the sun streaked up in glory from the east.

Thus *Wavebreaker* sailed towards the light, carrying her passengers to hell.

I rousted Thessy out of his bed with a cup of tea, then went to my own bed as he took over the wheel. I slept, dreaming of *Masquerade* sinking through waves of steel into torrents of fire.

I woke just before lunchtime to find *Wavebreaker* still sailing eastwards. Ellen was showing Rickie Crowninshield all the elaborate electronic toys that only Ellen wholly understood; the radios, radars, weatherfaxes and satellite receivers, and Rickie was being surprisingly attentive, but as soon as he saw me he scowled and clamped a pair of headphones over his ears as though to make sure that he did not have to hold any kind of conversation with me. Ellen shrugged at his rudeness.

"How's the weather?" I asked her.

"No change."

I squinted through a porthole and saw the sky was scraped blue and bright above an empty sea. "You faxed a chart?" I asked Ellen.

"Sure did." She handed me the sheet of grey paper with its synoptic chart which had been transmitted from Florida just a few moments before. I pretended to despise such modern aids, but that was really a defensive reaction because I knew I could never afford such frills for *Masquerade*. I saw that there was not even a ripple of low pressure off to the east, which was the reassurance I wanted, for a depression to the east could swiftly twist itself into a full-blooded storm.

"Good morning, Rickie," I said loudly, wanting to demonstrate that I held no grudge for his behaviour in the night.

121

"Yo." His voice was surly, but suddenly he twisted round to face me and took off the headphones, and I thought he was going to apologise for his rudeness of the previous night, but instead he demanded to know if it was true that we were out in the open ocean and were not planning to make a landfall for some days.

"That's true," I said.

"But I wanted to do some scuba!" he said in outrage.

"There'll be a chance, I promise."

"Jesus!" he said in exasperation, then turned abruptly away. I waited to see if he would say any more, but he evidently did not want my company. I grimaced at Ellen, then went topsides where I found the ship being steered by its automatic pilot and Thessy and Jackson Chatterton perched halfway up the mainmast with reels of rigging wire from which Thessy was fashioning a parallel set of starboard shrouds. I wanted to double up all *Wavebreaker*'s standing rigging, just in case we did try to take her across the ocean. There was no sign of Robin-Anne who was presumably asleep. Chatterton climbed down to the deck and told me that Robin-Anne had eaten a huge breakfast.

"What about Rickie?"

"He just played with his food," Chatterton frowned, "and that means he must be over the crash period, which means his behaviour's going to be difficult."

"Even more difficult?" I asked with dread.

The big man laughed. "Nick, you ain't seen nothing yet."

It seemed that Jackson Chatterton was right, for we were all witnesses to a dreadful metamorphosis in Rickie. When he had joined the ship he had been nothing but eagerness and smiles, romping about like a new puppy, but now he had turned unrelentingly morose. At lunchtime he scowled at his sister who, wrapped in a dressing gown, fell on the sandwiches as though she had not eaten in weeks. "I'm famished!"

Rickie would not even try a sandwich, but instead pushed his plate away and lit a cigarette. He sipped at his can of diet soda and grimaced at the taste. "Have we got any beer on this boat?" he suddenly asked.

"No," Ellen said placidly. "Doctor's orders."

"Fuck the doctors." No one responded, which merely annoyed Rickie. He stared at his sister whose pale face was made even paler by the sun-block ointment she had liberally smeared on her skin. "You like this shit-for-drink, Robbie?"

Robin-Anne nodded, but was too busy eating to take much notice of her brother, though she did manage to mumble that she thought the diet soda was really kind of good.

"I think it's really kind of crap." Rickie turned his truculent gaze on me. "You must have some liquor aboard, Nick?"

"Not a drop," I lied.

"That's very un-British of you." He attempted an atrocious imitation of my English accent. "I thought all British ships were fuelled by rum, sodomy and the lash. Isn't that what they say?"

"That's what they say." I kept my voice friendly, for I was determined not to be drawn by his provocation.

"Are you gay, Nick?" Rickie suddenly asked me in what purported to be a tone of serious enquiry. I did not answer, while everyone but Robin-Anne, who was too busy eating, seemed embarrassed. Once again the lack of response infuriated Rickie who, seeking some other means of provocation, hurled his can of soda across the deck. "Shit-juice!" he shouted.

Ellen caught my eye, and we stared at each other for a sympathetic fraction of a second, then I looked away to see that the sticky liquid had sprayed across the teak planks. "Clean it up," I said mildly.

"Rum, sodomy and the lash!" Rickie chanted at me with a sudden and extraordinary vindictiveness.

Jackson Chatterton stirred as though he proposed to clean up the mess himself, but I waved him down and kept my eyes on Rickie. "Clean it up," I said again.

"You clean it up. This is our vacation! I didn't suggest coming on this heap of a boat to work like a house-servant, isn't that right, Robbie?"

Robin-Anne just went on eating.

"Clean it up," I told Rickie again.

Rickie seized Thessy's can, pulled open its top, and hurled it messily after the first. "Now what are you going to do? Flog me?" He suddenly laughed, then looked at Ellen whom he perceived as a possible ally. "You can never tell with a Brit, can you? It's either a flog or a fuck."

Ellen said nothing to encourage him. Robin-Anne ate stolidly on, while poor Thessy looked terrified. Only Jackson Chatterton seemed comfortable with Rickie's display of petulant temper. "The man said clean it up," Chatterton said calmly, "so clean it up!"

But Rickie was long beyond sense. "This is a vacation!" he screamed at me, "so why are we out here? I want to see a beach! A beach, you know what a beach is? Sand? Surf? I want to go board-sailing, maybe do a little water skiing. I want to do some scuba, for Christ's sake!"

I ignored him, fetching instead a mop and bucket from one of the big stern lockers. The bucket had a rope attached to its handle and I skimmed it over the stern to haul up a gallon or so of sea-water which I slammed down in front of Rickie. "The deck needs cleaning, Rickie, so do it." I threw the mop at him.

He ignored the mop, just staring at me, and I saw him take a breath ready to defy me so I spoke before he could. "Either you clean the deck, Rickie, or I'll scrub it with your hair."

He began to weep. Robin-Anne glanced at him, then smeared mustard on a roast beef sandwich. "It's real good food," she said enthusiastically.

"I'll help you," Ellen said to Rickie, then she took his hand and placed it on the mop handle. "Come on," she said gently.

Thus, as Rickie feebly dabbed at the deck and as his sister ate, our happy ship sailed on.

When, before we had sailed, I had tried to anticipate the cruise-cure, I had naïvely foreseen it as a difficult but intrinsically rewarding experience. I had fondly imagined that the Crowninshield twins, repentant and eager, would work about the ship by day and, exhausted by sea air and honest labour, would sleep all night. I had imagined them as willing partners in our efforts to help them, and I had been encouraged in that optimism by the knowledge that Rickie himself had suggested this drastic therapy of isolation from drugs by going to sea.

Yet, in the event, I was right about only one thing; it was difficult. We spent aimless days beating up and down the endless wind, carrying our cargo of resentment and despair, and though I worked to strengthen *Wavebreaker*'s rigging for a notional crossing of the Atlantic, in truth I was rehearsing the arguments I would use to convince Senator Crowninshield that the cruise-cure could not ever work.

At least not for Rickie, for Rickie was my problem. The cruise-cure might have been his idea, but now that he had embarked on the experience he had no wish to co-operate with it, and instead his moods veered between a cringing self-pity and a vituperative defiance. His weapon of choice became the tape deck on which he played an appalling cacophony of rock music at a level well judged to be loud enough to annoy, but not quite loud enough to provoke me into open hostility. Jackson Chatterton asked me why I simply did not disconnect the tape deck from the boat's electrical supply, but I suspected that such a move would merely persuade Rickie to transfer his battle to another piece of the boat's equipment, and one which, unlike the tape deck, might be necessary to *Wavebreaker*'s survival. I asked Chatterton how long we could expect Rickie's anti-social behaviour to last, and the big man smiled. "For ever, Nick."

"For ever?" I sounded appalled.

"I think he's just being himself," Jackson Chatterton said sourly, "an eternal jerk."

"And his father might become President," I said sourly.

"Glory be!" Chatterton said mockingly, and began to laugh. "I tell you, Nick, if that man's serious about winning the jackpot, then the sooner he puts Rickie in a straitjacket, the better."

Yet Rickie did have better moments when he seemed to realise just what a jerk he truly was, and in those moments he would ineptly try to help with the working of the ship, and he would even apologise for his obnoxious behaviour, though the apologies were usually addressed to Ellen, Chatterton or Thessy, and rarely to me. I suspected that there was something inherent in my character or appearance that irritated Rickie, because I noted how even in his lucid and calmer moments he took care to avoid me. Only once did he deliberately seek out my company, and that was when he fetched a chart up to the cockpit and asked me to show him where we were. I pencilled a cross to mark our estimated position and showed him how we had been beating up and down in the open ocean, parallel with the islands but always out of their sight.

"What's the point of that?" he asked, with only a trace of his usual hostility.

"It's a good way of shaking everyone down," I said. "If we were constantly anchoring and going ashore then no one would fall into a shipboard routine." I hesitated, wondering how much truth he could bear, and decided he might as well hear it all. "I thought the whole idea of the cruise-cure was to isolate you. How can I do that if we're in and out of anchorages?"

"Yeah, sure, sure." He brushed off my explanation and stared at the pencilled cross I had made on the chart. "But we will go back to the islands?"

"Of course." I should probably already have taken *Wavebreaker* back to the islands, for our hopelessly inadequate watchkeeping arrangements were making Thessy and me more and more tired. Yet, if I was honest with myself, I knew my weapon of choice against Rickie was to keep him out at sea. He used the cassette player and I used navigation. It takes two to fight.

"So when do we go back to the islands?" he demanded.

"In a few days?" I was deliberately vague.

"I want to do some scuba, right? Have some fun!" He said the last three words in an outraged voice, as though 'fun' was the birthright of a rich American youth, and I was being unnaturally cruel in denying it to him. I said nothing, which only annoyed him. "Or do you think I'll run away if we go ashore?"

"Would you?" I asked.

"I just want to do some scuba!" He was still outraged. "OK?"

"OK," I said placatingly.

"And soon, you know?" He snatched the chart away from me and roughly folded it. "I mean, like before next year?"

"A week at the very most," I promised him.

He bad-temperedly chucked his cigarette end towards the sea, but it fell into the scuppers and I saw the flicker of pride cross his face as he was tempted to leave the smoking and glowing butt to make a scorch mark on the wood, but then he saw my expression and, behaving as though he had never intended to do anything else, he stalked to the gunwale and contemptuously flicked the cigarette over the side. He went below without another word and two minutes later I heard the nauseating sound of the Pinkoe Dirt-Box Band crashing through the boat.

Robin-Anne had the capacity to be entirely more pleasant company, except that she had fallen into a torpor of careless inactivity. She abandoned her heavy eating, picking listlessly at her meals instead. She seemed self-absorbed and almost as short-tempered as her brother, yet she made far more effort to be sociable, and when a half-dozen dolphins one day decided to keep *Wavebreaker* company I thought I saw Robin-Anne enjoy a moment of pure innocent pleasure as she watched the lovely creatures dive and leap in our quarter-wave. She took a particular liking for Thessy, and the two of them would often sit close together, talking and talking, and there was something curiously touching about the sight. I asked Thessy what they spoke about, and he told me that he was trying to lead her to

Christ, then complained that Robin-Anne would never listen to his evangelism because all she ever wanted to do was talk about cocaine.

I smiled. "I know."

I knew because it had become Robin-Anne's habit to come on deck each night and there to use me as a sounding-board for her obsession with the drug. I heard how, in the dark hell of anhedonia, an addict took alcohol or barbiturates or any other thing that might alleviate that terrible Godless empty black hole of dopamine exhaustion. She told me about the seething paranoia of the addict; how they feared that someone else might be cheating them of their supply. She told me how the addicts fought and stole and lied and whored to find the money to feed their habit. "And in their sane moments," she said, "they hate themselves for what they're doing, but the only sure escape from that self-loathing is to use still more cocaine."

I had wanted to ask her if she had ever been driven to desperate measures to find cocaine herself, but I did not like to put the question which, in any case, her next words implicitly answered. "Rickie and I were always kind of popular," she said wryly.

"Because you had money?"

"We've always had lots of that," she said with attractive deprecation. She was staring to starboard, where gargantuan clouds shrouded the stars and cast a black pall across the sea. Despite the massing clouds the wind was still steady from the south-east, the seas were long and smooth, and the weather forecast untroubling. Robin-Anne smiled. "You always have plenty of friends if you've got lots of money to buy them cocaine."

That smile was one of the last she gave me for, night by night, she had been plunging ever deeper into what Jackson Chatterton called the abstinence phase. Robin-Anne tried to explain what he meant as she sat curled in the swathing oilskin jacket. She looked very calm and her voice was softly placid, but I could see her pale, long-fingered hands flexing and twisting as she spoke. She had, as usual, brought me a cup of coffee that I was letting cool on the binnacle shelf as she told me that the first stage of withdrawal was marked by the anaesthesia of sleep and the pleasures of food, but that easy first phase was replaced by the torture of abstinence; a time of wakefulness and torment. Robin-Anne's torment was the memory of the blissful drenching of her soul with sudden euphoria, the glorious dependability of a chemically induced heaven. It was a memory, Robin-Anne said, that prowled and snarled and clawed at her resolve, begging her to give it the blessing of just one more sniff of cocaine, wheedling to her that one small hit of the magic powder could not possibly hurt.

"And how long," I asked, "is the abstinence phase?"

"If I'm real lucky, three months. Two years if not." Her huge eyes looked almost liquid in the small light glinting from the binnacle. "And very soon," she went on sadly, "I'll begin to hallucinate about the drug, to dream about it, and to lust after it more strongly than I've ever wanted anything in all my life. Nothing will matter to me except the drug. If I was in love I would forget my lover, and if I was a mother I'd forget my children, because all I would think about was the drug." She stared forward, to where one bright star showed under the canopy of dark cloud. Earlier I had tried to get her interested in the sextant, challenging her to catch that one lonely star in its mirrors, but she had been too lackadaisical to make the attempt. Now she shuddered suddenly. "I hate being ill."

"Ill?"

"I've got a chemical dependency, Nick. That's an illness. It isn't a character weakness, but an illness."

I sipped the coffee and grimaced as I realised she had added gobs of sugar and forgotten the milk. "What happens when the abstinence phase is over?" I asked.

She spread her hands in a simple gesture of benison. "It will be over when my brain no longer resurrects the memory of the drug's effect, and when that happens I shall be properly alive again, like you and Ellen and Thessy."

"May it be soon," I said, but Robin-Anne did not respond to that dutiful scrap of piety. Instead she went below and a few minutes later, as I went down to fetch a proper coffee, I saw her sitting in front of the tape deck, a set of earphones clamped over her short and so very pale hair; she was rocking obsessively back and forth, back and forth as though she could drive the clawing scrabbling hateful demon out of her soul with a scorching blast of her brother's fearsome music. I was watching someone I liked slip into a poisonous hell, and I was helpless.

An hour later Thessy relieved me. I gave him the course, shared a bacon sandwich with him, then went below to sleep.

Ellen woke me an hour after dawn. I was groggy with sleep and fumbled for the light switch, but instead Ellen swept back the curtains to flood grey daylight into the small cabin. "Trouble, O Captain, my Captain!" she said cheerfully.

"Oh, no." I sat up. Ellen held out a grey weatherfax sheet which showed that the isobars had shrunk and wrapped themselves into a depression during the night. The low pressure was far away east in the Atlantic, but Ellen had been right to wake me for we both knew how swiftly such depressions could develop into storms that could move with lightning speed across the sea. I pushed hair out of my face and frowned at the chart which, I saw, had been transmitted just moments before. "Oh, bugger." I said.

"Two syllables even!" Ellen mocked me. "Wow!"

I scowled at her, tried to find some crushing retort, but yawned hugely instead.

"I must say," Ellen adopted a southern accent, "that you are just the prettiest sight in the morning, Nick Breakspear. Is that what I have to look forward to all the way across the South Pacific?"

"You're not exactly a ball of fun yourself first thing in the morning," I reminded her, then looked up at the wind-gauge repeater that was mounted on the cabin bulkhead. I saw that the wind speed had dropped a fraction, hovering now on the cusp between force three and four, but there was little comfort to be taken from that reading for the wind direction had moved a fraction southerly and the barometer mounted next to the wind-gauge betrayed that the pressure had dropped even since I'd gone to sleep. I leaned across the bed and tapped the glass and watched the needle fall even further. "We'll have to run for it," I said.

"Bad as that?" Ellen asked with what I suspected was a tinge of enthusiasm for a taste of rough weather.

"It isn't a hurricane," I said dismissively. It was too early in the season for a hurricane, but the small depression could quickly grow into a tropical storm and, under the lash of such a storm, it was hard to tell how it differed from a hurricane. Nor did I want to take any chances with a tired and short-handed crew, and, as shelter was not so very far away, prudence dictated that I should turn our bows westwards and find a hurricane hole where we could safely ride out whatever nastiness the weather brought. I swung my legs to the floor and reached for my shorts. "Is there any coffee?"

"On the stove, great leader."

"Would you tell Thessy to run due west? And tell him I'll bring a proper course in a moment."

"Your every wish is my command," Ellen said, then took good care to leave before I had time to articulate one of those wishes. I rubbed the sleep from my eyes, then pulled on one of my old army shirts before picking up Thessy's much battered Bible that lay on the small table between our beds. It was an ancient Mission Bible, given to Thessy by his father, and bound in stiff black boards that had been discoloured by salt spray and creased with too much use, but the binding was still sound and its red-edged pages intact. Thessy had been instructed by his father to read his way through the whole book, ploughing indiscriminately through the dirty bits, boring bits and bloody bits alike, but he was finding it hard going and had shyly told me that he was much looking forward to reaching the Gospels. So far he had only managed to reach a very minor and remarkably gloomy Old Testament prophet. I kept a finger to mark the particular

131

doom-laden passage that Thessy was now reading, and turned back to Psalm 55. 'Cast thy burden upon the Lord,' I read, 'and he shall sustain thee.' I read the familiar psalm for comfort, and felt the ship wear round as I did so. There was a smack as a wave caught her on the beam, and a crack of the sails, then Thessy had her running hard and strong, and I smiled as I thought how good a sailor Thessy was, and how good a person he was too, then I went to fetch myself a coffee and to work out a course that would lead us to shelter.

"What's happening?" Rickie had been sitting at the single sideband radio, perhaps eavesdropping on traffic.

"It's your lucky day," I said. "By dusk we'll be at anchor."

"Yeah, man!" His face showed some of the delight he had demonstrated on the morning he had first joined the ship. He snapped his fingers in celebration, then turned away to probe the radio waves still further.

I plotted a bearing for San Salvador, then went topsides and gave the new course to Thessy. The wind, which had fallen away, was piping up again, and I suspected the day would soon be lively. The sky was clouding fast, and the sea was rising, reminders of just how quickly a depression could twist into a storm. Not that we were in storm conditions now, and we were nowhere close to shortening sail, but the long wave crests were flecking white and *Wavebreaker* was beginning to roll as she ran in front of the freshening breeze.

I braced my legs against the roll. Thessy slackened the mainsheet, and grinned as our bows chopped into a chunk of water that exploded into white fragments and spattered back down the deck. Two hours later the same motion drove the bows under and I felt the long hull shudder as she tore herself free, then I watched as a great sweep of green water rolled down the deck to shatter at the cockpit coaming before pouring thick out of *Wavebreaker*'s scuppers. Thessy whooped for sheer joy as the main boom touched the starboard-side waves to draw its own miniature and water-splintering wake through the darkening sea. I shared his happiness, for it was a marvellous day's sailing; exhilarating and quick.

By mid-afternoon the sky was darkly overcast and the seas had built into great crinkled monsters that looked far more threatening than they actually were. They were big enough to impress Jackson Chatterton who brought a camera on deck and asked me to take his picture against a backdrop of the looming grey waves. "Photographs always make the waves look smaller!" I shouted to him over the rush of wind in the rigging.

"What?"

"Doesn't matter, Jacko. Stand there! Smile!"

The water thundered past, but we were safe, running miles ahead of the storm. The whitecaps spilt angry tangles of foam down the waves' faces, but the wind was no more than force seven, gusting eight, and we still did not need to shorten any sail. Ellen made a big plate of sandwiches, but only Chatterton, Thessy and I were tempted. The twins seemed as oblivious to the food as they were to the magnificent seas. At one point I went below to fetch the radio direction finder and saw Robin-Anne glance out of the stateroom window to where a shaft of sunlight briefly glinted through a rent in the clouds to cast a wash of silver brilliance on the crumpled water as it heaped and rushed on past the hull, but for all the notice Robin-Anne took of the sight she might as well have been blind. Her face was blank, and her thin body was slumped on the stateroom sofa with a discarded book beside her. Rickie had disappeared and I had an unworthy wish that perhaps he was spewing up his belly with seasickness.

I took a mug of tea to Thessy who did not want to be spelled at the wheel because he was finding too much pleasure in steering the schooner through the great onrush of wind and wave. "How long till landfall, Nick?" he asked.

"Maybe a half-hour?"

In fact it was nearer forty-five minutes for, as we closed on the islands, a rainstorm blotted out our visibility. The sea surged up behind, lifting and carrying *Wavebreaker* forward. Thessy, his face shining from the rain, grinned with delight. He saw the land first, or rather he saw the great white stone tower of the Dixon Hill light high over San Salvador.

The rain became harder, bouncing off the deck and cascading thick off the sails. "Do you want a slicker?" I shouted at Thessy.

He shook his head. I was more tired, or else older, or perhaps more feeble, and decided that I wanted to change into dry clothes and so I left Thessy at the wheel and dropped quickly down the main companionway into the incongruous luxury of our main stateroom where Robin-Anne, stirred from her lethargy, was trying to tune the television to a Bahamian transmitter.

She nodded a distracted greeting to me, then, turning away, screamed with fright.

She screamed because her brother had suddenly appeared in the companionway that led from the forward cabins. Blood was pouring from his nose.

"Jackson!" I shouted, then ran forward to where Rickie was reeling back against the bulkhead. "What happened? Did you fall?"

"Get lost." His one good eye was glazed, and its pupil huge. He must have come from the heads, for the door was swinging and I could see a smear of blood on the edge of the toilet bowl, and I guessed he must have been vomiting into the bowl when a lurch of the ship cracked his nose against the edge.

"Come on, Rickie!" I tried to ease him away from the bulkhead towards one of the chairs, but he thrust me away.

"Fuck you." His voice was extraordinarily hoarse, a dry and croaking voice like some cartoon monster. Blood dripped from his chin on to the stateroom carpet. His forehead was greasy with sweat.

Jackson Chatterton came running from the galley, then slowed as he saw Rickie's face. "What have you done?" he asked Rickie, but in an oddly accusatory tone.

"All of you," Rickie encompassed the whole world with a wave of his hand, "fuck off. Really." He had begun to weep, his thin shoulders heaving with enormous sobs.

"I think he must have fallen," I said.

Chatterton shot me a look of withering scorn. "He never

fell! Look at him! He's high! He ain't even bruised! He's just burst a blood vessel, that's all!" He twined a big hand in Rickie's hair and thrust the boy's head towards me. "Look!" Chatterton's voice was harsh and ugly, full of hatred.

I looked to see tears streaming down Rickie's slack face to mingle with the blood that was dribbling on to the sole. He was grizzling like a small child, and staggering as the big seas rolled *Wavebreaker*'s long hull.

"Look at the turkey's nostrils!" Chatterton shouted, and I realised his anger was not directed at me, but at Rickie.

I looked. Blood was filling and welling from Rickie's nasal cavities, but at either side, on the very edges of his nostrils, there were traces of white powder.

"Oh, God," I said.

"Fucking jerk!" Chatterton pulled Rickie away towards their cabin. "You miserable poxy jerk! You've got it, haven't you? You smuggled your stuff on board!"

"He's got cocaine on board?" I asked naïvely.

"He's been fooling us!" Chatterton laid Rickie on the bed, but not roughly, and I began to see that much of the black man's rage was aimed at himself for not being more alert to Rickie's condition. He had assumed that Rickie was going through the turmoil of the abstinence phase, when in fact Rickie had just been oscillating up and down the euphoric scale between heaven and hell.

Robin-Anne shrank back into the sofa, abandoning the television that hissed an untuned signal at us. She looked scared. She had been struggling against her abstinence phase all week, and even perhaps daring to hope that she was winning her battle, but Rickie had not tried at all. Somewhere on board *Wavebreaker* there was a supply of his cocaine. "Oh, damn," I said tiredly, then went to stand in the door of Rickie's cabin. I watched as Jackson Chatterton staunched the blood and began probing Rickie's nose with a paintbrush. The big man worked with an extraordinary gentleness. "What are you doing?" I asked.

"Why don't you put on dry clothes?" Chatterton asked me

in return, but when I did not move, he held up the small bottle of oily liquid into which he had been dipping the paintbrush. "It's an anaesthetic. You sniff enough cocaine, Nick, and the stuff eats away your nasal septum and your vocal cords till you don't have a nose or a voice any more, do you?" This last question was snapped at the weeping Rickie. "Instead you'll look like a leper, with a saddle-nose that's nothing but a rotted cavity full of snot and stupidity!" He spat the words at Rickie, yet his hands were still very tender. "So where are you hiding your nose-candy, Rickie?"

"Fuck off," Rickie shrieked at Chatterton. I remembered Robin-Anne telling me how the threat of deprivation drove cocaine users into a bitter paranoia, and I was seeing that madness now in Rickie's frenetic reaction to Chatterton's questions. More than frenetic, for Rickie suddenly lashed out at the big man.

That was a mistake. Chatterton rammed Rickie back on to the bed and thrust his face close to the screaming boy. "Oh, baby, you in trouble! You are *in* trouble! You nothin' but white meat in a bad jail, Sweetpea. You ain't got the brains of a tick! You go on like this, you be a big, dumb, blind motherfucker with your brains trickling out a hole in your dumb face!" Chatterton's voice, honed to savagery by years of the army, utterly cowed Rickie who could only stare in shocked horror at the face so close above him. "You be such a dumb-ugly piece of shit, boy, that not even the blind prisoners want to rape you! You hear me?" Chatterton waited till Rickie, sobbing, nodded softly.

Ellen, puzzled by the commotion, had appeared in the doorway beside me. She frowned, still not understanding. Rickie, oblivious to her presence, was racked with tears.

I told Ellen the good news; that we had an overdosed Rickie and some hidden cocaine aboard.

"I searched the turkey's luggage!" Chatterton complained to us as he went back to working on Rickie's nose, "and I did a good search, a real good search! I know he couldn't have smuggled enough stuff aboard to do this to himself, I know!"

"He probably didn't." Ellen stared dispassionately at Rickie, and then, in a very commonplace voice, suggested the obvious solution to our mystery. "But I suspect someone else did."

"Oh, God!" I spoke to myself. I was remembering a tall, handsome and laconic man, a southerner who wore a badge saying 'Just Say No!' I had asked Ellen to search the ship after Jesse Isambard Sweetman had trespassed on *Wavebreaker*, but that search had been to discover whether any item might have been stolen and it had not occurred to either of us that perhaps Sweetman had come to hide something aboard the schooner. But who else could it be?

"Sweetman," I said aloud.

I felt like an idiot. We had gone to sea in such innocence, with such high hopes, and with such good intentions, and all the time Rickie had been laughing at us because his friend Jesse Sweetman had salted away the candy before Rickie even came on board.

So now all we had to do was find it.

We anchored that evening in the good shelter of Sea Rat Cay's lagoon. Sea Rat Cay is a flat, nondescript and uninhabited patch of land where palms, casuarinas, slash pines and sea-grape grow. The lagoon has a sandy sea-bed that lets an anchor dig in hard, and is deep enough for a boat of *Wavebreaker*'s draught. The Cay itself is never more than ten feet above sea-level, but shaped like the letter C to give wonderful shelter from every wind except a rare westerly. By nightfall Thessy and I were content that our three anchors were well bedded against the rising wind that was tossing and clattering the palm fronds. Scraps of broken palm were whipping across the lagoon water that was rippling like a miniature angry sea, but at least the rain had stopped, though the dusk sky was foully black. I watched the wind tearing at the vegetation, then went below and saw that the pressure had stopped its steep fall.

I copied the barometer reading into *Wavebreaker*'s log, then went back to the main stateroom where Jackson Chatterton was systematically taking apart every scrap of furniture. He was finding nothing. He had already combed the cabin he shared with Rickie and had discovered nothing except a few black and glossy pills that he said were Methedrine. "Better known as speed," Chatterton told me. "The turkey probably had them in case he ran out of cocaine. And those are Dexamyl." He showed me yet more pills he had since found in the main-cabin, but what he had not yet discovered was any cocaine. He searched diligently. Ellen watched him with folded arms. She seemed embarrassed by the proceedings, while Robin-Anne was dully oblivious to the whole drama. Rickie, his eyes still wet with tears, vociferously protested that the search was unnecessary. "I haven't got any! None! Jesus! Why won't you believe me?" He lit a cigarette, even though another was trickling smoke, barely lit, in the ashtray beside him.

"Where did you meet Jesse Sweetman?" I asked him.

"Get lost," he said; then, in a reversion to an earlier insult, began to chant at me in a singsong voice. "Rum, sodomy and the lash. Rum, sodomy and the lash."

Thessy crouched at the foot of the companionway stairs, his eyes showing white and scared, so I went back to stand beside him and thus to give him encouragement.

"You like a bit of black bum, do you?" Rickie jeered at me.

"Oh, shut your silly face!" Ellen suddenly snapped at him.

Rickie was astonished at Ellen's hostility, and he turned to defend his point of view. "He's a Brit!" He explained to Ellen but pointing at me. "Rum, sodomy and lash. Black bums and buggery!" He began to laugh, and I started walking towards him, my anger ready to explode in appalling force, but Ellen, just as she had averted my violence when Sweetman was aboard, now did so once again.

"If I was hiding drugs aboard this boat," she said in a very reasonable tone of voice, "I'd hide them in the one place where a person can be alone."

Chatterton frowned at her, then looked to me for amplification.

"Try the heads," I said, wondering why I had not thought of it earlier.

138

"Oh, damn you all," Rickie said despairingly, and thus confirming where we should look.

We all seemed to meet in the doorway of the heads, all but Rickie who had gone the other way. He was still crying. He went to the radio desk where he clamped a set of earphones over his skull as though he could blot out the whole world and all its misery. And misery it would be, for we had found his cocaine.

Chatterton found the first bag inserted in the toilet-roll holder, threaded inside the spring which tensioned the holder in its bracket. Another bag was taped deep behind the drain outflow under the small washbasin, while a third was concealed behind the panelling where it was attached to *Wavebreaker*'s steel hull. We could find no more of the drug, though Chatterton warned us of the addicts' cunning. "I'll keep looking," he offered.

I carried the three plastic bags into the stateroom. It was the first time I had ever seen cocaine at close quarters and it looked so very innocent. It was more crystalline than I had expected, with a glint like rock-salt, but it took an effort of the imagination to realise just what pure evil I held in my hands. Robin-Anne stared at the bags, then what little colour was in her face seemed to drain away as she recognised the powder. She licked her lips.

I walked past her and tapped Rickie's shoulder. He was hunched furtively over the microphone of the VHF, its headset tight over his ears. He flinched away from me, so I roughly pulled the headset away from his ears. "I want you."

"Go play with your black boy, Breakspear."

I hit him hard across the head; a smacking ringing bang of a blow that rocked him violently sideways. He opened his mouth to scream, but before he could utter a sound I had seized his shirt and pulled him harshly out of his chair and then, still one-handed, I spun him round and hurled him against the bulkhead. He crashed into the panelling, his black hair flopping with the whiplash of the impact. His nose had begun to pour blood again, and his eyes were wide with terror. I was holding the cocaine in my left hand, so I used my right to hit him in the belly. He uttered a moaning gasp and folded over. I grabbed his hair and forced him to stand upright against the bulkhead. "Make one more sound," I hissed into his astonished and terrified face, "and I'll beat you so hard that you'll wish you had never been born."

"Nick?" Ellen said tentatively, then louder and with a note of warning in her voice, "Nick!"

"Leave us alone," I warned her. Ellen was clearly hating the violence, while Robin-Anne seemed not even to have noticed that it was happening. Jackson Chatterton, watching from the door of the heads, made a circle with his thumb and middle finger and offered it to me as a gesture of approval.

Rickie's breath was coming in huge lung-hurting gasps. Blood bubbled at his nostrils and trickled down to his chin. His blind eye was sheened by the lights, while his good eye was bloodshot and scared. He made not a sound, not even a sob, as I gripped his shirt and pulled his face towards me. "You're coming on deck with me."

He nodded. I doubted that anyone had ever used physical violence against Rickie Crowninshield, and he was stunned by it. He was also as meek as a milksop now, and eager to please by hurrying after me up the companionway stairs. His nose dripped blood on to the non-skid treads, then on to the teak deck as I led him to the portside rail. Spits of rain were being carried on the wind that was hissing across the sheltered lagoon now ragged with scraps of vegetation torn from the trees and bushes on the darkening Sea Rat Cay. The wind was shrieking in *Wavebreaker*'s high rigging, trembling the masts and making the long hull tug against her anchor rodes.

"Watch me," I said.

Rickie whimpered as, one by one, I tore the three bags open and tossed their contents to the wind. The keys of heaven's gates were scattered to the sea and the angry wind and the malevolent sting of rain. God knows how much that cocaine was worth, but enough to make even Rickie Crowninshield cry as he watched the powder vanish into the dusk. When all three plastic bags were empty I washed them in a bucket of sea-water, tossed the fouled water overboard, then stuffed the clean bags into the gash bucket. "Is there any more on board?" I asked Rickie.

"No," he said quickly, eager to please me. "None. Really."

"If I find any more," I told him, "I'll hurt you properly." At that moment I hated him. I hated his weakness, his tears, his money, his misused privilege, his deceit, and his utter uselessness. "So tell me about Sweetman," I said. "He put that stuff aboard?"

"Yes, he did. Yes."

"So who is he?"

Rickie seemed puzzled by the question, as though he expected everyone to know who Sweetman was. "He's our supplier," he said at last.

"Your supplier? You mean at home?"

"Yes, sure."

"But you're two thousand miles from home. What the hell is he doing here?"

"I don't know." Rickie was crying harder now. "I just don't know."

"Why the hell did you want to come on this boat if you weren't going to make any effort to give up?" I asked angrily.

"I do want to give up! I do, I do, I do!" He was grizzling pathetically; a tall crumpled broken boy.

"Go away." I could not hide my revulsion, but I don't suppose he noticed. He just crept below.

I stayed on deck as night fell, and I told myself that I stayed there to make sure that the anchors were holding, while the truth was that I simply did not want to go down and look at Rickie's tearful, bloody face or at Robin-Anne's soulless vacuity. So instead I sat in the cockpit, hunched against the splashes of rain, and watched the night fall black across the fretting lagoon. I sensed that the storm had either passed us to the south, or else that it had not worked itself into its full frenzy.

"So just what did you expect of Rickie?" Ellen's voice interrupted me. She had silently appeared in the companionway, holding a spare oilskin jacket that she now tossed at me.

"I don't know." I pulled the jacket round my shoulders as a protection against the small rain that was falling, then shifted down the thwart to make room for her.

Ellen sat and brought a bottle of my Irish whiskey out of her oilskin's pocket. "You didn't hide the bottles as well as Rickie hid his cocaine." She poured three fingers into a glass. "So just what did you expect of him?" She handed me the glass.

"A little effort," I said. "This whole goddamn mess was his idea."

Ellen groaned. "Come on, Nick! This isn't a Boy Scout cruise! He's a very sick boy!"

"Then he should be in a hospital!" I spoke very bitterly. "He shouldn't be here. We're not trained to deal with Rickie's kind of crap."

Ellen poured herself some whiskey, then stared across the break in the lagoon towards the open sea. It was almost full dark, but we could just see how the wind was whipping the exposed waves into a churning mass of whitecaps. "I suppose," Ellen said after a while, "that you're planning to tell the senator that we can't cope with Rickie?"

"Something like that," I confirmed her guess.

She gave me a rueful look. "I could really use the three months' money, Nick."

It had not been so very long since Ellen had savaged me for lumbering her with the company of rich junkies, yet now she was arguing for continuing with the cruise-cure. "I just can't take three months of Rickie," I said very fervently.

"What you really hate in him," Ellen said in a most prosaic voice, "is that he reminds you of yourself."

"Don't be ridiculous," I snapped, and meant obnoxious as well.

"He's just like you," Ellen said flatly. "He's rejected the

world of his famous father. I've often thought that the real silver spoon in this world is not how much money you're born to, but how good an address book you inherit. I can't really believe that all those second-generation actors and politicians and writers are born with natural talent, they're just born knowing the right people, and familiarity means they're not afraid of their parents' trade, while the rest of us poor saps have to work our way up the hard way. But you rejected your father's world, just as Rickie is rejecting *his* father's world. I admit the rejections take different forms, but rejection is almost always graceless. I doubt your father enjoyed you being a marine, any more than the senator likes Rickie smoking crack."

"I am nothing like Rickie," I said very clearly.

"You're a rebel," Ellen said, "only your rebellion took the perverse form of seeking out respectability. Why did you become a marine?"

I sought for a flippant answer, but none came, so I offered Ellen the truth. "Because my father marched to the American Embassy to protest against Vietnam, and he was in the Campaign for Nuclear Disarmament, and the one thing he always professed to hate was militarism. So." I shrugged, as though the rest was obvious.

Ellen smiled. "Sweet, handsome Nick." She said it very fondly and with what seemed to be some pity. "Could you have been an actor?"

"No."

"But you probably wanted to be, and you probably felt horribly inadequate against your father's excellence, and that's just what Rickie is feeling now. Rickie has probably felt inadequate all his life, and right now, when he's been given into our care, all he finds is this horribly competent Brit who scowls at him, and makes him feel useless, and shouts at him not to tread on the sailcloth or to wind a line the other way round a winch, and is it any wonder that he's as miserable as a cat in a rainstorm?"

I growled, reluctant to accept the criticism.

Ellen smiled. "Be nice to him. Find something to praise!"

"What am I supposed to do?" I bridled. "Tell him his hair looks nice?"

"At least he has a comb and makes an effort," Ellen said pointedly. "No, but you have to start somewhere. He's fascinated by the boat's electronics, so why don't you praise him for that? He spent two hours experimenting with the radios today, and perhaps he'd like to hear you say how clever he is for having mastered the equipment?" She smiled encouragingly at me. "The journey might be a thousand miles, Nick, but it begins with a single step."

I said a few very rude words to show what I thought of such sententious rubbish. Ellen, for all her sour wit, had moments when she tried to swamp the boat in American niceness.

She sighed. "Just give him a chance, Nick."

"Sod him."

"So eloquent, you English, so very eloquent." She stared briefly into the sky as though seeking inspiration, then looked back to me. "You shouldn't have hit him."

"Why not? He deserved it."

"No one deserves to be hit. Violence has never solved anything, it merely suppresses and disguises truth. Your father, whatever else he might or might not be, is surely right in his hatred of militarists."

"My father" – I wearily leaned my head against the cockpit's coaming – "would march to support the Movement to Burn Babies if he thought it was fashionable. I didn't rebel against his beliefs, because he doesn't have any. I rebelled against his lack of truth."

Ellen sighed. "How very strict you are, Nick. That's probably why Robin-Anne is so besotted with you."

That made me snap my head upright. "Besotted?"

"She's in love with you," Ellen saw my astonishment and laughed at it. "She thinks you're the strong man who'll protect her from the demon drug. You've become her solution now, her magic potion." Ellen mocked me with a smile. "Congratulations, Nick, you can marry six million bucks! You can be son-in-law to the President! Wow! You can invite me to the White

144

House for a plastic chicken dinner! All you need do is pop the question."

"It isn't like that," I said feelingly. "Robin-Anne talks to me about cocaine, but not about anything else. If she's in love with anyone, it's Thessy! They're inseparable. She's certainly not in love with me!"

"Oh, but she is. What do you think she talks about with Thessy?"

"Jesus and cocaine. He told me."

"Jesus, cocaine and you," Ellen corrected me with a smile. "Ask Thessy if you don't believe me. She pumps him for information about you; what your star sign is, your favourite colour, what you like to eat, that sort of thing." Ellen grinned, but I could see she was being deadly serious.

"Oh God." I leaned my head back again to let the spitting rain strike my face. "Then that's all the more reason," I said softly, "to abandon the cruise. Robin-Anne has to learn to beat drugs without me."

"Oh, that's very pious!" Ellen poured me more whiskey. "But very callous, too. This kid is trusting you, Nick!"

"Oh, shit." I did not want the responsibility.

Ellen laughed. "Three months, Nick, that's all you have to give them, and at the end of three months we'll pick up our big fat cheques and we'll sail your boat across the Pacific. Is it a deal?"

I turned my head and smiled at her. Somehow, after the last few days, that dream of the South Seas had faded almost to unreality. "Are you really going to sail with me?" Ellen had already said as much, but I wanted to hear her say it again.

She pretended to think about it, then nodded. "I like you, Nick Breakspear, because you reinforce my convictions about men."

I smiled. "I take it that isn't a compliment?"

"No," she returned the smile. "They say a woman needs a man like a fish needs a bicycle, but I guess I'm just the odd fish out, and I have a hankering for bicycles, and especially for old-fashioned, upright and honest bicycles." She paused. "And do you want me to be really honest?"

"Of course."

"Your father was the most handsome Hamlet that ever was." She let that one sink in, then laughed, blew me a kiss, and was gone.

Ellen had made me feel better, and she had also left me the Irish whiskey, though I did not drink any more that night. Instead I waited till I was completely certain our three anchors were holding, then I went to bed, but via the forward hatchway so that I need not see either Rickie or Robin-Anne who were slumped in front of the television in the main stateroom.

I took one last look through the cabin port. The wind had slackened, so that the anchor rodes were no longer thrumming like harp strings. The rain seemed to have stopped altogether. A rift opened in the clouds beyond Sea Rat Cay and a weak shaft of moonlight touched the island so that the nearest pines looked as though they had been dipped in molten silver. "The worst of the storm's gone," I told Thessy, "so we'll be off first thing in the morning."

"God villing." He looked up from reading his gloomy minor prophet.

"Tell me" – I tried to make my voice very casual – "but does Robin-Anne talk about me to you?"

The poor boy had obviously not wanted to tell me before, and now looked horribly embarrassed, but he could not tell a lie so he nodded. "All the time, Nick. She says you say poetry in the dark."

I laughed, then shook my head to show Thessy that he should not take Robin-Anne seriously. "Ellen says we should persevere for the full three months." I wanted to know how Thessy would react to such a prospect.

He frowned in serious thought, then nodded. "I think if God vanted us to give up, Nick, he vould not have let us begin."

I supposed that made sense. "Thank you, Thessy."

"Sleep vell, Nick."

And, surprisingly, I did. To dream of *Masquerade*, and cleanness, and of far-off northern seas as cold as steel. I dreamed of home.

I woke early to hear the wind sighing in *Wavebreaker*'s shrouds and clattering the palm fronds on Sea Rat Cay, but I could tell, even without looking at the wind-gauge, that the storm was dying. Thessy was snoring gently in the other bed, so I rolled quietly out from under the sheet, pulled on a pair of shorts and went on deck. It was the break of day and a wan watery light was leaching into a sky that was ragged with clouds touched leprous yellow by the rising sun. *Wavebreaker* fretted to her anchor rodes, but with no great force. The foetid stink of wet vegetation was wafting from the island on a wind that was still blowing the open sea ragged, yet the barometer was rising and I saw no reason why we should not be under way within a couple of hours.

I went below and made myself an instant coffee and used the rest of the hot water to fill a shaving bowl that I carried back to the deck. I propped a mirror against the binnacle, and scraped happily away. I tunelessly sang myself some cheerful song as the wind snatched the foam off the razor's edge and whirled it quivering into the scuppers. The same wind was thrashing the trees ashore and crashing the seas against the outer coral so that the waves shredded white into airborne foam, yet, and despite the wind's remaining strength and my own rendition of 'Oh, What a Beautiful Morning', the dawn suddenly struck me as strangely quiet. That thought made me pause, razor poised by my throat, so that for an instant I must have looked uncannily like a man contemplating suicide.

Why was the morning so quiet?

I straightened up as I realised what was missing from *Wavebreaker*'s usual dawn chorus; it was the hollow clatter of the wire halliards tapping against our metal masts. For a second or two I wondered whether Ellen or Thessy had woken in the night to stretch the halliards away from the masts to silence their insistent racket, but that was not the answer. Instead, when I looked, I saw that we had no halliards any more.

There had been halliards the night before, now there were none.

I stared stupidly into the rigging, the cut-throat razor forgotten in my hand. There were no halliards left, none. Not on either mast. I went to the foot of the mainmast and worked the sailcover back from the gooseneck and found a stub of wire protruding from the sail's peak. The wire had been sheared clean so that its severed end shone with the brightness of newly exposed metal.

I turned, still gaping. All the halliards were gone, every single one. The halliards were the lines used to hoist the sails and, once hoisted, to hold the sails aloft, and they had all disappeared. At the bows, where I had left the jib, staysail and storm jib halliards snaphooked on to the pulpit rail, there was now nothing except a pair of bolt-cutters that were a part of *Wavebreaker*'s rigging kit and which had no business lying abandoned by the hawse hole. I picked up the bolt-cutters, reasoning that Rickie must have used them in the dark as he worked his way round the deck to cripple *Wavebreaker*. It had to be Rickie.

I swore. None of the other rigging seemed to have been touched; only the halliards. It was a piece of mindless stupid vandalism. I had hurt Rickie, so he had hurt the boat to gain his puerile revenge. Playing the Pinkoe Dirt-Box Band too loud was not enough, now he had to creep about in the night, cutting the wire halliards from the sails then casting the bitter ends off their winches before, presumably, dropping them overboard. I imagined him laughing at the chaos he knew he would cause.

Then damn him, I thought, because if his desire was to stay in the lagoon and wait for the sun, then I would disappoint him by taking *Wavebreaker* out to sea on her twin motors. Before leaving the lagoon I would thread lightweight lines through the masthead sheeves so that we could easily haul replacement halliards through the blocks. I knew we had coils of spare wire stowed away below so that, even though Rickie's vandalism was a nuisance, it was not fatal to the boat. By the day's end, I thought, we should have made good all the damage and be once again safely under sail.

I went forward and started the diesel generator which not only powered the ship's heavy electrical equipment like the air conditioners, anchor windlass, sail-furlers and bow thrusters, but also performed the daily chore of charging the ship's batteries. My anger at Rickie had settled into a grim determination that he would not beat me. Instead I would give him an uncomfortable day at sea by driving *Wavebreaker* hard into the wind and waves, and I would threaten him with ten kinds of horror if he dared lay a harmful finger on the boat again.

Thessy, woken by the throbbing of the generator, came yawning from the companionway. "I need you," I startled him by the sudden energy in my voice. "I want messenger lines put through every halliard block. You find some lightweight line and I'll dig out the spare halliard wires. We've got work to do!" Poor Thessy stared at me as though I was mad. "We should look on the bright side, Thessy," I went on, "and be grateful for a chance to replace all the halliards before we take this tub across the ocean."

"Halliards?" He looked at the mainmast, then back to me. "Vot happened?"

I showed him one of the cut stubs. "I suspect it's our friend Rickie. But if he thinks he can beat me, Thessy, then he will have to think again!"

Thessy frowned. "You think Mr Crowninshield did this?"

"Can you think of anyone else?"

Thessy looked sad at such evidence of human sinfulness, then glanced up at the ragged clouds that scudded over the lagoon. "It'll be brisk out there today!" He spoke with relish.

"The brisker the better!" I wanted to take Rickie out into my element; out into the great heaping wilderness of an ocean after storm, and once there I would keep him on deck and make him work. He might not be fit for the intricate jobs like splicing the rope tails on to the new wire halliards, but he could do his share of hauling and lifting, and I did not care how sick he might feel or how much his nose bled. I would make him do some real work for a change. I would sweat him. "That's where I've been wrong," I told a bemused Thessy,

149

"I've let the twins laze about as though this was a holiday cruise. It isn't. They should be working! They've got to take some responsibility for their own lives instead of flopping around like lap-dogs. We'll give Rickie a proper watch to keep as a deckhand, and Robin-Anne can help Ellen with the cooking, and ..." My voice tailed away to nothing because the generator had missed a beat, then it missed another, and I turned and stared forrard as the small engine gave a horrible groaning sound, then seized to a dead halt. It suddenly seemed very quiet on *Wavebreaker*'s deck. "Oh, no!" I walked forrard.

"The fuel?" Thessy suggested.

I prayed he was right, but I doubted that a mere fuel blockage would have created that terrible groan. I opened the hatch and dropped down into the steel-walled generator compartment. The fuel came from the main tanks which were deep amidships and the feed-line was equipped with a glass-bowl trap designed to float out any water that might have contaminated the diesel fuel. The trap was full of the reddish oil, showing that there was no blockage upstream of the glass bowl, yet, strangely, I could see some odd whitish specks suspended in the fuel.

I unscrewed the trap, dipped my finger into the diesel oil and brought out one of the specks. It had a white crystalline appearance, not unlike the cocaine I had scattered to the winds the previous night, and for a mad second I wondered if Rickie had hidden yet more of his drug in the fuel tanks, but then I tasted the speck and knew this was not cocaine. I fished another crystal speck out of the bowl and offered it on my fingertip to Thessy whose anxious face peered down from the hatchway. "Taste that," I suggested.

He gingerly licked my finger, then instinctively screwed up his face until he realised what he had just tasted. "Sugar?"

"The bastard," I said. "Oh, the bastard."

The generator was useless now. Rickie had poured sugar into our main tanks, and the engine, sucking the sugar down the fuel lines, had super-heated the sweet granules into a burnt and sticky treacle that was now blocking the engine solid. *Wavebreaker* needed to be taken to a dockyard where the generator could be stripped and cleaned, and her fuel tanks and lines scoured of the last traces of sugar.

"Oh, hell," I said bitterly and unhelpfully.

"At least it isn't the main engines." Thessy was trying to look on the bright side.

"I'll kill him!" I hauled myself out of the hatch and gave an entirely useless and somewhat painful kick to a ventilator hood.

Thessy was holding out my cup of cold coffee, as though that would placate me. "But the main engines are all right," Thessy insisted, and of course he was right, but the main engines were useless without fuel and all of our fuel, so far as I could tell, was fouled with the sugar. I could probably siphon some clean diesel off the top of the tanks, filter it, then rig up a jury supply to run the main engines, but it would all take time, as would re-rigging the halliards. I swore again, knowing that we were stuck in Sea Rat Cay's lagoon for at least the next twenty-four hours.

"There's only one thing that consoles me," I told Thessy as I stumped down the deck and pulled open a locker. "We're stuck here now, and he'll have to go cold turkey, and I hope he suffers the pains of hell. I hope it hurts!" I had taken a length of one inch rope from the locker. It was one of the lines we sometimes used as a spring when mooring alongside a dock, and now, to Thessy's puzzlement, I quickly tied an intricate and rarely used knot at one end of the line. I tossed the rope to Thessy. "Hang that from the lower spreaders, Thessy, then we'll make ourselves a proper breakfast before we start work."

Thessy stared dubiously at the rope I'd thrown him, but climbed the ratlines to the mainmast's lower crosstrees where he obediently suspended the hangman's noose. It lifted to the now useless wind and I half wished that I dared to use it.

But instead I fried myself some eggs, and I fried Thessy his favourite breakfast which was a mash of bread and bananas, after which, much fortified, we both got down to work.

*

We did not see Rickie all day. Robin-Anne took him some sandwiches late in the afternoon, and he must have eaten them, for later on I saw the empty plate in the stateroom, but we had no other evidence of his continued existence – except from Jackson Chatterton who offered to drag Rickie on deck so that I could make use of the hangman's noose. Chatterton confirmed that Rickie had admitted the vandalism, but had offered no reason for it other than a general complaint that shipboard life sucked, and that I sucked in particular. I let the little swine suffer in the uncooled humidity of his dark cabin, for, in an effort to save electricity on a boat that now had no means of recharging its batteries, I had played merry hell with the fuse locker. I had disconnected everything except the VHF radio. We had no television, no hair dryers, no electric razors, no cabin lights, no air conditioners, no refrigerator, and, most blessed of all, no Pinkoe Dirt-Box Band.

Robin-Anne was embarrassed by her brother's actions and even offered me an apology. She asked me what would happen now, and I told her we would have to sail *Wavebreaker* back to her home port to have her fuel lines cleaned and generator repaired.

Robin-Anne frowned. "So you're abandoning the cruise?"

"I don't have much choice."

"So Rickie will go to jail?" she asked me, as though that decision was in my gift, but I could offer her no answer other than a shrug. "But what about me?" she wailed.

"You're doing just fine," I tried to reassure her. "You don't need us or this boat, you're doing wonderfully!"

"I'm only succeeding because of the boat! Because of you!" Her solemn face threatened tears. I saw Ellen watching us, and I did not know what to say, so I just turned away and muttered that I had to get on with the repairs.

I might not be able to offer Robin-Anne what she wanted, but at least I could take refuge in hard work. By mid-afternoon all the halliards were replaced, and each was properly equipped with a neatly spliced rope tail, and I celebrated that achievement by hoisting the mainsail and letting it flap impotently in the wind that had become little more than a strong breeze.

Thessy had done most of the work on the halliards, while I had fitfully made progress on rigging a new fuel supply system. The spare fuel tanks I had installed while docked in McIllvanney's yard were a godsend, and I succeeded in siphoning the best part of sixty gallons of filtered diesel oil out of the contaminated tanks and into the new tanks before the first traces of sugar appeared. Thessy and I then spent the rest of the afternoon and the best part of the early evening rigging new feed lines through *Wavebreaker*'s bilges. The last connection had to be made under the engine room, and Thessy held a flashlight while I wriggled under the gratings to manoeuvre the final jubilee clip into place. Ellen, standing in the engine-room door, was pleading with me to restore power to the microwave so she could heat up some defrosted lasagne. She had to shout at me because the bilge was surprisingly noisy with the sound of waves throbbing beyond the steel hull.

"If this system works," I called back to her, "and the engines start, then you can have all the power you want." The ship's batteries could be charged from either the generator or the main engines. "But not lasagne, for God's sake. You must have something edible in that damned freezer?"

"I'll put you in the damned freezer," Ellen threatened. "There is nothing wrong with my lasagne!"

I decided not to pursue that argument. Instead I gingerly worked the screwdriver towards the jubilee clip. "If I drop the screwdriver," I said to no one in particular, "then I will know there is no God."

Something clanged on the hull. Ellen, believing it was the sound of the screwdriver falling, laughed.

"That wasn't me," I said. The screwdriver's blade was in place now, and the clip was tightening nicely. "Did either of you launch the power skiff?" To me the clang had sounded like a metallic object striking *Wavebreaker*'s hull from the outside, and the aluminium skiff was the likeliest contender, except that both Thessy and Ellen assured me that the skiff

153

had still been hanging from its davits when they last looked. "It must have been a floating log," Ellen suggested. "The lagoon's full of flotsam."

"Probably." I finished tightening the clip. "That's done, so it seems there must be a God after all." I wriggled backwards and suddenly the whole hull rang like a giant bell, then, through the bell's lingering and deafening echo, I heard something heavy scrape harshly down the ship's side, and I realised that the throbbing I had noticed earlier had not been the sound of waves, but rather the underwater sound of a propeller. "We've got visitors." I sounded surprised.

Thessy was still holding the torch, so Ellen ran back to the companionway steps. I began to ease myself up through the hatch in the engine-room gratings when suddenly I heard the clatter of footsteps on the deck above my head. I grimaced at Thessy, suspecting that we were about to be the victims of a US Coastguard search, but as I pulled myself free of the hatch I heard a man's voice shouting in urgent Spanish. Ellen, halfway up the main stairs, seemed to sink back with a look of sad resignation on her face. Then she gave a small scream.

"What the hell . . ." I began, but then a man appeared on the companionway steps, driving Ellen backwards, and I understood why Ellen had screamed. The man was carrying a Kalashnikov rifle.

And Rickie, I realised, had been cleverer than I. Rickie, I suddenly knew, had won.

I realised, too, that it was my own fault. I should have known that an addict like Rickie would not have risked days of deprivation by disabling a ship. Instead he had crippled *Wavebreaker* because he had known that his supplies were coming to Sea Rat Cay and, in that knowledge, he dared not let the ship move away from the rendezvous. And I also understood now why Rickie had taken such an interest in the ship's radio equipment, for he had always planned to use the radios to summon his friends to his side.

"Oh, God." I picked up a two-foot-long steel wrench, but it was a forlorn gesture in the face of a Kalashnikov assault rifle.

The gunman had already reached the foot of the stairs. He was wearing jet-black fatigues and had a blue scarf about his neck. He was a young man, whose darkly tanned face had a scarred chin and dumb animal eyes that made his gaze terrifying. He jerked the Kalashnikov's barrel upwards, indicating that he wanted all three of us on deck. When we hesitated he shouted at us in Spanish.

"Ve have to do vot he says, Nick." Thessy was resigned to the defeat and was sensibly trying to accustom me to its reality.

The man shouted again, presumably ordering Thessy to be quiet and to move quickly, then he looked at me and gestured that I should drop the wrench. I let it go, and the sound of its fall was the humiliating knell of surrender.

The gunman stepped back as I walked out of the engine room. He was giving me no room to attack him, but instead kept the gun's wicked-looking barrel aimed firmly at my belly. He jerked the gun again, indicating that I should follow Ellen and Thessy up to the deck.

I obeyed, to find that the evening sun was slanting prettily across Sea Rat Cay. The wind was almost gentle now and the sea beyond the lagoon's narrow entrance had calmed to a long and shivered swell. A frigate bird, its wide wings and forked tail silhouetted handsomely against the wash of red sunlight, swooped above the island. An osprey was fishing the far end of the lagoon, its talons scraping a white line of foam across the darkening still water. All that remained of the storm were a few high scraps of cloud which, touched red on their undersides, flew west as though they fled the night.

And there, on *Wavebreaker*'s deck, like the pirate-conqueror of a captured ship, was the white-coated, black-dressed and ponytailed Jesse Sweetman who bowed with pleasure as Ellen appeared from the companionway. "My sweet soul's rare delight," he greeted her, "my dearest lady. The last time we met, you lit such a blaze in my soul that you were forced to extinguish it, but with what, my delicious one, will you extinguish my ardour now?"

Ellen said nothing.

Behind Sweetman two armed men watched us with wary, hostile eyes while alongside *Wavebreaker*, and grinding against her hull, was the dazzle-painted boat that bore the number of the Beast on her sharp-nosed prow. *Dream Baby* had fetched us into nightmare, and Rickie, emerging in triumph from his cabin, crowed with delight.

There were four of them, including Sweetman, and all four were armed. I saw two Kalashnikov rifles, one with a wooden stock and the other with a metal folding stock, an American M16 rifle, two pistols, a pump-action shotgun, and an Israeli-made Uzi equipped with the 64-round magazine. For all I knew there might have been other weapons aboard *Dream Baby*, or in the sea-bags that the gunmen had dumped amidships on *Wavebreaker*'s deck, but what I saw was more than enough. Two of the gunmen were evidently peons; mere thugs brought along as muscle; while the third, whom Sweetman addressed as Miguel, visibly carried some authority. He gave orders to the peons and was treated with evident respect by Sweetman. Miguel had a merciless slash of a mouth, a steeply receding forehead that suggested something simian and unfeeling, and oddly blank eyes. He carried the pump-action shotgun.

There were four of them and there were four of us. Ellen, Chatterton, Thessy and myself were made to stand in the cockpit with one of the peons on the deck in front of us, and the other by the mainmast behind us. I had spent much of my adult life close to guns, I had fired them in anger and been fired on in return, but I had never before known the sheer bowel-watering fear of standing unarmed in the face of weapons held by men who, so far as any of us could tell, had no scruples about using them. If I was scared, and if Jackson Chatterton, who had known war, was also scared, then I could only guess at the terror which Thessy and Ellen must have been enduring.

There were four gunmen, four of us, and then there were

the twins. At first they both stood close to Sweetman, and I saw Rickie explaining to his sister just what was happening and why, or rather I assumed that was what he was doing for he spoke too softly for any of us to overhear his words, but suddenly Robin-Anne broke away from her brother and ran to our group where she impulsively threw herself against me and wrapped her arms around me. I put a protective hand about her thin shoulders. "I'm not going!" Robin-Anne turned and shouted at her brother. "I'm not, I'm not, I'm not!"

Sweetman laughed at her defiance, while Rickie was gibbering with delight at the sheer drama of the moment. The first thing he had demanded when he reached the deck was a hit of cocaine, which Sweetman had happily provided from a black leather pouch that was strapped to his belt. I had watched Rickie snort the powder, then, moments later, I had watched the extraordinary change of mood sweep over him. He was suddenly manic, on top of the world, able to do anything.

What he really wanted to do was to hurt me, but Sweetman and Miguel restrained him. "There'll be time, dear Rickie," Sweetman said, then gave Rickie the Uzi to hold. Rickie pointed it across the darkening lagoon towards the palms and squeezed the trigger, but the weapon was not cocked and would not fire. Sweetman ignored him, and I watched, terrified, as Rickie tried to work out how to make the sub-machine-gun function.

Miguel had gone below to search the boat, and he must have found the missing fuses for suddenly the deck-lights, mounted just beneath the lower spreaders on both masts, came on to flood *Wavebreaker*'s long deck in a brilliant pool of yellow brightness. Rickie, the gun now slung on his shoulder like a totem, was boasting to Sweetman of his cleverness in disabling the schooner, but Sweetman was only half listening; he was staring at Robin-Anne who, quivering and hunched, was still holding me tight. "Come here," Sweetman suddenly said to her.

"No." Robin-Anne gulped the word, then repeated it more strongly as though each repetition reinforced her desire to stay away from Sweetman's evil. "No, no, no, no!"

"Poor Robin-Anne." Sweetman smiled at her, then he took from his pouch the shining black flask from which he had dispensed cocaine to Rickie. Elegantly, unhurriedly, he stepped over the cockpit coaming and thus down to our level. He kept his mocking eyes on Robin-Anne as he unscrewed the cap of the flask, then he stooped and laid a trail of white powder along the cockpit floor, and he continued it across the cushioned thwart, then he climbed back to the deck and, after streaking a line of cocaine across the cockpit's teak coaming, he trickled the powder across the deck and all the way back to where Rickie was standing. Sweetman must have used a small fortune in cocaine to lay that beguiling trail.

Sweetman capped the flask, then took from his pouch a small white straw that he scornfully tossed at Robin-Anne's feet. "Come, sweet one," he crooned in his deep attractive voice, "come to me, Robin-Anne, you know you want it, you know you've been missing it, loving it, wanting it, and it's here! Free!"

I held her tight, clasping her to me, but I felt her twitch as she looked down at the white trail.

"Robin-Anne!" Ellen was beside us, and spoke warningly. "Don't!"

"You hold fast, girl!" Jackson Chatterton said.

"Dreams are made of this, Robin-Anne." Sweetman, like some evil Prospero, passed his hand across the trail of cocaine. "It's the best Bolivian rock, pure as ice and with a taste of paradise. And that is where we are going, my darling Robin-Anne, your brother and I are going to the land of heavenly plenty, where there is always abundant joy, and where you will never be alone again and where you will never be bored again and where you will never need worry again. But if you stay here, who will look after poor Robin-Anne when we're gone? So come, my darling, come."

"No!" I said.

"Don't listen to him!" Sweetman's handsome strong face smiled on Robin-Anne who had twisted her head to look into his dark eyes. "Come to me," Sweetman went on, "because

158

you're one of us, Robin-Anne. You're not a dull mud-person; you're better than that, you're finer than that, you're purer than that! People like us are not tied by convention, we're not hampered by caution. We have dreams, and we have daring, and we fly to the heavens while the mud-people disapprove of us and hate us because we are so very beautiful and they are so very, very dull."

"No, Robin-Anne," I said, but she shook my hand away from her shoulders and stared huge-eyed at the trail of powder; staring at it as though she had never seen such a substance before. She seemed mesmerised by Sweetman's crooning voice, and I moved forward to hold her again, but immediately the thug in front of me jerked his Kalashnikov round and raised it to his shoulder so that I was staring dead into its threat. I froze.

Robin-Anne had not even noticed the gun or its movement. She was transfixed by the powder, lusting after it and hating it, and I heard her give a very faint moan, then suddenly she dropped to her knees and seized the straw and grovelled down to sniff a three-inch section of Sweetman's long line.

He laughed.

Robin-Anne was on her knees, head on the deck, her bony backbone clearly visible through her thin shirt. She seemed to be crying. I stooped to pick her up, but the gunman fired, making Ellen cry aloud and Thessy gasp. The bullet whined overhead; a mere warning, but sufficient to make me straighten up, leaving Robin-Anne on her knees.

"So very simple," Sweetman said scornfully. The wind fluttered the end of his ponytail's black ribbon. If it had not been for his round metal badge with its anti-drug slogan 'Just Say No!', he could have been an adventurer from the days of swashbuckling swordsmen and Spanish treasures.

Robin-Anne took a huge breath, as though she was coming to life, and suddenly her head jerked up and I saw that, though her eyes were wet with tears, she was laughing. She seemed hugely relieved, as if some terrible ordeal was at last over. She stood and, her feet inadvertently scuffing the powder, she climbed to where her brother waited for her under the harsh yellow deck-lights.

"Robin?" Ellen called sadly.

"It's OK, Ellen" – Robin-Anne turned her sweet face towards us – "it's really OK now." She smiled at me. "It's OK, Nick, I promise. Everything's going to be OK!"

Sweetman gestured at the rest of the cocaine, his hand describing an arc of courteous invitation. "Would anyone else care to try my dream potion? Darling?" This was to Ellen.

Ellen said nothing.

"Why don't you come here," Sweetman tried to entice Ellen, "come to me."

"This is ridiculous," Ellen said in her most practical voice; the voice of a sensible liberal who knows that reason and good sense will always prevail, "you must know that you can't maltreat us."

Sweetman was delighted with the word. "Maltreat? My darling sweet treasure, I shall never maltreat you. I may make you moan with passion, and I may entice you to taste heaven in my arms, but maltreat you? Never."

"You jerk." Ellen's liberalism evaporated somewhat, then she screamed in fear because the shotgun had suddenly blasted below decks. I heard Miguel pump the action, then the gun fired again.

"The radios, I expect," Sweetman said helpfully. He took the Uzi from Rickie and, with a confident familiarity, cocked its bolt. I thought, for a horrid moment, that he was going to give the prepared gun back to Rickie, but instead he slung it on his shoulder and lit one of his pale blue cigarettes. "We shall lock you up," he said, as though he had finished having his fun with us, "and in the morning we shall leave you. Rickie, of course, will come with me. That way he won't have to endure the tedium of standing trial, will you, dear boy?"

It had clearly all been arranged. Rickie had suggested the cruise-cure because it would secure him the return of his passport and bring him to the Bahamas where his friend Sweetman would 'rescue' him from the courts. The only snag to Rickie's plans had been my insistence on going out to sea, where even Sweetman could not find us, but even that inconvenience had been mitigated by Sweetman's secret cache of cocaine. Rickie had never wanted to give up the drug, he had never wanted to face reality and he had certainly not wanted to face a judge; all he had ever wanted was to swamp himself in cocaine's euphoria and Sweetman was arranging it. Doubtless, in return, Rickie had promised Sweetman a portion of his inheritance – perhaps he had promised the whole legacy, for six million dollars could buy a lot of chemical heaven. And twelve million dollars – I looked at Robin-Anne who now smiled on us with a vacuous benignity – could buy an awful lot more.

"But before I dispose of you for the night –" Sweetman drew on his cigarette, "will someone tell me what that is?" He pointed to the hangman's noose that I had forgotten to take down and which now hung foolish and limp in the bright glare of the deck-lamps. "Well?" he insisted.

"I was expecting you," I said with a very feeble defiance.

"Oh, you are so very droll." Sweetman turned his thin handsome face to Rickie. "Reward him for being so very droll, Rickie."

Rickie laughed, then jumped down into the cockpit. He approached me very slowly, betraying his nervousness, but he must have felt confident that I would not fight back so long as the guns were pointed at me.

I saw the scorn on Sweetman's face and knew that he was inviting Rickie to make a fool of himself, but Sweetman's amusement did not mean that I would be allowed to make a fool of Rickie.

"Go on, dear boy!" Sweetman encouraged Rickie, "hit him."

Rickie hit me. He put all his strength into that first blow, but I rocked my head to meet the punch and it hardly hurt. He began flailing at me, fist after fist, but he had no skill and cocaine had sapped his young strength, and as it dawned on him that he was neither hurting nor harming me he became even more desperate to do both. He spat at my face, thumped

161

a feeble fist into my belly, and when I smiled at his impotence he launched a massive kick at my groin, but missed altogether and ignominiously thumped down to the cockpit floor.

He sat there, panting. The gunman facing us was grinning with gold-capped teeth as Sweetman shook his head with mock despair. "I shall have to show you how it's done, Rickie."

"No!" Ellen protested. "No!"

Robin-Anne giggled. "It's OK, Nick!" she called, and I did not believe that she knew where she was or what was happening. She looked like some wan relic of flower-power stranded twenty years out of her time on *Wavebreaker*'s deck.

Sweetman, the gun still dangling from his shoulder, jumped down into the cockpit where, with scant courtesy, he dragged Rickie away from my feet. Rickie, out of breath and with grazed knuckles, stayed on the cockpit's floor from which he took a pinch of cocaine that he inhaled as though it were snuff. I heard an air conditioner come on below decks, its current surge momentarily dimming the deck-lights, and I supposed that Miguel was going from cabin to cabin to see what he could find, explore or destroy.

Sweetman stood close to me, and raised the Uzi in his right hand so that its short barrel was pointing at my belly. He stared into my eyes, and smiled. I could see beads of sweat on his forehead and smell the tobacco on his breath. I thought he was going to drive the Uzi into my solar plexus, then the look in his eyes suggested he would pull the trigger and empty the magazine into my stomach. Rickie, who was still on the cockpit's decking, must have thought the same for he froze to watch the effect of the small bullets ripping into me, but instead, and with the force of a striking snake, Sweetman reached out his left hand and seized Ellen. He stepped back swiftly, dragging her off balance and putting her in front of himself like a shield.

I had instinctively moved to help her, but Rickie was in my way and Sweetman's Uzi still threatened me. Ellen was gasping with pain or shock, while Sweetman, pleased with his cleverness at thus surprising her, was smiling over her shoulder. He was keeping her body in front of him like a shield. She strained against his arm that was tight about her, but he merely backed another step away from me, and effortlessly took Ellen with him.

"You don't want to spend the night in a chain locker, do you, my sweet one?" Sweetman asked Ellen. "Wouldn't you be happier in my arms?"

"God damn you!" She struggled again, this time with enough force to make him use both hands to restrain her. He was forced to let the Uzi dangle from its sling as he put his right arm about her torso. He hugged her into stillness, then, with a malicious smile and to show how helpless she was, he ran his hand across her breasts.

"Do you want to have her, Rickie?" Sweetman asked. Rickie grinned, but said nothing. Sweetman undid the top button of Ellen's shirt. "If you're very good to me, my darling" – he slid his right hand inside the shirt and I saw Ellen's eyes widen either with fear or outrage – "then I'll keep you to myself, instead of sharing you with my friends. Poor Miguel won't like that, but he can be so vilely horrid with girls. He makes them bleed."

Ellen, enraged by the threat, moved with sudden and astonishing effect. She slammed her right elbow back into Sweetman's ribs, then raked her heel down his left shin and on to his instep. Sweetman's threat of rape had unleashed a demonic force in her. She was crying with frustration, but she was also hurting her captor. She rammed her elbow back again, and lunged forward to escape him, dragging him a step forward as he clung on to her. The gunman in front of us was moving to help Sweetman, while the one behind was laughing at the sight of the girl's frantic struggles. Sweetman was snarling and swearing at Ellen, and still trying to pull her backwards.

She screamed and wrenched at him once more, and this time she managed to unbalance and half turn Sweetman who shouted, not because she had hurt him, but because he had seen me moving forward. Jackson Chatterton was also moving, and he was doing the right thing by moving away from Ellen and me, thus dividing the enemy's aim. Chatterton was also taking care of Thessy by dragging the boy away from the guard who was standing behind us.

The gunman in front of us swung his Kalashnikov towards me, but Rickie blocked the man's aim by reaching up to obstruct me. I slammed a knee into Rickie's skull, driving him down, but his feeble lunge had tripped me and I fell on top of him, but not before I had succeeded in reaching out to snatch at the Uzi which still dangled from Sweetman's shoulder.

I caught the gun's webbing sling and tugged. Rickie screamed as I fell on him. Chatterton was shouting. A gun fired. God knows I had not wanted to start a fight against such overpowering odds, but we were committed now. Sweetman tried to snatch the gun back, then bellowed because Ellen had kicked him in the groin, and suddenly the Uzi was free and in my hands and all my old training took over. I was terrified, my mind was cringing away from the expected bullets, but at the same time I was rolling and turning, my right hand was groping for the trigger, and I was seeking targets. I saw the gunman to my right, the one who had been moving to help Sweetman but who had not dared fire for fear of hitting Sweetman or Rickie and I rolled up to my knees, pulled the trigger and saw the pale muzzle flames and felt the stuttering and astonishingly light recoil of the small gun.

The Uzi seemed to make very little noise, or perhaps its sound was drowned by Ellen's screaming. Robin-Anne was gasping and sobbing with terror. Another gun fired from behind me and it seemed as though a sheet of blood whipped up over my head like a great wing of scarlet horror. The gunman I had shot was down and sliding across the deck, his feet kicking with involuntary spasms. I twisted towards the gunshot I had heard. Rickie, frozen by terror, lay curled beside me.

"Nick!" Chatterton shouted. There was something frantic in his voice, but I could neither see nor help him.

"Nick! Run!" That was Ellen, who was free again, and though she must have been shouting at me it was Sweetman who obeyed her and who zig-zagged away from me to take refuge in the companionway. He held one hand clasped to his groin and his face was contorted with pain.

A Kalashnikov fired and I heard the bullet whiplash over my head. The second gunman had found cover at *Wavebreaker*'s stern and I suspected he was sheltering on the swimming platform and using the deck as a firing step. I guessed he could not see me because of the cockpit coaming, but he was probably just trying to keep my head down until Miguel or Sweetman finished me off.

I saw Ellen off to my left. She had run to the ship's rail. She looked briefly back, then jumped a split second before a burst of bullets splintered the rail where she had been standing.

"Nick! Hurry!" That was Jackson Chatterton again. He was free and running, a shadow somewhere at *Wavebreaker*'s bows beyond the bright deck-lights. I saw him jump overboard and heard the splash as he hit the sea.

I looked for Thessy, but could not see him, and I guessed he must have gone with Chatterton. Sweetman had disappeared below decks and I had not seen Miguel for minutes. Rickie was whimpering under me while Robin-Anne was cowering and screaming by the mainmast. The first gunman was taking a long time to die in the starboard scuppers; his blood was draining overboard and his feet were twitching. He was gasping and sometimes uttering small despairing cries, but it was his shoes that caught my attention for they were an incongruous pair of black leather brogues that looked as if they should have been worn with a pinstripe suit. The shoes were tapping the deck to mark the man's death spasms. He was a long time dying, and he was the first man I had ever shot, and I was feeling sick. I was trained to this, I had even been reckoned a weapons specialist in the Marines, but to the best of my knowledge I had never shot anyone.

I swallowed hard, then looked at the sight-holes in the Uzi's magazine to see I had about thirty rounds left. Enough for three seconds of fire, and enough, I hoped, to get me safely off the ship. "Thessy!" I shouted. Before abandoning *Wavebreaker* I wanted to make sure I was not abandoning Thessy.

The only answer was the tap tap of the dying man's shoes. I heard a noise in the companionway and fired a half-second burst in its direction. The noise stopped. The shoes still tapped. I wished the man would die. In films men died so easily, but this man was jerking in his long death throes. I heard a swimmer splashing beside the boat, then the distinctive sound of an assault rifle being cocked below decks. "Thessy!" I shouted again, but the only answer was a single shot fired by the gunman at the stern. The bullet whipped overhead, struck the anchor stock at the bows and ricocheted up into the dusk.

Rickie tried to jerk away from me, so I slammed an elbow down on his skull and told him to shut up unless he wanted half a magazine of bullets emptied down his gullet. He whimpered, but stayed still and silent. Moths flew thick about the bright yellow floodlamps that lit the deck so garishly and showed me that the cockpit floor was awash with cocaine and slick with blood. The blood was not mine, and I did not think it was Rickie's. I heard voices below decks and knew I had to break the stalemate. I pulled off one of Rickie's shoes and tossed it on deck, and sure enough the gunman aft took the bait and fired as he heard the sound.

I stood up, snarling, and saw the muzzle flashes sparking beside the life-raft container. The gunman was standing on the swimming platform so that only his head and shoulders were visible above the main deck. He was the man in black with the blue scarf. He saw me and began to swing the Kalashnikov towards me, but I was already firing, using my left hand to check the Uzi's swing, and I forgot my nausea as I watched the Uzi's bullets snatch across his chest to colour his blue scarf red, then my bullets splintered his gritted teeth, and suddenly the gunman was gone, hurled backwards, and all that I could see of him was a lightning pulse of blood that fountained high in the night sky to splatter *Wavebreaker*'s ensign with a new and redder dye, then I heard the stateroom skylight shatter behind me and I swivelled to see Miguel's shotgun thrusting up from the broken panes and I squeezed the Uzi's trigger one last time, but only to hear the bolt clatter on an empty chamber.

166

I heard Sweetman shout to give himself courage, and I suspected he was charging up the companionway with the M16 and so, abandoning valour for safety, I ran as fast as I could for the rail, and the shotgun crashed at me and I felt the lash and sting of pellets hitting my arm and back, but then I was at the gunwale and I half fell and half folded myself over the varnished rail and let myself and the empty gun drop into the astonishingly warm water.

In which, suddenly and blessedly, I found silence.

Jackson Chatterton's hand seized me and dragged me hard into the shelter of *Wavebreaker*'s steel hull. Ellen was already there. We were safe enough for the moment because neither Miguel nor Sweetman, leaning over *Wavebreaker*'s rail, could fire past the hull's convexity, but nor could we swim away from the hull for, within seconds, we would become the easiest of targets. Yet I knew we had to swim away from the schooner for surely Miguel or Sweetman would soon come hunting us in *Dream Baby*.

"Where's Thessy?" I asked.

Ellen was treading water beside me, and Chatterton, who had pulled me to safety, was staring up into the glare cast by the deck-lights.

"Where's Thessy?" I insisted.

"He was with me," Chatterton replied irritably, as though I annoyed him with an irrelevant question. "We've got to get out of here! Shit!" A burst of automatic rifle fire smacked water not twelve inches from Chatterton's face. The sound of the gun was obscenely loud. I heard the magazine being ejected and a new one slapping into place, then the gun fired again and I saw a stream of cartridges tumbling towards us through the yellow light, and I knew that whoever fired the weapon must be holding it far out from the ship's side and angling its barrel back in, thus making the bullets come perilously close to us.

"Go forward!" I told Ellen and Chatterton. "Take a big breath, then dive for one of the anchor chains, understand? Use the chain to pull yourselves away from the ship. Get well out into the dark before you break the surface and you should be safe."

The automatic weapon fired again, spraying bullets at the sea in an indiscriminate pattern. Some struck the hull just above our heads and whined away to leave scars in the paint. The shotgun crashed as well, forming an instant and miniature maelstrom above which I could see the cartridge's faint smoke residue drifting away in the bright cast of *Wavebreaker*'s deck-lights.

"You're coming as well?" Ellen wanted my reassurance.

"I want to look for Thessy."

"I told you! He's all right!" Chatterton spoke too loud and the rifle's bullets swerved towards us. We all ducked under and I saw, astonishingly, the stitch of air bubbles where each bullet drove into the water to be immediately cushioned into impotence. The water had been turned yellow by the flood-lamps.

We swam forward, keeping close to the ship's side, and once under the steep overhang of the bows we took turns to dive for the nearest anchor rode. Sweetman and Miguel seemed to have lost track of us, for they kept firing at the water amidships, and the noise of their guns covered the smaller sounds we made as we pushed hard away from *Wavebreaker*'s side.

I dived last, kicking away from the ship and swimming deep so that the anchor chain was a silhouetted black streak against the shimmering yellow mirror-bright surface of the water. I panicked that I would miss the chain and that my head would break surface close to where the gunman stood on *Wavebreaker*'s deck, but then I clasped one of the slippery links and desperately hauled myself hand over hand away from *Wavebreaker* until my lungs were bursting, and only then did I let go of the chain and swim up to break the lagoon's black surface. I gasped for breath and flinched against the bullets I expected, but then discovered that I had sur-faced well beyond the pool of light thrown by the schooner's deck-lamps, and that our enemies were still firing down by the ship's side. I turned towards the closest shore and decided not to think about sharks. I saw Ellen's gleaming head close by, and Chatterton's further inshore.

The lights on *Wavebreaker* were suddenly doused. Robin-Anne had begun screaming in a sustained shriek of terror that was abruptly cut short as though someone had slapped her face. I saw that the daylight had not entirely faded; and that it had only been the brightness of the deck-lights that had made it seem as though night had fallen.

We swam for the shore. Our heads must already have melded with the encroaching blackness of the dusk, for we were not seen. The Kalashnikov and the sharper-toned M16 fired a few random bursts and their bullets flicked wildly and uselessly across the lagoon, but none came close to us. It was only when the three of us crawled up on land and blundered noisily into the dark bushes that the bullets became threatening.

Yet still none of us was hit, and after full dark the shooting became much wilder and more sporadic. *Wavebreaker*'s decklights came on again, doubtless as a precaution against our trying to recapture the ship, while *Dream Baby*, hitherto moored on the far side of *Wavebreaker*, briefly cruised the lagoon with its searchlight raking the bushes and palms, but whoever was on board did not see us, nor did they try and come ashore, and I realised that Sweetman and Miguel must be scared half to death of us. They, after all, had gone into the fight with an arsenal of weapons, while we had none, yet we had killed both their gunmen and then got clean away; and, so far as they knew, I still had the sub-machine-gun, and their imaginations must have been worried that I still had a bullet or two left in its magazine. In fact the empty Uzi lay on the lagoon bed beneath *Wavebreaker*, but our enemies would not know that we were unarmed. We were also blessedly uninjured except for the shotgun pellets in my back and arm, and the myriad of bites from the mosquitoes that began to plague us as soon as we crawled up on to the beach.

We crossed the tail of Sea Rat Cay, pushing through spiny dark bushes until we reached a small beach on the ocean side of the island where a reassuring lump of limestone lay between us and the weapons still on board *Wavebreaker*. We crouched in the boulder's comforting protection, catching our breath and listening to the surf's monotonous grumble. A palm arched above us like a great sheltering arm, and it was there, beneath that tree and staring at the restless and shining sea, that I learned how grievous our injuries truly were; far more grievous than a few mosquito bites or shotgun pellets.

For Thessy was dead.

Ellen half gasped and half screamed when she heard the news. She was suddenly in shock; crying and shivering and I held her very tight while Jackson Chatterton told us what had happened.

Thessy had died in the very first seconds of the fight. He had died quickly, with a Kalashnikov bullet in his skull. I closed my eyes, knowing that it must have been the blood of Thessy's dying that had sheeted over me like a great red wing in the dusk.

Jackson Chatterton had tried to save him. He had dragged Thessy away from the threat of the gunman at the back of the boat, running forward to join Robin-Anne in the belief that the gunman would not open fire for fear of hitting her, but the gunman had fired all the same, and his bullets had hit Thessy. Chatterton, wiser in the ways of man's brutality, had twisted down to the scant cover of the scuppers, and had pulled Thessy down with him, but by then the boy was already dead.

"Are you sure?" I asked.

"God, man, he was dead. He got two in the spine and one here." Chatterton spread a huge hand on his own skull to demonstrate the size of Thessy's wound. Ellen did not see the gesture. She was sobbing, while I, for all my horror and grief, was obstinately dry-eyed. Thessy had been my friend, and still I could not weep. "He felt nothing," Chatterton said bleakly, and at least we could be grateful for that.

Chatterton blamed himself for Thessy's death, saying he should have thrown the boy overboard in the very first second of the violence, but Ellen, between sobs, said that it was her responsibility because she had begun the fight, but I told them that if it was anyone's fault, it was mine, for I had encouraged Ellen's fight by joining in, and it had been I who had taken the gun from Sweetman and escalated the horror. "I killed the bastard who killed Thessy," I said softly, as if that was some consolation, but there could be no solace for such a death. Thessy had been so very innocent, and his passing had torn a great hole in my universe; a great damned stupid Godless waste of a hole.

171

So I sat there, unable to shed a tear, yet unable to imagine Thessy dead. I kept thinking that every rustle of leaves or clatter of palm fronds was the sound of his coming to join us, and so I kept looking round, expecting to see his face or hear his anxious voice, but the movements were just the night shadows being wind-stirred among the leaves and the sounds were only the crash of the sea falling on the reefs and the sigh of the warm uncaring wind.

I told myself that if I had fired the gun quicker, or moved faster, then Thessy would still be alive. And why Thessy, of all of us? Thessy, so earnest and so good, so unworthy of this death, and I closed my eyes and prayed that there truly was a heaven where an honest boy from Straker's Cay would find eternal happiness.

And I prayed that there was a hell, too, a real hell, worse even than the cocaine addict's anhedonia; a place of demons for Sweetman and his kind.

"He hadn't even reached the Gospels," I said suddenly, and somehow the thought of Thessy's serious face frowning over his ancient Bible broke the dam of my tears and I began to sob like a child. I was also shaking with the delayed terror of the fight, and Ellen reached for my hand and pulled my head down to her shoulder.

Above us were a million stars, stretching for all eternity, their light coming from the time before history and perhaps, I told myself, beneath those stars, Thessy's soul was arrowing towards the happiness his faith had promised him. There could be no such happiness for us. We snatched a few moments' sleep, but not much, for the guns on *Wavebreaker* fired intermittently throughout the darkness, and we were galled, not just by the threat of Sweetman and his crew, but by our responsibility for Thessy's death. In the rare minutes of sleep I dreamed of guns, of snatching up the sub-machine gun and finding it empty in the face of the Kalashnikovs, and I woke shaking and sweating and with Ellen scratching and cursing at the sand flies.

I dozed again just before dawn, but was startled into full

wakefulness by the cacophonous din of *Wavebreaker*'s sound system. Rickie was playing one of his 'English music' tapes at full blast and Sea Rat Cay's birds screamed in protest from the trees. Nature's storm had passed, leaving the world calm. Beyond the reefs the sea was a gun-metal grey, hammered flat and waiting for the sun's annealing light.

"I'm going to kill them," I greeted the new day.

"Amen," Jackson Chatterton growled, "amen."

And the sun came up on an empty sea.

Wavebreaker looked very pretty that morning as she lay in the encircling arms of Sea Rat Cay. The three of us crept across the island to keep a watch on our enemies, and we lay hidden under the palms and stared at the glory of a tropical lagoon in which the schooner's long white hull and slender masts were reflected as cleanly as though the water was a sheet of polished glass.

Rickie came on deck, carrying the Kalashnikov. He unfolded its stock and began firing randomly, sending bullet after bullet into the palm trees. He fired a whole magazine at a lumbering pelican, and missed. Robin-Anne brought him a mug of tea or coffee and flinched away from the gun's noise before taking her own mug to the bows where she sat looking hunched and miserable. Rickie obsessively fired on, exhausting magazine after magazine. The noise was obscene. "I hate guns," Ellen said beside me, "I do so hate guns."

An hour after dawn Miguel fired up *Dream Baby*'s motors. The powerboat was still tethered to the schooner. The blue smoke of her twin exhausts drifted across the water. It was evident that they were leaving, for Rickie and Sweetman dragged plunder from *Wavebreaker* and lowered it to Miguel on *Dream Baby*. Some of what they stole was practical, like the outboard motor from the skiff, but mostly they just collected whatever glittered or took their fancy; the television, lamps, pictures, and even the rugs from the stateroom. Robin-Anne ignored them.

Rickie climbed down on to the powerboat's deck as Sweetman dragged the body of the gunman across to *Wavebreaker*'s gunwale. The body was that of the man whose shoes had beaten a dying tattoo in the scuppers, and now his corpse was unceremoniously tipped down into *Dream Baby*. Rickie leaped away from the dead man, but I saw Miguel apparently push the corpse into a locker. It seemed they were taking their own dead away, but I saw nothing of Thessy's corpse and I felt again the idiot, wonderful, helpless hope that he might yet be alive.

Sweetman took the Kalashnikov from Rickie, then went and stirred Robin-Anne by nudging the small of her back with the gun's flash-suppressor. She looked round and he pointed her towards the waiting *Dream Baby*, clearly indicating that it was time for her to leave. For an instant I hoped Robin-Anne would show some reluctance, and that she might even call my name to let us know that she left *Wavebreaker* against her will, but she jumped to her feet and strolled back down the deck with Sweetman, and she even held the Kalashnikov for a moment while he lowered the last of McIllvanney's scuba sets over *Wavebreaker*'s gunwale and on to *Dream Baby*'s afterdeck. Robin-Anne returned Sweetman the gun, then climbed gingerly down into the sports-fisherman. I saw Miguel turn and speak to her, then heard her laughter come clean and clear across the water. Overnight, it seemed, Robin-Anne's resolve to say no had been melted in the fierce heat of cocaine's euphoria.

Sweetman alone stayed on board *Wavebreaker*. He went below decks and stayed out of sight for about five minutes, then he reappeared and swung his long legs over the rail. He lit a cigarette, then unslung the Kalashnikov and began firing burst after burst into the island's shoreline.

"Jesus!" Jackson Chatterton swore. This firing was far more purposeful and far more dangerous than Rickie's earlier random shooting. Sweetman was methodically raking the shadowed edge of the beach, guessing that we would be hidden somewhere just above the high water line, and his bullets ripped like saws through the leaves as, burst by burst, the rounds came nearer to us. I heard Sweetman change the magazine, then I put my arm over Ellen's shoulder and held her down low as the next burst cracked wickedly above our heads. Scraps of brittle palm rained down on us. Bullets smacked and whined off a limestone outcrop while a thousand birds were screeching their objection to the sky.

The firing suddenly stopped. I hardly dared lift my head for fear Sweetman would see the movement, but then I heard *Dream Baby*'s engines thud into gear and I looked up to see the gaudily camouflaged powerboat accelerating away from *Wavebreaker*.

Which was sinking.

For a second or two I thought I must be dreaming, then I realised Sweetman must have opened *Wavebreaker*'s seacocks while he was below decks. The schooner was delicately heeling towards us, and I could see she was already settling at the stern, and I knew that within a very few minutes she would lurch down to the lagoon's sandy bed. The big sea-water inlets that fed the engine's cooling pipes must have been wrenched away and the water would be gulping up into the bilges and over the engine-room gratings.

"Oh, the bastards," I breathed.

Dream Baby, the 666 of the Anti-Christ dark on her bows, slowly circled the lagoon; Miguel was at her wheel, while Sweetman had climbed to her flybridge from where he was peering into the green shadows on shore. Chatterton wriggled backwards as I forced Ellen's head down again. I think we all stopped breathing. I heard the throb of the powerboat's motors come very close to us, and I waited for the ripsaw sound of the assault rifle's automatic fire, but we must have been too well hidden for there were no shots. Instead, Miguel took the boat very slowly and very gingerly towards the rocky beach sixty yards to our left. I was certain that Sweetman planned to come ashore, and I was wondering how the three of us were to escape his execution when I saw that Sweetman had exchanged the Kalashnikov for a boathook and, standing now at *Dream Baby*'s bows, he was fishing in the water for the body of the second gunman; the one I had blasted off the swimming platform.

It took all Miguel and Sweetman's strength to haul the body on board. Rickie refused to help, and Robin-Anne must have stayed below in *Dream Baby*'s cabin. I still half expected Sweetman to land and try to hunt us down, but he must have feared what could happen to him in the dark tangle of steamy vegetation that covered Sea Rat Cay for, once the second corpse was securely aboard, Sweetman ordered Miguel to reverse *Dream Baby* away from the shore. Jackson Chatterton breathed a sigh, while Ellen was crying softly with relief at our escape.

Miguel steered *Dream Baby* under the schooner's canting stern and Sweetman, a cigarette in his mouth, raised the rifle and fired a long burst into the belly of the power skiff that was still hanging from its davits, then he raised the barrel and fired another derisive burst to riddle the red ensign with bullet holes.

"The bastard," I said.

"Don't be so ridiculous," Ellen said, "it's only a flag."

Then, with one last derisive burst of bullets that were sprayed indiscriminately into the trees, *Dream Baby*'s engines were given full power and she seemed to stand on her stern as she accelerated into the lagoon's narrow entrance. The motors screamed as her stern drives churned the sea to spray, then she was gone.

Wavebreaker creaked as she settled further over, while the waves of *Dream Baby*'s wash foamed and broke in the lagoon entrance. I stood and walked to the water's edge.

"Mind those turkeys don't come back, Nick," Chatterton sensibly warned me. If *Dream Baby* had suddenly reappeared at the lagoon entrance then I would have made an easy target, but I could hear the receding beat of the boat's engines going further and further away from Sea Rat Cay. I stood at the water's edge and watched *Wavebreaker* sink.

She took twenty minutes, but then, with one last graceful fall, her masts canted over until they were pointing towards the tops of the island's tallest palm trees. A wave of blue water pulsed away from the hull to break on the lagoon's shore.

Thessy and I had rerigged her well. Even when she finally toppled, her topmasts did not break. She settled on her starboard flank, her port side just out of the water and her long masts reaching out across the lagoon. I waited till I was sure she had settled firm, then I swam out to her, hauling myself up her almost vertical deck to perch on her rail that was just four feet above the lagoon's rippled surface. I sat there, feeling the misery of a man who has lost a boat. I had never been very fond of *Wavebreaker*, but she had still been mine to command, and now she was a sad sunken wreck.

Ellen and Chatterton followed me. "We can't refloat her," I greeted them. Doubtless *Wavebreaker* would be salvaged, for she was hardly damaged, but we had none of the equipment that was needed to rescue her. "So we'll have to call for help."

Ellen gingerly climbed up to sit beside me. She looked nervously around, and I guessed she was frightened of seeing Thessy's body, but there was no sign of it. There was a big streak of blood on the patch of exposed deck beneath us, but no corpses.

"What do we do?" Ellen asked dully.

"First we find some fresh water and food, then we get the hell out of here." I was trying to sound optimistic, but Chatterton and Ellen seemed sunk in gloom. I left them, slipping off the rail and swimming down the deck, past the cockpit, then down to the huge lockers which opened on to the swim platform. Beneath me, in the astonishingly clear water, I could see a Kalashnikov lying on the sand. Near the gun were the piles of cut halliard wires that Rickie had dumped overboard. A ray flapped its wings to swim across the heap of wires as I opened the portside locker where Rickie's scuba equipment had all been stored. All three sets had been stolen, but Sweetman had left the old face masks that Thessy and I had sometimes used when we dived to check that our anchors had bitten into uncertain ground. I pulled one of the masks free and fitted it over my eyes.

I swam back to the sunken companionway above which I took a deep breath, then kicked my way down to the galley. It was dark as Hades inside the sunken boat and I lost my bearings and began to panic. I flailed to find an exit, hurt my arm on the stove's edge, then saw a dim green light filtering from the companionway stairs. My chest was bursting, but I kicked my way to the stairs and shot back to the surface where I gasped for breath and found myself shaking.

Ellen had donned the other mask. She took a breath, jack-knifed, and dived elegantly down. I followed more clumsily, this time pushing back the hatchway's sliding coaming to allow more light into the galley area. I sank down to join Ellen and saw that she was already opening the supply lockers. Air bubbles dribbled from her mouth to join the mess of cornflakes and flour that floated around her. She turned with two bottles of Perrier, and I thrust myself back out of the way so as not to obstruct her.

The three of us sat on the rail and breakfasted on Perrier. We were thirsty as hell. Afterwards I swam to the stern and pulled the lanyard on the life-raft's canister, which opened like a fibreglass clamshell to expose the expanding orange-coloured raft which began to unfold as its gas canisters automatically discharged into the inflatable tubes. The raft had a canopy, so would offer us shelter from the sun, and it also had some iron rations and two flasks of bitter-tasting water. Best of all, though, it had an Epirb.

Sweetman and Rickie had forgotten the Epirb, or perhaps neither had known that it existed. "What the hell is an Epirb?" Jackson Chatterton asked as I towed the raft towards the exposed patch of *Wavebreaker*'s hull.

"An emergency position indicating radio beacon." I offered him the full name, then unfolded the device's radio aerial and simply tossed the buoy into the water. It floated there, already transmitting its distress signal to any passing satellite or air-craft. "Within about five minutes," I told Chatterton, "the US Coastguard in Nassau will know we're here, and they may think we set the beacon off by mistake, but they'll still send someone to take a look."

178

Two hours later, as we still waited for rescue, Ellen suddenly remembered her notebooks. "I've got to have them," she insisted.

I knew she kept her precious writer's notes in the stern-cabin that she had shared with Robin-Anne, but I did not want her to risk her life by swimming back to that cabin where she could so easily be trapped underwater. I tried to dissuade her by saying that the notebooks would surely be soaked and illegible by now.

"I'm not a complete idiot," she said with a touch of her old asperity. "At sea I keep the notebooks in a waterproof plastic case." Even so, she saw the danger of trying to swim from the companionway back to the stern-cabin, so instead suggested that we break the big stern windows.

"It'll take something very heavy to smash them," I said dubiously, then I remembered the heavy bolt-cutters that I had found on deck just twenty-four hours before, and which I had put back in one of the lockers built into the cockpit coaming. I donned the face mask again, dropped down deep into the water, then tugged back the locker's heavy metal lid.

And Thessy floated out.

I gagged, swallowed water, retched, then kicked desperately to the surface where I choked and gasped on the warm air. Beneath me, with an obscene sluggishness, Thessy's body bumped over the locker's sill and floated slowly upwards. The sea-water had washed the huge hole in his skull clean and bloodless. I swam frantically clear, as though the corpse was somehow threatening.

Ellen screamed.

Overhead, suddenly clattering and driving the sea into a frenzy, was a US Coastguard helicopter. The Epirb had done its magic, but too late for justice, for *Dream Baby* had long vanished among far islands.

So we rescued Thessy's body, found Ellen's notebooks, salvaged the bullet-ridden ensign, and flew away.

Thessy was buried on Straker's Cay, close to the small church where he had worshipped all his short life and the small seapool in which he had been baptised. The little church had a red-painted corrugated tin roof and a white wooden belfry and blue-painted walls in which huge unglazed windows were covered with palm-leaf blinds. Lizards clung to the walls and to the tar-soaked beams that held up the roof. The pews were old park benches made of wooden slats slotted into cast-iron frames, and every seat was taken and still more islanders crowded in to line the walls and fill the aisle. Ellen and I were the only white faces, and there was no face with dry eyes. We sang till we were hoarse, and then Bonefish wanted to sing some more, and so the congregation rocked back and forth as though the very strength of our voices and the rhythm of our clapping could propel Thessy to his better place beyond the river where one day we would all gather to be dressed in glowing silks and to live for ever in the place where there would be no more crying and no more sin and no more grief and no more death, but only sweet joy eternal.

Flowers were piled by Thessy's coffin, and more were heaped on the Mercy Seat above which the preacher stood to promise us the Resurrection, and the congregation shouted Hallelujah, before – still singing, and with the feet of the islanders stamping dust from the path that led from the church to the graveyard – we carried Thessy's coffin to the sandy cemetery with its painted wooden crosses and cheap jars of wilted flowers and its herd of goats and its view of the long, long sea beating eternally from the east; the sea that Thessy had loved and sailed so well. Jackson Chatterton helped carry the flowers, while Bonefish insisted that I helped carry his son's coffin. Bonefish still called me 'sir', and his son's coffin weighed so very little. Thessy's head was resting on the defaced and bullet-torn ensign that I had rescued from *Wavebreaker*. It was not the flag of the Bahamas, but it was the flag that Thessy had sailed under, and he had been proud of it.

Bonefish spoke by the grave. We would meet Thessalonians again, he promised, in that blessed land above, and we should not mourn for his son, for he had been translated into glory, gone to be with Jesus, and all the voices called Hallelujah – or rather all the voices except for that of Denise Harriman, George Crowninshield's black aide from Washington, who had arrived late to represent the senator at the funeral, but who now looked desperately embarrassed by the ritual as though the primitive faith that now entrusted Thessy's soul to God was an affront to her Washington sophistication.

We lowered the box into the scrabbling dry soil, and we threw handfuls of sand that rattled on its lid, and then the minister read the twenty-third psalm as the flowers were heaped at the foot of the slowly filling grave. The senator had sent a wreath of white lilies and a handwritten note that expressed his deepest regret that he could not be present, but he promised Bonefish that he would visit Straker's Cay soon, and he would try to make some sense, if any could be made, of Thessy's death.

Bonefish and Sarah, Thessy's mother, were on their knees beside the grave, weeping and rocking, and I knelt beside Bonefish and tried to say how sorry I was, but I could not speak because my throat was hoarse and lumpish. The sun beat on my bowed shoulders as Bonefish put his arm across my back and said how grateful he was that I had been a friend to Thessy, and how I had been a hero to Thessy, and all I could think of was that I had let Thessy die and I began to cry. I could hear the sea crashing and scraping at the nearby beach, and I was glad that Thessy would have that noise in his ears for all eternity, or at least till the graves were opened and the dead flew up to meet their Lord.

We piled the last of the flowers on the new dry mound of sandy soil. John Maggovertski, who hardly knew Thessy, had sent a wreath, but nothing had come from Matthew McIllvanney, and, more surprisingly, nothing from the owners of Cutwater Charters. McIllvanney had cursed me when I told him of the boat's loss, then he had gone to fight his battles with the insurers. I had been told that *Wavebreaker* was being salvaged and she would probably soon be back at her dockside, but I would not sail on her again, and neither would Ellen for

McIllvanney had fired her. He did not actually have the power to fire me, but he hardly needed to, for I had lost any chance of a job when *Wavebreaker* sank. Instead of flowers, McIllvanney had sent a message demanding that I visit his office to sign the necessary forms for the loss adjuster and salvage company. I had thrown the message away.

When the funeral was over and the mourners were making their slow way back to Bonefish's house where the singing would go on all day, Ellen gently steered me in the opposite direction. "I just want to talk with you," she said. I had not seen Ellen since the morning we had been rescued from *Wavebreaker*, after which I had become entangled with the police. As soon as the police had reluctantly released me, I had come straight to see Bonefish, and thus Ellen and I had not seen each other until today when she and Jackson Chatterton had arrived on the morning ferry. When she had first disembarked I had not recognised her for she was wearing a dress. The dress was a very dark wine-red colour with a long full skirt and it made her look oddly unfamiliar and wondrously beautiful.

If Ellen wanted to talk to me in private she was to be disappointed. Jackson Chatterton, suspecting we wanted to be alone, had the tact to walk away, but Ellen and I had hardly been ten seconds together before we were waylaid by Denise Harriman. The senator's aide had been joined by a tall, short-haired man who had not been in the church, and whom I had not spotted at the graveside. He was in his early middle-age and had a tanned hatchet face with gunfighter eyes. "This is Warren Smedley," Denise Harriman introduced us, "Mr Smedley is an agent of the Drug Enforcement Administration in Washington DC."

Smedley nodded, but did not offer to shake hands. There was something very sharklike in the economy of his movements and in his silence. He was wearing a dark blue suit, a starched white shirt and a sober grey tie.

"The senator asked Mr Smedley to talk with you," Denise Harriman explained the agent's presence, then paused as though to let Smedley speak, but the DEA agent just stared out across the long shoaling lines of foam that ran white and ragged from north to east. We had all stopped at the shoreline and were standing in awkward proximity. Ellen, her eyes red from too much crying, took my hand and pulled me a pace backwards.

"Did you know that Robin-Anne telephoned her father's office?" Denise Harriman suddenly asked me, as though to break the embarrassing silence.

"No," I said. "Did she want him to rescue her?"

"The very opposite. She called to say that she and her brother are entirely safe and happy, but are not coming home." Denise Harriman took a pair of sunglasses from her handbag. "She refused to tell us where they were hiding. They're very stupid children."

"It was all planned," I said tiredly.

"We imagine so, yes." Denise Harriman did not sound very interested, or perhaps she was just nervous of the silent and glowering Warren Smedley who was listening to our conversation but contributing nothing towards it.

"I think Rickie only suggested the cruise-cure so he could get his passport back and join his drug friends," I said. "He fooled us all, didn't he?"

"Especially the senator," Denise Harriman said very tartly, as though any inconvenience that the rest of us might have experienced as a result of Rickie's machinations were as nothing compared to the senator's sufferings. "Senator Crowninshield personally put up the half-million dollars cash for his son's bail."

Ellen made a scornful noise, and I suspected she was about to compare the level of bail with the millions of dollars that the senator spent on his own election campaigns. "Damn Rickie," I blurted out before Ellen could say anything. I was thinking of Bonefish's loss, which was so much greater than any the senator had suffered.

Smedley turned on me suddenly, as though my words had alarmed or intrigued him. "Are you apprised of Rickie

Crowninshield's present whereabouts?" he asked in a very nasal but oddly toneless voice.

"Of course I'm bloody not." I was annoyed with Smedley for being so rude to us, and I had no intention of making his life easy or my answers to him pleasant.

"At this time we are searching for the senator's children" – Smedley was quite unmoved by my anger – "and our best indications of their whereabouts will surely come from tracing Jesse Sweetman. What can you tell me about Sweetman?"

I said I merely knew Sweetman was an American, a southerner, and that Rickie had claimed him as his drug dealer.

"He's a very fashionable dresser." Ellen added the detail sarcastically, but Warren Smedley took out a notebook and solemnly wrote down the sartorial information before continuing with his questions. Had either of us heard the dead gunmen's names mentioned on board *Wavebreaker*?

No.

And Miguel. Could we add to the description we had given of Miguel to the Bahamian Police?

No.

And *Dream Baby*?

"You can't miss *Dream Baby*," I said bitterly. "It must be the most over-painted boat in the islands!"

Smedley dutifully wrote the words 'over-painted' in his notebook, but I sensed that the DEA agent was merely going through the motions and did not really expect to learn anything new or useful from us. "Do you have anything to add to the statement you made to the Bahamian Police, Mr Breakspear?" He asked. "Or you, Dr Skandinsky?"

"No," Ellen and I answered at the same time. Like me, Ellen had made a very full statement to the police, and we had both tried to identify the men who had boarded *Wavebreaker* by searching through huge piles of photographs, but neither of us, nor Jackson Chatterton, had recognised Miguel or the two gunmen I had shot. The police had shown most interest in my story, and for two days they had kept me locked up in 'protective custody'. I had confidently believed that the baleful

Deacon Billingsley was behind my incarceration and I had spent the whole two days expecting to be charged with murder when, quite suddenly, the entire affair had evaporated. No one was to be charged with any killing; indeed the police had dismissed the two dead gunmen as my fantasy for, they said, no bodies had been found and no complaints had been received. Thessy's murder, which was indisputably real, was written off as being caused 'by a person or persons unknown'.

It was suddenly as if nothing untoward had ever happened in the lagoon of Sea Rat Cay. Nor had any newspaper taken any interest. No journalist had known that the famous Senator Crowninshield's children were aboard the schooner, so the senator had been spared that embarrassment. No American citizens had died so no mainland newspaper was curious about the boat's sinking, and the island papers could not get exercised over the death of one teenager from Straker's Cay. Thessy was not the first innocent islander to be murdered by drug-runners, nor would he be the last, and the only newspaper which had even mentioned his death had shown no indignation at his murder.

The whole matter had thus magically subsided. I had been released from jail and given back my damp passport which had been among the items already rescued from the stranded *Wavebreaker*, and now it was evident that the senator, or at least his aide, was welcoming that utter lack of interest. "We would appreciate it if the two of you would exercise some reticence about these events?" Denise Harriman said to Ellen and me. "We've been most fortunate in the lack of media interest so far, and we would prefer it if none was provoked until the senator can satisfactorily resolve the situation. I hope you understand me?"

"Entirely," I said bitterly. "You want us to shut up."

"Exactly so." Denise Harriman rewarded me with a cold smile.

"Tell me," I said, "was it pressure from the senator that had me released from custody?" It suddenly made sense that George Crowninshield would try to avoid any publicity about

185

his children's escapades. The events at Sea Rat Cay could have denied him the presidency, and I wondered just how he planned to recover from their effect for, though there had been no publicity yet, there would surely be a flurry of press interest when Rickie Crowninshield did not turn up for his court appearance.

Denise Harriman was not interested in discussing it with me. Instead she looked at her watch, then made some pious and predictable remarks about the day's sad duty. I began to repeat my question about whether the senator had been responsible for hushing up the whole business, but Ellen nudged me into silence, implying that I wasted my breath because the answer was obvious.

Denise Harriman stepped away, and I thought our business was done, but Warren Smedley still had a surprise for us. "At this time" – he was clearly one of those Americans who thought that using the word 'now' betrayed a lack of education – "we have a duty to alert you against the possibilities of reprisal activities."

I gaped at him. Ellen frowned. "I'm sorry?" she asked.

"It is probable that the men who accompanied Jesse Sweetman will wish to exact a revenge for the deaths of their companions. The drug-trafficking business is mostly conducted by families who take a particular pride in avenging the deaths of any family members. The best advice of the DEA at this time is that you both leave the islands forthwith. I trust I make myself clear?"

"You mean they'll try and kill us?" I asked, not because I had failed to understand Smedley's warning, but because it seemed so fantastic.

"Precisely that, Mr Breakspear. And not only will they be seeking revenge, but you are the only witnesses who can testify against them in a murder trial." Smedley gestured towards Thessy's grave.

I felt no particular fear because Smedley's warning seemed merely dutiful; a warning that the Drug Enforcement Administration would give to anyone who happened to find

186

themselves on the outskirts of the drug trade's savagery. My own feeling was that Sweetman and Rickie, having got what they wanted, would not provoke further trouble by another display of violence. "I'll keep a watchful eye open," I said lightly.

"You'd do better to leave the islands," Smedley said, but without any real force, then he stepped back and turned away without another word. Denise Harriman nodded icily at us, then fell into step beside the DEA agent. The two suited each other; they were as spare and cold as two scalpels lying on a surgeon's tray.

"God damn them!" Ellen glared after the retreating couple. "Do you get the feeling that Thessy died for nothing?" There could be no satisfactory answer and, in hopeless resignation, Ellen put her hands on my shoulders and rested her head against my chest. I could smell the scent of shampoo in her hair. "Oh, God," she suddenly said, "I never knew there were so many hymns," then she began to cry. I held her and tried to soothe her. At the far side of the graveyard, uncomfortable in a black suit, Jackson Chatterton had been trying to stop the goats from eating the flowers on Thessy's grave, but was now being questioned by Warren Smedley.

"Walk with me." Ellen sniffed back her tears, took my hand and led me along the shore where the small lagoon waves broke amidst a rubble of dead coral and broken limestone. "Do you think they'll really try to take revenge on us?" she asked, not with any fear in her voice, but rather with a note of almost academic curiosity.

I shrugged. "I suppose it's possible."

"So what will you do?"

"I won't run away. I've got a boat to mend." I had never finished the fortnight's shakedown cruise, so the senator had not needed to assume responsibility for *Masquerade* which was still propped up in Bonefish's yard.

Ellen and I walked on in silence until we reached the deep rock pool where Thessy had been baptised. Two lizards stared at us from the pool's stony margin, then darted away as we came too close. We stopped by the pool and I stared out to sea where the white bridge stack of a bulk carrier showed just above the horizon. "You should leave the islands," I said.

Ellen smiled. "Male chauvinist Nick. I'll never change you, will I? You'll stay, but I should run away."

"I'm not the one with intellectual reservations against the use of violence," I said, "but you are."

"But evidently not when I was threatened with rape." She spoke grimly, then let go of my hand to crouch beside the baptistry pool into which she idly flicked small scraps of broken shell that sideslipped through the clear water to the sandy bottom. "I'm probably leaving Freeport anyway," she said.

"You are?" I could not hide the note of disappointment in my voice. I did not want to believe that the loss of *Wavebreaker* would mean the end of our friendship. I had already lost Thessy, and now Ellen?

"The Project wants someone to do some field research on Great Inagua" – she spoke of the Literacy Project – "and I'd really like to do it. And I'd be safe there. No one will look for me on Great Inagua."

"You'll hate it," I said fervently. "It's nothing but salt works and mosquitoes as big as seagulls."

She made a face at the thought of the mosquitoes. "My other alternative is to boat-sit for Marge and Barry." Marge and Barry Steinway were a married couple who had both lectured at Ellen's university, and who, on retirement, had bought a thirty-six-foot catamaran called *Addendum* which they sailed between the Florida Keys and the Bahamas. "They want to visit their new grandchild in Vermont," Ellen explained, "and Marge is lecturing at a summer school in New Hampshire, so they asked me to look after *Addendum* for a few weeks. I thought I might even sail her to the Keys? It would be good practice, wouldn't it?"

"For crossing the Pacific?" I asked with a ridiculous surge of anticipation.

"I can't think what else it would be good practice for, can you?" Ellen twisted to smile up at me. "I know I can't use the sextant properly yet, but I'll use the Loran, and it will be my first night all alone at sea. And I'll be safe in the Keys, because no one will know where I am, and perhaps I'll go and explore the Dry Tortugas because I've always wanted to see them." Ellen seemed to be talking to stop herself from crying. "To be honest I'd rather have a job that paid real money, and Marge and Barry said I mustn't worry if one was offered to me, because *Addendum* will be safe enough in its marina, but I'd like to do it. I'd like to prove I can do a voyage on my own."

"You'll do fine."

"At present it's either *Addendum* or Great Inagua." She stood and brushed shell scraps from her hands. "I'll probably make up my mind on the ferry tonight. I'd really like to earn some money, but no one seems to be hiring."

"You could stay here," I said hopefully.

She smiled at me, but said nothing. Instead she began walking back towards the graveyard.

"Couldn't you?" I pressed her.

"There's no work for me here, Nick." She held out her hand, inviting me to catch up with her. "So what will you do?"

"I'll work on *Masquerade*."

She frowned. "Won't they look for you here?"

"I'll be careful." We walked slowly beside the sea. A plane took off from the airstrip, drowning the island in its noise, and I supposed that it was taking Denise Harriman and Warren Smedley back to the mainland. The din of the aircraft temporarily scared the goats away from Thessy's grave.

"Where shall we meet?" Ellen asked suddenly. "I mean for our voyage?"

"Miami? Fort Lauderdale? Key West? I'll write to you if you give me an address."

"And when shall we leave?" she asked.

"Sometime in late September," I guessed. "Maybe October."

She stopped and cradled my face in her dry warm hands. "Till then, Nick, take care."

"Of course."

"Because we're going to sail away for ever and a day." She smiled, and I suddenly realised just how much in love with her I was, and the knowledge almost broke my heart because a ferry was taking her away from me this very evening.

"You take care, too," I told her.

"I shall, of course I shall," she said, then she took her hands from my face because Jackson Chatterton was coming to join us. "I suppose we'd all better go and sing some more hymns," Ellen said sadly, and so we did.

PART THREE

The mourners were still singing in Bonefish's yard as I walked Ellen and Chatterton to the stone pier where the Straker's Cay passengers waited for the ferry's arrival. The bay was too shallow to let the big boat come right up to the pier, so all the passengers and freight had to be shuttled out in a red-painted motorboat that was moored at the foot of a precariously narrow iron ladder at the pier's seaward end. One of the adventures of landing on or leaving from Straker's Cay was negotiating that rusting and perilous ladder.

We arrived at the pier at dusk. There was no sign of the ferry yet, though that was nothing unusual for the boats were often hours late in edging into the small bay, but for entertainment there was always the islanders' conversation as well as a small palm-thatched hut where lukewarm Coca-Cola and thin beer could be bought. "Don't wait," Ellen said to me, "we'll be fine."

"I don't mind waiting."

"Don't, please," she said, and I realised that the prospect of waiting with me, with so much to say and no real privacy in which to say it, was troubling Ellen, and so I said goodbye to Jackson Chatterton, who was going back to his clinic in America, and then I kissed Ellen.

"It seems stupid," I said, "that it should end like this."

"Think how much worse it is for Thessy," she said with an apparent callousness that was designed to keep her from crying, but the design failed, and the tears began to run as she hugged me one last time. "I wish I'd remembered to bring some jeans," she said suddenly, "because it's going to be so embarrassing to climb down that ladder wearing a dress."

"But a thrill for everyone else," I said, then I hugged her close and advised her not to go to Great Inagua, but to sail *Addendum* to the Florida Keys instead.

"I probably will," she sniffed.

I shook Jackson Chatterton's hand again. "Safe home," I told the big man. "And take care of Ellen."

"I will, Nick, I will."

I walked back to *Masquerade* alone. The night was noisy with insects and bright with stars. The kerosene lamps at Bonefish's house were lit and at least a score of mourners still sang under the lemon trees, but I wanted to be alone and so I skirted the house. A noise erupted in the bushes to my right, sounding like a heavy body charging straight at me, and I turned, heart thumping with adrenalin, but it was only one of Bonefish's pigs that swerved away from me and ran squealing towards the light.

Masquerade was a great shadowed bulk in the darkness. I clumsily climbed the nine-foot wooden ladder and pushed back the tarpaulin which had failed to keep Bonefish's chickens from roosting in her cockpit. The big timber baulks that cradled my boat creaked as my weight shifted her hull and as I slid back her hatch and dropped down into the cabin.

It was stiflingly hot below decks. I edged into the fore-cabin, which I had rebuilt as a workshop and store, and pushed open the forehatch. Back in the big main-cabin I took out the companionway's washboards so that the night's small wind could blow clean through the two sweltering cabins, then lit a candle that I placed under a lamp's glass chimney. The small dancing light reflected back from the glossy white paint and deep varnish that preserved *Masquerade*'s cabin from the ravages of salt and sea. It was strange to be in my boat again. If I closed my eyes and tried to blot out the sound of the hymn singing, concentrating instead on the beat of the surf, it was almost possible to imagine that *Masquerade* was afloat, and then the wind gusted to make the hull move a creaking millimetre inside its cradling and the illusion was almost perfect.

The booming call of the ferry's siren announcing the ship's late arrival in the bay made me open my eyes. Palm fronds clattered above the companionway, belying my dream that I was at sea. I opened the locker above the sink and took out a warm bottle of beer. The beer, with a tin of fruit cake left over from Christmas, would make my supper.

194

It was still cruelly hot inside the boat. The wind was not finding its way down either hatchway so that the sweat was running in rivulets down my back and belly, and I knew I would have to rig a canvas windscoop before I tried to sleep. Then I forgot the discomfort of the heat for the boat had shifted again, but this new movement was not caused by the wind, but rather because someone or something had stepped on to the ladder. I froze, then there was the unmistakable sound of a shoe scraping on one of the crudely carved rungs. "Who's there?" I called.

There was no answer, only the creak of the ladder as my visitor climbed towards *Masquerade*'s cockpit. "Who's there?" I called, but again no one replied, and I thought of a drug lord's revenge, so I pulled up the cabin sole and groped deep into the bilge for the big clumsy pistol, yet even if I found the Webley I knew it would be too late, for I had protected the hidden weapon with a thick waterproof wrapping of taped plastic and it would take me precious seconds to disentangle the gun, by which time the intruder would have found me. I felt my blood run cold with the fear of imminent horror, then I wondered whether the bastards had already found Ellen and I cursed myself for abandoning her on the pier.

I found the gun and pulled it towards me, but my intruder was already standing at the top of the companionway ladder, blotting out the stars and staring down to where I sprawled helplessly in the small yellow light of the guttering candle. I let the plastic-wrapped gun drop back into the bilge.

"I didn't want to go home," my visitor said, and her wine-dark dress rustled as she climbed down into the cabin. I stood up to meet her and to hold her. Then I kissed her, and my own eyes were closed because I was so very glad that she had come back. "I'm not a cook any more, am I?" Ellen asked, and her voice was little more than a whisper.

"No," I said, "you're not."

"It's hot in here."

"Yes," I said, "it is."

Her dress rustled as it dropped to the cabin's sole. Above *Masquerade* the stars blazed.

And I blew out the candle.

In the morning I found Ellen sitting by the lagoon, hugging her knees and watching the sea. Her flaming red hair was twisted into a bun. Apart from a book to read on the ferry she had brought no luggage to the island, for she had not expected to stay beyond the one day, so she had nothing to wear except the red dress. In its place she had found a pair of my old shorts and a T-shirt, both of which hung from her like a suit of barge sails draped on a racing dinghy, but even my misshapen clothes could not diminish Ellen's beauty. I smiled at her with the shyness new lovers have on first waking, and Ellen smiled back, but it was apparent she did not want to talk; instead she just took my hand and gave my knuckles a swift kiss as though to tell me that everything was well.

I made coffee on the spirit stove, and offered her a slice of the tinned fruit cake for breakfast. Startlingly white egrets were flying up from the far mangrove trees. "Are there flamingos here?" Ellen broke the silence.

"I've not seen any."

"What were you thinking" – Ellen turned a very serious face to me — "when you had to kill those men on *Wavebreaker*?"

I wondered where that question had sprung from. "I was too scared to think."

"Scared?" She still frowned as though she did not believe me.

"Scared and sick," I admitted. "As thugs go, you see, I'm remarkably inexperienced." I spoke lightly, though in truth I still woke sweating in the night as I imagined what would have happened if I had not managed to seize Sweetman's Uzi and kill the two gunmen before they turned the Kalashnikovs on us. My other nightmare was my firm conviction that if I had only fired at the second gunman first, Thessy would still be alive. "The best quality for a soldier," I said sadly, "is to have no imagination, none."

But I had imagination enough to know what would happen if Jesse Sweetman or his friends found us and so, after breakfast, I unwrapped and cleaned the big Webley. Ellen watched me do the chore, but made no comment. When it was cleaned I pushed the gun into a pocket of my shorts, but after an hour my own sense of looking ridiculous made me take the gun off and hide it again in *Masquerade*.

I spent the rest of that morning with Bonefish, not doing very much and not even speaking about Thessy very much, but just trying to repair the reed-valve on Bonefish's old outboard motor. I did promise to write to some of our old charter customers to enquire if they had any photographs of Thessy, for the only picture that Bonefish and his wife possessed was one that had been taken when Thessy was about eight years old – though, as Ellen remarked, he hardly looked a day different to when he was seventeen.

It was a sweet weekend, despite the sadness that had brought Ellen and me so close. I did some work on *Masquerade*, but mostly Ellen and I just walked or swam or talked. The best day we had was the Sunday, Ellen's last full day on Straker's Cay, when we sailed Bonefish's skiff to one of the deserted outer islands where nothing but the sea and the birds and the iguanas and the palms existed. We swam naked in the lagoon and watched a Spotted Eagle Ray's languid beauty as it rippled above the sandy sea-floor, and I turned my head to watch Ellen swimming and I wondered if ever again I would know such happiness, and then I remembered that once *Masquerade* was in the Pacific we would spend our lives wandering between palm-fringed beaches and forgotten islands.

We let the sun dry us, and we made the silly talk that lovers do. We astonished ourselves at our own joy, and believed that no one else had ever known such bliss. I thought of Robin-Anne's dismissal of all pleasure as nothing but the brain's unromantic secretion of chemical traces, and I supposed that love could be similarly dismissed as a cocktail of genetic impulses and seething testosterone, but I did not believe it. This was happiness, a glorious happiness, a taste of heaven. I did not know why I loved Ellen; I thought half her opinions were mad, and she probably thought all mine were, yet we laughed together and we had found a care for each other and for each other's dreams and lives and hopes.

Ellen had brought her book to the deserted island, but was too hot or too happy or too lazy to read it. "*A Feminist Symbolist's Perception of Goethe,*" I read the title aloud. "Bloody hell, woman."

"You wouldn't like it," Ellen said lazily, "on account of its utter lack of pictures."

"You can buy me the comic-strip version." I flipped through the book, seeing where Ellen had made notes in her tiny precise handwriting. The author was described as being 'chairperson' of a Women's Studies Department of a Californian university. "Why is there no such thing as a Department of Men's Studies?" I asked.

"We leave the study of mindless brutes to the animal behaviourists," she pounced with undisguised glee, then laughed at her small victory. "Would you like to be studied?" she asked me.

"No."

"But I study you." She turned over on to her front. We were both still naked and our warm skin was flecked with sand.

"What have you learned about me?" I asked.

"How very desperate the big tough Nick is for approval and love." She pronounced the verdict very seriously, then lightly touched my face with a finger. "What happened to all the other girls?"

"What other girls?"

She sighed and rolled on to her back. "He was a marine, and he's a virgin?"

I laughed. "Some were good, some were bad. Some just wanted to use me as a means to meet my father."

"So you learned to distrust them?"

"Maybe." I thought about it. "Some just wanted me to be more ambitious. One girl said she wouldn't marry me unless I became an officer."

198

"And why didn't you become an officer?"

"Because that would have been expected of Tom Breakspear's son."

"Ah!" Ellen said triumphantly. "So you joined the Marines solely to annoy your father! You wanted his attention. He ignored you as a child, didn't he?"

"No more than he ignored anything or anyone else," I said. "In my father's heaven there is only one star."

"Poor Nick."

"No." I did not need pity. I had, after all, grown up in the most lavish wealth. I had lived in a succession of beautiful houses, from English manors to exquisite French châteaux to a vast Beverly Hills mansion. I remembered the hours of loneliness in Beverly Hills, the echo of the marble hallways, the splash of the fountain in the swimming pool and the subdued laughter of the servants in their rooms over the big garage. Once, when I was eight, my father had bought everything in a toyshop and had it all shipped to the mansion. I had rewarded him by putting every single toy into the swimming pool until the blue water was heaped with tin trains and teddy bears, awash with building blocks and cowboy outfits, littered with bicycles and dolls' houses. "My father," I said slowly, "should have beaten the living daylights out of me."

"Silly Nick." She cut open a mango and pushed a slice towards me. "I suspect I would like your father."

"You would like him if he wanted you to like him. He has the ability to be whatever anyone wants him to be, and if you wanted him to be modest and kind and erudite and learned, then that's what he'd be for you, and you'd never believe it if I told you that he screws anything that moves, regardless of gender, and has a mind like a cesspit."

"But you love him."

"Yes."

"And you're his favourite child?" The guess was a little more tentative than her previous assertion, but it was no less true.

"Probably," I conceded, then watched as Ellen, satisfied

with her cross-examination, lay back and closed her eyes. "So what about you?" I asked.

"What about me?"

"Who were your lovers?"

It was an awkward question, born of a lover's clumsy jealousy, but Ellen did not seem to mind it being asked. "Academics and activists." She shrugged, as though none of them had left a mark on her soul. "They told me they were above lust, that their interest in me was purely to share the cause and explore the cosmos, but all they ever really wanted was a fuck."

"You can't blame them," I said, maybe a shade too warmly.

Ellen turned her head and looked very gravely at me. I thought I was about to be reprimanded for levity, but instead she smiled. "Poor Sir Tom," she said gently.

"To have me as a son, you mean?"

"To be denied you as a son," she corrected me, then drew my face down to hers.

The waves rippled the sand. The wind was a warm sigh. The world was at peace. I was in love.

We went back to *Masquerade* and I built a fire and cooked freshly caught mullet for our supper. I had not taken the Webley revolver to the deserted beach, but I kept it beside me as we ate. Ellen hated the sight of the weapon, and claimed we did not need it. "That man Smedley didn't say that Sweetman's friends would take revenge," she told me that evening in her most no-nonsense tone, "only that there was a possibility that they might. I reckon they won't, because if they really wanted to kill us, then they would surely have tried already. I think Smedley is just trying to earn his salary by being pompous."

I was more concerned than Ellen. I was far less sanguine than I had been when the DEA agent had first uttered his lackadaisical warning. I felt fairly safe on Straker's Cay; the island was so small, the islanders were watching out for us, and no stranger could have landed without our knowing of their arrival within minutes, but it was that snug safety of the place which was undoubtedly contributing to Ellen's growing sense of security, and that worried me. It especially worried me that she was insisting on returning to Freeport the next day, and so, after we had eaten, I again tried to persuade her not to leave Straker's Cay at all.

She shook her head. "I can't do a proper job here, Nick. I'd want to feel useful."

"I can teach you some carpentry."

"Thank you, but no," she said very deliberately, then laughed at the very thought of handling a saw or a chisel. "It'll be OK," she reassured me. "I'll sail *Addendum* to the Keys and hide there like a little bunny in its hole."

"Then at least let me escort you as far as *Addendum*," I urged her.

She turned her head to look at me. The fire was burning low and its dark light shadowed her face wondrously. "I am not in need of a nursemaid, Nicholas Breakspear." She always used my full name whenever she wished to chide me, which was usually at those moments when she thought I was exhibiting the cardinal male sin of being over-protective.

"I just want you to be safe," I explained.

"I want myself to be safe, astonishingly enough," she said tartly, "so I shall sail away from here on a safely crowded ferry, safely collect some clothes from my apartment, say a safe goodbye to the Literacy Project, then safely disappear on *Addendum*. Does that safe agenda meet with your approval?"

"I'd still rather come with you to make sure that you'll be all right," I said stubbornly.

"You've no reason to travel to Freeport." She leaned forward and tried to stir some life into the fire. "I'm a grown woman, not some shivering female in need of protection."

She was adamant, so late that night I walked to the village and, without Ellen knowing, tried to telephone the Maggot. In truth I had little hope of reaching him, for using the Bahamian inter-island telephone system is akin to bouncing messages through far galaxies towards an alien starship that might or might not exist. The system was a mixture of bakelite tele-phones, fibre-optics, old-fashioned operators, microwave links, and VHF radios, and it was a rare day that any two com-ponents meshed smoothly. However, fate was being kind to me that Sunday night and the whole system worked beautifully and, even more miraculously, the Maggot was actually at home. I asked him a favour, and the Maggot, being a kind man, gave it to me. "But don't tell Ellen!" I warned him.

"Not a word," he promised, "not a word."

Which meant, whether Ellen liked it or not, that I had done the male chauvinist thing, and she was protected.

I slept badly, dreaming of Thessy's body bumping across the locker's drowned sill, then of the dying man's shoes beating the deck like a drummer's tattoo.

I woke Ellen with my restlessness. For a time we lay silent, listening to the night waves breaking on the reefs beyond the lagoon, and to the clatter of the palm fronds above our grounded boat. The windscoop drifted a fitful breeze through *Masquerade* that stirred the black mesh of the insect screen that Ellen had rigged across the hatchway. "I don't want Thessy to have died for nothing," I said at last, explaining my unrest.

"Are you dreaming of revenge, my noble and silly Nick?"

"Yes."

She traced her fingers across my chest. "Leave it to the law."

"The law won't do anything. It's been corrupted by money."

"So what will you do?" Ellen challenged me. "Go in shoot-ing? Nick at high noon? Gunfight at the Sea Rat Corral? And you'll end up just like Thessy, nothing but a mound of dirt in a cemetery."

"Thessy's not a mound of dirt," I protested, "he's in heaven, where he doesn't have to read gloomy minor prophets any longer and he gets fried bread and bananas every morning, and God has given him a lovely boat to sail in a challenging wind all day and every day, and he's got lots of friends and he keeps telling them about this wonderful couple called Nick and Ellen who'll one day be joining him."

Ellen laughed, then kissed me, and a tear fell from her cheek on to mine. "So what are you going to do?" she asked softly.

"Nothing." That sad truth was forced on me by reality, not by inclination. "I don't even know where to find Sweetman, so I can't do anything."

"Good," she said, then rested her head beside mine. "Sleep now."

I woke tired, and after breakfast I worked on *Masquerade* while Ellen read her book in the shade of the cradled hull. Her ferry was not due till the evening, but at midday, just as he had promised, the Maggot's aircraft swept low overhead. Ellen frowned as the dirty plane sank beyond the palm trees. "I hope that's not who I think it is."

"The Maggot?" I managed to sound very innocent. "He's not such a bad fellow."

"For a maggot," Ellen said, "he's a louse."

Twenty minutes later the Maggot walked up to Bonefish's yard, looking as innocent as any man wearing an appallingly garish Hawaiian shirt could look. He pretended that he had simply dropped by the island to see me, and feigned surprise on discovering Ellen was with me, though he could not resist imbuing that surprise with a foully suggestive leer. "Having a good time?" he asked Ellen.

She smiled glacially. "Why don't I leave you two good old boys to grunt at each other in peace. Maybe you could indulge in a mutual grooming session?" She snapped the book shut, and stood ready to leave, but I managed to stop her by feigning a sudden and brilliant idea.

"Are you flying back to Freeport?" I asked the Maggot, knowing full well that he was.

"I sure am, Nick." It seemed to me that he was over-acting, but Ellen did not notice.

"It's crazy for you to take the ferry," I said to Ellen. "You'll get home much quicker if you fly! And you'll save money. You won't charge her, will you, John?"

"Not a red cent," he said, like the good trooper he had agreed to be, for on the phone he had nobly undertaken not only to fly Ellen to Freeport, but then to drive her from the airport to her apartment, and from her apartment to the marina where *Addendum* was moored. Ellen, whether she wished it or not, was going to be guarded, though whether she would permit the Maggot to drive her round the island once she reached Freeport was debatable. Still, by making the phone call to the Maggot I had done what I could to look after her.

She still hesitated before accepting the Maggot's offer – though I was certain she would accept – for Ellen disliked the ferries, and flying was a far more convenient method of moving around the islands, but the long duration of her hesitation was an eloquent measure of her dislike for the Maggot. However, she finally nodded and even found it possible to thank him politely. "It's really very kind of you, Mr Maggovertski."

"It's all my pleasure, honey. You'll be ready in an hour?"

The 'honey' put a skim of ice on to Ellen's voice. "I shall indeed be ready, Mr Maggovertski."

The Maggot scratched deep in his beard. "Call me Maggot, honey, everyone does."

"Not me, Mr Maggovertski, not me." She stalked away.

The Maggot watched her until she was out of earshot then shook his head wistfully. "You lucky bastard, Nick." He took a half-cigarette from behind his ear and relit it. "I've never seen her looking so well! You can just see that she was shrivelling away for lack of a bedding, can't you now? I know she might be a professor, but under the skin she's just another bimbo."

There were times, I thought, when Ellen was entirely accurate in her judgement of the Maggot, but I was still grateful to the huge man, so I ignored his crudities and instead thanked him for donating his time, fuel and aeroplane.

"Hell, Nick, it's a pleasure. But do you really think you're in danger?" He sounded very sceptical. When I had telephoned the Maggot I had described my fears of Sweetman's reprisals,

204

and now I forcefully reiterated my conviction that Ellen was in danger. The Maggot, though plainly reluctant to believe me, was polite enough not to scoff at my tale of possible revenge. He was also curious about the events at Sea Rat Cay, and made me tell him the whole story.

"Have you ever seen *Dream Baby*?" I asked him when I had finished describing the fight on board *Wavebreaker*. I thought it entirely possible that the Maggot might have seen the oddly painted powerboat during one of his flights about the islands.

He shook his head. "I'd remember a boat like that, Nick."

"You're sure?"

"You think I could forget a boat called *Dream Baby*? With a camouflage paint job?" He shook his head, then frowned. "Does it matter very much?"

"I'd just like to know where they are, that's all."

The Maggot gave my shoulder what he thought was a light punch, but which was more like being whacked by a piledriver. "Don't worry about where they are, but just make sure they don't know where *you* are."

An hour later the three of us walked to the Maggot's plane that stood baking in the shimmering heat. The plane looked horrible, oil-streaked and filthy, and Ellen shuddered at the sight of it. "Is it safe?" she asked.

"Hell, yes," the Maggot said. "Mind you, you can never tell what's safe, can you? I remember when the New Orleans Fruits, that's the Saints to you, honey, had a fourth and one against us, and they decided to run it, and we reckoned it had to be safe because those toads couldn't float a fairy fart down a sewer, but —"

"Maggot," I said, "shut up."

"I think it's time we went." He climbed on to the wing and opened the plane's door. I helped Ellen up. She was not going to kiss me in front of the Maggot, but she gave me a smile he could not see and, once she was inside the plane, she secretly blew me a kiss.

"I'll write to you from Florida!" she called.

"Soon! Please!" I called back.

205

The engines hammered into life, driving scraps of grass and chips of coral back from the propeller's wash. I stepped back as the plane lurched forward, then watched as it hurtled down the runway and lifted smoothly and safely into the air. The Beechcraft climbed up over Thessy's grave and I watched my love go, watched till the plane was just a scrap of light in the northern sky, and I went on watching till the faraway plane winked out into distant invisibility. I turned away and felt very much alone, and very much in love.

As it turned out I did have reason to go to Freeport after all, and had I known that good reason I would have had no problem in persuading Ellen to let me accompany her.

Because, once I had watched her fly away, I went to the village post office, which operated in what had once been a chicken shed, to discover that a letter had come to me from McIllvanney's boatyard. McIllvanney's secretary, Stella, apologised that she had not sent the money Cutwater Charters owed me for the proctologist's cruise, but sadly Mr McIllvanney would not authorise the release of any funds until I turned up at the yard to sign the necessary insurance and salvage forms for *Wavebreaker*.

I swore in frustration. I should have known that McIllvanney would muck around with the money he owed me! And if I had just visited the post office before taking Ellen to the plane I could have flown with her to Freeport. Now I would have to waste a day and two nights making the journey by ferry.

Poverty dictated that I make the journey so, two days later, I clambered down the pier's dangerous iron ladder and was carried out to the waiting ferry. I changed boats in Nassau, reaching Freeport early on the Thursday morning. I caught a bus to McIllvanney's boatyard and found the man himself standing on a floating pontoon next to his sleek forty-two-foot motor yacht called *Junkanoo*. *Junkanoo* was one of McIllvanney's own charter boats, but he was plainly about to use her himself for her motor was burbling away and he had been busy untying her stern warp as I arrived. It was also plain that he had company aboard for there was a pile of luggage on *Junkanoo*'s stern deck and I suspected that the pink garment bag and lavender suitcase were not McIllvanney's choice of travel gear. Leaning on the suitcase was a tennis racket in a lavender slip case that was embroidered with a big initial 'D'. McIllvanney, it was apparent, had a girl aboard his boat, which perhaps explained the lack of warmth in his welcome. "So what the fock do you want, Breakspear?"

"You wanted me to sign some papers," I courteously explained my presence. "So here I am."

"So come back next week, your Holiness."

"Just forget it," I walked away from him. "I'm only in town today, and that's it. So please yourself. I'll send you a writ for the money you owe me."

"Wait, you bastard!"

I waited. He made fast *Junkanoo*'s stern warp, then jumped aboard to kill her engine. Almost immediately the door from the main-cabin opened and the tall, fair-haired girl I had met in McIllvanney's Lucaya apartment walked on to the stern deck. She was still wearing high heels and very little else. She recognised me and gave me a wholesome and welcoming smile. "Nick! It's just so very good to see you again. How are you doing?" She asked the question with that earnest rising inflection by which Americans seem to imply a genuine curiosity for what is otherwise an entirely formal greeting.

"Very well, thank you, and yourself?" I matched her politeness, but I was also trying to remember the girl's name. Her body, clad in its barely existent bikini, was entirely unforgettable, but her name had disappeared into the space between the stars.

"I'm doing good, thank you," the girl said with heartfelt enthusiasm, "real good!"

I still could not place her name, and my only clue was the big 'D' embroidered in shiny pink thread on the tennis racket's lavender case. Debbie? Dolly? Denise? Donna, of course! "It's very nice to meet you again, Donna," I said.

"You're just going to have to forgive me for one little

moment, Nick," she said as though our meeting was the most important thing in her world, then she turned a worried face on McIllvanney. "I just thought you ought to know, Matt, that the air conditioning went off."

"Of course it went off, you silly cow, because I turned the focking engine off, and you can't have the air conditioner on unless you're generating some focking electricity because it drains too much current from the focking battery."

"Oh! How silly of me! I should have known!" She gave me another gladsome smile, all teeth and sparkle. "Are you coming aboard, Nick? We've got some champagne in the cooler."

"No, he's focking well not coming on board, he's coming with me." McIllvanney jumped on to the pontoon. "Just wait for me, woman."

"It's been so good talking with you again, Nick," Donna called as we walked away.

"Are you poaching the firm's inventory?" I asked McIllvanney when we were safely out of Donna's earshot.

"I'm just doing a delivery job, all right!" He turned, clearly upset by my jocular accusation. He rammed his fingers towards my eyes as though trying to blind me, but instead forcing me to take a backwards step along the pontoon. "I'm just delivering the bint to a client!"

"OK! Forget I spoke!" I said placatingly.

"I'm just delivering her to a client, and when he's used the stupid cow, I fetch her back. Either me or Bellybutton fetches her back, but there's no funny business, you understand?" He walked on, simmering with fury. *Starkisser* rocked gently beside the pontoon and I noted how skilfully Bellybutton had painted the silver star on her long glittering bow. He had added a lipstick-red cupid's mouth at the very centre of the shooting star. Bellybutton himself had sidled away from my unexpected arrival, scuttling away up the office stairs as though he was desperate to avoid me.

McIllvanney took the same stairs two at a time, while I hobbled behind him. Bellybutton, as I entered the office, was finishing a telephone call. He gave me his usual sly and maniacal grin, then edged about the room towards the door. Stella had already found the necessary papers in the filing cabinet and now spread them on McIllvanney's desk. "Sign wherever there's a pencil cross," McIllvanney curtly ordered me. Bellybutton, the door safely reached, gave one last mocking smile and was gone.

I began reading the top form.

"Oh, for Christ's sake!" McIllvanney complained, "but are you going to read every word before you sign them?"

"Yes."

He growled, but there was nothing he could do. Stella, with a friendly but nervous smile to me, had slipped out of the office to buy some milk, leaving me alone with McIllvanney who stared angrily out of the window while I methodically read through the small print and sub-clauses and obfuscations of the various forms. Yet, despite having been written by language-murdering lawyers, the forms were straightforward enough; mere formalities to do with insurance and with *Wavebreaker*'s condition on the morning she sank. I began signing the forms, first authenticating my own qualifications to prove that the boat had been under competent command, though that, I thought, was a dubious assertion, for in fact *Wavebreaker* had been pirated before she sank. "I hear you're salvaging her?" I said to McIllvanney.

"Aye." He was adding his own signature to some of the forms and, for a moment, he seemed reluctant to say any more, then he decided that a modicum of politeness might hasten the scribbling of my signatures, and so he grudgingly elaborated. "They say they'll have her up by tomorrow night."

"I'd be grateful if you could find Thessy's Bible for me, and ask Stella to send it on to his father?"

I thought he would refuse the favour, but then he nodded curtly before sweeping the signed papers into an envelope. Donna was doing aerobic exercises on *Junkanoo*'s rear deck, a sight to provoke cardiac arrest. "Do you know what the hell has happened to Ellen?" McIllvanney asked me. He had his back to the window as he wrote an address on the envelope.

So far as I knew Ellen was on board *Addendum*, and hopefully in the Florida Keys by now, but I had no intention of letting McIllvanney know anything about her travels. "Has Ellen been away?" I asked ingenuously instead.

McIllvanney responded to my mock-innocent question with a filthy look. "Of course she's been away. She went to the funeral, and she hasn't been seen since. I know that, because I went to her flat on Sunday, but she wasn't there."

"Why don't you just leave her alone?" I asked with rising anger. "She's not for hire. She's not going to become one of your whores, so just forget her!"

"It's none of your focking business why I want to talk to the bint, and –"

The clashing noise of the pistol's cocking action stopped his voice cold. He looked up, and for once I actually saw McIllvanney go pale. He was staring into the cavernous black muzzle of my .455 Webley pistol. It is a very frightening pistol. For a start it fires an enormous bullet, so the barrel gapes alarmingly, and the gun is built on a gigantic scale. The weapon is almost a foot long. As it happened the gun which was threatening McIllvanney was not loaded, but he did not know that, and the sweat was prickling at his forehead. "Ellen is not for hire," I said again, but this time very slowly and very distinctly.

"Jesus goddamn wept." McIllvanney, still pale, stared in horror at the gun's gaping muzzle. "Christ in his heaven, but why the hell are you carrying that, you fool?"

"Because there are men out there who might want to take revenge for the deaths of the guys I killed. It's like a family feud, but I'll be damned before I make it easy for them to finish me off." The gun had made a hard uncomfortable lump at the small of my back, and I had been glad of the chance to take it out and thus remove the pressure from my spine.

Now the unloaded gun was pointing directly at the bridge of McIllvanney's nose. He was shaking, and I was using both hands to train the gun, just as if it really was primed to go pop and I was preparing for the mule-like kick of the recoil. "Ellen is not for hire," I said a third time. "Do you understand me?"

"Bloody hell fire!" McIllvanney stared wide-eyed at me, and his voice took on the aggrieved tone of wounded innocence. "I only wanted to do the girl a favour! Ned Carraway needs a cook on board *Hobgoblin* because his girl has caught the pox or something, and Ned phoned me to ask if Ellen could step in for a few days!" Ned Carraway was the owner and skipper of a beautiful locally built schooner, *Hobgoblin*, which was a few feet shorter than *Wavebreaker* and several light years prettier. *Hobgoblin* was built of wood and was bereft of almost every modern comfort except the sheer loveliness of sailing blue seas in a proper wooden boat, though the price that Ned and his American wife paid was to spend most of their spare time painting the beast or coaxing its ill-tempered and dangerous petrol engine into brief and reluctant life.

So Ned had needed a replacement cook? I stared at McIllvanney who, sensing my discomfort, pushed the telephone towards me. "If you don't believe me, phone him!"

"Oh," I said, feeling stupid and lowering the gun.

"You're focking mad!" McIllvanney said fervently. I had scared the daylights out of him, which was something of an achievement, even though I now felt like an idiot.

"Ellen's got a job looking after a friend's boat," I said helpfully, "so I don't know if she can work for Ned, but if she's in touch I'll pass on the message."

"Ned's probably found someone else by now. He was pretty desperate, so he was." McIllvanney was still shaking with the fear that had made him loquacious. It really is very unpleasant indeed to stare into a gun's muzzle.

I held the gun loosely in my left hand. "It wasn't loaded," I told McIllvanney, as though that might make him feel better.

"I don't give a toss! You should be locked up! Who the hell do you think is coming after you?"

"Sweetman. And the other fellow, Miguel. The guys who

211

were on *Dream Baby*. Which reminds me. Can you remember where you saw *Dream Baby*? Because if I can find her, then I'll find the guys who were responsible for Thessy's death."

"You're mad! You think that boat is still around? They'll have got rid of *Dream*-focking-*Baby* long ago. They'll have sunk her, so they will. They don't want trouble, you fool, any more than the rest of us want trouble."

I pushed the gun into the sweaty space at the small of my back, then let my shirt fall like a curtain over it. "You want me to post your letter?" I offered.

"You're a lunatic." McIllvanney was beginning to recover his equilibrium. He opened his window and shouted down at Bellybutton who was pretending to do some work on the pontoons, but in reality was ogling the lubricious Donna. "Hey, Bellybutton! If you ever see Nick Breakspear in this yard again, you run him off, you hear me? Run him off!"

Bellybutton and Donna both stared in surprise at the office window. McIllvanney, pleased with himself, slammed it shut, then glared at Stella, his secretary, who was standing in the doorway with a carton of milk. "And that goes for you, too," he told her, "if you see this bastard in my yard again, call the police."

"Yes, Mr McIllvanney." Stella said nervously.

"Now you," he pointed at me, "fock away off."

"Give me my money first." I did not dare ask him for the money I had earned on the Crowninshield charter, guessing that a sunken schooner had probably voided that contract, but I still wanted my slice from the proctologist and the lawyers.

McIllvanney scribbled me a cheque that he bad-temperedly threw across the desk. I smiled my thanks, then, obedient to his wishes, focked away off.

I went directly from McIllvanney's office to the bank, determined to cash his cheque before perversity decided him to stop payment. With that precaution successfully accomplished I was left with the best part of a day to kill before I could catch a return ferry, so I found a public telephone that worked and dialled the Maggot's number. I was half hoping that the big man would offer to fly me home to Straker's Cay, but I also wanted reassurance that he had delivered Ellen safely to *Addendum*'s marina. Or perhaps I just wanted to talk to someone about Ellen; I had the disease of all lovers, the need to spread my happiness to whoever could be persuaded to listen.

But that was not to be the Maggot, for all I reached was his answering machine that first belched at me, then chuckled, then instructed me to lay the word down on him. I complied, saying that I would try to reach him later and would buy him a beer if he was free at lunchtime.

I then bought a copy of the *Nassau Guardian* and took it to a bar where, under the soft thump of a revolving ceiling fan, I sipped a pale beer and read about the new Health Clinic on Great Exuma, and about how the Combined Baptist Choirs of Great Abaco would be raising their voices to the Lord in a Concert of Praise on Sunday next, and how the dead body that had been discovered on the east coast of Andros had now been identified as that of an American tourist, Jackson Chatterton.

I stared at the newspaper. It was shaking, but whether it was my hand or the draught from the fan I could not tell.

The newspaper reported that Jackson Chatterton had drowned, and that his body had been in the water for some time before it was discovered. His remains had now been delivered into the care of the American authorities. It was a little filler of a story, a squib to take up space, but it left me quaking with horror.

Oh God, no, I prayed. No, please God. I closed my eyes very tight, but that did not help, so I opened them again and stared at the small story that was so very bland, and I supposed that Chatterton's killers must have been waiting on the ferry, because they had surely assumed that all of us would be leaving Straker's Cay on the next sailing after Thessy's funeral. But instead they had only found Jackson, which meant they must still be looking for Ellen and me, and I remembered Warren Smedley's warning, that I had treated so lightly, and I felt stark naked and very vulnerable in that hot, brightly painted bar; I looked frenetically around me, but there were only two men playing dominoes, a dog that was twitching in its flea-ridden sleep, and a barman who gave me a very odd look as though he suspected I was already drunk.

I tore the story from the newspaper and shoved it into my pocket. The gun was a cold hard lump in my back. I felt certain that everyone could see its obvious shape beneath my shirt. My heart was thumping. I was frightened. I was still having difficulty in coming to terms with the news.

Jackson Chatterton was dead. The big, stolid, angry, gentle man was dead. I remembered his childish delight in being photographed in front of the great seas that had been running before the storm, and I felt a surge of impotent anger at the men who had killed him, and doubtless they were the same men who would be trying to murder Ellen and me. They were not just taking revenge for the deaths of the two gunmen, but destroying all the witnesses to Thessy's murder.

And suppose I was the only witness left alive? Suppose that Ellen had not sailed away? My blood was running cold with terror as I abandoned what was left of my beer and went into the sweltering street. There were no taxis. God damn it, there were no taxis! The street was crowded with cheerful American sailors, come ashore from one of the naval ships engaged in Exercise Stingray, and the sailors seemed to have taken all the cabs. I pushed through the crowds on the pavement, balefully watching for any face that watched me. I saw no one suspicious, but I did see a taxi suddenly swerve to drop three sailors outside a massage parlour, and I shouted at it, waved, then commandeered it by climbing inside.

I paid off the cab at the marina where *Addendum* had been moored, and from where Ellen should have sailed two days before. The marina's gate was open and unguarded. Next to the gate was a small office, but, though its door was open and a small battered radio was playing rock music, the office was empty.

I ran down to the pontoons. I could see a score of monohulls, and the usual cluster of gleaming motor yachts, but there were no catamarans moored in the marina. I felt a surge of relief that Ellen was safe, for I knew our enemies would never find her if she was at sea, lost in or beyond the Gulf Stream and among the swarms of other pleasure craft; but then, just as I felt myself relaxing from the panic that had besieged me, I saw her.

I saw *Addendum*. The big white catamaran lay alongside the very last pontoon. Her name was painted in fake black oversize typescript across the transom of her starboard hull, and she had the forlorn air of abandonment.

The panic returned then, but I told myself there was still hope. There had to be hope, for I could not bear the thought of what I most feared. Perhaps Ellen was still provisioning the boat? I went to the end pontoon, then climbed aboard *Addendum* to discover that no one else had been aboard the big catamaran in days. Litter had blown from the marina's yard to collect in a leeward corner of her capacious cockpit, while a spider had made a thick white web across the louvres of the padlocked cabin door. A dishrag had been hung to dry from the ensign-hooks on the signal halliard and the dishrag's folds had stiffened to the consistency of dry chamois leather.

I dutifully rattled the cabin door, then peered through one of the windows into the vast cabin. It was empty. I went forrard and tried the forehatch, but that was as well secured as the main companionway. A dry brown palm frond had been blown on to the netting which was rigged between the bows of the twin hulls. I crouched next to a Dorade ventilator box and put my fingers by its vents to feel the whisper of heated air coming from *Addendum*'s stifling interior. I sniffed the air, dreading that I might smell the awful stench of a body left to rot, but the exhausting air was merely musty. Ellen was not here and, so far as I could tell, she had never been here.

I heard a sudden blast of music, and I turned to see a workman wander out of one of the marina sheds. He was a Rastafarian, carrying a vast music box on one shoulder as he half danced and half shuffled his way across the yard.

"Hey!" I shouted at the man.

He stared at me in complete astonishment, as though I was an angel come down from paradise. Then he turned and stared towards the open gate before looking back to me, thus slowly convincing himself that I was real person who had arrived through the gate and not some heaven-sent apparition. "What are you doing, man?"

"Is this the Steinways' boat?" I was trying to convince myself that there might be two catamarans called *Addendum*.

The man switched off the music. "That's Barry Steinway's boat. You a friend of his?"

I climbed on to the pontoon and walked slowly towards him. "Have you seen a girl on board *Addendum*? A pretty girl? She should have been here two days ago. She's got red hair and good legs."

He grinned at my last words, but shook his dreadlocks. "No, man. I ain't seen no red girl." He danced two self-absorbed and silent steps before offering me a toothless grin. "She real pretty?"

I took out a five-dollar bill. "She's tall," I said, "and sun-tanned, and she was supposed to be looking after the boat for the Steinways. She was going to sail it to Florida. Has she been here? Have there been any telephone messages for her? Her name's Ellen."

"I told you, man! I haven't seen no girl!"

I gave him the five dollars, which he treated as a paltry reward for his ignorance, then I asked if I could use the telephone in the marina office. He gave me his grudging consent.

I dialled the Maggot. Once again I got the answering machine, but this time I left no message.

Ellen was gone. Jackson Chatterton was dead. Thessy was in his grave. And I was scared.

I hurried to the school where the Literacy Project had its office, and where I found the Project's secretary to be a tall, light-skinned and grey-haired Bahamian woman who seemed bowed down by her insuperable problems. She introduced herself as Lillian Malleson and, assuming that I had come to talk about her troubles, immediately blamed them all on the television. "We can't compete with it," she said despairingly, "why did they ever invent it? That's what I'd like to know. Why?"

Unable to answer her query, I explained my own; that I was looking for Ellen Skandinsky.

"She was here at the beginning of the week." Lillian Malleson closed a window against the ear-splitting noise of the children in the school's dusty playground. "I think it was Monday. She said she'd been on one of the out-islands for the weekend."

"Did she say where she was going?"

Lillian Malleson frowned at me, almost as if she was noting my presence in her office for the first time. "You're Nick?"

"Yes."

"Ellen mentioned you. She likes you. Are you interested in the Project? We do need help." She crossed the room and tugged open the humidity-swollen door of a tall cupboard, then stared with quiet sorrow at the heaps of reading primers that mouldered on the shelves. "None of them are any good." She plucked a book at random and held it out for my inspection. "See for yourself."

She had given me *The Gospel Story Retold for Little Christians*, the cover of which showed a group of golden-haired and blue-eyed children sitting at the feet of a very white-skinned and well-fed Christ. A couple of plump rabbits and a bluebird were also listening to the Gospel message. Lillian took the book from me. "This is supposed to compete with *Miami Vice* or *The Cosby Show*?" She tossed the book back in the

217

cupboard, and brought out another called *Our Furry Friends From Far Australia*. "I think this one was donated by the British High Commission," she said, "and, if I recall correctly, we've got a thousand copies. If you want to know something about koala bears or kangaroos then please feel free to take one of those books away, or even a thousand if you wish." She went back to her table that was covered with a dreadful litter of letters, books, file cards and ashtrays. In pride of place, at the very centre of the desk's muddle, was a very modern American telephone with an inbuilt message recorder. Lillian stared at the sleek instrument as though seeking inspiration. "I do remember Ellen saying she was sailing a boat somewhere," she said suddenly, and reverting to the question I had put to her a few moments before. "Might she have said she was sailing a boat to Florida?"

I already knew that Ellen had not done that. "What about Great Inagua," I asked instead. "Wasn't she thinking of doing some work for you on Great Inagua? Perhaps that's where she is?"

"I'm sure she's not." Lillian shook a cigarette from a packet. "I know I shouldn't," she said tiredly, "but my husband's a doctor, and he does, and I think if Freeman can smoke, why can't I? It isn't a fair world when you think about it, is it?"

"Did someone else go to Great Inagua instead of Ellen?" I asked, but only after agreeing that it was not, indeed, a fair world.

"No one." She lit her cigarette. "We didn't have the money for the fare, you see. The salt company on the island offered to pay all our costs, but I'm not entirely sure I replied to their letter. Do you think I should write and remind them of their offer?" she asked me with great seriousness.

"Oh, yes," I said with equal seriousness, "I think you should." I paused. "Perhaps Ellen went with her own money?"

Lillian shook her head. "She didn't take the questionnaire if she did, and there's not much point in going there without the questionnaire. At least, I don't think she took the questionnaire." She went to an antique filing cabinet and dragged out a broken drawer. She puffed smoke as she hunted through the chaos of papers, while I looked round the lizard-haunted walls which were smothered with posters designed to teach the alphabet; 'O is for Oliver, Asking for More, while P is for Puffer-Train, Making a Roar'; then Lillian found the Great Inagua file and mutely showed me that the United Nations Educational Scientific and Cultural Organisation Standard Literacy Attainment Questionnaire, English Language Edition, Number 34, published 1961, To Be Filled In With Indelible Ink ONLY, was still in the file. "It's the only copy of the form that we have," she said, "so Ellen can't have taken another."

I stared out of the window. Small children were swinging from a climbing frame that was thick with rust. "She's disappeared, you see," I explained bleakly.

Lillian's shrug seemed to suggest that these things happened and that it was foolish to seek any explanation.

"If you see her," I said, "would you please tell her to phone John Maggovertski?" I wrote down the Maggot's telephone number, but I had a feeling that I was wasting my time, or perhaps it was just that I had been infected with the general air of hopelessness that pervaded the Literacy Project.

I asked if I could use the Project's phone to make a local call, because I wanted to see if the Maggot had reached home, but it seemed the telephone was not working. "They sent an engineer last week," Lillian Malleson said, "and he said this telephone is too modern."

"So get another telephone?" I suggested.

"It was donated." She stared at the splendid instrument. "It seems that it can be adapted to the system, but . . ." Her voice tailed away.

"The engineer couldn't read the instructions?" I hazarded a guess.

She blinked at me. "If I see Ellen," she said instead of answering me, "I'll ask her to phone you."

I thanked her, then went out into the playground of shrieking children. Ellen was gone.

*

Ellen was gone, but all I could do was go on looking for her. I could find no taxis near the school so I caught a bus that dropped me near the Straw Market, and I ran through the alleys and into the courtyard and up the stairs to Ellen's small apartment. I thumped on her door.

There was no answer. A child cried across the courtyard and a goat bleated at the foot of the staircase. A woman screamed at a child, a dog howled in pain, and in the street a truck's brakes hissed like an attacking puff-adder. The televisions in the various apartments were mostly tuned to an American talk show on which chainsaw-voiced women were screaming their opinions about the desirability of geriatric sex.

I kicked at Ellen's door and only succeeded in chipping away some loose flakes of yellow paint.

I looked under the broken piece of balustrade where Ellen kept her spare key, but the key was not there, so instead I tried to break down her door. The flimsy lock proved unexpectedly resilient and I bruised my right foot as I kicked and kicked again, but at last the lock broke and the door swung open.

I need not have bothered, for Ellen was long gone. Her bed was empty, her bathroom was empty, and there was nowhere else in the tiny flat to search for her. "Hell," I said. The room was as untidy as ever, so I could not tell if anyone else had searched it, but it did not look as though there had been any kind of struggle in the room for the bed was made neatly enough and nothing had been overturned or spilt. Her father's crucifix hung black and still against the wall through which the sounds of the neighbouring apartment came depressingly clearly. A plant on Ellen's table was desperate for water and I fetched a glass from the bathroom. A cockroach scuttled across the floor and I slammed down my heel and squashed it with a lucky hit.

I looked in cupboards and drawers, not really certain what I was searching for, but unwilling just to stand in the room and give way to the threatening despair. I found a letter from Ellen's mother in Rhode Island and I copied down the telephone number in the sudden hope that Ellen might have gone home.

I felt a flicker of hope because I found none of her precious writer's notebooks, but that really meant nothing; Lillian Malleson had already confirmed to me that Ellen had done what she had told me she was going to do; namely fly to Freeport, collect her baggage from this apartment, say goodbye to the Literacy Project, then sail away. Except she had never reached the marina.

The despair was creeping up on me. I badly needed to talk to the Maggot. I turned in the tiny space of Ellen's apartment, seeking any clue as to what might have happened to her, and finding none. I kicked at one of the boxes of African literacy leaflets in my frustration and the violence of the motion dislodged the gun from my waistband. It clattered harmlessly to the floor.

Ellen's neighbour, a man who worked a night shift as a cashier at one of the island's casinos, had been disturbed by the noise I had made breaking down Ellen's door, and now came to see just what or who had caused that commotion. He arrived as I was picking up the gun from Ellen's straw matting and, seeing the weapon, he backed sharply away and made noises as though he was trying to restrain a horse. "Whoa! Whoa! It's OK, I ain't curious! Not me! You just break in, don't you care about me, man! I ain't curious, oh no!"

"It's OK!" I ran on to the balcony that connected the small apartments and tried to placate him. "I'm just looking for Ellen. I'm her English friend, Nick."

I was not sure he believed me. Certainly the glimpse of the evil-looking gun had unnerved him. He raised his hands to ward me off. "I ain't seen Ellen for days, man! Not for days! It ain't my business. That's what I told the other gentlemen."

"What other gentlemen?" I had pursued the casino cashier almost into his apartment.

"Just people! They were here last week."

"White people? Hispanic? Blacks?"

"All sorts, man, all sorts. I don't know who they are, and I can't tell you more!" The cashier had backed inside his tiny apartment where a television flickered. I caught a glimpse of a girl's dark and naked legs curled on a sheet printed with a tiger-skin pattern, then the cashier slammed the door in my face. "You go away!" He shouted through the door as he slammed its bolts shut. "Go away!" I heard the girl asking questions, but the cashier was more concerned with getting rid of me. "Go away!" he shouted again, his voice shrill with fear, "just go away!"

I went away. I suspected that the visitors the cashier had described were McIllvanney and Bellybutton. McIllvanney, after all, had already told me that he had visited Ellen's flat.

I went into the street and used some of the money I had cashed that morning to buy a hasp, a padlock, eight screws and a screwdriver, then I went back to Ellen's apartment and, after leaving her a note apologising for the mess I had caused and begging her to telephone the Maggot if she came home, I made good the damage I had caused. I scribbled another note for the cashier next door, apologising for scaring him, and asking him to leave a message at John Maggovertski's number if he heard any news of Ellen. I wrote down the Maggot's phone number and address, and added that I hoped to be at that address later that day. I hid the padlock's key in the place where Ellen normally hid her own spare key. The casino cashier watched me through a crack in his curtains, but pretended not to be home when I knocked on his window, so I slid the message under his door and left him to the girl on his bed and the harridans on his television.

I needed a telephone. The public phone just outside Ellen's apartment block had been used as a public urinal, and its handset torn away, so I walked down to the waterfront, then along to McIllvanney's yard.

"I'm supposed to call the police and have you thrown out," Stella greeted me cheerfully, "but do you want your mail and a cup of tea first?"

"Thanks." I went to the window and stared down into the yard. *Junkanoo*'s pontoon was empty, evidence that McIllvanney had taken Donna to her client. There was no sign of Bellybutton. *Starkisser* rocked gently at her berth. The marina looked strangely empty without *Wavebreaker*'s towering presence. "Can I use the phone?" I asked Stella. "It's long distance."

"Call the moon for all I care, Nick. I don't pay the bills." I called Ellen's mother in Providence, Rhode Island. I did not want to alarm her so I merely described myself as an old colleague who happened to be in America and wanted to speak with Ellen. Her mother told me that Ellen was in the Bahamas. I thanked her. Another escape route of hope was thus blocked.

I dialled the Maggot, but again I only reached his irritating message. "John?" I said to the damned machine, "this is Nick, and I've lost Ellen, and I need to talk to you. If you come home, then for God's sake don't leave till we've spoken. I'll keep trying to reach you." I put the telephone down. "Shit."

Stella had heard the message I had dictated to the Maggot's machine. "You lost Ellen?"

I nodded. "She's not at her apartment, she hasn't gone back to her mother, she's not on her friends' boat, and she's not working for the Literacy Project." I shrugged. "So I don't know where she is."

Stella heard the despair in my voice and tried to cheer me up by saying that Ellen was a survivor and a tough girl. I smiled my thanks for her efforts, and tried to believe her. Then I sat in McIllvanney's chair to read my small pile of mail. Most of it had been forwarded from England. A journalist from London had written to say he was writing my father's biography and he would be most grateful if I could spare him some time to share my memories. One of Her Majesty's Inspectors of Taxes wrote to remind me that I had not filed an Income Tax return in three years, and that consequently Her Majesty would appreciate hearing from me pronto. A bank wanted to send me a credit card. "Stuff 'em." I screwed the mail into a ball and tossed it at the garbage can.

Stella gave me a mug of coffee. "I know the man tried to see Ellen on Sunday." 'The man' was McIllvanney.

"He told me," I said, then, thinking of the cashier's assertion that there had been more than one man trying to see Ellen, I asked whether Bellybutton had accompanied McIllvanney. If McIllvanney had gone to Ellen's apartment alone, then the men the cashier had seen must have been Sweetman's friends.

Stella, who did not like Bellybutton, shrugged. "I don't know." She frowned suddenly, then pointed at me with a teaspoon. "But when you came to the yard to sign those papers this morning, Bellybutton made a phone call. It was about you. I heard him say your name."

"What else did he say?"

"I couldn't hear." She suddenly gave me a guileless smile. "But you can always ask him."

"Bellybutton's still here?"

"He's playing poker in the sail loft." Before I could stop her Stella had opened the office door and was shouting down into the yard. "Hey, Bellybutton! I want you! Get your lazy bones up here!"

I would have preferred to approach Bellybutton in my own way, but Stella had precipitated the moment, so I went past her on to the outside staircase just as Bellybutton emerged scowling from the sail loft. "What is it, woman?" he was shouting, then he saw me. "You!" He pointed a threatening finger at me. "You're not supposed to be here! You get the hell out of here!"

"You answer Nick's questions, Bellybutton, you hear me?" Stella demanded stridently.

"You shut your black mouth, woman!"

"Listen –" I tried to intervene.

"You get your white ass out of here!" Bellybutton screamed at me. "You got ten seconds! And I'm counting!"

"I only wanted to ask you . . ."

"Bellybutton!" Stella screeched at him. "You remember your good manners!"

"Fuck my good manners." He looked back to me. "Five seconds! You're not asking me nothing! You're getting out of here! That's what Mr Mac says you're to do, and that's what you're going to do! Three seconds, two, one!" Suddenly, and with alarming speed, he drew a knife from his belt. It was a heavy-bladed filleting knife that he pointed towards me as he advanced to the bottom of the stairs. "You want to give me aggravation? OK, I don't mind aggravation. My Mama weaned me on to aggravation!" His three poker-playing friends, two of them still holding their playing cards, had come to the sail loft's door. Bellybutton, evidently needing to show off in front of this small audience, began climbing the stairs towards me.

"You go back!" Stella ordered him. "And you put that cutter away!"

"Shut your filthy black mouth, woman!"

"I only want to ask you some questions . . ." I began, trying to introduce a little civility into the yard, but I could have saved my breath.

"OK, man! You're in real trouble!" Bellybutton began taking the stairs two at a time.

So I drew the gun.

Stella screamed and fled into the office. She slammed the door.

One of the poker players shouted a warning at Bellybutton, but the warning was hardly needed for he had already seen the gun and his eyes had widened to the size of eggs. He had also stopped cold. "No!" he said.

"I just want to ask you . . ." I began again and in the same civil, unfrightening tone.

"No! No!" Bellybutton backed away, stumbled on a step, then took a flying leap from the staircase to land in an ungainly sprawl on the yard. A stray cat fled in terror.

"Listen!" I shouted.

"You're mad! Mad!" Bellybutton picked himself up and ran towards the pontoons. His friends were making themselves scarce, fleeing towards the gate and scattering their cards to the warm wind.

"Stop!" I shouted at Bellybutton. I was running after him, but he was much faster and was already unclipping *Starkisser*'s cockpit cover. He had the boat's keys on a chain hanging from his belt.

I took a couple of the big cartridges from my trousers' pocket and shoved them into the Webley's cylinder. I closed the gun, then cocked it. "Stop!" I shouted again.

Bellybutton used his knife to slash *Starkisser*'s warps. He thrust the boat away from the pontoon. I was running closer, but stopping to load the heavy gun had cost me time. "I only want to ask you a question." I was pleading with him.

Bellybutton fumbled the key into the ignition, turned it, and *Starkisser*'s twin drives crackled into deafening life. A startled pelican flopped off a pontoon stake, and pigeons clattered up from the yard's roofs. Bellybutton twisted his panicked face towards me, then rammed the twin throttles hard forward so that *Starkisser* skidded away from the dock like a terrified horse.

"Damn you! Stop!" I fired, not at the boat, nor at Bellybutton, but into the water ahead of *Starkisser*. I could hardly hear the gun's report over the snarl of the engines, but I saw the bullet spurt up a white fountain, then Bellybutton was snatching at the wheel to stop the sleek blue craft from slip-sliding into the rock wall that was *Wavebreaker*'s empty wharf. I fired again, this time blasting a small puff of rock dust from the dock above Bellybutton's head, and at the very same moment *Starkisser*'s polished stern struck the wharf with a crack that must have been heard halfway to Florida, but the boat did not falter. Instead she just dug her rear end into the water and took off like a jet-fighter overdosing on afterburners.

"Shit." Bellybutton had known something, I was sure of it, but I had lost him. Or perhaps he was just plain terrified of guns. Whatever, he was gone, and I pushed the gun back into my waistband. The water in the dock was slopping and churning from the turmoil of *Starkisser*'s stern drives.

Stella, reappearing at the top of the office stairs, had a hand over her mouth as she tried to stifle a scream. "I'm sorry, Stella." I went to the bottom of the office steps. "I'm sorry."

"It's OK, Nick."

I told her that if Ellen telephoned then would she please ask her to get in touch with the Maggot. I gave Stella the Maggot's address and telephone number, but I could feel hopelessness rising around me like a great cold flood. I gave the Maggot another call, but his answering machine just offered me its flippant, crude message. Stella called me a taxi. I had two places left to search, after which I faced the anhedonia of despair.

McIllvanney's cheque had given me more than enough money to pay for the long taxi drive to West End. I could have saved myself the cost of the cab by telephoning, but the very act of moving about the island engendered its own hope. Motion staved off despair.

It was lunchtime when the taxi dropped me off at the Harbour Hotel. I bought a bottle of beer before walking back along the straggling waterfront from where I could see that *Hobgoblin*'s mooring was empty, or rather that it was occupied only by Ned Carraway's cream-painted dinghy. Ned Carraway's cream-painted house was shaded by a huge bougainvillaea. Everything Ned and Julie owned was painted cream; the boat, the house, the furniture, the bicycles, the van, even the children's home-made building blocks. *Hobgoblin* was a wooden boat that needed paint to save her from the sun's destruction, and Ned had bought a job lot of cream paint from a bankrupt building merchant, and he now owned enough cream paint to last a dozen lifetimes. Julie claimed that she dreamed of cream paint. I opened the cream-coloured gate and immediately a tethered piglet tried to charge me and only succeeded in tripping itself up and squealing with sudden fright. A slew of nappies were hanging to dry on a washing line at the side of the house. I banged on the screen door. "Julie!"

"Nick! It's my dream man!" Julie Carraway came to the door with her latest baby propped on her hip. The baby was the colour of *café au lait*, while Julie, who was a plump and cheerful girl from Cincinnati, was the colour of melded freckles. "Don't tell me," she said, "you've come to take me away. You've got a Rolls-Royce waiting at the Star Hotel, a private aeroplane on the strip, and a bottle of champagne hidden behind your back?"

I brought out my half empty bottle of beer. "Will that do?"

"Story of my life." She plopped on to a half-broken chair on the cream-painted verandah and unselfconsciously bared a heavy breast for the baby. "He's a hungry little devil. Takes after his father." She grinned from the baby to me. "Sit down, Nick. Don't mind the madhouse. If you want another beer there's some in the kitchen, but don't bother with the fridge because it's broken. The bottles are in a zinc bucket under the sink." I could hear those children too small to be at school playing behind the house. Julie had six children; all of whom she happily called her half-and-halves. One of the smaller half-and-halves looked solemnly at me from the edge of the cream-painted screen door, then, with a grin, ran off to join her siblings.

I perched on the verandah's edge. "I'm looking for Ellen."

Julie must have heard the despair in my voice for she offered me a sympathetic look, but she could offer me nothing more. "I haven't seen her in weeks, Nick." Then her antennae must have detected something else, for she gave me a very shrewd glance. "Are you two suddenly sweet on each other?"

"Yes."

"That's great, Nick! I always thought you and Ellen should get together. You're just like Ned and me, unlikely enough to make it really work!" Julie's pleasure was genuine and touching.

That pleasure made me smile, but sadly. "She's disappeared, Julie, and that bastard McIllvanney said that Ned had phoned because he needed a replacement cook on *Hobgoblin*, and I was wondering if that's where she's gone?"

"Ned called Matt McIllvanney?" Julie sounded incredulous, for McIllvanney was not noted for showing any kindness to his rivals, even to rivals as unthreatening as Ned and Julie, which made it somewhat odd that Ned might have asked the Ulsterman for help.

"McIllvanney says Ned called him," I insisted.

"When?"

"Sometime last week?"

Julie frowned. "Ned was having a problem with Gwen. Do you know Gwen?" Julie had herself been *Hobgoblin*'s cook till she became the first mate's mate, after which she and Ned had bought the boat as a home for their marriage, though now, because most charter customers don't take kindly to being overrun by the skipper and cook's small children, Julie lived ashore and Gwen, who was one of Ned's distant cousins from the Family Islands, cooked superb meals on *Hobgoblin*'s antiquated charcoal stoves. I said I knew Gwen, and Julie shifted the sucking baby to a more comfortable position. "Her mom was ill, if I remember. Ned called me eight days ago, but he didn't say anything about Ellen. He wasn't even phoning about Gwen, really, but because he'd had to go ashore to get a new gasket for the air-tank compressor. I remember he said that Gwen was worried, but he didn't mention replacing her, and they were way away, Nick! All the way down in the Turks, for God's sake! He called me from Sapodilla Bay!"

Sapodilla Bay was in the Turks and Caicos Islands, five hundred miles away. "Can you talk to Ned?" I asked her.

Julie hooted. "We're not rigged like *Wavebreaker*! Ned's got one antique VHF that only works if you kick it, then sing it the 'Star-Spangled Banner'! I'll hear from him when he gets back, and not before, unless he has a problem and has to phone me from one of the islands."

"When is he back?"

"The day after tomorrow."

"Ask him to give me a call at the Maggot's." I frowned, trying to find a scrap of hope in anything Julie had said. "Are you sure he didn't mention Ellen at all?"

"Not a word," Julie said patiently. "He talked about the compressor, he mentioned Gwen's mom, and he told me that I was the girl of his dreams, but that if a handsome Brit came along it was quite all right for me to run away with him." She paused to let me laugh, but I was too worried, and so she reached over and patted my arm. "Nick! I wish I could help, but I don't see how she can be with Ned! He'd have told me! I've been away, but he knew where to reach me."

"You've been away?" I was snatching at the frailest straws of hope; dreaming suddenly that Ned might have reached Ellen without Julie's knowledge.

"I took the kids to Nassau for the weekend." Julie grimaced. "I went to see the Dreadful Parents who won't visit us here because they think the toilets are dirty, so they pay me to stay in a nice clean hotel in Nassau. They were trying to persuade me to get a divorce, abandon the half-and-halves, then go home and marry a nice white stockbroker called Elmer who plays golf with Daddy, drives a BMW, and has a mortgage." She laughed at the very thought. "But Ned knew which hotel we were staying at, and he didn't call me. Mind you," she added cheerfully, "Ned wouldn't talk to the Dreadful Parents if he could possibly help it, and I can't say I blame him. I'm not really sure why I talk to them myself any longer."

"Damn," I said, but speaking of Ellen rather than Julie's parental woes, and I tilted my head back to stare up into the bougainvillaea. Even the bougainvillaea was cream.

"Is it that bad?" Julie asked.

"It could be," I said bleakly.

Julie paused. "Is it to do with that trouble on *Wavebreaker*?" The gossip had clearly run the island's waterfronts like wildfire, and I could not blame Julie for being curious, so I gave her a brief account of what had happened at Sea Rat Cay, and talking of it made me think of Jesse Sweetman and his peons, and of Thessy shot, and of Jackson Chatterton drowned, and of happiness snatched away. Not three weeks ago I had thought myself so close to paradise; with nothing but a boat to mend and a girl to take to the farthest corner of the world, but then the senator had persuaded me to help his kids and now I was bereft and close to utter despair. I took a pull at my beer that had at last warmed to a drinkable temperature. "If Ned had wanted a cook" – I was worrying at this one like a bad tooth – "would he have called for Ellen?"

"Of course he would! Ned's always had an eagle eye for a pretty girl." Julie laughed with pleasure at the thought. "And if Gwen has had to leave *Hobgoblin* then he'll be desperate because he's got a dream of an off-season charter at the moment – a whole lot of scuba fanatics from Germany, and I know he'd love them to book again next year – but I tell you, Nick, he would have called me if there had been a real problem with Gwen because I'm the one who would have had to arrange her replacement."

"But not if you were in Nassau?"

"He'd have called me!" she said patiently.

It was hopeless. I stared down at the verandah's wide floorboards as Julie tried to cheer me up. "She'll turn up, Nick! Ellen's an independent girl!"

"Yeah, she'll turn up," I said without enthusiasm or belief.

"You want some lunch? Soup and a spam sandwich? Warmed-up baby muck? Minced turnips and custard? Name your pleasure."

I shook my head. The gun was a hard lump in my back. "Can I use the phone?"

"Go ahead." She hospitably waved me towards the house.

"It's only to call a taxi." I was reassuring her that I was not planning to call London.

"Where are you going?"

"To the Maggot's house."

"You don't want to pay for a taxi." She stood up. "We'll pile the half-and-halves in the back of the van and I'll drive you. It will be nice to see the Maggot's ugly face again."

"I don't want to be a nuisance."

"Shut up and hold this." 'This' was the baby, which took one look at my face and burst into tears.

I prayed to God the Maggot was home. I had searched everywhere and found nothing, but the Maggot had been with Ellen on the day she had disappeared so if anyone knew what had happened to her, then surely the Maggot was that person.

If the Maggot himself was still alive. Which now we drove to find out.

The Maggot's house was built in a filthy section of a failed and dilapidated industrial park which was a wasteland of used cars, broken buildings, and toxic wastes. A tidal creek wound its way through this depressing landscape, but it would have been stretching matters to say that the creek was filled with water; it was in fact a noxious sludge of mud-edged chemical horror. The Maggot's house overlooked this oil-slicked sump, in which his fishing boat was berthed, thus enabling him to boast of his 'sea-views'. He claimed that the neighbourhood could only improve, and that its undoubted proximity to the sea made his 'house' into a prime investment.

The prime investment had once been a frozen-food warehouse, which meant that its only windows were in the old upstairs offices facing the creek. The rest of the building had hugely thick concrete walls and heavy steel doors which suitably protected the Maggot's rare collection of firearms. Yet even the Maggot was dimly aware that living within a concrete and steel box was not wholly desirable, so he had bought some lumber from one of the failed businesses in the industrial park and made himself a verandah on the creek side of the box. From the verandah he enjoyed a fine view of the oil-storage facilities on the far bank of the chemical soup.

Julie braked outside this elegant dwelling that still carried a faded sign on its gate ordering deliveries to the left and collections to the right. There was no sign of the Maggot's red Firebird, indeed the only sign of life was the Maggot's immense Rottweiler that began barking and chewing at the chain-link fence as soon as Julie's van stopped by the gate. I wound down the window. "Tatum! Shut your face!"

Tatum was reputed to kill anyone who did not know his name, but merely slobbered over those who did. The dog now whined and writhed with the pleasure at being recognised. The huge beast certainly did not look starved, but that did not mean the Maggot was at home, for I knew he had an arrangement whereby someone came by and hurled offal over the fence when he was away. "The place looks kind of deserted," Julie said uneasily. "Are you sure you want to wait here?"

The place seemed more than deserted; there was even an air of menace in its stillness, but I was desperate to see the Maggot, so I said I would wait. "Will you let me pay for your petrol?" I asked Julie.

"Get out of here, Nick Breakspear!" She laughed, offered me a kiss, then enjoined me not to be a stranger.

I climbed into the heat as the half-and-halves chorused their obedient goodbyes. "Invite me to your wedding!" Julie shouted, then she grated the worn gears as she drove the half-and-halves off for the treat of an ice-cream.

Tatum was shivering with the anticipation of having someone to swamp in dog-dribble. The gate was chained and padlocked, but I knew the Maggot kept the key under a chunk of concrete that anchored one of the fence posts, so I found it, let myself in, and was immediately assaulted by half a ton of amorous Rottweiler. It was like being raped by a fur-coated Sherman tank, but I fought the brute off and, inch by inch, made progress towards the verandah stairs. Tatum finally allowed me to climb to the broad deck with its seductive views across the skim of oil that made a shimmering prism of the creek's surface. *Bronco-Buster*, the Maggot's long-decked fishing boat, was berthed at the end of a short concrete wall that carried a sewage overflow pipe to its outfall into the creek. The smell of the sludge was fairly overpowering, but this was high summer and, as the Maggot liked to say, you could not expect a prime real-estate investment to have everything.

A second key was hidden on one of the rafters that supported the verandah's canvas roof. That second key fitted a padlock which secured what had once been an upstairs office window, and was now a makeshift entryway into the Maggot's kitchen. I struggled through the metal frame, then helped myself to a beer from the refrigerator and a tin of tuna from a cupboard. A steel door led from the kitchen into the rest of the house, but the Maggot did not make the key to that door available to casual visitors. He reasoned that his friends were welcome to drop by when he was not at home and more than welcome to avail themselves of his verandah, kitchen, beer, and scenic views, but he would keep the rest of his house private, and thus the steel door stayed locked unless the Maggot was in residence.

I opened the beer and the tuna, found a fork, and took my makeshift lunch back to the verandah. I extracted the gun from my waistband, not as a precaution, but because it was uncomfortable, and laid it on a wicker table. I sat in the Maggot's favourite chair, which he had bought from a company that specialised in dismantling old aircraft; this particular chair had come from a Boeing B52's cockpit and was wondrously comfortable.

The oil-storage tanks quivered in the heat. The scum on the creek slowly curdled the shimmering oil. The tide was dropping, leaving a greasy gunge on the newly exposed rocks that lined the channel. Rats scuttled along the near bank. The Maggot liked to sit on this verandah with some of his guns and blow the rats away, but for every one he killed it seemed a dozen came back. That was another reason the Maggot liked this house; he could fire guns to his heart's content and no one complained of the noise for no one lived anywhere near. A few people worked in what was left of the industrial park, but only the Maggot lived here. I drank the top off the beer, and waited for the rest to reach a decent temperature. Tatum had gone to sleep in the shade under the verandah's deck.

A truck whined and rattled on the road that was hidden from me by the bulk of the Maggot's house. Nothing more moved for a half-hour until a car came up the road, and I hoped it was the Maggot, but instead the car drove into the warehouse next door where solvents were stored. I went back to the aircraft seat and stared at the tank farm across the creek.

I did not want to admit the possibility, but suppose Ellen was dead? Suppose the Maggot had died with her? Perhaps they had been ambushed after leaving the Literacy Project office when they were on their way to *Addendum*'s marina, except that surely such an ambush would have made the newspapers? So perhaps they were alive? Perhaps their car had been stopped and they had been taken away at gunpoint? Supposing she was alive and . . . I could not even face that contingency, and I momentarily closed my eyes tight as though I could drive the horror of such a fate out of my mind.

Maybe nothing had happened to her? Maybe she had just wanted to visit her friends in America? Perhaps she had gone back to the university where she had taught? I tempted myself with hope, while beneath me Tatum whined in his sleep, then growled softly. I tipped the beer bottle to my mouth.

I tried to reassure myself that the Maggot would soon be home, booming with life and obscenities, telling me that Ellen had abruptly changed her mind and decided to fly to the United States. Perhaps she had sent me a postcard from the airport, which postcard would even now be waiting in the tiny post office on Straker's Cay. The Maggot always called it Streaker's Cay. He had a nickname for everything. The Denver Fairies, the Chicago Chicken-shits, the Philadelphia Sugar Plums, the Tampa Bay . . .

Tatum barked, breaking my idle chain of thoughts and bringing me bolt upright in the pilot's seat. The barking was frantic, but when the dog paused to draw breath I heard the twang of a chain fence under stress off to my right, and I turned that way, but could see nothing until Tatum suddenly appeared from under the verandah, accelerating into killing speed, and barking as he went; then the poor dog just seemed to disintegrate into blood, fur and offal as a shotgun crashed obscenely loud, and I realised that men must be breaking through the wire out of my sight round the corner of the house. I snatched up the gun and dropped to the floor. The violence of my motion spilt the heavy chair on to its side. I left it, crawling instead to the verandah's edge. Tatum was a bloody mess on the dirt, but at least the dog had died instantly and was not twitching and whining in agony.

The property beyond the chain-link fence was a dumping

ground for dead cars. The sun reflected dazzlingly from a myriad scraps of peeling chrome. I could see no one trying to cut their way through the fence, nor any gaps already cut in the wire. I could see no one at all, but then the shotgun fired again from its vantage point among the wrecked cars.

The shotgun fired a third time, pumped, fired once more, then fired a last time. The shots filled the stench-laden air with noise and swamped the verandah with a storm of lead pellets that whipped overhead, smashing the glass of a hurricane lamp that hung from the verandah's rafters, but otherwise doing no harm. I was down behind the heavy timbers of the balustrade. There were small gaps between the timbers that let me watch the car graveyard, but I still could not see my enemies.

All I could see were the heaps of rusting cars and the unbroken chain-link fence. Nothing more. I realised I was holding my breath, so I let it slowly out. I was alive. I was unhurt. I fumbled in my trouser pocket, found a handful of bullets, and loaded all six of the Webley's chambers. I cocked the gun, then looked again through my small loophole. Tatum's body was already busy with flies. Paraffin was dripping from the punctured reservoir of the hurricane lamp behind me. I could see no gunman at the chain-link fence.

The hairs on the back of my neck prickled. The dog had been attracted to the fence because of the noise of the wire being cut or stretched, yet the fence was undamaged and my attackers had evidently retreated into the piles of scrapped cars, and I suddenly realised that they had merely used the noise of the fence as a decoy to draw the dog and my attention one way while they attacked from the other, and I rolled on to my back, sat up, and levelled the gun towards the top of the second flight of stairs which led up to the far side of the verandah. I was aware of being frightened, but I noted that my hands were utterly still.

I could not see if anyone was climbing those far stairs. Nor could I see the concrete wall which edged the left-hand side of the property. That wall formed the rear of the small warehouse complex in which the industrial solvents were stored. I had watched a car roll into that yard only moments before, but I had thought nothing of it. The warehouse had a corrugated tin roof. Doubtless my enemies had crossed the roof under the cover of the shotgun's fusillade, and were now approaching the verandah. Would they assault the stairs or try to fire up through the stout timbers of the deck? I dismissed the latter fear. I knew I had to concentrate on the likeliest threat, eliminate it, then worry about what else the ungodly might do.

The fear was quivering in me. The beer and tuna were acid-sour in my belly, my left leg was shivering, my bowels were like water, my heart was racing; yet I had a gun, and my hands were rock steady, and I reasoned that I was facing the men who had hurt or killed Ellen, and all my consciousness seemed trained on the patch of light that marked the top of the far stairs. I was in shadow, but anyone who attacked me must come through that light and thus make themselves a target. That thought gave me confidence.

Except they threw a grenade instead.

I saw its silhouette and knew I had lost.

Except they threw too hard and the grenade thumped against one of the rafters and dropped sharply down to lodge just behind the solid lump of the Maggot's fallen aircraft chair, which now protected me like a blast wall. I was counting the seconds since the grenade had appeared. I opened my mouth to equalise the blast and drew up my knees to protect my midriff, but I did not take the gun away from the bright space at the top of the far stairs.

Which bright space was suddenly cracked apart with noise and flame. The canvas roof billowed, ripped and tore away as hot air punched at me with an appalling violence, but no shrapnel came at me. The heavy pilot's chair slid six feet towards me, and the table was blown on to its side, but I was unhurt. The spilt paraffin had caught fire, its flames flickering across the verandah's deck. The sound of the explosion still echoed, and it was during that echo that my attackers charged up the far stairs.

I could not see them clearly, for the sunlight was too bright and I was half dazed by the explosion, but a part of my brain had gone back into its training and it was telling my body what to do. My enemies were charging up the steps and one of them was shouting like a fiend either to give himself courage or to intimidate me. I could only hear the one voice, but two pairs of boots. I also knew that my attackers would not see me immediately for I was in shadow, and the verandah was a chaos of fallen furniture, flame and smoke, and that blessed small scrap of my brain that had been programmed in the lethal skills of soldiering told me to hold my fire until I was certain of a kill.

The first man, the one who was shouting, hurled himself on to the verandah. He was a young black man, short-haired, muscular, and carrying a Kalashnikov. I unthinkingly registered the distinctive shape of the curved magazine, and I saw the muzzle's pale flames pricking the brightness as he began spraying the verandah with bullets, but like most inexperienced men he was firing too high. I knew there was a second man behind him, and I guessed the second man was the marksman. The first man had been committed to draw my attention, while the second was the expert, the executioner who would kill me while I was distracted by his noisy companion, so I shifted the heavy Webley a fraction to the right and waited for the second man, and I did not otherwise move a muscle, because movement attracts fire, and I waited for a full second while the first man hammered the verandah with bullets. I was inwardly gibbering with fear as I waited, but then the second man appeared. He could have been the first man's twin brother. He panned his rifle round the verandah, saw me, and shouted a warning to the first man who had still not spotted me. I pulled the trigger.

I was terrified, yet still the training held good. I was using both hands to steady the gun and I had taken my time. I had given myself all of a half-second to aim, and at that range a trained soldier could not miss, and I fired, and I saw the bullet shatter the second man's throat and his shout turned into a wet gulp as he became airborne, flying backwards, his blood filling the open verandah in a sickening spray that was turned to incandescent red by the sunlight. The first man began to turn his gun back towards me, but the hammerlike recoil of the Kalashnikov's automatic fire had been spinning his body and his aim away from me, while my arms had already soaked the massive blow of the revolver and were steady again and I knew he was going to fall to his right in a desperate attempt to escape me, so I fired that way and saw the dark fleck where the bullet hit his ribs. His whole chest quivered with the seismic shock of the bullet's strike. The blow thumped him hard against the cement-block wall of the Maggot's house, and there he stayed, suddenly leaning on the wall with dull eyes staring at me and the now silent gun hanging by his side.

Then he sighed. His lips were drawn back from his teeth, and he looked as though he was going to cry. He tried to lift the rifle, but it was as heavy as lead in his nerveless hand. He suddenly looked very young and very sad, like a child deprived of a toy. There were tears in his eyes that brimmed, then poured down his cheeks. He stared reproachfully at me, then made one last supreme effort to lift his assault rifle. I watched the muzzle rise towards me, felt the sudden panic, and so I fired a last time. The Webley's heavy bullet obliterated the man's face, wiping away his tears for ever. He slid down the wall, leaving a slime of blood on the concrete.

Silence. The paraffin flames flickered blue. Bile was sour in my throat. Sweat stung my eyes. I noticed that my hands had begun to shake.

I thanked God they had not been waiting in ambush when Julie had dropped me at the gate, for God knows what slaughter they would have made had they fired at her van. But how had these men known where to find me? That was not a difficult question to answer, for I had spent all day telling people that I could be reached at the Maggot's house, and doubtless my enemies had known ever since early morning that I was on the island. Who else could Bellybutton have telephoned? And who had he phoned? Billingsley? But if the policeman wanted me dead, why had he not killed me when I was in custody? Because too many questions would have been asked as a result of such a death. The conjectures flickered through my consciousness, even as I listened for a sound, any sound, that would betray the next move of my enemies.

If they made any move at all, other than to escape, for they must have realised that their first attack had failed disastrously. If they had any sense they would cut and run now, just as I should cut and run before the police arrived. I expected the police at any moment, for surely someone must have heard the gunfire and called the authorities? I could smell blood. So much blood. Dog blood and man blood. The world stank of blood and burning kerosene; a mingling stench that even overpowered the reek from the channel behind me.

I rolled over, expecting a shotgun blast.

Nothing. The first man I had shot was out of my sight, blown back down the steps, but the second was still lying slumped at the foot of the wall. He was dressed in black fatigues. I edged across to him, skirting the paraffin flames, and took his Kalashnikov, which was the East German version with the pimply black plastic stock. The gun was sticky with the dead man's blood, which I tried to wipe away. I took the two spare magazines that were jammed into a pouch attached to his webbing belt. The paraffin had set fire to the wicker mats that carpeted the verandah and the flames were suddenly brighter and fiercer.

I changed the assault rifle's magazine. That gave me thirty rounds. I was crouching low. Puddled in the dead man's blood were some cartridges ejected from the Kalashnikov. They were made of green-lacquered steel like those I had found on *Hirondelle* so long ago. That coincidence did not mean that these men had also killed *Hirondelle*'s crew because the Eastern bloc, just like the West, was flooding the world with weapons. Talking peace is good for a politician's image, but selling weapons is good for employment figures and foreign earnings. I was moving towards the side of the verandah which faced the car graveyard, towards the chain-link fence. No police had come yet.

The heat of the burning wicker was increasing and its smoke was thickening, but that smoke was not going to help me because it was rising into the air instead of clinging to the ground like a screen. The burning wicker would drive me off the verandah, but only into the aim of the surviving gunmen. To burn or be shot? I was as indecisive as Hamlet. Be shot, I decided, and so I stood up, keeping my back against the wall of Maggot's house and pushed the Webley into my trouser pocket. Nothing moved in the yard of scrapped cars. I could just see the far-off open sea above the piles of shimmering crushed metal. My back hurt where the pellets had hit me on board *Wavebreaker*; those shotgun pellets had all been removed and the wounds were almost healed, yet suddenly they felt raw and painful.

I cocked the Kalashnikov. I used to teach marines how to strip and fire a Kalashnikov, the theory being that one day they might have to fight with captured weapons. The Kalashnikov was a good gun. You could stamp on it, burn it, drown it, and still it goes on working. I edged down the stairs, expecting the blast of a shotgun at any second. The stench of dog blood was thick, and the buzz of flies even thicker. Sweat trickled down my face and stung my eyes. I cuffed it away. No one fired. I reached the ground and ran like a hare to the sewage outfall wall where *Bronco-Buster* was moored. The wall's top was curved, like an arch over a pipe, and the concrete was crumbling. The stink of sewage and oil and smoke and blood was overpowering. I stumbled desperately off the wall's curvature to land heavily on *Bronco-Buster*'s aft deck. She was thirty-two feet long, had a flying bridge and a tattered fighting chair that did not look strong enough to withstand the tug of a stickleback. I crouched in her open wheelhouse, watching the shore.

Fire and smoke still showed on the verandah, but much more feebly now, for the wicker mats had burned out and the rest of the structure was built of timbers so massive that it would need a blowtorch to set them on fire. The charred remnants of the canvas awning, blown ragged by the grenade, lifted in the warm and idle wind. I doubted that the flames would spread to the Maggot's house, for the old cold-store was built of materials that would not ignite easily.

Still no police had come. Nothing living moved except three turkey vultures that circled overhead. I was slowly concluding that I was safe, that no gunmen were left to fire at me, but that did not mean I could relax. The police must surely come, and to avoid their questions I decided to take *Bronco-Buster* to sea, though that notion depended on the boat's engine starting. I decided I would run for Straker's Cay. I could think of nowhere else to go. It was not safe to stay here, for my enemies would be sure to return, and if not my enemies than it would be the police. All that was left was to salvage *Masquerade* and go. There was nothing else. No Ellen.

I thought I heard a car accelerate away, but was not certain. I waited ten more minutes, then straightened up in the wheelhouse. No one fired at me. *Bronco-Buster*'s engine and fuel tanks were all under padlocked hatches and her ignition needed a key, which meant I would have to hot-wire the boat, but first I had to make sure she was fuelled. I used the Kalashnikov's flash suppressor as a jemmy, ripping a hasp and padlock out of the spongy wood to lift a locker lid and reveal the boat's main fuel tank.

She was almost empty. A sight glass ran down beside the big fifty-gallon fuel tank, and it showed hardly a quarter inch of fuel remaining. That was just enough to reach McIllvanney's yard where I would beg, borrow or steal *Starkisser*.

I began levering at the engine hatch, needing to turn on the seacocks that fed the motor's cooling system, when I heard the creak of the Maggot's gate. I looked up.

The Maggot had come home at last. I felt an avalanche of relief crash through me as I watched him climb out of his red Firebird to open the gates, then I shouted to warn him that gunmen might still be lurking in ambush, but he was too far away to hear me over the sound of his car's engine so I fired the Kalashnikov into the air, and that alerted him. He dived back into the Firebird and I saw him leaning towards the glove compartment, presumably to find a gun.

I clambered off the boat on to the awkward slope of the wall. The Maggot accelerated into his yard, his tyres spinning a smokescreen of dust into the humid air. No one fired at him. He skidded the car to a stop beside the body of his dead Rottweiler. Flies buzzed. The Maggot did not spare the dog a glance, but just ran up the verandah steps with a fire extinguisher he had snatched from his car. "What the hell happened?" he shouted at me.

"Where the hell's Ellen?" I shouted back. Fire hissed as the Maggot released the chemical extinguisher. A noxious mist, foul as the stench of the creek, reeked away from the verandah. "Where's Ellen?" I shouted again as I reached the foot of the verandah steps.

"Ellen?" The Maggot turned and frowned at me as though he did not really understand the basis of my question. "She's with you, isn't she? That's where she said she was going!"

And with those words all hope went.

"We went to her apartment, OK? She fetched her things, went on to the Literacy Project, then she reckoned that she didn't want to sail that heap of junk to the Keys, but wanted to go back to you, so I dropped her off at the ferry terminal."

"You just left her there?"

"Sure! She insisted she was OK." The Maggot, kicking the last sparks of the fire dead, sensed my unspoken criticism that he should have been more protective, and that he should even have flown Ellen back to Straker's Cay. "I had a booking to fly three Venezuelans to Rodentworld." Rodentworld was the Maggot's nickname for Disneyworld; so called because it was the place where people dressed as mice to welcome the tourists. "The charter had been booked for weeks, Nick," he went on defensively, "and I couldn't let them down."

"I know. I'm sorry." It was unfair to blame the Maggot for what had happened. He had done his best.

"And frankly –" he forced a very unconvincing laugh, "Ellen wasn't really happy in my company. You know how she reacts to me? Like I was something thrown up by a hog?"

He backed down off the verandah that was still wreathed in smoke and fumes, though the last of the flames had been extinguished.

"Ellen never arrived at Straker's Cay," I told the Maggot, but then a sudden and searing pulse of hope shot through me. "Unless she's there now? Maybe she arrived after I left?"

The Maggot shook his head. "I've just come from there. I went looking for you." He had gone to the body of the gunman who had fallen backwards down the stairs and now he crouched beside the bloody corpse to search its pockets. This dead gunman, like the other, was dressed in the quasi-military black fatigues.

"You went looking for me?" I asked the Maggot.

"That senator – Crowninshield – wants to see you," the Maggot explained carelessly, as though US senators were always demanding my company, then he suddenly cursed and twitched back from the dead body as though it had bitten him.

"What?"

"Jesus!" The Maggot tossed me the wallet he had taken from a pocket of the fatigues. Till now the Maggot had displayed a remarkable insouciance in the face of the flames and death that had polluted his house, but now he was suddenly showing real alarm.

The wallet was stuffed with money, but it was not the cash that had alarmed the Maggot. It was the warrant card. The dead man with the flies in his mouth was a policeman. I had just shot a policeman. I had probably just shot two policemen.

"Oh, my God." I was shaking.

The Maggot stood up. His red Firebird made a ticking noise as its engine cooled, but otherwise there was silence. The other gunman or gunmen had fled. The gate of the warehouse yard was open and tyre tracks showed on the road where they had spun their wheels in their hurry to get away. They had left their dead behind. Dead policemen. The Maggot stepped backwards. He was going to abandon me, I was sure of it and I could not blame him.

"Deacon Billingsley," the Maggot suddenly said.

"That's not Billingsley," I said. I was still shaking. It was slowly dawning on me just how much trouble I was in. The world had jumped its gears. Just a month ago I had been helping to film a Pussy-Cute commercial, and my biggest worry had been keeping the bloody cats from marooning themselves up *Wavebreaker*'s rigging; now I was a cop-killer and that meant an eternity in jail, or even worse. "Do they have capital punishment in the Bahamas?"

"Billingsley must have sent them." The Maggot had taken the wallet back from me and was pulling out the wads of money. "For God's sake, Nick, think! You were a witness to Thessy's murder. They want to get rid of all the witnesses."

I stared at the gunman. Flies were thick on the awful throat wound. "They weren't here on police business?" I asked, still in shock.

"Of course they were not damn well here on police business." The Maggot had grabbed the corpse by its boots and was dragging it under the smoking verandah where it would be hidden from the road. "Even the Bahamian Police are not yet officially drug-smugglers. And for God's sake, don't just stand there! Help me get the hell out of here!"

"Help?" It was dawning on me that the Maggot was not going to leave me to my grim fate, but was planning on helping me. I felt a flood of gratitude for the huge man.

"Sooner or later their pals will come looking." The Maggot found his keys and unlocked the door. "So for Christ's sake, let's go!"

He began hauling green canvas bags from inside his house and told me to stack them into the boot of his car. The bags were heavy and clanked metallically, as though they were filled with golf clubs, then I realised the Maggot was rescuing the best of his astonishing gun collection. "Are you abandoning this place?" I asked him.

He paused for a second. "Two dead policemen in my house? You bet I'm getting the hell out of here." He tossed out two plastic garbage bags of clothes, a briefcase, then a silver-framed photograph that showed a delicately beautiful brunette dressed in a body-stocking and leg warmers. He had plainly been prepared to make a moonlight flight, knowing just which possessions he wanted to rescue and which he wanted to abandon. Then, leaving the house door open, he shouted at me to get in the car.

I still held the photograph. The engine snapped into life, the back wheels spewed dirt and dust as the Maggot let out the clutch, then we were fishtailing out of his compound and on to the road. He accelerated away.

I looked at the portrait. The girl had a fragile loveliness, raven-dark hair, bright eyes, and an impudently cheerful smile. Her body was lithe and taut. "Pittsburgh?" I asked the Maggot.

"Yeah." He spun the wheel hard and I heard the guns shift in the boot.

"She's very beautiful," I said in real tribute.

"Yeah. Except now she's giving blow jobs in the back room of a peep-show." The Maggot's voice was grim as death. "That picture was taken before she found cocaine. They don't look so damn good afterwards."

God damn it. I closed my eyes as though I could obliterate the misery in darkness. Ellen. The thought of her suddenly swamped me, making me want to cry. She had tried to catch a ferry to come back to me, and it was from the ferry that Jackson Chatterton had been pushed to his death. It had all gone wrong.

And now we were running.

We loaded everything into the Maggot's Beechcraft. That, at least, he could take with him when he left the Grand Bahamas, though he was resigned to losing the car. He was fond of his Firebird. It had a bumper sticker which read 'This Might Not Be The Mayflower, But Your Daughter Came Across In It.' The Maggot tried to peel the bumper sticker away, claiming he might never find another like it, but the paper tore in his big fingers.

"For Christ's sake!" I snapped. "Let's get out of here!"

"I've got to file a flight plan yet. You wait." He at last abandoned the bumper sticker and, snatching up a chart and a pile of papers, strode away towards the airport buildings.

I climbed into the Beechcraft. It was like a Turkish bath inside the plane, which was standing in the full sunlight, but at least I had the illusion of being hidden. I was nevertheless scared, expecting to hear the visceral wail of a police siren at any second. I watched a helicopter come beating in from the north, its rotors flashing light, and I was sure that it was bringing men to arrest me. I slunk down in my seat as the machine landed not far from the Maggot's plane. I waited for the helicopter to disgorge uniformed men, but instead a hugely fat man in Bermuda shorts climbed out of the helicopter and, without a glance in my direction, walked away.

The Maggot seemed to have disappeared. Sweat was pouring off me. By now, I thought, the police would have found the bodies of their two colleagues. They must have found the bodies. The men who had fled the scene must surely have reported the killings and my description was doubtless already clattering out of telex machines in dozens of police stations across the islands. It was such an easy description: just look for Hamlet, Prince of Denmark. "Shit, shit, shit!" I swore aloud, pounding the plane's broken dashboard, willing the Maggot to reappear from the control tower. He still did not come.

Two black men in white overalls strolled towards the Fire-bird. They stood admiring the car's lines. The overalls were too clean, I decided. Each man wore the logo of an oil company, but I was sure they were policemen. One of the men lit a cigarette. Where the hell was the Maggot? I shrank down in the seat.

Ellen was gone. I had lost *Masquerade*. All I could now hope for was to get out of the islands alive, and then to run from the extradition lawyers. It was my own fault. Ellen had warned me not to get involved with the drug lords; she had warned me on the morning I had found the floating wreckage of the *Hirondelle*, but I had not listened to her, and now she, like Thessy and Jackson Chatterton, was dead. Or probably dead. Or worse. I shivered suddenly, not with cold, but with horror. I knew my grief was in a kind of suspense and that when it came it would be hard to bear, but not so hard as the ordeal that Ellen must already have endured.

The two white-overalled men strolled away. I could hear them laughing. A big passenger jet thumped down on to the main runway. Its engines went into reverse thrust and the thunder bellowed across the field. Where the hell was the Maggot? "Jesus!" I swore impotently. "Come on! Come on!"

Then a police car drove into a car park just a hundred yards away and a uniformed constable climbed out. He stared directly at me, then, as though drawing out my torture, he yawned and stretched his cramped arms. I was tempted to run. Not only would I be charged with murder, but probably with gun-smuggling as well, for the Beechcraft was crammed with weapons. One of the guns, astonishingly, was a Kalashnikov PKM, the general-purpose Russian machine-gun, which the Maggot claimed to have bought off a collector in Florida. The Beechcraft even had boxes of ammunition for the Russian gun, each box containing belts of one hundred rounds. The rope-handled boxes, I noticed, were all labelled *Oficina Económica Cubana*. Another bag held a clutch of little Czechoslovakian Scorpion sub-machine-guns, toylike weapons that were lethal at close quarters. What kind of a mind, I wondered, thought it important to salvage such things when doing a moonlight flit? And what kind of a man would strand me in his plane for so long? "Come on!" I encouraged the invisible Maggot.

The policeman turned and strolled towards the airport terminal. Dust blew across the tarmac. Ellen, Ellen, Ellen. The reality of her fate had not sunk in yet, or else the horror of what had happened to her was so great that my mind refused to face it. Sweetman had surely had her killed, or kidnapped. I tried to think of something I could do to find her, or to avenge her, but there was nothing. I was utterly helpless for I did not know where Jesse Sweetman was, and even if I did know I was not sure what I could do, and then I suddenly wondered just why the Maggot had been so certain that Deacon Billingsley had sent the policemen to kill me at his house. I had never learned of any connection between Sweetman and Billingsley, so why had the Maggot assumed there was?

The Maggot at last appeared in the far doorway. He strolled towards me as though he had all the time in the world, even stopping to chat to the men in white overalls, then wandering with blithe unconcern around the plane as he inspected its wings and tail. "Nothing's fallen off," he reassured me as he climbed into the cabin, "and we've got clearance for Fort Lauderdale."

"Thank Christ for that."

"Not that we're going to Fort Lauderdale, of course. I thought we might visit Coffinhead Porter instead. Do you know Coffinhead?"

I knew Coffinhead, though not as well as the Maggot did. Coffinhead was a Bahamian who had become rich through years of lucrative smuggling, though of late he had retired to a small, but legitimate, marina in the Berry Islands from which he ran a very quick fishing boat and a fleet of diving boats. Coffinhead, whose nickname arose from his oddly elongated and boxlike skull, had sometimes helped out our charter clients by taking them to dive on some especially exotic coral reef, but so far as I knew Coffinhead Porter was not a lawyer, so he could not fight a murder charge on my behalf, and nor did Coffinhead Porter own an airline, so he could not fly me away from Deacon Billingsley's vengeance. "Just why the hell are we going to see Coffinhead?" I asked the Maggot in a very bitter voice.

"Because Senator Crowninshield's there, of course," the Maggot said as though that was the most obvious answer in all the world, "so hold on to your underwear and we'll see if this thing flies."

The thing flew, and it felt wonderful as the wheels left the ground and, second by second, we climbed higher into a police-free sky. Yet I knew there would be more policemen wherever I landed, and I wondered if I would ever be free of their pursuit. I stared regretfully down at the impossibly blue sea that was scarred with the white wakes of pleasure boats and tried to make sense of all the things that had happened to me since the morning. Nothing clicked into place, nothing. "What on earth is Crowninshield doing at Coffinhead's place?" I asked the Maggot.

"He wants to see you. Perhaps he likes you?" The Maggot offered me a suggestive simper.

"Maggot, what the hell is happening?"

He looked at me as though I was mad. "What the hell do you think is happening? The senator wants to get his children back. He's asked me to help him, and I said I wouldn't do it unless you were included in the fun and games. That's why I know Ellen isn't at Streaker's Cay, because I went there to find you."

"Does the senator know where the twins are?"

"Of course he does!" The Maggot was astonished that I needed to ask.

I felt the day's first pulse of hope, though it was a very feeble pulse. If the senator knew where the twins were, then that was surely the place where Jesse Sweetman could be found, and where Jesse Sweetman was, so also was Ellen, if she was alive. As a straw it was not very strong, but it was something to cling on to all the same. "How the devil did the senator find out?" I asked.

"He didn't find out. You did." He banked towards the

250

south, lancing bright sunlight across the cockpit. Cool air was at last venting out of the nozzles.

"I did?" The world was out of joint.

"There," the Maggot pointed to one of the back seats where, among his papers and guns, a brown envelope lay.

I opened the envelope to find that it held a sheaf of black and white photographs. They were the pictures I had taken of Murder Cay on the last occasion that I had flown with the Maggot.

They were not good photographs. One was a distant view of the island, but the picture was so hazed by heat that it was difficult to see anything except the outline of surf and coral and a mass of palm trees on the island itself. There was a reasonable photograph of the dog-leg entrance channel, and there was a perfect picture of two of the island's houses, which looked much bigger than I remembered, and both of which had lavish swimming pools, tennis courts, elegant land-scaping, white stone terraces and satellite dishes on their pantiled roofs; but most of the other pictures were horribly blurred, though I could just make out one of the two trucks which had been parked to block the island's runway and, beyond the truck, the elongated painted cross at the end of the airstrip.

"I grant you're good at blowing away *narcotraficantes*," the Maggot grinned at me, "but you're pure dogshit with a camera."

I grunted acknowledgement of that truth as I sifted quickly through the rest of the prints, many of which had been flared into obscurity by the bloom of the sun's reflection on the plane's windscreen. The very last picture in the pile was the one I had snapped just as the Maggot had desperately side-slipped to evade the machine-gun fire. As a consequence the picture was skewed and one edge was a blur which I assumed was a part of the plane's cockpit. I had been trying to photograph the boats in the island's anchorage, but all I had captured was a sailing yacht and a white working boat with a stubby little wheelhouse. The shadows of the boats showed dark on the pale clear sand of the lagoon's bed. I looked at the Maggot who was lighting himself a cigarette. "So?" I asked. I had rarely seen a worse set of photographs, and I did not understand how they could possibly have identified Murder Cay as the place where the senator's twins had taken refuge.

"Have a look at that last picture again," the Maggot shouted above the engine noise. I looked. It was the skewed and blurred photograph which showed the yacht and the working boat. "How many boats can you see?" the Maggot asked me with evident enjoyment.

"Two."

"And how many shadows on the lagoon bed?"

I looked, I counted, then I blasphemed. "Good God," I said in wonderment.

"Bingo." The Maggot grinned at me. "Two boats, but three shadows. Well snapped, Nick."

I gazed at the photograph. At a casual glance there did indeed seem to be just the two boats in the picture, but three solid hulls were indisputably shadowed on the sandy sea-bed, and the moment I noticed that third shadow I saw the third boat that was floating just above and to one side of it. That third boat was a sports-fisherman which had been camouflaged with dazzle paint, and the camouflage had melded the boat into the sun-chopped water and rippled lagoon-bed sand with an extraordinary efficiency. It was *Dream Baby* and, once disentangled from her background, she was so glaringly obvious that I wondered how I had ever missed her with my first casual look. I could even make out the antennae splaying from her upperworks and the white straps on her fighting chair.

"You found *Dream Baby*," the Maggot said. "She ain't there now, of course, but she was the day that you and I flew over Murder Cay, and I'll bet you a case of whores to a thimble of cold beer that your friend Sweetman lives on Murder Cay."

And Billingsley, I remembered, had a house on Murder Cay, which explained why the Maggot had been so sure that the policeman was behind the attempt to murder me. It all made sense. Sweetman wanted to cover his tracks, and he had called in his favours from the big policeman to do it. And Ellen? I closed my eyes in sudden fear. "How do you know *Dream Baby*'s not there now?" I asked the Maggot in an attempt to take my mind off Ellen.

"Because the senator pulled strings in Washington, and he got some surveillance photographs taken two mornings ago. They're in that blue folder."

The folder bore the embossed seal of the Drug Enforcement Administration. I pulled it out from under the canvas bag that held the Russian machine-gun and extracted the photographs. The first picture showed the whole anchor-shaped island surrounded by the coral reefs of the Devil's Necklace. The next picture was an oblique view of the eight lavish houses that were built on the anchor's shank, then there was a set of prints showing details of the individual houses which, like the palaces of ancient Rome, were built about pillared courtyards. They had swimming pools, tennis courts, private docks, servants' quarters and terraced views across the western part of the lagoon. The largest house was topped by a blunt tower which sported a small radar aerial. There had once been a ninth house, closer to the airstrip and built right on the beach, but at some time that house had been half demolished and its ruins now stood like some part-excavated archaeological site. The remaining eight houses all stood on the western side of the narrow spit of land, while the eastern half formed a long and narrow nine-hole golf course, complete with sand traps and beside which a skeletal radio mast sprang incongruously from a stretch of sandy wasteland.

The prints were all in colour. The shadows in the photographs stretched westward, and the sprinklers on the golf course were venting huge sprays that sparkled in the low-angled sunlight. None of the householders was visible, only their servants. A maid swept a tiled terrace with a besom. A black gardener watered urns of flowers, while another man scooped leaves from a swimming pool with a long-handled net. A cook washed some fruit in a back yard while, beside

253

her on the edge of a well, a tabby cat yawned. Clearly none of the servants had been aware of the surveillance aircraft that must have been tens of thousands of feet high, yet still the pictures were of a startling clarity; I could even see a clutch of tennis balls lying discarded in the corner of a court, while in another photograph I could read the title of a newspaper, *El Espectador*, that had been discarded on an upholstered lounger beside a tiled pool. More ominous was the photograph of a jeep that had a half-inch Browning machine-gun mounted on a pintle in its rear bed.

"Some place, eh?" the Maggot said. "You have to be a drug-smuggler or a quarterback to be rich enough to own one of those houses."

"And you think Sweetman owns them?"

"No!" The Maggot was scathing. "The island belongs to a Colombian family called the Colóns!" He grinned his pleasure at the Spanish name which was amusing only in English. "They manufacture cocaine and smuggle it to the Bahamas. Sweetman works for them, and the senator thinks he must own one of the houses. We do know that Deacon Billingsley and the cabinet minister have each got a house on the island, while the biggest house, the one with the radar aerial, belongs to the Colón family. You met Miguel Colón. He was the charmer who helped Sweetman sink your boat."

And a charmer, I thought, who had arranged some wonderful insurance for his family. Not only did one of the Bahamas' most senior policemen have a vacation mansion in this drug lord's private paradise, but a cabinet minister was housed there as well. Doubtless the Americans would love to have searched Murder Cay; they would want to swamp the island with their screaming Blackhawk helicopters and Blue Thunder patrol boats, and send in drug-sniffing dogs and men in bullet-proof vests carrying bullhorns and rifles. The Americans doubtless wanted a mini Grenada or Panama and they would probably have arrested anyone on Murder Cay who was found in possession of so much as an unlicensed aspirin, but they were helpless as long as they needed Bahamian permission to operate on Bahamian soil, because the Colón family had the insurance of having a top policeman and a senior politician on their payroll.

"So" — I looked at the Maggot — "the senator is going in on his own?"

"No." The Maggot grinned. "He wants us to go in with him."

"Jesus," I said; not swearing, but praying. I was thinking of that half-inch Browning mounted on the jeep pintle.

The Maggot grinned at me. "The senator's paying well! And if you're anything like me then a bit of cash won't come amiss."

But I would not help the senator because of his money. Instead I was remembering my feeble straw of hope that perhaps Ellen was still alive and being held captive by Sweet-man. The hope blossomed impossibly, for I could not bear to think of her dead. I stared westwards across the heat-hazed sea. Somewhere over there was the island where perhaps Ellen was being held. Perhaps. Beneath me, their prows sharp as blades, American warships sliced the blue water to cream.

Twenty minutes later the Beechcraft's wheels thumped down from the wings as we circled to get downwind of our landing field. I felt the sweat prickle at my skin. I was frightened that the police would be waiting for me. "Fear not" — the Maggot sensed my apprehension — "for I am with thee." He grinned, then launched into his customary litany of landing. "Thank you for flying Maggovertski Airways; please return the steward-ess her pantyhose and restore her to the upright position, and kindly pray that the tyres don't blow."

The wheels bounced and spewed smoke.

The tyres did not shred on the coral, nor were any police waiting. There was only a taxi that we loaded with the guns, and which then took us to find the senator.

George Crowninshield was waiting for us in the palm-thatched office of Coffinhead's small marina. He looked horribly out of place for, despite his media-advisers' insistence that he dress in cowboy boots and drench his speeches in down-home folksi-ness, he was not a man who was at home with the common folk. The senator was more of a white-wine-and-finger-food politician than a cakes-and-ale populist. He was also missing his herd of advisers and aides, for he was quite alone in the small office. "I'm not here on official business," he explained his solitary state, "but privately, just as I was when I first came to see you about the twins." He shook my hand. "Thank you for coming, Nick. Truly, thank you."

I forbore to say that two dead Bahamian policemen had given me small choice in the matter. Instead I shrugged away his thanks and asked just what exactly he wanted of me. "I don't want any trouble, Nick, you understand that? No trouble! I just want to visit Murder Cay tonight and talk to the twins and see if they'll come away." He stared through the window to where the Maggot was unloading the green canvas bags from the boot of the taxi. "And it would be just great if you could come and help me," the senator added.

I thought of the fearsome firepower that the Colón family would undoubtedly unleash in defence of Murder Cay. "Why don't you just telephone the twins?" I asked him.

"I've tried." The poor man was desperately nervous, but that was understandable for it was not every day that a father sought a confrontation with drug-runners. "There's only one telephone line on to the island and the man who answers pretends not to understand me. I even had a Spanish-speaking staff member try for me, but she got nowhere. We were lucky," he suddenly added.

"Lucky?" I did not follow the train of thought.

"That the photograph you took showed that camouflaged boat."

The senator was even luckier, I thought, that the Maggot had thought to inform him of the photograph. Which was odd, in a way, for the Maggot seemed to have no liking for the senator. "Are you quite sure the twins are on the island?" I asked the senator.

"It seems the obvious solution." Crowninshield was sweating profusely. "We think that Rickie wants to buy one of the empty houses. He could live in a drug heaven, you see, but he can't have bought the house yet because he doesn't inherit his money till next week."

"And is that why we're going to Murder Cay?" I challenged him. "To protect your family's fortune? And to make sure you don't lose the half-million dollars you put up for Rickie's bail?"

Crowninshield looked angry and flushed, and I thought for a second that he was about to protest at my accusations, but instead he suddenly seemed to crumple inside. "Probably," he admitted, "and why not? You think I should just let the money go?"

I had nothing to say, so kept silent. The senator frowned at me, seeking to broaden his justification for going to Murder Cay. "But it isn't just money, Nick. If there was no money involved, and only my children's lives at stake, I'd still go. Even if by going I lose my career, it's still something I have to do." He stopped, evidently seeking words that would convince me, and when he spoke again his voice was more measured, as though making the speech was calming his frayed nerves. "I simply want to reach my children and talk to them, Nick, and perhaps persuade them to make another effort to live without drugs. I'm not going as a senator, I'm not doing anything official, I'm just a father trying to save his kids." He smiled ruefully, offering a glimpse of his famous charm. "Everyone on my staff says I'm mad. They say that what I'm doing today is political suicide, and perhaps it is, but Robin-Anne and Rickie are my kids, and no one else will save them."

There had been a noble and convincing ring of truth to his words, but I was still not wholly persuaded. "And the twins are worth the White House?"

He stared at me, a half-frown of puzzlement on his handsome face. "You're not a father?"

"No."

"If you were a father," he said heavily, "you would know."

The door of the office opened and the Maggot, grinning broadly, staggered in under the weight of the assorted machine-guns and ammunition, which he dumped on Coffinhead's table. George Crowninshield scowled at the awesome

257

display of weaponry. "I'm sure we're not going to need all that firepower, Mr Maggovertski."

"The trick of kicking ass, senator, is to equip yourself with a very heavy boot. And some bullet-proof vests." The Maggot carried three flak-jackets that he now added to the arsenal.

Like the senator I stared with some alarm at the guns. "I thought you didn't want any trouble."

"I suppose we ought to be ready for trouble?" the senator said tentatively.

"Then buy some yachting smoke-flares off Coffinhead," I advised him, "because if those bastards start shooting then the best thing we can do is hide, not shoot back. Or else we get in the plane and get the hell out of there!"

"We're not flying there," the Maggot said. "Remember those trucks they keep parked on the runway? If we fly there, Nick, we'll all be hamburger meat by midnight. No, we're renting one of Coffinhead's inflatables."

"Which is why we wanted your help," the senator said, "to navigate for us? And of course we would appreciate your advice." Using one of Coffinhead's inflatable boats made good sense.

Coffinhead used the boats to carry diving parties to the coral reefs, but they were not much different from the rigid-raider assault boats I had used in the Marines. The big boats were fast, but best of all their rubberised gunwales gave very little purchase to a radar impulse, and that could be important for Murder Cay was equipped with radar. I sorted through the DEA's colour surveillance photographs until I found the picture which showed the radar aerial mounted on the tower of the biggest house. I was trying to tell from the size of the aerial just how sensitive the island's radar would be.

The senator divined my worry. He had another identical blue file at his elbow, and now he opened it and leafed through the papers inside. "We've registered that radar's electronic signature, Nick, and we know that it operates at ten thousand megahertz on a three-centimetre wavelength with a zero point five microsecond pulse length."

"Oh, thank God for that," the Maggot said with heavy sarcasm, "I thought it might be a problem."

"What he means," I explained, "is that it's a recreational radar, like the kind you see on weekend powerboats, but it's still dangerous."

"But the inflatable boat –" the senator began.

"Will probably slip under that radar without being noticed," I confirmed for him. Inflatables, with their curved hull shape and low freeboard, were notoriously hard to detect on radar. "But vanishing from the radar doesn't mean that you'll reach the island. It's going to be dark tonight! There's not much moon. How the hell do you think you're going to see the channel?"

"With these." The Maggot smiled and held up a pair of passive night-goggles.

"I think we've anticipated most of the problems," the senator said modestly. He paused then, hoping to hear my assent, for I had still not told either man that I would travel to Murder Cay that night. I kept silent and the senator translated that silence as a reluctance to help him, so he took out the big photograph which showed the whole of the island and used it to demonstrate the foolproof nature of his plan. "We thought we'd land there" – he pointed to a small beach which lay close to the radio aerial and very near to the entrance channel – "and we hoped that you would stay with the boat, Nick, while we cross the golf course in an attempt to find Rickie and Robin-Anne . . ." He hesitated, then offered me an oddly strained smile, "And you can be sure that we'll seek news of Ellen as well, and if we discover that she's being held against her will then we'll call for help. No one can hold an American citizen prisoner without due process."

"Hold on!" I said. I had not told the senator anything at all about Ellen's disappearance. "How did you know she's missing?" I asked him, and could not hide the tone of accusation.

"Because I told him," the Maggot admitted cheerfully. "I telephoned from the control tower before we left Freeport!"

"Of course." I felt very foolish.

"Nick?" The senator's voice was very tentative, and I sensed he was about to offer me sympathy. "I didn't know," he said, "that you and Ellen were –"

"It's OK, senator," I said, interrupting him. I know he meant well, but I did not think I could cope with his heavy-handed sympathy.

There was an awkward pause. A sea-breeze blew through the unglazed window, beyond which pelicans perched on the pilings that held Coffinhead's boat slips where his small fleet rocked gently under the palm trees. I thought how happy a man could be in a place like this, yet every Eden had its serpent, and the serpent in the Bahamian Eden was the proximity of America's hunger for drugs.

"Our biggest problem" – the senator tried to restore our attention to his plans for the night – "will be the guards. Warren Smedley of the DEA tells me that he's certain there will be guards, because it's likely that there's several million dollars' worth of cocaine stored on the island. The guards are probably based in the Colón house, that's the one with the radar." The senator leafed through the photographs I had brought from the Maggot's plane and showed us the house with the small tower.

"I am hopeful," the senator went on, "that the guards won't even be aware of our presence. I am also hopeful that we know in which house the twins are staying. I suspect it's the northernmost house. One of my aides spotted a cassette tape which he recognised as one of Rickie's favourites. It's an English group. Something about a dirt-box. Here, you can see the tape box if you look closely." He found a picture of the northernmost house and laid it on the table. "There." He pointed at a lounger on the terrace. "If you've got good eyes you can probably see it without a magnifying glass."

Then I stopped listening to the senator and looking for the wretched Pinkoe Dirt-Box Band cassette, because I had seen something else in the photograph. It was something I had missed when I had cursorily leafed through the prints in the aeroplane.

I had found a boat.

Not *Dream Baby*, but another boat.

The northernmost house, like all the others on Murder Cay, had a private dock that projected into the lagoon. The water at the dock was clearly not deep enough for the larger boats like *Dream Baby*, but shallow-draught craft could safely be moored to the pilings, and the camera had caught one such boat moored at the northern pier. The angle of the sun and the coincidence of a tangle of palm shadows half obscured the boat, which is why I had missed it on my first casual glance, but now I saw the fantastic flourish that had been painted on the boat's long bows. That flourish was a shooting star embellished with a cupid's pair of lips. *Starkisser*. My blood was suddenly running ice cold. The photograph might mean nothing, yet somehow it meant everything. *Starkisser* had been at Murder Cay on the very day after Ellen had disappeared, and why, earlier this day, had Bellybutton run from me in such abject terror? Did Bellybutton know that McIllvanney had delivered Ellen to Murder Cay, and was that why he had fled from my anger?

"Nick?" The senator, who had been talking, had evidently asked me a question which had blown straight past me.

I looked up at him. "I'm sorry?"

"I just wondered what chance of success you give us tonight?"

"Success?" I had to laugh. "None at all, senator. Your aides are right, and you're not just committing political suicide, but real suicide! Your idea doesn't have a prayer. It doesn't stand a cat's chance! You've fallen out of your tree, the pair of you. Those bastards on Murder Cay are going to chew you up and spit you out, both of you."

The Maggot showed no reaction to my pessimism, but the senator looked appalled. "Does that mean you won't help us, Nick?" For answer I yanked the Russian PKM machine-gun free of the other weapons, unfolded its butt, dropped its bipod, crashed its feed mechanism open and shut, then cocked it. It had been years since I had trained on this particular model, but the familiarity flooded back instantly, and the

261

harsh sounds of the gun's oiled movements echoed sharply and efficiently in the small room. I pulled the trigger to let the bolt fall on the empty chamber, then I slammed the gun down on the table. I had been showing off; demonstrating my slick competence with guns and letting the senator know that I had been a Marine, and a good one, and that he needed me. "Of course I'm coming," I said. "I want to kick some ass."

The senator's smile of relief was very flattering. He held out his hand. "Thank you, Nick."

"Way to go!" the Maggot said, and gave me a high five. My father, in one of his rare moments of giving me sober advice, had once warned me against an excessive dependency on emotions. Such a dependency, he claimed, was a luxury only to be indulged in by inadequate actors, children, and clergymen. The rest of us had a duty to think before we jumped and to consider the consequences of our actions. I do not think Sir Tom believed a word of what he was saying – he was probably rehearsing some thoughts from a play he was reading at the time – but, despite the hypocrisy of its histrionic delivery, I had always remembered the advice. I had rarely acted on it, but I had remembered it. Now, staring at the photograph which linked Matthew McIllvanney with Murder Cay, I forgot that good advice. I forgot it because I knew McIllvanney had been stalking Ellen, and suddenly it was all so patently obvious. McIllvanney had kidnapped Ellen and taken her to Murder Cay, there to give her to our enemies, so all I now wanted to do was to take the vicious Russian gun and use it to cry havoc to an island. I did not care what chaos I engendered, I just wanted to hurt the men who had hurt Ellen.

But I should have remembered my father's hypocritical advice. The senator must have known that three men were not sufficient to challenge the malevolence of the *narcotraficantes*. Yet the senator was going to Murder Cay.

I should have known that the senator would not lightly put at risk his glorious political future. Yet the senator was going to Murder Cay.

And what part was the Drug Enforcement Administration

playing? I did not ask myself that question, yet I knew they had provided the surveillance photographs, and it now seemed they had even read the signature of the radar set on Murder Cay. So what else had they done?

And the Maggot, for all his crudities, had an appetite to enjoy life, yet he too was going to Murder Cay. And where did the Scorpion guns come from, or the PKM, or the flak-jackets? Or the passive night-goggles?

I asked myself none of those questions. Instead I told myself that I was couching a lance for Ellen, just as the senator was charging home for his children, and just as the Maggot was revenging a once dazzling girl who now danced empty-eyed in a Pittsburgh peep-show.

Thus fools rush in where angels fear to tread.

The little Scorpions came with either a ten- or twenty-round magazine, and I helped myself to six of the bigger ones which I taped in pairs, back to back, so that when one magazine was exhausted I would only have to reverse a taped pair to have the gun ready to fire again. I also took handfuls of Coffinhead's smoke-flares which, while not as good as smoke-grenades, could still generate a useful screen.

The senator refused to carry any weapon, saying he could not provoke violence, while the Maggot loyally chose the American M16 and two American-made Ingram sub-machine-guns. The Maggot and I carried all the guns down to Coffinhead's dock and stowed them in one of the rigid-raiders. Coffinhead himself was filling the gas tank. He cocked a curious eye at the guns, but knew better than to ask any questions. Instead he wanted to know when the senator was paying him.

"Before we leave tonight," the Maggot promised, and I wondered just how much this night's escapade was costing the senator. Certainly Coffinhead was making a fat profit, not just on renting the boat, but he was also charging the senator for the tarpaulin that hid the guns, for the compass I would use to navigate the last few miles to the island, and for the bag of emergency smoke-flares that I had stored under the tarpaulin in the inflatable's rigid-bottomed hull.

Once the boat was loaded, the Maggot and I wandered to the end of the dock. The light was shading into evening as we stared through the narrow channel that led from Coffinhead's marina to the open sea. The water was being glossed gold by the setting sun and it was hard to believe that the coming night could bring gunfire.

The Maggot lit a cigarette, then offered me a wry look. "You must be tired, Nick."

"A bit." In truth I was utterly knackered.

"I'm glad you're coming, though." He spoke softly.

"I'm only doing it for Ellen," I said bitterly. "Nothing else."

"Sure, Nick. That's what I reckoned." He drew deep on the cigarette, then blew a stream of smoke towards the water.

"What I don't understand," I said, "is why you're doing it. You don't like the senator, and you'd hate his son."

"I'm doing it for the same reason you're doing it," the Maggot said, then he paused and I thought he was not going to elaborate, but suddenly he shrugged. "I was married to Pittsburgh." He made the confession abruptly.

"Oh, God." I was suddenly overwhelmed by the sadness of it all. We have just one life to live, only one, and so many people seem to piss the gift away. I thought of the girl's vivacity, and I tried to imagine such a beauty being wasted in a sleazy stinking pit of a peep-show.

"I guess I'm still married to her," the Maggot continued quietly. It was hard to read his facial expression behind the tangle of beard, but his voice was full of a most bitter grief. "Her name is Wendy," he went on, and I sensed that he had not talked about his wife for many years. "Wendy Maggovertski. I met her in a hotel in Cleveland. We'd gone there to play the Browns, and she told me we were going to get our hides whipped. We did too, and she married me ten days later. Just like that. I thought the sun and stars shone out of that lady, Nick."

I stared at him, wishing that Ellen had seen this vulnerable side of such an apparently invulnerable man. "I'm sorry, John," I said inadequately.

"She could make people laugh, know what I mean?" He stared blindly across the lovely stretch of water. "When she walked into a room it was like an extra bulb had been switched on. Now she gives blow jobs to buy herself cocaine."

"Oh, God," I said, so very inadequately.

"It was a fag dancer who trained at her health club who gave her the first cocaine. He gave me some too. I thought it was just another piece of being alive, a piece of fun, but it never touched me like it touched Wendy. She suddenly wanted nothing but cocaine, then more cocaine, and when I stopped giving her the money for it she left me to make her own money." He sucked on the cigarette again, so deeply that its tip glowed a hard, brilliant red. "I killed the little bastard."

"Who?"

"The fag dancer." There were tears in the Maggot's eyes. "No one knows, of course, and I'd deny it if you told anyone, but I broke the pansy faggot's neck." The spleen in the Maggot's voice was of a terrible intensity. "It didn't help. It didn't bring Wendy back. She'll never come back now. She'll just die. But tonight I'll take some more revenge on the bastards who took her away from me. Fuck 'em, Nick! Let's go get 'em!" He howled the challenge into the darkling lagoon, then thumped one huge fist into a massive palm, and I thought this was how he must have been just before a football game, hyped up and emotional, except that tonight we were playing with guns, and any defeat would be for ever.

Because tonight we would both be fools for love.

At Murder Cay.

PART FOUR

The passive night-goggles turned the world into a dreamy green place of smeared liquid-light. I had donned the goggles as we neared Murder Cay, thus turning the silver and black into jade and lime. I was aiming the inflatable towards the island's radio mast that speared like a dark green line drawn against the paler green of the sky in which the stars showed as bright emerald sparks. The Devil's Necklace, which lay like an outer defence about Murder Cay, was betrayed in the goggles by the brightness of the water breaking on the coral heads, while the crooked passage through the reefs was revealed as a smoothly shining green-black path which led to the black, unlit bulk of the island itself.

Nothing moved on the island and no light showed there. If any light had been burning it would have sparked brilliant and cruel in the night-goggles' screen, but the navigation light on the island's southern tip, like the red air-warning beacons on its tall radio mast and the green and white airstrip beacon, was switched off.

I put the engine into neutral and let the boat drift a half-mile outside the reefs while I searched for any signs that our arrival had been detected, but no boats patrolled the lagoon and no jeeps moved on the single road. "What's happening?" the senator asked nervously.

"Just checking," I said.

"Is it OK?" The senator was more than nervous. He was scared. He fidgeted with the short rubber-sheathed aerial of the battery-powered VHF radio that he carried in a pouch of his bullet-proof vest. The senator had insisted on bringing two such hand-held radios, just in case everything went wrong and we needed to scream to the outside world for help.

"Playtime, children," the Maggot said with grim facetiousness and in an effort to spur me onwards, but still I let the boat drift on the rising tide. I was giving my instincts time to smell the night's danger.

It was dark. The moon was a sickle blade low in the south-eastern sky, though in my goggles it looked more like a freshly cut paring of the purest green light. We were in the small hours of Friday morning, the witching hours when the mind is at its most superstitious and fearful, yet so far everything had gone astonishingly smoothly. Coffinhead Porter had slung the loaded rigid-raider from a pair of davits at the stern of his big sports-fishing boat, then had ripped us across a jet-black sea to drop us thirty miles from Murder Cay.

Now, forty minutes later, we drifted a half-mile from the Devil's Necklace and I stared entranced at an emerald world. "Nick?" The senator, like the Maggot, had no night-goggles, and could see nothing in the darkness.

"It's OK," I said at last, then I let in the engine's clutch so that the big inflatable moved smoothly forward. The Maggot, crouching in the bows, slid the Russian-made machine-gun over the gunwale. On the goggles' screen the gun's belt of ammunition looked like linked green bars of glowing gold.

The water crashed and broke and seethed on the coral. I thought how the island's small radar set must pick up a lot of wave clutter from the coral heads, and how that clutter would hide us; then we were in the channel, moving slowly and almost silently. The channel was supposed to be bare of navigation marks, but I spotted a small buoy, nothing but a plastic bottle on a weighted line, which marked the dog-leg bend, then we were past the buoy and I turned the boat and accelerated slightly as a faint line of paler green showed me where the pebble beach lay at the foot of the radio mast.

The security lights on the island's houses were suddenly switched on.

The Maggot cursed, while I snatched off the goggles which had suddenly flared blindingly bright. The world reverted to a prosaic darkness slashed by the sudden line of arc-lights which stretched across the island to silhouette the trees and shrubs growing between the houses and the slender golf course. I had instinctively throttled the motor back as the lights came on so that we were scarcely moving as we cleared the landward end of the passage and started across the smooth black water that lay within the protective ring of coral. The lights were reflected on the blackness in long sinuously shivering streams of silver.

The senator was sitting straight up, staring with alarm at the brightly lit island, but, despite the security lights, nothing moved there and no guards were visible. I wondered if the lights were randomly switched on and off automatically. "Do you want to abort?" I asked the senator.

"I think perhaps we should." Crowninshield was in a plain funk. He was not trained to such escapades, and he had not imagined that the night would be like this. Doubtless he had hoped for a straightforward landing, a fortuitous meeting with his children, and a decorous withdrawal. Instead every moment increased the tension.

"We don't abort!" the Maggot said. "We go on."

"Maybe we'd better go on," the senator said, and I wondered if he always agreed with the last man to express a firm opinion, and I recalled the jibe that he was a politician without a cause. Or was he about to make the war on drugs the cause that would propel him to glory?

Then the island's lights went out.

"Someone there is awake," I forgot my doubts about the senator's motives, suggesting instead an explanation for the dousing of the security lamps, "but they're not suspicious. They probably have orders to switch the lights on for a few minutes every hour, but now that they've seen nothing they'll be going back to watching their dirty video." I hoped the video was very dirty indeed, dirty enough to keep the guards' eyes riveted on the screen as we negotiated the entrance channel. I pulled the night-goggles back over my eyes again. A bright strip of emerald light glowed in the tower of the house where the guards were posted. That strip of light had not been there a moment before, and I guessed that it marked where the guard had left the shutters or curtains cracked open after he had peered into the glow of the security lights. I looked northwards, to my right, and saw that the northernmost house, the one I was convinced was Sweetman's, lay in utter darkness.

271

"Let's go, Nick!" The senator was being tormented by the boat's sluggish speed.

I eased the throttle forward. The Maggot had discarded the machine-gun and picked up his rifle and I heard the clatter of its bolt as he worked a round into the chamber.

"Put the gun on safe!" I said warningly. I did not want an accidental shot disturbing our enemies.

"You put a hole in both ends of the egg, then suck? Is that right, Nick?" The Maggot grinned at me. His face, like the senator's and mine, had been smeared raggedly black with a foul-smelling camouflage cream that was supposed to double as an insect repellent. We were all wearing flak-jackets over camouflage shirts and trousers. I superstitiously wished I had my old beret.

It seemed unreal to be back in a rigid-raider. Sometimes, in the Marines, we had been encouraged to make a silent, creeping approach, while at other times we would simply point the rubber boats towards the enemy shore and let the things tear the sea into white shreds. This night's adventure still seemed like one of those long-ago training exercises, an illusion helped by the smell of the gun oil and the rank camouflage cream. I aimed the inflatable straight for the base of the towering radio mast, then we all lurched forward as the rigid hull of the inflatable struck a rock or shoal. I twisted the wheel and gunned the throttle so that the boat slithered and scraped over the obstacle into deeper water.

"Get ready!" I called softly.

We were travelling faster now, and showing a white wake at our stern. I wanted to drive the boat's bows well up the beach. I snatched off the goggles at the last moment, then cut the engine as the small wave that was pushed ahead of our bows broke white and loud on the shelving pebbles. "Hold tight!"

We struck the beach. There was another and fiercer lurch, a scraping noise that seemed hugely loud in the dark night, then we shuddered to a halt. The sound of the boat's rigid fibreglass baseplate sliding on loose stone echoed in my ears. "Go! Go!" I hissed the command.

The Maggot led the way. His feet crunched briefly on stone, then he was running awkwardly towards the black shadow of the radio mast's enormous concrete foundation. He was carrying the rifle and two sub-machine-guns that seemed tiny in his huge hands. He was also lugging a kit bag which held extra ammunition and a supply of smoke-flares. I heard the thump as he dropped the bag in the shadow of the concrete. "Ready!" he called softly.

"Go, senator," I ordered. "Good luck."

The senator stepped rather fastidiously out of the boat, then clambered up the shallow lip of limestone and turf that edged the small beach. There was just enough moonlight to show the soft swells of the nearest fairway on the golf course. A wind stirred one of the flags marking a green.

I lugged the machine-gun and as much ammunition as I could carry on to dry land. I made the boat fast, then picked up the Kalashnikov and two boxes of its ammunition. The Maggot and the senator were already crossing the golf course, going to find the twins. Somehow, in this darkness, that seemed a rather forlorn mission.

It also seemed much warmer on land, and I was sweating beneath my heavy bullet-proof vest. I mounted the gun at the corner of the radio mast's foundation, which was a concrete block four feet high and ten feet square. The huge lump gave me almost perfect protection from any gunfire that might come from the houses beyond the fairway. I lay down behind the gun, opened its feed tray and pushed in a new belt of ammunition, then cocked the mechanism. I raised the rear sight and aimed the gun towards the streak of light in the tower. I suddenly felt ridiculous; I was blacked up and armed, like an actor playing at war. I also felt dog tired. It seemed impossible that just twenty-four hours ago I had been on a ferry, and since then I had searched Grand Bahamas for Ellen, fought off an attempt on my life, then agreed to this nighttime madness.

I yawned. For two pins I would have rested my head on the Kalashnikov's butt and closed my eyes. The night insects were loud among the sea-grape that grew to the north, and the foam was incessant where it broke loud on the coral behind me, but otherwise the only sound to disturb the night was the muffled grumble of the island's generator. The senator and the Maggot were lost in the darkness, and again it struck me as perversely odd that the two should have made their unlikely alliance. How had the senator known that the big bearded man had such a fierce hatred of drugs? That question startled me into full wakefulness. And why was the Maggot equipped with ammunition from Cuba? Had it been part of the vast cache captured by the American forces on Grenada? Or had it come from the Panamanian arsenals captured when Noriega was arrested? But if so, why was it in the Maggot's hands? I began to realise that there were some very good questions that I should have been asking hours ago. Perhaps the most important question was why a man like Crowninshield would risk this adventure and thus hazard his tenancy of the White House. For his children? Would Crowninshield really sacrifice the White House for Rickie? My father would not have sacrificed a walk-on part in a beer commercial for the health of one of his children, and I suddenly realised what I had never realised before; that a politician must have an ego and an ambition every bit as massive as any great actor.

A dog began barking somewhere beyond the golf course.

My head jerked up as I slipped the gun's safety catch to automatic. The dog had begun to howl now, spreading its warning up and down the thin shank of Murder Cay.

The floodlights were switched on again. Their sudden blaze was blinding and terrifying, but I could just see the dark shape of the tower window beyond the floodlights' glare, and so I aimed the gun at that dark rectangle. I waited.

Then, seemingly all at once, I heard a truncated shout of terror, the belch of a sub-machine-gun firing, and the dog's howl turning to a scream that was chopped brutally short. A heavy machine-gun opened fire from the tower. I saw the gun's muzzle flash as a stunted dark red flame in the window, then I lost sight of that flame for I had pulled the Kalashnikov's trigger and my own muzzle was pulsing an almost invisible but intrusive light from which the green tracer rounds were spitting lazily away.

I had aimed high and left. I dropped the barrel, edged it right, and it seemed to me that my green fire was being swallowed in the dark shadowy hole of the tower window. The far machine-gun stopped abruptly.

I too stopped firing. I could smell the gun's propellant in the air; sour and thin. Adrenalin coursed warm through my blood. My heart was thumping.

I heard shouts. The sub-machine-gun fired again and I saw a floodlight explode. Sparks crackled from the broken light fixture. A second light went dark as the Maggot shattered it, but enough lights remained to turn the island into a deathtrap. I aimed at a light and extinguished it with a short burst, then heard the first whipcrack of return fire slash terrifyingly over my head. The enemy was firing at the source of my green tracer. A bullet struck the radio mast to ring the structure like a bell. I fired to kill another light, but still more lamps were being lit as people woke in the houses and turned on their garden floodlights. I hoped the senator and Maggot were already retreating because we had only one course of action now, and that was to pile into the rigid-raider and light out through the reefs at top speed.

Another machine-gun opened fire from my right, but the new gunner was disoriented and fired wildly across the golf course.

Then an explosion split the night with white fire and a noise like concentrated thunder. A brilliant streak of flame lanced skywards and I realised it had to be the fuel tank of the generator blowing up because a second or two after the explosion all the remaining lights on the island flickered and died. All that was left was the churning flames of the burning gasoline that lit the underside of a thick billow of dark smoke.

Smoke! When in doubt, use smoke! I took a handful of the flares from the Maggot's kit bag, scraped the cap off one to ignite it and hurled it as far as I could towards the golf course. Orange smoke plumed and thickened and was carried on the east wind towards me. I waited till the smoke was all around me, then, abandoning the machine-gun for a moment, I sprinted forward till I was close to the smoking flare. A machine-gun fired ahead of me and a stream of bullets whined and flickered somewhere to my left. I took another flare and hurled it forward again, thickening the smoke and trying to make a corridor down which Maggot and the senator could escape. I had reached the coarse grass of the fairway now. I hurled a third flare, then turned back towards the radio mast. A stream of tracer bullets sawed through the smoke. I heard the bullets crashing and whining in the metal lattice of the radio mast to sound like a mad orchestra of steel percussion.

The bullet stream jerked towards me and I dropped flat. The second enemy machine-gun fired wildly above my head, then I heard the thud of boots running to my left. "Maggot!"

"I'm here, Nick!"

I clambered to my feet and ran towards the safety of the radio mast's huge concrete base. The Maggot was already there, his rifle levelled above the concrete. The senator was hunched low, breathing hard and looking as though he wished he had brought a rifle. Or stayed in Washington. The sky was a cacophony of bullets. "What happened?" I shouted at the Maggot.

"Guard dog!" he shouted back. "I had to shoot the bloody thing when it attacked us! Then I dropped a flare into their generator fuel tank."

"Well done!"

The senator half stood beside me and cupped his hands to shout over the sound of the gunfire. He was shaking and his voice had risen an octave in his fear. "I lost the radio! Where's the spare?"

"In the boat!" I shouted.

He turned and looked towards the beach, but the space between us and our boat was laced with enemy tracer and bullets. "Jesus!" I saw him mouth the profanity. He was quivering with terror and I could not blame him. The senator had never before experienced the concentrated fire of automatic weapons. The hammer blows of the machine-guns' noise was enough to unsettle the brain, let alone the genuine threat of death in the more sibilant passage of their bullets. The senator was just lucky that the bastards weren't slinging artillery at us.

"We don't need a radio!" I yelled the reassurance to him. "As soon as things calm down we'll get the hell off the island! It won't be long! They can't keep using ammunition at this rate!"

"It was the dog!" the senator shouted, as though it would be useful if he explained precisely how he had lost the radio. "It came for me and I panicked. I dropped the set, you see, and ran."

"It doesn't matter!" I still needed to shout, for the night was cracking with bullets.

"But we need the radio!" The senator was veering towards hysteria again. "Don't you understand, Nick, we've got to have the radio!"

"We don't need a radio! We just need to get the hell out of here!"

Our chance to get the hell out of Murder Cay came just seconds later when, one by one, the various guns opposing us died away. The Colombians, or whoever it was that fired at us, must have ripped through a ton of ammunition, and now they were calming down. Or perhaps they believed us all to be dead. I waited a few seconds to make certain that the firing really had subsided, then I gestured for the senator to run back to the boat. "Keep low! Wait for us!"

I lay down behind the machine-gun, ready to offer covering fire if it was needed. The thinning orange smoke still provided protection enough to hide the senator's lumbering run, for the enemy did not open fire again. Once I saw that the senator had safely reached the boat I tapped the Maggot's shoulder. "Now you," I said, "go!"

But my voice seemed to unleash a new torrent of enemy gunfire that screamed and whiplashed over our heads. The fire clanged on the mast and ricocheted off the concrete. A tracer bullet whined off one of the mast's wire guy ropes to soar high and scarlet into the night sky. The Maggot had sensibly stayed under cover, and I crouched low beside him, and hoped to God that the senator was also flat on his belly. One of the enemy's machine-guns had a very harsh, deep and menacing sound, and I guessed it was the half-inch Browning. I knew no flak-jacket could stop one of those rounds, and the best thing we could do was to lie still and pray that our enemies would soon become bored with playing at soldiers.

"Nick!" The senator was suddenly shouting at me from the beach. "Nick!" He had to scream to be heard over the sound of the gunfire.

I turned and swore helplessly.

Out in the lagoon was the white bone of a bow wave and the plume of a high-speed wake. A powerboat had circled the southern part of the island and was now speeding to cut off our retreat. "Stay still!" I shouted to the Maggot and the senator, hoping that immobility would hide our exact position, but I could have saved my breath for suddenly a trail of sparks twisted and climbed into the night from the approaching boat. The trail was the wake of a parachute flare that cracked open to illuminate the whole sky with its brilliant white light. The flare also served as a signal for the guns in the houses to cease their fire. The white light illuminated the whole western coast of Murder Cay, sharply revealing our beached and stranded boat in a pitiless white glare.

I was turning the machine-gun, settling its bipod and rearranging its heavy tail of bullets. I was slow, but the Kalashnikov really needed a two-man crew. "Fire at it, Maggot!" I shouted, but the men on the boat fired first and I saw their tracer, green like mine, flick low across the water. The senator was running towards us, his face a rictus of terror, but the gunner in the powerboat was not aiming for the senator, rather for our inflatable, and his aim was all too good for I could hear his bullets pounding and tearing at the stiff fabric tubes of the big rigid-raider. More and more of the bullets beat and thrashed at the dying boat.

I opened fire and my green tracer crossed theirs, and I

dipped my line of green fire just as the men in the boat saw the danger and rammed their throttles forward. They were too late. My Kalashnikov's jacketed bullets sliced into the power-boat like a chainsaw, and I saw the craft shuddering and twisting under the impact, then the boat accelerated crazily ahead so that its own machine-gun was thrown off balance and spewed its stream of tracer fire high into the air.

I paused to thread a new belt into the Kalashnikov. The powerboat turned away from us. It was running at full speed now and I guessed that the frightened helmsman was trying to find the channel through the Devil's Necklace, but instead he hit a submerged coral head and the boat reared up into the air, aiming for the moon, and I saw the transom come clear of the water and in the dying light of the white flare I could see the whole open cockpit displayed towards us. A man was falling clear. The Maggot whooped at our victory, which was really no victory for we had lost our own boat. The enemy's boat was also lost. The water spraying from its twin jet drives looked exactly like two rocket exhausts trying to hurl the sharp-nosed hull up to the stars, but then gravity won and the whole sleek craft turned on its back and crashed sickeningly down into the sea. White water splayed outwards, then the parachute flare died and we could see nothing more.

"Oh, my God! Oh, my God!" The senator seemed to be hyperventilating

The smoke was clearing ahead of us, thinning and shredding above the golf course's narrow fairway. The generator's fuel tank still burned, but less fiercely now so that it cast a much smaller light.

I walked back to the water's edge. Our enemies beyond the golf course had been blinded by the parachute flare, so for a few seconds it was safe to risk the open ground. I jumped down to the beach to see that our boat had been effectively destroyed. The inflatable had been equipped with seven separate air chambers, and any three were sufficient to keep the hull afloat, but only one of the compartments had survived the flail of bullets. Most of our ammunition seemed intact, and I hurled those boxes ashore. The big Thermos of coffee was shattered, and the sandwiches I had made on board Coffin-head's boat had been soaked by salt water.

The senator joined me in the tangled sodden mess and, with a cry of triumph, produced the spare VHF radio, which had been protected from the sea by a waterproof case. He extended the radio's stubby aerial, then crouched under the tiny bluff that edged the beach. "Stingray, Stingray," I heard him gabble, and I guessed that the adrenalin and fear had curdled his memory.

"The word you want is Mayday!" I called to him.

"Mayday, Stingray. Acknowledge please." He spoke with frantic urgency, so much so that it seemed to me that he must have lost his marbles, but then he offered me a curiously reassuring smile. "It's OK, Nick, help will come."

"Sure," I said. "God will send a flight of killer-angels." I cupped my hands and shouted at the Maggot to join us. "Bring the machine-gun!"

"What do we do now?" The Maggot asked when he reached us. The senator was fumbling with the transmit button, still desperately filling the airwaves with his message.

"We'll work our way south." I nodded towards the scrub-land that edged the airstrip. "We'll carry as much ammunition as we can, and dump the rest. We'll cross the island and steal one of the boats from the anchorage." I grinned, pretending a confidence I did not feel.

"Nick! Nick!" The senator interrupted me. "It's the radio! It's not working!"

"You want Channel Sixteen," I said patiently, "and just shout Mayday into it, then tell whoever answers that we're under attack on Murder Cay."

"But it's broken!" the senator insisted, and I could see he was close to panicking again. I took the radio from him and found that a neat hole had indeed been punched clean through its casing. The radio must have been hit by one of the rounds fired from the powerboat, and it was now useless. "But we need it!" The senator stared at me, appalled.

"Forget it!"

"We'll be stuck here!" The senator was shaking again.

"We won't be stuck here! Trust me!" I pushed the Maggot's bag of spare ammunition at the senator. "Carry that. We're going to be all right, I promise! Let's go!"

We hurried south, leaving the shattered boat behind. Our enemies, their night vision still not recovered from the flare's brilliance, did not see us leave for, after a moment or two, they resumed firing at the base of the radio mast. I heard their bullets ring clear in the night, then a more muffled sound made me turn and curse.

"What?" the senator asked worriedly.

But before I could explain a sudden explosion cracked huge and violent in the lagoon. The plume of smoke and water shot fifty feet into the air. "The bastards have got a mortar!" I said in astonishment. The muffled sound I had first heard had been the mortar firing.

"Not bad for a bunch of *narcotraficantes*," the Maggot said in wry admiration. "So where did they get that baby? Do you think they stole it from the Colombian army?"

"Who the hell cares?" The senator flinched as another bomb exploded far away. "I need a radio! I need a radio!"

"We're going to find a radio!" I snapped. "We're going to find a boat, and boats have radios. So come on!"

Our enemy had lost us for the moment, but I feared for our survival all the same. The mortar fired another bomb towards the base of the radio mast, but sooner or later the drug-runners would realise we had abandoned that shelter and then they would turn the lethal bombs towards the rest of the small island which offered precious little cover from the explosions. Which meant our best hope lay in finding a boat and then, ignominiously, running away.

We walked across the island, hidden from our enemies by the scrub that grew thickly to the north of the airstrip. The Maggot seemed excited by the gunfire, while the senator was merely desperate to find a radio. He had a moment's wild

281

hope when he noticed a twin-engined plane sitting under a crude palm-thatch shelter, but when the Maggot climbed on to the aircraft's wing and opened its door, he saw that all the aircraft's instruments and controls had been ripped out. "It looks like my plane," he announced cheerfully.

"I need a —" The senator began his demand, but I was bored with his whining insistence and cut him off too sharply.

"I told you! We are going to find a fucking radio on board a fucking boat!"

"It wasn't supposed to be like this!" the senator complained.

"Don't squabble, girls," the Maggot said, "not when we're having such fun."

Our enemies were having less fun than before. They still fired some sporadic shots across the golf course, and their mortar thumped another half-dozen bombs towards the beach where we had landed, but their firing was tentative, almost as though they were puzzled by our lack of response. Or perhaps they were merely distracted by their other problems, the chief of which was that the fire, which the Maggot had started by shoving a flare into the generator's petrol tank, was burning much more fiercely now. I saw a palm tree flash into sudden bright flame and spew sparks that whirled away across the island's narrow waist. The light of the fire was bright on the big house with the tower and the small radar aerial.

We were far beyond the light thrown by the crackling flames. Instead we were hidden deep in a cloaking darkness as we walked past one of the big black trucks that still blocked the island's runway. Off to our right we heard an engine start up, then a pair of headlights flared bright across the golf course and I suspected that the jeep with its rear-mounted machine-gun had been sent to find us, but the vehicle drove north, away from us, so for the moment we could safely ignore it.

We hurried on while, to our north, the jeep enfiladed the concrete foundation block of the mast and the heavy machine-gun pumped a stream of futile bullets into the shadowed space which we had long vacated. I knew it would only be seconds now before they discovered our absence, after which our enemies would begin searching the island in earnest.

But then, at last, the lagoon's anchorage stretched open and serene in front of us. A dozen boats floated on the water's sheer black surface that was glossed red by the flames. Closer at hand was the ruined beach house which offered a shadowed hiding place where the three of us crouched just a few paces from the water's edge. "What we have to do now," I said, "is swim to the nearest boat, turn on its electrics and call for help."

"I'll go," the Maggot said.

"No!" The senator insisted. "I will."

"You both go," I made the decision, "and I'll give you covering fire from here." One of us had to stay behind to offer protective fire. "Swim slowly." I took the Kalashnikov from the Maggot. "And don't splash. Once you're on board, stay there! If I can't reach you, then try and get yourselves the hell out of here."

The Maggot frowned at the note of resigned pessimism in my voice. "I'll stay with you, Nick."

"I don't need anyone to stay with me," I said petulantly. "They've lost us, so there's no immediate danger, but the sooner we're all on the boat, the better. One of us has to be arse-end Charlie, and that one's me. So go!" I turned away from them, intimating I had no more to say, and hefted the Russian machine-gun on to the makeshift breastwork of the ruined wall. I aimed the gun at the nearest house which was no more than two hundred paces away. The building was dark and seemingly deserted.

The Maggot and the senator abandoned their boots and flak-jackets; then, wearing only their lightweight fatigues, they waded into the lagoon and breast-stroked through the limpid black water. The Maggot had strapped the M16 across his back, but had left his sub-machine-guns on the beach. The closest motor-cruiser, a sports-fisherman, was no more than sixty yards away.

I watched them swim for a moment, then turned to stare towards the blazing fire which silhouetted the southernmost houses. Stingray. That was the word the senator had used on the radio, and Stingray was the name of the US naval exercise that had filled the Bahamian seaways with lean grey ships and the island bars with boisterous sailors. I turned and gazed at the two shapes which swam so soft and slow towards the powerboat. Stingray. And I remembered how, on the day that the senator had come to find me on Straker's Cay, he had gone on to a reception at the American Embassy in Nassau where he had met officers from the Stingray fleet. And that very same day he had turned up in the unlikely company of the Maggot. And that reminded me of an earlier question: exactly how had the senator found the Maggot?

The two men had reached the transom of the big sports-fisherman, and I watched as the Maggot's huge dark shape moved cautiously up the boat's stern ladder. A few seconds later I heard a splintering crack as the main-cabin door was forced. I guessed the Maggot was now searching for the electrical master switch. After that he would have to find the secondary switches to power the radio circuit, then discover the radio itself.

The senator climbed the stern ladder. None of the Colombians seemed to have noticed what was happening in the lagoon. What had the Maggot called the Colombians? *Narcotraficantes*, I had noted his use of that word, and wondered at it, because the Maggot was not usually a man to dignify someone with a proper noun when an improper word would suffice. I stared at the dark shape of the boat from which the Maggot was undoubtedly sending the radio message. But to whom?

Illusion, I thought to myself, everything is illusory. Truth is so slippery. The art of politics, like the art of the theatre, is to create a perfect illusion. It had taken a politician to make a simulacrum of Camelot in the twentieth century, and he had done it so perfectly that no one noticed that the Knights of the Round Table were being sent to be slaughtered in Vietnam.

The voters had wanted the illusion. "You have to remember," my father liked to say, "that the bard was wrong. Not all the world's a stage, most of it is an auditorium instead. Some of us are born to entertain, while the lumpen mass is born to be amused. But do remember, dear boy, that it is that lumpen audience which pays, and we performers who take their money. I make a bad audience, but am a great and rich performer; while you, Nick, are in danger of becoming a poor and astonishingly credulous spectator." He had despised my naïvety, wanting me to make the falsehoods of the stage into my avocation, but I had rebelled, preferring credulity to skill, innocence to knowledge, and naïvety to cynicism. I still preferred truth to lies, yet somewhere in this night's darkness I knew there was a great dark lie that I had been made to serve.

"Nick!" the Maggot suddenly hissed across the black water. "Nick! It's OK! Come on!"

The summons undoubtedly meant that the radio message had been successfully sent, and doubtless the sensible thing for me to do was to join the two Americans on the boat, but it was dawning on me that I had been tricked and harried into coming to Murder Cay to ride shotgun for a purpose that had never been revealed; and I sensed, too, that no one but me cared what might have happened to Ellen. The senator did not care if she was raped and had died, because he had his own agenda. But Ellen had become my agenda.

So I ignored the Maggot's summons.

Instead, I stood up, looped the belt of heavy linked cartridges around my neck, and picked up the machine-gun. While my enemies regrouped, I would find my woman. My cue had come at last, and it was time to leave the credulous audience and become a performer, making my entrance according to a stage direction I would write myself; enter from the night a deceived lover, armed and angry, seeking truth.

The Maggot hissed at me to join them on board their boat. I walked away. I was angry, but at who and what I was not sure. My anger made me careless. I made no attempt to hide, but just strolled up the beach carrying the heavy Kalashnikov.

My actions were not quite so foolhardy as they seemed, for the beach on the eastern side of Murder Cay was backed by a sand bluff nearly six feet high, and, by stooping, I could have walked almost the whole length of the island concealed from anyone who might have watched from the houses. But at that moment I did not care about concealment for the madness was on me; the insane conviction that I was armoured by righteousness and that no harm could therefore come to me.

A mortar bomb fluttered far overhead, dropping somewhere near the runway. A white parachute flare followed the bomb to explode over the island's centre before drifting down behind its straggling plume of brightly lit smoke. Another flare was fired to burn brilliantly above the ruined beach house. The flares cast shadows as black as the mouth of hell, and I was walking in one such inky shadow.

I was walking towards the northernmost house which I believed belonged to Jesse Sweetman and to which, I was sure, Ellen had been taken. Sweetman had made no secret of his lust for Ellen, and he could clearly afford to pay McIllvanney his pimp-price. I trudged clumsily, my boots sliding in the treacherous sand. I had to negotiate the awkward pilings which supported the wooden piers that jutted off the sandy bluff and led to the private docks. I tripped on a discarded sailboard and banged my head on the low slanting trunk of a palm tree that grew across the sand. The linked ammunition looped round my neck clinked with every step, and the Scorpion slung from my left shoulder kept swinging to crash tinnily against the Kalashnikov, but no one heard me through the din of mortar explosions and the crackle of random gunfire. I plodded heavily on, walking like a man in a dream, and I was still moving in that same dreamlike unreality when I reached

Sweetman's house. I took no soldierly precautions, but simply climbed the wooden steps from the beach and walked across the marble-paved terrace as though I was a welcome visitor. The madness told me I would survive, and perhaps the madness was right, for no one saw me, and no one challenged me, and no one fired at me.

Then the trance snapped as a shadow moved in the flowering shrubs off to my left, and I threw myself sideways, guns and ammunition crashing loud on the marble terrace, and I wrenched the machine-gun round to face the sudden threat, and the Kalashnikov's steel-clawed bipod scraped on stone as my finger took up the first pressure on the trigger.

Then I froze. Because the threat miaowed, then purred, then rubbed itself soft and warm against my right cheek. Sweat was pouring off me. "Oh, Jesus," I blasphemed softly, and laid my head on my left forearm.

An explosion jarred me back into alertness. It was a huge explosion, thumping my eardrums and pulsing a sheet of red flame high into the night. I guessed that the fire started by the Maggot had spread to a big tank of cooking gas that supplied the island's largest house. I could see men running in the garden of that house, fleeing from flames that were leaping as high as the radar aerial on the small tower. A bush crackled into instant fire to stream golden sparks into the night. Behind me the lagoon was being fingered silver by the falling flares.

Those flares were being sprayed haphazardly about the sky, just as the mortar bombs were now being scattered indiscriminately across the island's open spaces. The mortar seemed to be emplaced in the garden of the house just beyond the raging fire. I could hear men shouting in that garden. Every now and then a machine-gun or rifle would open fire, but without purpose. The *narcotraficantes* had lost us. They were night-blinded by their own fire and by their flares, and they neither knew how many enemy faced them nor where that enemy was.

The northernmost house lay silent and dark. A hot tub on its terrace seemed to be filled with molten silver where the crescent moon glossed its water. Beyond the tub was a black wall of glass in which one sliding window had been left open. A white curtain stirred in the gap, but I could sense nothing threatening beyond the curtain, and so I stood up and edged round the hot tub's gleaming water to the open glass door. No one challenged me. I paused by the billowing curtain, listening, but I heard nothing to scare me, and so I walked unopposed and undetected into my enemy's house. There was a distinct smell of perfume, as though an exotic woman had just left the darkened room. I stood, eyes wide, till a flare cracked apart in the southern sky to cast an eerie white glow through the open window, and I saw that I was in a long elegant room furnished with cushioned wicker furniture. More glass doors opened on to the central courtyard where a swimming pool reflected the flare's harsh fire. The walls of the elegant room were hung with fine antique prints; the home of a civilised murderer.

I stood utterly still. I was trying to sense danger in this perfumed house, using whatever primitive instincts were left to me, but then a door opened deep in the house, and I saw the flicker of a candle flame and I realised that someone was walking down a long corridor towards me.

One side of the corridor was formed by the glass wall that looked on to the central courtyard while the other was a lined with bookcases. Whoever walked between the books and the glass was shielding the candle flame with his hand so that his forward motion would not extinguish the small light.

It was Rickie, and he came unsuspecting towards me.

He was weaving slightly on the carpeted floor, and staring intently down at the candle. He had left the door at the far end of the corridor open and more candles burned in the room beyond, but I sensed Rickie was alone. He was humming to himself, concentrating on preserving the flickering fragile flame, then he saw the flash-suppressor of the machine-gun pointing at his midriff, and his eyes slowly came up to mine, and the candle dropped to extinguish itself on the floor.

"Hello, Rickie," I said gently.

He was shaking. He could see me well enough, because I

was illuminated by the candles in the room behind him, but I could only dimly see his face. What I glimpsed was not good. He looked ravaged and old before his time. His mouth opened and closed as though he was trying to speak, but he could not, then he began to back away from me with his hands held towards me. "You're dead!" he said. "They told me you were dead!"

"Your father's here, Rickie. He's come to take you away."

Rickie backed into the candlelit room and I saw just how pale and sick he looked. His one good eye was bloodshot and there were flecks of dried blood at his nostrils. A pulse was racing at his neck. He backed further from me, stopping at a table on which he sat as limply as a puppet loosed of its strings.

"You shouldn't be here!" he whimpered, and he held his hands towards the walls as though feebly trying to protect the room's contents, and the odd gesture made me realise just what was being stored in the big, high-ceilinged chamber.

It was the new riches of the Americas.

I was standing among the new gold that flowed to corrupt old nations; the new white gold of cocaine. I was in a room filled with cocaine; a room crammed with plastic-wrapped bales that must have been stuffed with the white crystalline powder. So much powder that I was crunching it beneath my boots because someone, I assumed Rickie, had slashed open one of the bales to pluck out a noseful of heaven.

There was money on the table behind Rickie, and a machine for counting banknotes, and there was also a knife. Rickie picked up the blade and held it towards me, but his threat lacked menace. It was merely a dutiful gesture, and it was no trouble to pluck the blade from his nerveless fingers. He shivered, perhaps thinking that I would attack him with the knife, but instead I went to the piled bales and slashed at their plastic wrappings. I sliced again and again, each cut of the blade spilling more wealth than had ever filled the hold of a galleon sailing from the Spanish Main. The cocaine glittered as it cascaded to the floor and covered the carpet in glinting drifts. I ripped open more of the bellying plastic sacks, burying my hand to its wrist in a flood of pure cocaine. Rickie, watching me, suddenly began to giggle, then to choke, then to laugh. "You're Nick," he said at last.

"That's right."

"They said they were going to kill you." He spoke like a small child who had trouble remembering exactly how the syllables should be joined together.

"They tried," I said, and I slashed into another bale and yet more cocaine hissed and seethed down to the floor. "Where's Ellen?" I asked.

"Ellen's pretty." Rickie was staring with awe at the cocaine that silted the carpet.

"Where is she, Rickie?"

"I have to tell them you're here, so they can kill you," he said in a very matter-of-fact voice.

"Of course you do." I stabbed at plastic, wrenched the blade and watched the powder fall. "But first tell me where Ellen is."

"You're a ghost! You're dead!" Rickie sounded suddenly alarmed, and he began to make curious weaving motions with his hands as though he was trying to ward off my unquiet spirit. His nose had started to trickle blood, and he was crying. He seemed to have disappeared into a private misery of hopeless despair. "You're dead! Dead!" he screamed at me, spitting sputum and flecks of blood that stained the snow-white powder drifts on the floor. "You're fucking dead and I hate you!" He hated himself, and he hated me, and he spat at me with pure loathing before shrieking at me to go away.

I dropped the knife into the cocaine, then fired the Kalashnikov. I aimed above and to one side of Rickie's head. The green fire of the bullets chewed into the wall and the gun's shattering noise echoed cruelly in the room. Rickie howled and covered his ears, then cowered down to the floor that looked as if it was covered with a new clean fall of snow. His blood was very bright on that new snow.

When the gun stopped firing he looked up at me, wondering

whether I was going to kill him or, worse, perhaps hoping that I would.

"Where's Ellen?" I asked again.

"They're all next door," he said in a voice that was as close to madness as any I had ever heard from a human being not on the stage. His words made perfect sense; it was the timbre of his voice that was insane. It was a whining and choking sob from the pits of despair. "All the women are next door in Billingsley's house. They were put there to keep them safe. I don't like Billingsley. I really don't like Billingsley, and he doesn't like me. No one likes me." Then he began to weep again, but I no longer cared. I was going next door.

I locked Rickie in the room with his fortune of cocaine, then I walked down the book-lined corridor, across the elegant and perfumed room with its antique prints, and so on to the moon-washed terrace. I climbed over the terrace's balustrade and edged warily down a steep grassy bank to a strip of sandy ground that separated the northernmost house from Deacon Billingsley's. The policeman's house formed three sides of a courtyard that faced towards the sea. The interior of the court was a swimming pool.

I ran up to Billingsley's terrace, but as I reached the top of the bank a match scraped and flared. I froze. I could smell cigarette smoke, then an armed guard strolled casually from within the courtyard to stand at the far side of the terrace. He did not turn towards me, but instead stared southwards at the flames which were now leaping high above the radar aerial on the tower of the big house. The man had a sub-machine-gun slung from his right shoulder.

He drew on his cigarette, then unzipped his fatigues and began to piss into an ornamental urn where a small shrub grew.

"Drop! Now!" I snapped.

The man turned, still pissing, and scrabbled for the Uzi that was slung on his shoulder, but I was holding the Kalashnikov high and the big gun was aimed directly at the guard's chest

291

and it slowly dawned on him that if he tried to use his small sub-machine-gun he was very likely to catch a bad case of bullet wounds, so he began to make calming motions at me with his hands and to utter small whimpering noises.

"Get down," I said, motioning with the big gun, and the man dropped to his knees. He wanted to zip up his fatigues, but when he dropped his hands I shouted at him to raise them again. He disobeyed me, but only to make the sign of the cross. He was shaking.

"Down!" I said again and he dropped flat on his belly. He was still making the small whimpering sounds. He lay just twenty feet away from me, his Uzi close to his right hand. To reach and disarm him I would have to walk in front of the open courtyard and, if any other guards waited in that courtyard, I would be dead.

Yet surely, I thought, the *narcotraficantes* would not have spared more than one man to guard their women? And I needed to disarm this one man if I was to go inside the house. "Throw your gun in the pool!" I ordered him, but he did not respond except with a quick burst of speech that sounded like a prayer. I supposed he spoke nothing but Spanish, a language I did not speak at all.

"In the pool!" I hissed at him, and made a motion with my own gun to show him what I meant, but he was lying flat and he could not see me properly, and so he did nothing. The Uzi was lying very close to his right hand, too close.

I edged to the corner of the courtyard, peered round, then dodged quickly back. No one had fired at me and I had seen nothing threatening in the deep shadows about the pool. The man on the ground had not tried to retrieve his gun.

I peered round again, this time pausing longer and sweeping the darkness at the pool's edges with the Kalashnikov. Nothing moved. The man on the ground, clearly terrified, did not move either. I felt the tension ebb out of me. The man was alone.

So I walked across the open flank of the courtyard. The man on the ground was shaking, expecting a bullet in his back, but all I did was to kick his Uzi away from his hand, then I kicked it again so that the weapon splashed into the swimming pool.

And just as it splashed into the pool, so the other gunman, the one who had stayed hidden in the shadowed courtyard, opened fire with another sub-machine-gun. And at that range, even with an inaccurate gun, the second gunman could not miss.

Six bullets struck me. I was standing with my left shoulder towards the house and the bullets whipped across me at chest height.

Five of the bullets struck my rib cage. Or rather they would have struck my rib cage, except that the bullet-proof vest stopped all five. The sixth bullet broke my upper left arm.

It was like being kicked by a carthorse, and I went down like a stunned calf. I gasped once with the shock, then there was a silence until the man who had shot me chuckled softly. Then I heard the click as he changed magazines.

There was no pain at first, just the astonishment of knowing I had been hit. The guard on the ground beside me was scrabbling away from me as though I might bring him bad luck.

I had fallen on top of the Kalashnikov. I rolled over and almost fainted from the pain that slashed at my arm and up into my left shoulder. The Scorpion had been hanging from that shoulder and I tried to reach it with my right hand, but then the man who had shot me was standing at my right side, towering over me, and he contemptuously kicked the little Scorpion away.

"You're a fucking clown, Breakspear," the gunman said in his easy, lazy southern voice, "and I hate clowns." Then he aimed his Uzi right at my forehead and I saw that my death was to be at the hands of Jesse Isambard Sweetman who was still clothed in his dramatic black outfit. His hair was unbound to hang loose either side of his handsome face.

He saw the recognition dawn in my eyes, and that recognition was all he needed to make his victory sweet and complete.

"Where's Ellen?" I asked him, and could not keep the pain from my voice.

He hesitated, then he smiled. "You'll never know, will you?"

"Please," I said.

"How very careless of you to lose her." He paused, watching me, then laughed softly. "I made her cry out in bed, Breakspear. She wanted it so badly that she cried out for it."

"Bastard —" I tried to heave up at him, but he stepped back and he levelled the gun again, and still he smiled.

"Carry a message to heaven for me. Just say no." And he pulled the Uzi's trigger and the small bullets flicked off the terrace by my left ear and slowly moved away from me because Sweetman had grown a third eye, a black and wet third eye, and he was falling backwards as he squeezed the trigger, and I stared up to see a jet of black glistening blood spurt from that third eye in his forehead.

The blood spurted to fall on me. The guard I had disarmed was scrambling to his feet, calling to the Virgin Mary for aid, but the M16 fired again from my left and the guard pitched forward to fall into the swimming pool.

"Ever since I got this damned gun wet," the Maggot said, "it won't fire in bursts." He climbed up from where he had been hidden by the bluff which edged the beach. "I thought you were coming to join us on the boat!"

I tried to kneel upright, but could not. I was feeling sick and dizzy. I wanted to tell the Maggot that the M16 was a notoriously unreliable weapon and that he should have used a Kalashnikov instead, but I suddenly could not speak. There was vomit in my throat and tears in my eyes. Ellen, Ellen, Ellen.

Then the Maggot was beside me and pulling me to my feet. He thrust the Scorpion into my right hand and took the belt of ammunition from around my neck. He tossed his M16 away and scooped up the Kalashnikov. "I've got to get you out of here, Nick." He turned me gently towards the sea.

"No." I jerked myself away, then almost screamed because

294

of the bolt of pain that seared up my left arm. I began walking towards the house.

"Nick!" the Maggot called.

"No!" My left arm was useless, and beginning to throb with a hellish pain. Blood was trickling inside my sleeve to drip off my fingers, but I did not care how much blood I lost or how much the wound hurt, just so long as I could get inside Billingsley's house where Ellen was. By the light of a flare I could see the dead gunman's blood spreading in dark wandering tendrils through the swimming pool. "I'm going in there," I explained to the Maggot and pointed towards the policeman's house.

"We got the boat's radio working," the Maggot said, "so it's OK! Help's coming."

"Sod your help," I said groggily, then I heard voices shouting from the next-door house, and I turned southward to see three men running towards us across a tennis court that lay between the house and the sea. I tried to raise the Scorpion, but the Maggot was much quicker than me. He used the Kalashnikov to sweep a green hose of fire across the court to drop all three men flat. One man stayed down, while the other two scrambled away. They were shouting for help and, even if I had been minded to take the Maggot's advice and retreat to the boat, it was now too late because we were cut off from the beach.

"Come on!" I shouted at the Maggot. He ran towards me. I could hear the bullets flicking overhead, then we were both in the shelter of the small courtyard. But we would not be safe for long, for our enemies now knew where we were.

A screen door in Billingsley's house was open. I stepped over the sill to see, across the room, and beyond an arch that led into a hallway, a sliver of candlelight showing under a door.

Behind me the Maggot's machine-gun began firing. He had his back towards me and I guessed that the men from the neighbouring house were swarming towards Deacon Billingsley's terrace. The Maggot hammered them with burst after burst of fire. A grenade exploded, but the Maggot survived for

I could hear the Kalashnikov continue to fire in short professional bursts. How did a football player learn that skill?

I walked towards the slit of candlelight. I went under the archway and found myself in a long central hallway. A door to my right banged open, revealing the outer darkness lit by the fire, and also revealing a tall man standing with a submachine-gun. I was in deeper shadow and the man did not see me till my Scorpion fired and its bullets lifted him clean up from the doorstep. The Scorpion had a twenty-round magazine and I fired it all, throwing the man back and cutting off his sudden scream of pain. His blood stank in the warm hallway. Women began screaming beyond the door.

"This is not healthy." The Maggot cannoned off the archway to join me in the hall. I held the Scorpion towards him and he obligingly took out the magazine, reversed it, and thrust the full magazine home.

"Put it on single shot, will you?" I asked him.

"Sure, Nick." He turned the selector to the '1', so that now the little gun would not empty its magazine in one blinding burst of fire.

"Now open the door." I nodded towards the telltale strip of light. I could not open the door myself because I was holding the gun in my right hand and my left hand was hanging bloody and useless.

The Maggot put his hand on the door, paused as he wondered what threat waited on the far side, then he threw it open and I dropped to my knee with the gun facing a candlelit room full of screaming and terrified women. "Shut the fuck up!" I shouted, because I was just as terrified as they were.

"Nick!" a girl called in astonishment.

"Shut up, get your heads down! Down! Down! All of you! Down! Down!" I was screaming the order as I crossed the threshold and searched the room for enemies, but there were no gunmen in there, only a group of women who huddled together for protection. I could see two beds in the room which was otherwise as bare and characterless as a hotel bedroom. I could not see Ellen. It was Robin-Anne who had recognised me. The Maggot was still in the hallway. He began firing the Kalashnikov and empty cartridge cases skittered across the polished wooden floor. Outside the windows I could hear a motor running, and I hoped to God it was not the jeep with its half-inch Browning.

"Grenade!" the Maggot shouted in warning, then threw himself backwards into the bedroom as the grenade exploded in the hallway, then the echo of the bomb's blast was drowned by the rending noise of the Browning half-inch machine-gun opening fire on us. The shutters and glass of the windows literally disintegrated, turned to splinters and sawdust and shards by the heavy bullets that now sawed at the wall of the house, chopping and chewing through it, even destroying the stone pillars at the edges of the windows. The machine-gunner was firing red tracers, and the fire was streaking across our heads to splinter and pierce the inner walls of the house. The Browning was powerful enough to fire clean through bricks and plaster and timber and sheetrock. The girls were screaming and sobbing, though the machine-gunner had fired too high and so far no one had been hit. Flakes of plaster and chips of wood rained down on us and the air was as thick as smoke with dust. The candles flickered in the gloom.

I scrambled over the room and provoked a shriek by treading on a naked pair of legs that belonged to a girl who was lying by an open window. She would not or could not move, so I knelt on her thighs as I pushed a fallen wrecked shutter aside to see the jeep standing no more than ten yards away. The machine-gunner, standing in the jeep's rear bed, was gritting his teeth as he played the stream of bullets back across the house.

He saw my face appear at the shattered window and he began tugging the Browning's heavy weight to face me, but I already had the little Scorpion resting on the splintered window-sill. I was sobbing and screaming myself with the pain, but I would be writhing in my death throes if I did not aim calmly and properly.

I fired my first shot and the Scorpion's recoil felt as feeble as a pop gun.

The Browning's bullets chopped towards me, filling the night with an appalling violence. I fired again. It was like using a peashooter against a cannon. I should have brought my Webley, I thought, then wondered why I had left it behind. The Browning's big bullets were destroying the night, splintering a whole world, and all I had was the Scorpion's puny single-shot power. I squeezed the trigger a third time as the plaster and timber of the wall began to explode in powdered wreckage about my ears, then suddenly the Browning's scarlet tracer jerked upwards to shatter Deacon Billingsley's rooftiles into thick red shards.

The gunner had disappeared backwards. The Browning's awful noise stopped dead and in the sudden silence I heard myself whining in agony.

"Nick?" A girl spoke from underneath me. It was not Robin-Anne's voice, nor was it Ellen's. "Nick?" the girl said again.

I ignored her. I was watching the jeep's driver who had taken cover behind the engine block, and I wanted to make sure that the man did not leap up to take over the now silent machine-gun. Behind me the Maggot fired a brief burst into the hallway, then there was an odd silence, except for the throbbing of the jeep engine, the crackle of flames and the moaning of a wounded man.

"Nick!" The girl underneath me was suddenly insistent, and even offended that I had ignored her so far.

"What the hell is it?" I asked irritably.

"You're kneeling on my legs, Nick. I really think you should know that you're hurting me." It was Donna, who sounded very aggrieved. "Please, Nick! If you could just try to be a little more thoughtful?"

"I'm sorry." I moved off her legs and wondered if she ever wore anything other than the flimsy bikini.

She smiled drenching forgiveness on me. "Good evening, Nick. And how are you this evening?"

"Donna?" I said blankly. I had recognised her, but I still could not quite come to terms with meeting her thus amidst the dust and smoke of this bullet-torn room.

"I'm good, thank you." She had assumed I had asked her how she was, which I had not, but nor was she 'good' either, for she was very close to hysteria, but Donna had been wonderfully brought up and even amidst the grenades and bullets she was doing her best to remember her Episcopalian manners. I looked back out of the window and saw that the jeep driver was still crouching behind his vehicle, then he suddenly showed his face because he was staring upwards towards a throbbing noise that seemed to fill the whole sky and I saw that the jeep driver was Matthew McIllvanney.

"Did McIllvanney bring you here?" I asked Donna.

"Of course he did!" she said brightly. "That's Matthew's job."

"So what's he doing here?" I had to shout because the throbbing noise had turned into the percussive blows of helicopters coming lower and lower, and some of the helicopters were equipped with bullhorns through which men were shouting in Spanish and English. They were yelling that we should throw down our guns and stand still. A searchlight sliced down from one of the hovering machines. "What's McIllvanney doing here?" I asked Donna again.

"He sometimes stays overnight, then tomorrow he'll take Dominica and me back to Nassau." She gestured at a tall and very pretty black girl who cowered at the foot of the other bed. "Dominica's my partner," Donna explained.

"Your partner?"

"At doubles. We play tennis with Susan and Felicity." Susan and Felicity evidently formed another part of the pile of lubricity that quivered on the wreckage-littered floor.

"What is this?" I asked. "Bloody Wimbledon?"

"It's the cabinet minister," Donna explained primly. "He pays us to play tennis in our altogether while he takes videos of us." She gave a little laugh of embarrassment. "And I have the most awful backhand," she confessed, as though the cabinet minister might have noticed.

"You play naked tennis?" I asked in utter bewilderment.

Donna nodded. "Yes, Nick. Though of course we all take care to put on some sun-blocking cream first."

299

"Fuck me," I said, but in astonishment rather than hope, then I stared round the bullet-shattered bedroom. A teddy bear, its stuffing disembowelled by a half-inch Browning bullet, lay close to a wide-eyed Maggot who seemed only just to have noticed the half-naked company he was keeping. Robin-Anne, looking like an orphaned waif among a company of princesses, was scrunched down at the far end of the room. "Have you seen a red-haired girl here?" I asked Donna. "Called Ellen?"

"Oh, no." Donna did not even need time to think of her answer.

I glanced out of the window. McIllvanney was on his feet, hands in the air. A helicopter's lights were just above him, and its rotor was thrashing the nearby palm trees and whipping dust up from the ground. "Stay here, John!" I shouted at the Maggot.

I almost screamed as I climbed through the broken window. My left arm hit the wall and the pain was suddenly blinding. Shreds of metallic insect screen and shards of glass caught and ripped my bloodied fatigues, but somehow I managed to get my right foot on the sill, hauled myself through the broken frame, and jumped down to the ground. A blinding searchlight immediately pinned me from the sky. "At this time," an American voice said, "you are required to stand still." The men in the helicopters did not know I was a good guy; to them everyone on the ground was a suspect. "Drop your weapon," the voice ordered me, "put your hands over your head, and stand still."

"Piss off!" I shouted. They could not have heard me for the metallic voice was now repeating the orders in Spanish. I ignored the helicopter. The Scorpion was in my right hand, blood and dust and plaster sheeted my left arm, and my ribs were hurting. I guessed that by dawn I would have bruises like hoofkicks all over my chest where the flak-jacket had stopped Sweetman's bullets.

"At this time . . ." the metallic voice began again in English, and I thought I recognised the flat nasal tones of the DEA agent, Warren Smedley.

I stared up into the blinding vortex of wind, dust and light. "Shut the fuck up, you illiterate freak!"

Amazingly, the illiterate freak shut up, or perhaps the helicopter pilot just moved the machine away towards more open ground, but whatever, I was suddenly left alone. But McIllvanney had also heard my shout, recognised me, and began to run. I ran after him. Ahead of us a helicopter landed and spilt armed men on to the fairway. A light had been set up to illumine the radio mast so that it would not prove a hazard to the aircraft. Everything, I thought, had been so well planned, then I saw McIllvanney jump to take shelter in a sand trap.

"Freeze!" I screamed at him, he looked back, and all he could see was the Scorpion in my right hand, and the sight of the small gun scared him into utter immobility. He stood petrified as I walked through the pelting wind of sand and palm scraps and smoke that was being lashed outwards by the helicopter's rotors. McIllvanney began shaking his head as I got close to him. "Down!" I shouted.

He dropped into the sand. I slid into the sand trap, then knelt on his belly and rammed the Scorpion hard into his face. "This time it's loaded," I shouted at him, "and I'll rattle bullets round your poxy skull if you don't tell me the truth. Where's Ellen?"

Another helicopter landed not far from us, its rotors kicking up a further slew of dust and sand. The bullhorns were bellowing their orders, trying to scare a whole island into quiescence. Blue-uniformed men with helmets, flak-jackets and M16s were jumping from the grounded machines, while yet more helicopters were flying in from the sea; their red, green and white navigation lights showing like bright jewels through the rifts of smoke that hung in skeins above the island.

"Where is she?"

"I don't know!" McIllvanney shouted. "I don't focking know!"

"You brought her here!" I was shouting like a maniac, and all around me the air was filled with the noise of engines and the stench of kerosene, and the smoke from the burning house

301

and the sound of men calling orders. "You're fucking lying!" I rammed the Scorpion's tiny barrel hard into the soft flesh under McIllvanney's right eye. "Where is she?"

"I don't know! For Christ's sake, I don't know!" He was terrified. "I didn't bring her here! On my honour, I didn't!"

"You lied to me!" I shouted. "You gave me all that garbage about Ned Carraway! All the time you were just wanting to bring Ellen here for these bastards to kill!"

He stared at me with what had to be genuine amazement. "Ned did call me!" he protested. "He couldn't reach his wife because she was with her parents, so he called me instead because he knew Ellen worked for me! But I haven't seen her since the day you left with the twins on board *Wavebreaker*."

I stared at him. Another helicopter reared back, flared its rotors and thumped down to spill yet more armed Americans on to Murder Cay's nine-hole golf course, which was beginning to look like Panama City on the day of the American invasion. Slowly I was beginning to see what must have happened. "Is Ellen here?" I asked McIllvanney, but more softly.

"No! They've been looking for her, just like they've been looking for you." He was almost crying in his eagerness to convince me of the truth. "They keep asking me where she is, but I don't focking know! Billingsley wanted to know, because he's the one who offered me money for a night in bed with her, and Sweetman never lets up about her, and now you're asking me, and I don't focking well know where she is! I just don't know! I'm not a magician! I can't make the bint appear when I don't know where she is!"

"She's not here?" I asked, not because I needed another denial, but rather in sheer astonishment.

"She's not here!" McIllvanney screamed, and I realised that Sweetman had lied about raping Ellen. He had lied because it had amused him to send me to my grave in abject misery, and he had very nearly succeeded.

McIllvanney had inadvertently spat at me in his desperate efforts to persuade me, but he need not have been so frantic for I believed him anyway. I had been deceived, but not by

McIllvanney, and not even by Sweetman – at least, not seriously. The illusions had been made by others. I flinched with pain as I stood up and shuffled away from him. I let the Scorpion drop into the sand. "You can get up now," I said.

"I've got nothing to do with the drugs!" McIllvanney shouted at me. He was still on the ground; still shaking. "You tell them that, Nick! You tell them! I've never messed with drugs! You know that! I just bring them girls. And they're good girls, the best!"

"I know," I said, then a man yelled at me from the edge of the sand trap to put my hands up, and another uniformed man jumped down to hold an M16 at my stomach while a third man grabbed my wounded left arm and, ignoring my yelps of pain, slapped a plastic handcuff about my bloody wrist then dragged my right hand down and cuffed my wrists together. The invading Americans were immobilising everyone; only later would they divide the black hats from the white hats.

"Don't move!" one of the invaders shouted at me, then thrust me face down beside McIllvanney who had been similarly cuffed. A vast Chinook thumped down beside a green, then disgorged a jeep which tore up the carefully manicured grass with its spinning wheels.

An American officer paused at the lip of the sand trap to speak into a small hand-held radio. "Stingray Alpha, Stingray Alpha, this is Stingray Dolphin, Stingray Dolphin. All secure in this area. I say again, all secure in this area. Dolphin out." The man gave McIllvanney and me an incurious glance then walked on.

"I'm not into drugs!" McIllvanney shouted after the officer, who ignored him, so the Ulsterman looked back at me. "Nick! You know me, I hate drugs, so I do! They're an abomination!" He evidently believed that by convincing me he could convince all the world of his innocence.

But I was not listening to McIllvanney. I was lying with my face in the sand and with agony ripping up my left arm, but I was also suddenly and sublimely happy. The word Stingray had confirmed all my suspicions. The senator had tried to radio Stingray, and now Stingray had come, because Stingray had always been meant to come, and that meant Ellen was safe.

And Ellen had always been safe.

The good guys had her, not the bad guys, but the good guys who had wanted me to help them. It had been the good guys who had caused Ellen to disappear, then encouraged me to take revenge for that disappearance by attacking Murder Cay. The Americans could not have legally searched Murder Cay because the Bahamians would not have given their permission, but the world would forgive the Americans if their forces, conveniently exercising close to the island, responded to an emergency call for help from an American senator who had travelled to Murder Cay on the innocent mission of seeking his missing children; and if the British government complained about such a Grenada-like invasion of the territory of a sovereign and Commonwealth nation, then the Americans would reply that they had also been rescuing the hide of a dumb Britisher who had only been trying to help the senator.

Thus had this whole night been planned. If either of the radios had worked then the cavalry would have ridden to our rescue long before the firefight developed, but the cavalry had always been waiting just beyond the radar horizon. Which all meant that I had been manipulated. The dictates of politics and public relations had decreed that this operation should look like a rescue mission, and my participation took away any suspicion that the operation had been planned in the Pentagon. The senator and I would be depicted as nobly heroic fools; Don Quixotes tilting at real giants and winning.

And the Maggot?

The Maggot, I imagined, would not exist. The Maggot would become invisible because the Maggot was surely an undercover man for either the DEA or the US Customs Service, or one of the myriad Task Forces that the Americans deployed against drugs.

"This one," I suddenly heard the Maggot's voice above and behind me, "you can shoot now. He's only a stray Brit and no one could have any possible use for him." Then he laughed.

"You bastard," I said, then the Maggot cut off my plastic cuffs and lifted me with an extraordinary tenderness. He took me to a medic who gave me basic field care, and who wanted to chopper me immediately to the operating theatre of a naval ship, but I refused to leave Murder Cay. I had questions I wanted answered, and to seek those answers I walked along the beach with Maggot. "Who are you?" I asked him.

"Maggovertski, John." He grinned through his black tangled beard. "Otherwise known as the Maggot. You know who I am, Nick. Failed football player, failing businessman, good old country boy, layabout, average pilot, extraordinarily talented beer drinker, gun collector, lover of loose women, lover of tight women, lover of any women, tennis coach extraordinary . . ."

"DEA?" I carried on the list for him. "US Customs? Special Task Force? CIA?"

"I kind of go deaf to some questions, Nick, on account of having banged my head against dickhead offensive linemen too often. But considering I'm just an easy-going party-loving animal with an aeroplane and a boat, you'd be amazed how many people confide in me their wishes and plans to introduce strange and narcotic substances into America."

We walked slowly on through the cloying sand. The small lagoon waves flopped feebly on the beach. The painkiller was making me light-headed, but not foolish any longer. "So where's Ellen, John?"

"So far as I know, Nick, she's in an Embassy guest house in Nassau. She's been well treated, though she didn't think so. We kind of denied her a telephone, and kept her on a leash, and she was unhappy about that. In fact she was as mad as hell. I know you're fond of her, Nick, but have you ever caught the rough side of her tongue? Jesus, she could strip the teeth of a running chainsaw! We were only keeping her in Nassau for her own protection, but you'd never have known it from the way she cussed us."

I smiled. "Were you the one who took her to Nassau?"

"Smedley did. You met Smedley, right? I kind of arranged

it, though." The Maggot had the grace to give me an apologetic look. "Sorry, Nick. But, Jesus, when you telephoned and asked for my help? You were just offering us temptation, and I was always kind of bad at resisting temptation."

"Screw you, mate," I said, but without malice, for I liked the Maggot, and he had been clever, so very clever. Instead of flying Ellen direct from Straker's Cay to Nassau he had taken her to Freeport and allowed her to complete as much of her planned itinerary as possible, thus making it seem even more plausible that she had been kidnapped. "But why couldn't you have told me the truth?" I asked.

"Think about it, Nick. If you'd known this whole party was being laid on and paid for by the US government, would you have put your miserable hide on the line for us?"

"No," I confessed wisely and truthfully.

"And you were just too good to overlook," the Maggot said with an indecent relish. "A trained soldier, and the son of the great Sir Thomas Breakspear! Even the Brits can't object to us rescuing Sir Tom's dear son from the *narcotraficantes*."

"But why did I have to do the killing?" I cut across his foolery with the bitter question.

He gave me a shrewd glance. "Because you were a marine, Nick."

"Not in your Navy."

He walked in silence for a few paces. "It's a war against drugs, Nick, and we're not going to win it unless we fight as cruelly and as pitilessly as the *narcotraficantes*. Not that we thought there'd be any killing here. Damn it, if the senator hadn't thrown his radio at the bloody dog, no one would have got shot! It wasn't meant to be like this."

"It never is," I said, and I thought that Ellen was right, and that this whole damn crooked business should be brought into the open so that no one could make profits so huge that they were worth the fighting and the dying and the lying and the stealing and the misery.

"Anyway, it's over now." The Maggot was uncomfortable with my dismay and hurried the conversation on. "I guess we

306

owe you a big thank you, Nick. Not, of course, that I speak for the US government, you understand. In fact, and you may quote me, the US government is just like any other government; a load of fat-assed faggot lawyers who only understand how to spend people's taxes but who can't even piss downwind unless their aides show them how to do it. So I would hate you to spread a rumour that I was in any way associated with those pin-headed dickbrains, and do I make myself plain?"

I smiled. "Yes, Maggot, you do. You don't exist, am I right?"

"You are so right."

Dawn was showing like a line of gun-metal above the horizon. The wind was rife with the stench of helicopter fuel, but beyond the coral reefs there would be a cutting cleanness to the air. I suddenly wanted to be away in my boat; just Ellen, *Masquerade*, and myself in great waters. I looked ruefully at my bandaged arm. "You've made it kind of hard for me to mend my boat, you big non-existent bastard."

"The boat's going to Florida tomorrow, Nick. You signed the papers, remember?"

I stared up into the Maggot's strong face. "When was all this set up? After Sea Rat Cay?"

"Sure. But even before that we kind of guessed Rickie might be making a play. It was all his idea to come to the Bahamas, remember? And the senator has been co-operating with the authorities for a few months now. In the first place he thought that by co-operating he could keep his son's sentence low, and in the second place he reckoned it might just pay off in a big stinking heap of publicity, and publicity to a politician is what cocaine is to Rickie. But I still didn't know if we were going ahead, even yesterday. We were kind of doing it by the seat of our pants, Nick, and I reckon if the bad guys hadn't come gunning for you, then my lily-livered lawyer superiors wouldn't have had the guts to turn us loose." The Maggot turned to stare back at the houses. The fire had been put out now, but in its place was a patch of brilliant white light that was evidently cast by the sun-guns of some television crews. "The press are already here," the Maggot explained, "on account that some of them were accidentally invited to watch a night of Operation Stingray."

"Accidentally invited by the senator?" I asked.

"I do believe his press office was involved. And I do believe that we may just have seen the making of a President." The Maggot lit a cigarette. "Of course, there'll be a whole lot more pressmen and television people arriving in a few hours, and they'll all want to talk to you. One of my jobs is to make sure you say the right things, Nick."

The helicopters carrying the press had landed on the island's northern promontory. From there the reporters had been escorted to see the tons of cocaine that had been waiting on the island for shipment to America, then the journalists were offered the senator as the hero of the hour. This would be tonight's lead television news story; how a senator's gallant attempt to rescue his children had led to the smashing of a Latin-American cocaine family. Good had triumphed over evil, the white knight had ridden deep into the valley of the shadow of death and had come out smelling of roses and his reward would be the White House rose garden. The politician had found his cause, America would have its illusion and the drugs would still flow in by other routes.

The press were not shown the bodies. One of the dead was Deacon Billingsley. He had been the man who had come to the door in the house and had there been killed by a full magazine from my Scorpion. Now, like the other dead, Billingsley had been zipped into a green rubber bodybag.

The press were not introduced to Rickie or Robin-Anne. Rickie was carried to a helicopter on a stretcher, while Robin-Anne walked beside him, her hand in his. "The rich are different," the Maggot said sourly as he watched the senator's two children being gently escorted away.

"How so?"

"Everyone else gets handcuffed and kicked around, but the bloody rich get choppered off to a five-star drug clinic. And doubtless the judge will be told that Rickie helped turn in the

Colón family, which means Rickie will only get a light tap on the wrist and told not to be a silly boy again." The Maggot spat into the sand as the Crowninshield twins were helped up into their helicopter.

The reporters were allowed to see the prisoners being led towards another waiting chopper. The cabinet minister was protesting his innocence, but Warren Smedley, the DEA agent, had already revealed to the press that a half-ton of cocaine had been discovered in the cabinet minister's house. It was clear that the island's distinguished hostages, designed to keep the Americans off Murder Cay, had been expected to share the island's dangers as well as its pleasures. Miguel Colón, stone-faced, was submitting to the plastic manacles with dignity, while Smedley, his captor, was looking like a sourpuss that had found the world's largest bowl of double cream. He even listened courteously as I passed on McIllvanney's protestations of innocence. "At this time," Smedley magnanimously responded, "we are recommending prosecution only against the island's inhabitants and their paid guards, not against their domestic servants or transient visitors."

"Not that any of it counts," the Maggot said to me when Smedley had gone. "The lawyers will have every single prisoner out on bail by this time tomorrow, and we'll be lucky if we can extradite even one of them."

The reporters were not introduced to the Maggot, who stayed well clear of their cameras and notebooks. His name would not be mentioned in any newspaper because, officially, he did not exist. Instead he walked unnoticed towards the airstrip where the navigation lights of yet more American helicopters strobed in the day's first feral light. "It's time I went," he told me, then he turned and stared briefly into the far western sky where, dark against the fading stars, a lone helicopter beat its way towards Murder Cay. "I guess you know what to say to the press, Nick?"

"The truth?" I suggested.

"That's usually dangerous." The Maggot grinned. "Why not say that only you and the senator came to the island, no one else, and you didn't bring any guns with you, you took the weapons off some careless guards who crashed their jeep. You'll see that we've tipped the damn jeep over for you, so the story will ring true. You don't say that the senator was pissing in his jockey shorts, instead you talk convincingly of his noble and self-sacrificing heroism and of his outstanding qualities of leadership. If you can sing a bar or two of 'Hail to the Chief', that would help. And, naturally, the two of you only fired in self-defence."

I smiled. "Naturally."

The lone helicopter was over the edge of the airstrip now, its landing lights bright on the stunted slash pines and sea-grape. The Maggot was not watching it; instead he was looking towards a small group of civilians who were being escorted by grinning Coastguards towards a big Chinook. "Dear Lord above." The Maggot's voice was suddenly hushed into an unnatural reverence. "Do you see what I see, Nick? Is that not pure essence of bimbo?"

I turned to see the group of girls being ushered towards the Chinook, but only one girl in that group could possibly have been a match for the Maggot's concupiscent dreams. "She's called Donna," I told him, "and she's an Episcopalian from Philadelphia, and she needs a tennis coach to look after her backhand."

"Nick, don't tease a friend."

"It's true," I said, "as God is my witness, she's worried about her backhand. Say you're a friend of mine, and tell her I said 'hi'."

"You are a great and generous man, Nick. And I do believe I have found myself a private pupil." He gave me an evil grin, then held out his huge hand with its heavy Superbowl ring. "I'll see you before we die?"

I took his hand, then held on to it to stop him from walking away. "One question, Maggot," I said.

"Try me."

I had to raise my voice because of the din being made by the landing helicopter. "The girl in Pittsburgh? Was she a lie too?"

He shook his head. "No, my friend. Wendy is all too goddamned real. She's why I do this."

I let go of his hand. "Good luck, Maggot."

"And to you, my friend!" He began running towards Donna's Chinook, then paused to shout back at me. "Tell Ellen I'll be glad to be the best man at your wedding! We'll have a blast!"

I laughed and turned away. The incoming helicopter had thumped on to the runway and its rotors were slowing to a halt. The drifting dust was touched red-gold by the rising sun. I saw that the first reporters had spilt on to this southern part of the island, and some were now heading towards me. It was time for me to add my corroborating testimony to the senator's instant legend. George Crowninshield; the winning warrior of the drug war, the senator who dared to act, the man to lead a nation in its crusade against the drugs that had threatened his own children. I could almost see the senator's halo as he strode about the island with the reporters and at the head of his newly arrived herd of aides and press secretaries.

Then a voice called from behind me and I turned, and I forgot the senator, and I forgot the reporters, and I forgot the Maggot, because Ellen had arrived on the lone helicopter, and her hair was red-gold like the new sun and her beauty brought a lump to my throat as I walked towards her. I held my arms outstretched, and she was running towards me, and I could see tears in her eyes and I knew she was happy, and I was just as happy; then we clumsily met, we clasped, we were laughing, and the embrace skewered a white-hot pain in my arm, but it did not matter.

"They wouldn't let me come," she said in breathless explanation, "because they said I might tell the truth to the press people, and I said if they didn't bring me I'd certainly tell the truth, the whole bloody truth, to the whole damned world, so here I am." She was laughing and crying. "Are you all right, Nick?"

"I am now," I said, "I am now." I heard voices strident behind me, and knew the press were almost on top of us. I

311

kissed Ellen. "I want to make you a promise," I told her.

"Go on."

"I will always tell you the truth."

"Dear Nick," she said. "Why do you think I'm here?" Her hands were warm in mine. A flash bulb cracked its brightness as she laid her head on my shoulder.

"Mr Breakspear! What happened?" A dozen voices demanded of me.

I turned and stared at the reporters. They were sweating and eager, hounds pressing on their kill. Sun-guns dazzled us, and microphones hedged us about. The journalists shouted insistent questions; demanding to know how I had met the senator, and did my father know I was here, and what had actually happened, and who was the girl with me, and how did I get the injury? But they went silent when I raised a hand. "I shall tell you the truth!" I made the promise in a stentorian voice, the voice of a marine sergeant shouting above the sound of a half-gale thrashing a parade ground, "and I shall tell you nothing but the truth." The senator had been momentarily forgotten by the press and his face showed pure horror at the prospect of my veracity. One of his newly arrived aides was thrusting through the crush of reporters in an effort to reach and silence me, but I had my audience now and I would not waste it. "Our revels now are ended," I said, but this time in the glorious voice of Sir Tom himself, the voice the old fraud had employed in his famous production of *The Tempest* at Stratford in '79, the voice that one critic had described as being like a golden-throated trumpet calling to the heart of a world's perplexity. "These our actors," I went on,

> As I foretold you, were all spirits, and
> Are melted into air, into thin air;
> And, like the baseless fabric of this vision,
> The cloud-capp'd towers, the gorgeous palaces,
> The solemn temples, the great globe itself,
> Yea, all which it inherit, shall dissolve
> And, like this insubstantial pageant faded,

Leave not a rack behind. We are such stuff
As dreams are made on –

I stopped abruptly, obedient to Sir Tom's adage always to leave the little darlings panting for more, and then I bowed, and then I laughed, and then I walked away. Ellen, her arm in my good arm, was laughing with me. The senator looked like a man reprieved from death, but not sure why. The equally puzzled reporters swarmed after me, shouting their questions, but I had nothing more to say. The isle was full of noises, but I had none to add, nor did I care what the world made of me, nor of Ellen, for we were bound for the long seas where high stars would guide us and a good boat would carry us, together and for ever.

BOOKS BY BERNARD CORNWELL

THE SAXON TALES

THE LAST KINGDOM

ISBN 978-0-06-088718-6 (trade paperback) • ISBN 978-0-06-112657-4 (abridged CD)

Set during the reign of King Alfred the Great, *The Last Kingdom* depicts a time when law and order were ripped violently apart by a pagan assault on Christian England.

THE PALE HORSEMAN

ISBN 978-0-06-114483-7 (trade paperback) • ISBN 978-0-06-078748-6 (abridged CD)

The exhilarating adventures of Uhtred and King Alfred the Great continue, as England is reduced to nothing but a small patch of marshland—and a beguiling sorceress and fearful Danish warrior complicate Alfred's desperate plans.

LORDS OF THE NORTH

ISBN 978-0-06-088862-6 (hardcover) • ISBN 978-0-06-114904-7 (trade paperback)
ISBN 978-0-06-088863-3 (large print) • ISBN 978-0-06-115578-9 (abridged CD)

After achieving victory at King Alfred's side, Uhtred of Bebbanburg returns to his home in the North, finally free of his allegiance to the king—or so he believes.

SWORD SONG

ISBN 978-0-06-088864-0 (hardcover) • ISBN 978-0-06-088866-4 (large print)
ISBN 978-0-06-137094-6 (abridged CD)

Alfred of Wessex has survived the Danish invasions, but though he now has an uneasy truce with his enemies, fresh Viking ships are arriving to plunder and enslave the Saxons.

THE RICHARD SHARPE SERIES

SHARPE'S FURY

Richard Sharpe and the Battle of Barrosa, 1811

ISBN 978-0-06-056156-7 (trade paperback) • ISBN 978-0-137416-6 (abridged CD)

Richard Sharpe has been sent by Wellington on a mission to Cadiz, now the capital of Spain, to rescue the British ambassador from a spot of undiplomatic trouble.

SHARPE'S TIGER

Richard Sharpe and the Siege of Seringapatam, 1799

ISBN 978-0-06-093230-5 (trade paperback) • ISBN 978-0-06-101269-3 (mass market paperback)

The first of Richard Sharpe's India trilogy, in which young Private Sharpe must battle both man and beast behind enemy lines as the British army fights its way through India.

SHARPE'S TRIUMPH

Richard Sharpe and the Battle of Assaye, September 1803

ISBN 978-0-06-095197-9 (trade paperback)

Richard Sharpe must defeat the plans of a British traitor and a native Indian mercenary army in this second volume of the India trilogy.

SHARPE'S FORTRESS

Richard Sharpe and the Siege of Gawilghur, December 1803

ISBN 978-0-06-109863-5 (trade paperback)

In this explosive conclusion to the India trilogy, Sharpe and Sir Arthur Wellesley's army try to conquer an impregnable fort in a battle with stakes both personal and professional.

www.bernardcornwell.net

SHARPE'S TRAFALGAR
Richard Sharpe and the Battle of Trafalgar, October 21, 1805
ISBN 978-0-06-109862-8 (trade paperback)

Having secured a reputation as a fighting soldier in India, Ensign Richard Sharpe returns to England and gets caught up in one of the most spectacular naval battles in history.

SHARPE'S PREY
Richard Sharpe and the Expedition to Copenhagen, 1807
ISBN 978-0-06-008453-0 (trade paperback)

Cornwell continues his popular series with Richard Sharpe's dangerous forays into Denmark, as he is fighting once again to keep the treacherous French troops at bay.

SHARPE'S HAVOC
Richard Sharpe and the Campaign in Northern Portugal, Spring 1809
ISBN 978-0-06-056670-8 (trade paperback)

It is 1809, and Sharpe finds himself once again in Portugal, fighting the savage armies of Napoleon Bonaparte, as they try to bring the Iberian Peninsula under their control.

SHARPE'S ESCAPE
Richard Sharpe and the Bussaco Campaign, 1810
ISBN 978-0-06-056155-0 (trade paperback) • ISBN 978-0-06-056095-9 (mass market paperback)

Sharpe has made enemies among the Portuguese, and when the British army falls back through Coimbra, he and Sergeant Harper are lured into a trap designed to kill them.

SHARPE'S BATTLE
Richard Sharpe and the Battle of Fuentes de Oñoro, May 1811
ISBN 978-0-06-093228-2 (trade paperback)

As Napoleon threatens to crush Britain on the battlefield, Lt. Col. Richard Sharpe leads a ragtag army to exact personal revenge.

SHARPE'S DEVIL
Richard Sharpe and the Emperor, 1820–21
ISBN 978-0-06-093229-9 (trade paperback)

An honored veteran of the Napoleonic Wars, Lt. Col. Richard Sharpe is drawn into a deadly battle, both on land and on the high seas.

THE NATHANIEL STARBUCK CHRONICLES

REBEL
The Nathaniel Starbuck Chronicles: Book One • Bull Run, 1861
ISBN 978-0-06-093461-3 (trade paperback)

When a Richmond landowner snatches young Nate Starbuck from the grip of a Yankee-hating mob, Nate turns his back forever on his life in Boston to fight against his native North in this powerful and evocative story of the Civil War's first battle and the men who fought it.

COPPERHEAD
The Nathaniel Starbuck Chronicles: Book Two • Ball's Bluff, 1862
ISBN 978-0-06-093462-0 (trade paperback)

Nate Starbuck is accused of being a Yankee spy. In order to prove his innocence and prevent the fall of Richmond, he must test his endurance and seek out the real spy.

BATTLE FLAG
The Nathaniel Starbuck Chronicles: Book Three • Second Manassas, 1862
ISBN 978-0-06-093718-8 (trade paperback)

The acclaimed Civil War series continues as Confederate Captain Nate Starbuck takes part in the war's most extraordinary scenes.

THE BLOODY GROUND
The Nathaniel Starbuck Chronicles: Book Four • The Battle of Antietam, 1862
ISBN 978-0-06-093719-5 (trade paperback)

Nate serves under General Robert E. Lee during the famous battle at Antietam Creek.

THE GRAIL QUEST SERIES

THE ARCHER'S TALE
ISBN 978-0-06-093576-4 (trade paperback)

Determined to avenge his family's honor after a band of raiders brutally pillages his village, Thomas joins the Hundred Years War and embarks on a quest for the Holy Grail.

VAGABOND
ISBN 978-0-06-093578-8 (trade paperback) • ISBN 978-0-06-621080-3 (hardcover)

Thomas of Hookton continues his quest for the mysterious relic, rumored to be the Holy Grail itself, as he weaves through the bloody battlefields of the Hundred Years War.

HERETIC
ISBN 978-0-06-074828-9 (trade paperback)

For three years, Thomas has fought alongside the English troops. But to reclaim what's rightfully his, he finds himself in a murderous race with a dangerous black rider.

ALSO BY BERNARD CORNWELL

AGINCOURT
A Novel

ISBN 978-0-06-157890-8 (trade paperback)

The inspiring story of that "band of brothers" who survives devastating hunger and disease only to face the horrors of the field of Agincourt.

WILDTRACK
A Novel of Suspense

ISBN 978-0-06-146264-1 (trade paperback)

Nick Sandman has nothing except his barely-seaworthy boat and his dream of sailing away from his troubled life. But to keep afloat, he strikes a devil's bargain with another sailor...

CRACKDOWN
A Novel of Suspense

ISBN 978-0-06-143837-0 (trade paperback)

Nick Breakspear thinks he's opted for the easy life when he accepts a job working on a yacht, but soon he's lured into a web of cocaine, cash, and cold-blooded killings.

GALLOWS THIEF
ISBN 978-0-06-008274-1 (trade paperback) • ISBN 978-0-06-051628-4 (mass market paperback)

A historical novel featuring a private investigator in 1820s London whose explorations into a mysterious murder case may help rescue an innocent man from the gallows.

STONEHENGE
A Novel

ISBN 978-0-06-095685-1 (trade paperback) • ISBN 978-0-06-109194-0 (mass market paperback)

An epic tale about one of the most mysterious and compelling monuments ever built, and the three men, brothers and rivals, who will be marked by its long shadow.

LISTEN TO
BERNARD CORNWELL

ON AUDIO CD

THE LAST KINGDOM

THE PALE HORSEMAN

LORDS OF THE NORTH

SWORD SONG

SHARPE'S FURY
Richard Sharpe and the Battle of Barrosa, 1811

ON DOWNLOADABLE AUDIO

THE LAST KINGDOM

THE PALE HORSEMAN

LORDS OF THE NORTH

SHARPE'S FURY
Richard Sharpe and the Battle of Barrosa, 1811

SHARPE'S ESCAPE
Richard Sharpe and the Bussaco Campaign, 1810

THE ARCHER'S TALE

VAGABOND

HERETIC

GALLOWS THIEF